Allen Ray Newton

THE BABYLONIAN
Book One in the "Eyes of Nimrod" Chronicles

To Pastor Vaughn:
For all the years
of great example &
teaching — Thanks!

Allen Ray Newton
Oct. 2014
II Cor 5:21

1

To my loving and very patient wife, Barbara. Her encouragement has been the bedrock of this book.

Chapter 1

Nimrod is back.

I finished my morning workout just as the sun's rays started defining the ripples on the Tigris. It was a ways off to the east, but I could make it out clearly from my present position; the flat roof of my family home. The water was high - normal for this time of year - but I knew the dry season was not far away.

The other inhabitants of Nippur were just stirring with the morning light, but I had been awake for a couple of hours. If the weather was good, I always spent my first moments of the day gazing into the night sky. It was an old habit; one I had developed because of a friend of my father. His name was Pul, and he knew all about the shapes that stars traced in the sky. I had been fascinated as he pointed out shapes like the *Hunter,* and the *Ram.*

My other motive for rising so early was to strengthen myself physically. I knew well that if one aspired to the great Babylonian army normal physical strength was not enough; and my desire went well beyond even that. I would attain to the elite palace guard of Nebuchadnezzar, mighty ruler of the world!

I could still remember clearly the sunlight gleaming from his magnificent armor. That was six years ago; I was only twelve at the time, but the impression was not easily lost. His father, Nabopolassar, was still on the throne then, but there was no doubt that this young general was destined to rule Babylon when the gods removed his father from this realm. At least that is how the religious types would put it. As for me; well, I lived in this realm, and I had great doubts about much that I had heard concerning the other. I had decided to concentrate my energies on things I could touch and feel; let the soothsayers debate the spiritual. Still... the stars always seemed to call me to consider other possibilities. But for now I was focused on reaching Babylon and the glory of her king.

It would have been just as natural for me to have hated him as it was that I admired him so greatly. After all, he was responsible for the suffering of our town at that time. A group of the farmers had rebelled against the kingdom, and Nebuchadnezzar was there to bring Nippur back into subjection. I could have hated him for all of the misery I saw around me. There were tales of people selling their children for food. Some said it was the same ones who were rebelling.

I could have hated him. But even at that young age I understood the need for authority in this enlightened time. The day when Nippur, Ur, Uruk and the other cities stood alone was well past. We had seen how poorly that system had worked. My father had told me many times how wise it was to be confederated under the able rule and protection of Babylon, and I had seen my city prosper under the rule of King Nabopolassar. His son was only doing his duty in trying to keep that prosperity alive for all of Babylonia. Great was my admiration for this mighty general.

That morning, as I spent those early moments gazing into the heavens, I remembered how Pul had pointed out three stars in fairly close proximity to each other that formed a straight line. They were, he explained, the girdle of Orion, a great giant of a man pictured by those stars and others nearby. I located them easily as they were always close to the horizon. I would often watch them fade away as the sun began its languid imposition upon the eastern sky. Pul had said that many people attributed the picture of the giant to a great leader; some saying it was one already in the past, others that it was prophetic of a great man to come. Some actually believed, said Pul, that they represented a great ruler of old who would return from the heavens to assume an even greater role.

He said, "Nimrod is back." He would say no more.

Since the day I became acquainted with the man who was now king in Babylon, Orion had symbolized Nebuchadnezzar to me.

It happened sooner and more suddenly than anyone had expected. Nebuchadnezzar was away on a campaign when the news reached him that his father was dead. There was much speculation - much fear in many cases - that Nebuchadnezzar would not return in time to maintain his right to the throne. Rumors spread rapidly. Within days, stories flew about an assassination. Some said that Nebuchadnezzar would not return at all. I suppose the prince had some uncertainty about the security of his ascension as well, for he returned to Babylon in short order and established himself on the throne.

Established? Now, in the ninth year of his reign, the word 'established' did not seem adequate for the man who ruled most of the world with the unusual combination of wisdom and might.

And I would be a part of that great empire. Nothing else was important to me. For the past six years I had pushed myself, making myself stronger by any means I could. Originally my desire was to ride beside him to war as a captain. Now that he was king, I still wished to be at his side. My early rising on this day was not unusual for me. It was difficult to find work these days, at least the kind of work I felt I needed to prepare my body for the rigors of the warrior's life. The palace guard was the final line of defense in the event of an attack on the capital city. Its members were chosen from the ranks of the army. Only those who excelled stood any chance of making the elite fighting force.

After the stretching exercises of the early morning hours I was ready for some real work. The docks at the Euphrates offered the best opportunity, so I headed for the river.

Our house stood close by to the canal that ran through the city. Father had explained to me that the Canal had been dug to control the flood waters. For a while, many years ago, he said, it had become the primary course of the Euphrates. Since then, a wall had been built around the city, a canal along its length, and the river had chosen the outside edge of the south wall as its new course. No one gave it much thought, but there was obviously a way for the water to flow under the walls and into the canal.

As was often the case, a boat was waiting at the Euphrates dock to be loaded with grain and other items to be taken to the other cities along the river, and to caravans for transportation away from the water. This was the kind of work I sought; the kind that had shaped my body into a condition not matched in Nippur.

No one questioned the superiority of my physique, but few knew of my reasons for developing it. My parents knew, but my mother did not approve, so it was not discussed much in our home.

Mother came from a different background than Father; different, in fact, than most around us. Her family was Shemite, as were the others, but hers was of a different clan. Father had met her in Ur while trading there. She had told him then of certain of her ancestors on her mother's side who left that city in times past, led, they believed, by the one true God. Mother had told me many stories about these people, now called "Hebrews," and that though she knew little about Him, she believed that there was but one God: the God of the Hebrews.

Her father was another story. She was always reluctant to speak of him or his heritage, but I knew instinctively that there was something special about my grandfather, even if I had never met him. Details were whispered between my parents when they thought my sisters and I were asleep. I heard one name repeated frequently - Haran.

As to the religious matters, Father cared little about them, and I even less. As far as I was concerned, the gods could take care of themselves; I was going to make the most of my life. What I had accomplished so far had convinced me that I could do whatever I needed to do to achieve greatness.

"Good morning, Kasher!" The cheery voice was from the boat's pilot, Utanin Urdak. I had helped him many times before, and we got along quite well. He was not a tall man, and he did not have the kind of obvious muscle that I did, but there was surprising strength in that small frame. Every time I had worked for him he was always involved in the actual loading of the boat, and there were few around the docks that could lift more than he.

His skin had a rough quality to it that was common to the men who worked on the river. His hair had probably been quite dark, and there was still a black strand here and there, almost completely superseded by the gray of his forty-plus years; not to mention the bleaching affect that so much time in the desert sun had brought about.

"Good morning, sir," I returned. "Any work for me today?"

"Always enough work for a good hand," he said. "Also, I'm short a trip man today. Any possibility you could ride with me and help unload? We plan to start the return trip next week."

Trying to mask my excitement, I asked, "Where to?"

His nonchalant answer brought a flood of images to my mind.

He said, "Babylon."

Chapter 2

"Babylon."

I had heard so many things from so many people about the great city that I felt I had seen it. In fact, I had never left Nippur; not unusual for a man of my years. There was much trade between the cities during this time of relative peace, but travel was still perilous in many ways.

The river was said to be alive, deciding for itself how to act and when to change its behavior. It was almost time for the floods - great for irrigation - which arrived in early summer. The canals had been in place for so long now that their origin was unknown. As long ago as the reign of Hammurabi, it was said, they had been in place, allowing not only for the watering of the fields but also for a partial taming of the rivers for navigational purposes. Nevertheless, many brave pilots had been lost beneath their waters, swollen from the melting snows in the mountains in the north combined with driving seasonal rains throughout the region.

The dry season was not without risk, either. There were times when the shallowness of the water made the river impassable in areas, and it was a long way between towns. Not a few men had disappeared in the desert, never to be found.

Then there were the thieves: usually nomadic bands of raiders with little regard for human life, and even less for the right of another to keep what he had. The traders would often anchor in midstream at night, but when the water was low, that offered little protection from the bandits.

All of these elements had created an atmosphere in which only those who had good reason dared to make the journeys along the Euphrates, and her sister, the Tigris to the east. My father had been a trader before my birth, but the responsibilities of a family had brought him to a decision to 'settle down' to the life of a farmer. It was not an easy life by any means, but much safer than braving the whims of the river. It was also much less exciting, challenging, and important as far as I was concerned. On long winter evenings he would often entertain us with stories of his time on the river. Mother would cringe, the girls would squeal, and I would cheer and beg for more as he told of the things he had seen and done. I could not imagine anyone giving up such a life as that for any reason.

Someone had to farm, that I knew, but I had decided very early that was not my life. I had worked the fields with my father until I my eighteenth year, and had not begrudged it too much. I was, however, very grateful that he had allowed me to begin another path at that age; another path that led to Babylon.

I could see it all in my mind's eye; the great avenues, the many palaces, the temples to the various gods, all overshadowed by one huge building, the Chamber of the Fates. It was said four chariots could ride abreast on the city wall. To experience it for myself so soon was more than I had hoped for; but, I was on my way!

In about two hours, our boat was loaded. It was typical of the boats along the river, and yet there were noticeable differences between it and the rest. It was about five cubits wide, the width staying the same for its entire length of about thirty cubits, and could hold a fairly valuable shipment, even of modestly priced goods. It was Utanin who had educated me about measurements, a very important part of loading a boat properly (a cubit being approximately the length from a man's fingers to his elbow, for example). Even though he always supervised the location of cargo on the boat, a general knowledge of how the weight should be distributed was helpful to anticipate his orders. He always seemed pleased to have me on the loading crew as I paid careful attention to how he wanted things done. Some of the others needed constant supervision, and even with it their loads often had to be adjusted for proper balance. The boat was shallow, allowing for the river work for which it was intended. There was nothing unusual in all of that.

Most of the boats were nothing more than reeds tightly lashed together; but not this one. It was plank-built, each board fitted to the next and sealed with bitumen. But that was not what made it stand out either. There were other plank-built boats around. The real difference was not something you could point to. There was simply a care in its construction that commanded attention. Even at first sight I could see that whoever had built this boat knew what he was doing; each board fitted expertly, all of the seams perfect. It was an old boat, but it showed little sign of wearing out. I knew also the extreme care that Utanin showed it.

He had shown me one day one of the secrets of his boat's stability. He revealed to me that he was not only the boat's owner, but he had, in fact, built it himself. We were alone at the dock just before sunset that day, and Utanin pointed out to me some reeds growing along the riverbank.

"This canal," he said, "was made by deepening a swampy area just here. The marshes still exist farther south, but the canals changed this spot forever. Once, right here, I met an old man from Susa. Nippur was once a part of that kingdom, you know. Anyway, this man saw my interest in boats and started talking to me about the old days before the canal was here. There were already other canals, but this area had been left alone. Nippur was abandoned for many years, and, during the time of his tale, it was just being rebuilt."

Utanin had a look on his face as if he were seeing the old man's story from his own memory. "He said the inhabitants at that time lived on what they could produce themselves - the conditions weren't favorable to trade yet. They mostly lived on fish they caught in the marshy water here, and they raised water buffalo for milk. The conditions here were perfect for rice, also, which they ate themselves and fed to their buffalo."

"He told how some of them used small, round boats made entirely of a flat mat of reeds; just big enough for one man. Though I've never seen it myself I've heard of tribes that still live that way, over on the lowlands near the Tigris."

"I didn't want to offend the old man, but I couldn't bring myself to believe that boats like that, just a thin mat of reeds, could hold a man's weight. I had been around boats all my life, and the only way to get a reed boat to float was to lash the reeds tightly together; almost forming a solid piece of wood. What he described would be flimsy. How could they support the weight of a man above the water?"

"I left him that day and spent the night in Nippur. The next morning, he met me at the river again. There, floating in front of him was a small, round boat, made of nothing but reeds."

"Without a word, he launched out into the water. I was sure he would sink – if not immediately, at least within a few moments. He didn't. The boat had obviously been thrown together quickly, and there was water around his feet, but the boat stayed afloat!"

"When he came back to shore he called me over to examine the boat closely, and I saw that he had sealed the ends of the reeds with bitumen.

Utanin continued quickly, obviously excited by his own story. "That day he and I started working on the design that eventually became this boat. Come; look!"

We boarded the boat, and Utanin went straight to the middle. There he knelt and pried a board loose. Only now did I notice that there was no bitumen showing on the inside of the boat. The seams were tight, but bare.

He lifted the board and called me over. I had expected to see either water or another layer of boards, but instead there were tightly bunched reeds. Utanin worked some of them up for me to see that they were placed in there about twenty deep.

"Our idea was that if the reeds by themselves floated, and together even sustained considerable weight on the water, then a quantity of them between layers of boards should increase a plank-boat's buoyancy. After considerable experimentation, we discovered that just the

14

two layers of wood - well sealed - would have the same effect; possibly even better. Apparently it is the air held in the reeds - and not the reeds themselves - that causes the floatation! I built one that way, and it worked great. Mine could carry much more cargo than other boats of the same size. The sealed chamber between the boards kept the boat higher in the water."

"So if you don't need the reeds, why do you have them there?" I asked.

"Well, one day, when the boat was loaded to its maximum capacity, I hit a submerged rock in the river. That seal was broken, the boat sank, and I lost a lot of cargo. After that I did some more experimentation, filling one with reeds like this. I loaded the boat heavy with rocks and broke its seal in shallow water. It sat down into the water and became sluggish, but it didn't sink! The water only came up to the top of the reeds. A cargo would have been saved in a real accident."

I was truly impressed by the results of all that experimentation, but what really stuck with me was the process. Utanin obviously knew how to put different ideas together to come up with something new and better. That was a quality I admired. I could learn a lot from him.

I went back to town to tell my parents that I would be gone for a while. I fully intended to return home with the boat. Little did I know that I was not to see Nippur for a long, long time.

Mother was working around the house; there was always much to do. My two sisters were only four and six, and still required a lot of care. As much as we

15

disagreed, I loved my mother dearly, and there were many things I admired about her. We were not all that different, really, both deeply committed - Mother to her family and her God; I to my ambitions.

As I drew close to the house she looked up. When she saw who I was, she started out to meet me. As she neared, she slowed, a worried look on her face.

"What's wrong?" I asked.

"That look in your eyes," she said, "is enough to concern any mother. What are you into now?"

"It's not what you think. I'm not doing anything mischievous. It's just that a great opportunity has come up. Utanin asked me to go along with him on this run. You'll never guess where we're headed!"

"Oh, son: not to Babylon! I know how thrilling it sounds, but there's so much wickedness in a big place like that. Who will watch over you?"

"Mother, I'm a grown man now. I don't need anyone to 'watch over me,'" I said, my heart growing heavy. "I thought you might be happy for me to have this chance. I guess I expected too much."

She caught my arm as I turned to walk away.

"Son, wait. You're right, and I am happy for you. I guess I was just giving in to my motherly instincts. But you're right, you are a man now, and besides, I must be willing to leave you in God's hands. He's much more capable than I of taking care of you."

"I don't need your god either, Mother. I can take care of anything I need to. Nothing has come along yet that I couldn't handle. Oh, maybe some small task that I couldn't do at first, but with a little more muscle, anything is possible."

"Kasher, I hate to think of what great problem will have to come your way before you see your limitations. You said you are a man, and so you are. But that's all you are, just a man; not a god. There are things over which the strongest man has no power. You will find this out. I only pray that Jehovah will have your attention before something really bad has to happen."

"I'm sorry Mother; I shouldn't have been so harsh. I do know that there are things beyond my power. And maybe there is a god, I don't know; but as long as I can handle the situation myself, I will."

"Yes, son, I'm sure you will, and I'm sure you're very capable of handling many of them. But when the time comes that you need help and your father and I aren't around, remember what I've told you about the one true God."

"I will, Mother; and thank you for caring. I must be going now. We are scheduled to start back next week.

I told her of Utanin's wonderful, unsinkable boat, hoping that would relieve some of her worries. It did seem to help.

"Tell Father 'goodbye' for me. I won't have time to get to the field and back to the boat before it must leave."

"Goodbye, Kasher, I will pray for you as always."

Her words trailed off as I ran toward the dock.

"I'll bring you something back from Babylon," I shouted back over my shoulder, "and something for the girls!"

The first part of the trip through town might as well have never happened, so intense were my thoughts of the trip ahead; and, of course, of our destination. Although I would not be permitted to enter the army until I was twenty, another year and a half, I felt sure that I could at least make some contacts in Babylon now that would help my placement when I was old enough to join. Although I was never considered a rude person, I was also not known to be shy. There would be no hesitation on my part to talk to anyone who would consider helping set me up in an army group that would see plenty of action. Those who did nothing would probably be known for doing just that. By the same token, those who were active would be seen and spoken of.

When I reached the market area my pace and my thoughts slowed. The market started a short ways up a small incline from the river, running down almost to the beginning of the main dock. Something about the early morning agitation there, so familiar to me, called to my mind. I felt a measure of shame that it had not come when I was saying good-bye to Mother, but the market seemed to define for me what Nippur was. It was all that I loathed and wanted rid of; and yet I couldn't deny the comfort I felt from its familiar sounds, sights and smells.

As I made my way through the stalls lining the road down to the river it seemed I was seeing it for the first time. The fruits and vegetables were the same as always, yet I had never noticed before how rich in color and texture they were. I paused for a moment at a table covered in dried dates. If someone had asked me before that moment what color dates were, I would have simply replied that they were brown. As I gazed down upon them now I saw a rich reddish-brown color, a strong contrast to the dullness of their surroundings. I looked slowly around me.

Beyond the market, looking into town, all was the same light brown of our soil. The houses blended in almost perfectly, as if they had risen spontaneously from the earth beneath them. Beyond the town, up and down the river, the irrigation had transformed the fields closest to the river into carpets of lush green which faded slowly into the brown of the desert as they spread away from the river. The farmers were anxious for the rains to begin, allowing that carpet to encroach farther upon the valley between the rivers.

As my attention came back to my immediate surroundings I began losing the romantic feeling the market had inspired. Reality returned to me first in the form of the noises one always heard here: sheep and goats bleating; heavy-handed stall owners screaming instructions to their workers; wheels that creaked and groaned, begging to be lubricated. The raucous chorus was reinforced by the smells: cheeses, already stinging the nostrils; pungent herbs; the harsh sweetness of fresh meat. Gaining strength in the sun's heat, all of this would soon have caused me to move away in disgust. Produce was removed from the carts, invariably leaving traces behind, already becoming acrid. The sun would evolve that smell as well, I recalled from many hot days in Nippur. As if the sounds and smells were not sufficient, all the beauty and color was quickly covered with the fine dust of the desert. The magic was gone. Everything was as it should be: brown, stinky and loud. I would not miss it all that much after all.

We cast off unceremoniously. Why should it be otherwise? This was just one of many boat launchings which took place almost every day in Nippur. Just another trader setting off for other places along the river. There was not even anything unusual about the fact that its final destination was Babylon. It was, after all, the center of everything; government, commerce, religion – the whole universe! I knew how normal our departure was, but it didn't stop my heart from pounding like a retreating army. I was sure that everyone who watched us casting off was sharing in my excitement. Surely the captain and crew were involved in my feelings of elation.

Reality (a new one; I was on the river!) hit me suddenly as Utanin called out, "Hey, Kasher. What do you think you are; a passenger? Get over there and do your part on the poles!"

Of course I had known that the trip would involve work. The boat had a sail, but even when the wind was sufficient to propel the craft well - which it wasn't at that moment - the crew would be constantly at work keeping debris away from the sides, watching for submerged sandbars and pushing off of them as they were encountered; not an unusual occurrence. Utanin manned the tiller, keeping us to the middle of the waterway.

As we moved north up the Euphrates toward the Shatt-en-Nil canal which would lead us to the other branch of the Euphrates – the one that ran through Babylon - Utanin called me back to his position.

"Let's see how much you know about your home city. What is that large wood structure there in the city wall?"

"That is the water gate for the city canal," I answered. "It is never opened these days, but it used to serve to fill the canal from the moat outside, or so I've been told."

I, like probably all the young people from Nippur, had spent hours exploring the city walls and the moat just beyond.

"You're right. A spring came up, sometime in the past, in the canal inside, making it unnecessary to bring water in through that gate."

"That, I didn't know," I said.

"What about that dark line just above the water level? What do you think that is?"

I looked hard. Finally, I noticed what seemed to be a small gap in the wood, obviously not like the joints between the other boards.

"I've never seen that before, but then, I've never been on this side of the gate."

"The larger structure of the gate was built that size in the beginning to let a lot of water pass quickly. After the inner canal was well established, a smaller opening was sufficient to keep the water level even inside and out. And, of course, even that is no longer necessary, so there is simply a wooden gate in the wall."

"How has the wood survived for so long?" I asked.

"It's made of the same wood I used to make this boat. It's called cedar, and it comes from up north in Lebanon. It will eventually rot from contact with the elements, but it has been known to last for amazing amounts of time, even in water."

"You would be surprised what can be of importance, Kasher. If you learn to be observant of your surroundings, the smallest thing can make a difference at times. That line is the top of the small door in the water gate. It was placed there by a great man of Nippur early on in the city's history. He was able to take great advantage of it for more than just equalizing water levels. During several sieges, food and weapons were brought into the city through it undetected. One of his enemies found out about it, eventually, and it became his downfall. The very thing that had enabled him to keep the city eventually allowed the enemy in as well."

About noon we reached the convergence of the canal and the river proper. There were small towns on both sides of the river here. Utanin explained that these towns, collectively known as Eresh, but independent from each other in their business, were flooded every year when the rains came. Someone always came back, though. It was an ideal spot for boat crews to rest as there was an army post nearby, discouraging thievery. The distance was not enough from Nippur to here for us to think about it, but if we had come all the way up from Ur, it would have been a good stopping point. I could see that most of the buildings were Inns. There were benches in front of most of them that were being used by young women. I was not very experienced with the opposite sex but I was pretty sure of their purpose there.

Utanin must have seen where I was looking as he said, "Not today, boy."

"Of course not," I answered, somewhat indignantly. "My mother taught me to treat women with respect."

"Good for her. These poor women don't get any of that, I can assure you."

"Why do they do it then?" Even as I asked the question I felt a twinge of guilt for being so judgmental. Utanin's response made my guilt sting even more.

"They don't have a choice, Kasher. They're slaves."

I mulled that information over for a while in silence. I had seen slaves before, and I had seen harlots in Nippur, but I had not encountered anything as vile as this. In my mind, a woman who chose to sell her body was worthy of scorn; but being forced to do so... that was a new kind of evil to me. I tried to put it out of my mind by concentrating on the boat work. Thankfully, we had some extra to do navigating the confluence. There were several other boats at the juncture too, so we had to be extra attentive, and the plight of those poor women was soon relegated to a back corner of my mind.

We travelled well into the dusk of the first day before stopping. We pulled up to a clear stretch of shoreline on a deserted stretch of the river. Jalen, one of the older crewmembers, had a fire going in no time, and I was grateful. I was imagining all sorts of bandits coming after us in the night. I asked Jalen about that and he told me that, while it was always possible, Utanin kept good track of where the dangers were along the river at any given moment.

"Remember when we passed Eresh?" he asked. Did you notice him talking with other river boat captains?"

"Yes, but to be honest I didn't pay much attention to their conversations. It seemed they were just being friendly. In fact, I heard him talk to some in a language I didn't understand."

Jalen smiled. "Those boats come from as far south as Eridu and from as far north as Nineveh. That covers a lot of languages. Our captain speaks them all. The boat captains keep each other informed about the dangers – and opportunities - on the river."

While Jalen was starting the fire another crewmember whose name I did not yet know slipped away down the bank of the river. In just minutes he returned with several large fish which we proceeded to roast over the fire. I was beginning to see a side of river life I hadn't known. Each of these men could no doubt have been successful on their own, but they had become something of a spontaneously developing community. There was no need for Utanin to bark out orders. Each man saw something that needed to be done and went at it. I was impressed to say the least. I remembered Utanin's advice about noticing what goes on around me. I believed I was learning valuable lessons from these men.

Even with Jalen's reassurance, I did not sleep very well. It was the first time I had slept in the open like this. Also, the excitement of what I was doing and where I was going had not even begun to wear off.

As I lay on my back looking into the night sky I found many of the star pictures my uncle had shown me. I knew by now something of their paths as they changed position daily, and even during any given night. Orion still held the greatest fascination for me, though I did not know why. As I looked at him, I saw something that took away what little drowsiness I had.

For years afterwards I would wonder if I had really seen it, If it had really happened, it had only lasted for a very short moment. By the time my eyes fixed on the spot I believed it to have occurred, it was gone.

I could only describe it as a flash, but it wasn't like a spark from the fire. It wasn't even like a falling star. It had appeared (if it really had) just below the three stars that make up Orion's girdle.

Eventually I fell asleep; entranced would probably be a better word. The last thing I remembered was still trying to focus on that spot in the sky, waiting in vain for another appearance of what I had seen. I would look for it for many nights to come.

The following morning came too soon for me. There was movement in our camp as soon as the sun began to light the horizon.

Myself included, we had a crew of six, plus the captain. Going upriver as we were, we would make four or five landings on our way, Utanin had said; not to unload, for our cargo was all destined for the capital. Our stops would be to rest and provision for the next leg of the trip. It was hot right now, very hot, and food did not last long. We took a little less than we expected to need each day, relying on fish we could catch to supplement our rations. We carried a small amount of wood as well, and, when the opportunity afforded itself, we stopped along the bank to prepare meals.

The time went by fast for the first two days. Utanin showed me a papyrus map of the canals and rivers of the area. He pointed out how we would travel along the inner branch of the Euphrates until it and the outer branch met, just before our third stopping point at Dilbat. There was always much to do which required my attention, so I had to limit my scheming to our times ashore. That was enough, though, to allow me to come up with many ideas. I had it all figured out by the middle of the third day. I was in complete control. Nothing could stop me now. I was on my way to Babylon!

And then the wind changed direction.

Chapter 3

As a boat captain of many years, I noticed the shifting of the wind almost immediately. My name is Utanin Urdak, named after some god or other to whom my mother was devoted. She had told me all about it once, but that was a long time and many thoughts ago. My belief in the gods was pretty basic, just like my ideas about most areas of life. The gods probably did exist, but since I had never seen one, they must not have been too concerned about me. And why should they be? I minded my own business, took care of people I found in need, and tried not to cheat anyone. Not too much, anyway.

I suppose everyone has a thought from time to time about the afterlife. My travels had brought me into contact with religions of many varieties, all of whom had one aspect in common. As far as I was concerned, they were much too worried about what happened after death, and not enough about the time before. The people I admired - and, admittedly they were few - were the ones who involved themselves with making their own part of the world a little better.

Occasionally, although very rarely, one encountered a man who seemed to have taken the good of religion and brought it down to earth in a practical manner. Nebuchadnezzar was just such a man in my opinion.

Some said he was a god himself, though I had never heard of his claiming deity for himself. On the other hand, I had never heard of his denying it, either.

Nebuchadnezzar grew up as the son of a king, and as such, he was not known in a personal way by a great number of people. It just so happened that I was one of the few who had spent time with him in his youth.

Of those who shared my life now, few knew anything about my days before the river work. Sure, I could have used it to my advantage in some situations, but there were still those, hard to believe, that did not share my admiration for the son of Nabopolassar. I suppose that anyone in power was bound to have enemies, and Nebuchadnezzar was no exception. No one spoke openly against him of course, but if certain factions found out about my connection, I could be in danger; and, more importantly, there was the potential that I might be used against the king somehow. Such things had already happened since his father died. Things were different now; much different for all of us…

"Utanin, come in here, please." The prince spoke, though not in the form of a command, with authority; as always. He was of kingly stock, and it showed. His father, King Nabopolassar, son of Nebuchadnezzar I, was proud of him, and justifiably so.

"Yes, what is it?"

"I just received this note from the palace. It says I'm supposed to receive the 'Scepter of Princes' tomorrow at noon."

"Isn't that supposed to be given on your eighteenth birthday?" I asked, reaching for the note he held out to me.

"Yes, and I don't think this is a good omen. Father is a stickler for protocol; especially in respect to the crown. He is a Chaldean you know."

Nebuchadnezzar was at that time only sixteen, his next birthday not for four months.

"So what do you want from me?"

"Listen, just because your father builds boats for my father…"

"The most wonderfully built boats in the world, you mean."

"Be that as it may, it does not give you the right to address me with disdain." Nebuchadnezzar spoke with mock harshness; then, in a normal tone, "But back to your question, I just thought that since you are out and about more than me, you might have heard something, and that as my friend, you might be able to help me prepare for this meeting I have with my father."

"Well, as a matter of fact I have heard something, although I don't know for sure if it pertains to your message. It is widely reported that the king, Nabopolassar the mighty, the ever glorious, the magnanimous, the…"

"All right, I think we have established who we are talking about. I do know him pretty well, you know."

"…king of all Babylonia, is not happy with the way his major conquests are going at the moment. It seems that, although his armies are winning most of their battles, the actual subjection of cities is moving at an 'unacceptably slow' rate."

"And you think that this has something to do with me?"

"Only a hunch. I must admit, though, that I don't see a clear connection between these problems and the scepter."

"Well, now that you bring up these details, I do," said the prince, rising to his feet. "The giving of the scepter is traditionally accomplished immediately before the king sends his son to his first army command."

"Ah, so you are to straighten out the 'conquest' problem. A little royal blood ought to fix things up in no time!"

"Very funny, Utanin: son of the royal boat-maker, royal joke-maker to the prince." Nebuchadnezzar said with a low bow.

"No, I'm serious! You have been exceptionally well prepared. You've caught on to the concepts of war with remarkable ease and quickness, and the bit about royal blood? That wasn't a joke either. I don't believe that it gives you any special abilities in itself, but there are many within the realm that do; and within the army there are quite a few who might just need a special presence to do a better job."

"You might have something there, Utanin. Listen, you've been here in the palace for what, four years now? What do you think my chances of commanding well are? All prejudice and friendship aside. I am only sixteen, you know."

"Nebuchadnezzar, if there was ever a sixteen-year-old who could do the job, it is you. I'm not saying it will just fall into your lap; it will be work. But I think that your father - your realm - needs you for this moment. This region is too unstable. I can understand why so many resist being taken over, but I'm convinced that it is in their best interest to ally with Nabopolassar. I think that most of the common people want to be part of Babylonia, but no king, no matter how small his territory or his army, is going to give up his kingdom without a fight. If what you said about the scepter holds true, I believe that, soon, you will be the major force that brings the world together under your father's rule. Meaning, of course, eventually *your* rule."

"Yes, that has not been far from my thoughts during this whole conversation. It is a sobering thought, as always."

"That is one reason you will be a great king. Your idea of ruling is not simply the concept of power, but of the great responsibility that power brings. Never lose that, and you will rule well."

"I must head toward the 'Chamber of Fates' now for this meeting. You will not be permitted inside, as you have no official status, but I would appreciate it very much if you would walk with me."

As we walked through the city, we talked little. Most of what was said was about the past few years we had spent together. I suppose that Nebuchadnezzar thought that my brooding was for the same reason as his; the impending change of his status in the realm. No doubt that was in my thoughts, but not foremost. My primary musing at this time was about my own future.

We passed the great monuments in silence, both of us looking on them as if we had never seen them before - or as if we might never see them again. Every once in a while one or the other of us would make some comment about one of them, especially the ones we had seen built ourselves. There were not many that had a great deal of age.

They formed a kind of corridor leading to the steps of the great hall, steps which first went down into a small garden with stone seats, and lamps hanging from the branches of magnificent trees. From there, the wide marble stairway led upwards to the massive cedar doors of the 'Chamber of Fates'. The great tower of Etemenanki rose up immediately behind.

We had a little time before the prince was due to enter, so we sat in the garden and spoke in low tones. There was no one else in the area, but it just didn't seem the place for loudness, nor was it necessary to raise your voice, so intense was the quiet there. The fact that the garden had been built below the level of the ground around it, along with the trees planted there, gave the effect of blocking out the normal sounds of life in the city. It was wonderfully cool there, even now in the middle of a summer afternoon.

The prince spoke first.

"I'm going to build gardens like this all over Babylon when I become king. No, not like this: bigger, grander gardens that will endure forever!"

"But the plants will die someday, won't they?" I asked.

"Yes, but the gardens I envision will be remembered and spoken of long after they have passed from the earth. In that way they will remain forever."

"Your reign may have just that effect itself."

"Utanin, I've been giving it a lot of thought; not just now, but for quite a while. I would like to have you as my aide when I become a general."

"I am indeed flattered, my prince, but I'm afraid that would be out of the question. You see I..."

"Oh, I know, you're afraid of it because you have no official training. Well don't let that bother you. I think you have wisdom beyond your years, and the areas where your education is lacking can be patched up in no time."

"Nebuchadnezzar, if you have one problem that is going to rise up against you more than any other, it is your inability to patiently listen to a matter to its conclusion. I was not going to say anything along those lines. What I was about to say was, I've made a decision to follow a different path. My father has offered me a boat of my own, and has set me up with some good prospects for the shipping business. Don't ask me why, I just believe this is the right course of action for me."

"Utanin, don't you realize what it is I'm offering you? I could bring you right into a governorship or something when I become king. And life might not be too bad in the meantime. It would mean some military life for a while; but things would be pretty nice for you between campaigns."

"I've considered all of that - and I am grateful, believe me, that you would offer me so much. But I'm convinced that I've chosen the right direction. Who knows, maybe I will be able to be of greater service to you as a boat captain than constantly at your side."

"I can't see how that might happen; although the gods could bring it about I'm sure. Nevertheless, I respect your decision without completely understanding it, and I wish you the very best. You realize, of course, that my preparation will take up most of my time until I am sent out on campaign. I think I shall not see much of you from now on."

"Yes, I realize that, and I've just decided to go ahead and move out of the palace now. Father said I could take the boat whenever I was ready, and I think I will start getting things together tomorrow."

"Well then Utanin, my good friend, I shall take this moment to say goodbye. Our friendship need not end though our relationship will no longer be close. I shall look for you when I ride the banks of the rivers. I make no promise of the future, but I believe the gods will bring us back together in their time."

"I sincerely hope so, Nebuchadnezzar. If there be any gods, I hope they guide you. I shall remain your most loyal of subjects. Goodbye, my prince."

Chapter 4

Utanin was already moving from the tiller to the sail by the time I realized there was a shift in the wind. We had been feeling a cool breeze from the mountains in the northeast since the night before, but now the desert - never far from the shores of the Euphrates - made its presence known in a real way.

The days had been quite pleasant. We had been making good time according to Utanin, and we needed two days at most, probably one good one, to reach Babylon.

Only a short distance from the west bank of the river was one of the most disagreeable pieces of land known to mankind. It stretched, in varying degrees of hatefulness, all the way to the Jordan River. Most of our agriculture was done between the Tigris and the Euphrates: that area washed fertile by the combination of the twin waterways and the irrigation ditches between, in some places connecting the rivers. The only ones who ever ventured far from the 'land between the rivers' were the wandering nomads, military men on a mission and the hardiest of caravan traders. These knew only too well the sudden hot windstorms which drove sand before them with devastating force. They were ready at all times to dig themselves into the sand and ride out the storms.

As I found out later, Utanin had weathered a few of these storms himself, having lived along the river for so long. But there was something wrong, now. One look at Utanin's face revealed both resolve and deep concern. Resolve, because he knew what had to be done. Concern, well, that was turning to outright fear.

"Too sudden," he was saying. "No time - it's coming too fast this time."

I could hear only that much. The wind was already swallowing up the rest of his mutterings.

The problem was that we were just passing an island in the middle of the river at that point. If we had been able to reach the actual east bank, we could have traveled away from the water and the desert quickly, and so diminished the amount of blowing sand we had to deal with. This island interjected a problem.

We could all see the problem; the rest of us not as quickly as the captain. As we were just beginning to grasp the whole situation, and bent our poles pushing away from the island, Utanin was already frantically working the sail - trying to use even the contrary wind to somehow keep us moving forward.

Then the worst happened. Just as the wind was reaching full force, we rounded the north end of the island. It looked for a moment like we might retain control of the boat and bring it to shore. Then we struck a submerged sandbar.

The boat, like all good river boats, only required about a cubit of water under the keel. We were heavy - even for this special boat, and with the wind stirring up the water, we struck the bar hard and lodged solidly.

As Utanin was still trying to get all the benefit he could out of the wind, the sail was completely unfurled.

When we ceased making headway all of a sudden, the wind - blowing so hard from our left - began immediately to turn the boat over. Looking away from the wind as the boat began to roll, we saw with dismay that we were still a long ways from shore. Above the din of wind and splintering wood I heard Utanin shout, "Jump!"

It only took a second for my mind to assimilate the command, grasp the good sense of obeying, and instruct my body to act - but it was almost too much time. The boat was coming over fast when I gathered all the strength in my legs beneath me and pushed out. Almost instantly, the boat crashed upside-down behind me, its cargo flying in all directions.

I had cleared it well enough, and I found I could stand in the water and keep my head above; but just barely. Looking around I saw only the capsized boat. After a closer look, however, I saw a thrashing motion at the near edge of the vessel. Making my way toward the movement (slowly, as I was fighting the wind and the water), I saw it was a hand that was stirring the water, but the one to whom the hand belonged was completely submerged. Fortunately, I was still able to stand with my head out of the water as I reached that flailing hand. I grabbed, and pulled, and, after what seemed like minutes, a body became visible through the murky water. As the head cleared the surface, I recognized the face of Utanin - but it looked strange. It was a bluish-purple color, and it was obvious that he was not breathing.

Dragging the dead weight of humanity behind me, I made quickly for shore. It didn't take long, the wind now more or less at my back, but knowing that Utanin was not breathing made it seem an eternity. Just as we reached land, I heard coughing behind me. For a moment, I was afraid to look back, but when I did, I saw Utanin was on his side, hacking and heaving violently.

He collapsed, and I laid him out as best as I could on the shore. He had stopped the coughing and was still now, but I could see by the swell and recession of his chest that he was breathing, although still with occasional shudders. I looked around to see if there was any place to get out of the ferocious wind. The powdery sand was blowing so hard it felt as though it would shave my skin right off, and it was already beginning to cover one side of Utanin as he lay on the shore.

There was nothing for shelter; no vegetation - not even a rock to hide behind. I was elated that we had survived, but I was completely out of strength. I simply couldn't go any farther. The sand piled higher on Utanin's unconscious body. I had to do something or he - maybe we - would be buried.

Utanin's talk about the water gate as we left Nippur came back to me in that moment. "Notice your surroundings!" I shouted at the wind. I began looking around for anything that could be of help. There were a few reeds low in the water along the shore. Those hollow reeds – like the ones between the boards of the boat! I struggled to the water's edge and pulled two of them, hollow in their middles, from below the surface of the churning river edge. I put one in Utanin's mouth and closed his lips around it as best I could. I had little hope that he would breathe through the reed well, but I had to try. I tore a part of my sleeve off, making a cover for his eyes and nose. Having done the same for myself, I pushed in close to him, put the reed in my mouth, and settled in for I knew not how long.

In some ways, I envied Utanin. He had no way of knowing what was going on. I fully expected that we would both die. The reeds might not be long enough; they might break; my hand which held the reed in his mouth might get tired. If we died, Utanin would know nothing about it. I, on the other hand, would be spectator to the entire process. He would go to the next life ...

What was I thinking: The next life? Did that exist? I had always been quite sure that there was no other life; that I had only this one to do with, only this one in which to make a name for myself. But now, so real was the confrontation of death for the first time in my life, I was not so sure. Maybe mother's religion was right, maybe the beliefs of the Chaldeans, maybe some combination of them and others. All I knew for certain was that I was facing the situation mother had spoken of so recently. I could not, for all my great physical strength, do anything to save myself. I was in the hands of fate, or God, or something; but not my own. I was frightened.

"God...if you exist...I don't know, I just don't know! I don't want to die. So many dreams; so many ambitions. Do you speak to people? Do you control the wind? Are you killing me, or is it just circumstances? It's getting harder to breathe...I'm scared...Sand in the reed!...I can't breathe.."

It was dark, but not the utter absence of light I was expecting. There were shadows - a few. I could still hear the wind, but it seemed much more distant. I tried to move my hand, and it moved without restriction. No sand! I was conscious, but was I still in the same life? Was this another world?

A light suddenly moved across my left cheek, and I turned my head quickly toward the source. My head spun; my vision was blurry, but I made out the shape of a person. At least it looked like a person. My eyes slowly began to clear, and I could see the form moving in my direction, something in its hand. A voice spoke. I recognized the language as my own, although there was a slightly different accent. Slowly my head began to clear.

I was in a tent; or rather in a room of a tent. The figure moving toward me was a woman, or a girl; her age I could not yet distinguish. The voice had the high quality of femininity to it, and so I decided the voice and the figure were related.

I tried to rise, but the voice - smooth but firm - directed me to lie still. My head agreed with the voice. It took a few moments for the spinning to settle down. My mouth was dry; so very dry. I tried to speak, but could only make a few unintelligible sounds. My mind wasn't much more intelligible, but I began to remember the wind - the water - Utanin!

"Utanin!" I croaked.

"Is that your friend's name?" asked the female voice, very clear now.

"Yes, did he make it? Is he all right?"

"Stay calm. Yes, he made it through fairly well. He's still unconscious, but that's not surprising, considering what you two went through. In fact, I'd say you both should be very thankful to even be alive."

"I can still hear the storm outside," I said. "Someone found us in time."

"Yes, that was my father and his men. They had lost a few goats just as the storm came up, and were looking for them when they stumbled onto you in the sand. They thought you were dead at first, but when they discovered you weren't, they brought you here."

"And where would here be?" I asked, able finally to look around a bit. I could see her now; young, about my age. I'm sure the circumstances had something to do with it, but if I was ever to see an angel, I thought it was now.

"You are in the tent of my father, Ibni-amurru, the greatest man in the Udhayb valley."

"Not only in his tent, but forever in his debt. What about the other men from the boat?"

"No one else has been found so far, I'm afraid."

"My name is Kasher. I come from Nippur. I was working my way to Babylon. How far is it from here?"

"Not far at all. We spend a great deal of time in the markets there. Even with our herds and carts it is less than a day's travel. We have smaller tents that we take to stay in while we are there. We were to go tomorrow, but the weather seems to have other ideas. God willing, we will go in a few days."

"You talk of the will of God. Is that just an expression to you or are you one of those religious types?"

"Oh, it is not merely an expression to me. I believe in the God of Abraham, Jehovah. He is the All-powerful One, the only true God."

"Listen, I really appreciate the fact that you and your family have saved our lives, but you should know that I don't believe in gods. You saved me, not some 'super being.' My mother follows that Abraham thing too, but I didn't see Jehovah or anyone else reaching down out of heaven to get us out of the sand and water."

"Kasher, I know I can't prove the existence of Jehovah to you, and I won't waste time trying. I am sure, though, that our finding you was no coincidence. Only time will tell what all this will reveal. Right now you need to rest. Drink this soup and we can talk later."

As soon as she had arranged things for me to eat, and made sure my comfort, she turned to leave.

"Wait," I called after her. "I don't even know your name yet."

"Ruhamah."

Her name floated back to me like chaff on a gentle breeze; and then she was gone through a flap into another compartment of the tent. I knew I was being influenced in part by what I had been through, but I had never experienced such strong feelings about a member of the opposite sex. Not that I was in any condition to begin a courtship, but this was special.

The soup she gave me was thin, obviously made so in order to not upset my stomach as I had been some time without food - unless you could count the large quantities of sand I had ingested. Thin the soup was, but still very tasty, and filled with strength-replacing meat broth. My throat was raw, but little by little I was able to coax the soup down, enjoying the taste of it in my mouth as much as anything I had ever eaten. How long had I been unconscious to react so to this meal? I considered calling for Ruhamah, as much to see her again and confirm my initial reaction as to get more information from her. But as I was pondering the wisdom of such a move, the warmth of the soup began to spread through my body, slowing my thought process. I set the bowl down on the low table beside my bed.

The next thing I knew I was awakening to the same voice that had brought me alive earlier. The difference was that this time it was singing softly, accompanied by a stringed instrument of some sort. Now I was sure – I was either dead and in some sort of paradise, or I was still under the sand dreaming, because the sound of that voice singing like that could not possibly correspond to the world I knew.

I sat up a little too fast and swooned a bit, groaning involuntarily. Ruhamah, in the next room, heard, and ceased her playing and singing. The flap between the two rooms was pulled back just as I managed to sit up on the bed. Ruhamah came through accompanied by a man who looked to be in his fifties. The girl stepped aside for him to come to me first, and he held out his hand in greeting, the smile on his face genuine, but not completely hiding other emotions. He appeared to be concerned for what I had been through, but I thought I detected some caution as well; as though he was wondering what kind of people he had brought into his house.

"How do you feel, young man?" He asked in a voice hard from years of outdoor work, softened as much as he could for the occasion.

"Quite a bit better now, thank you. The soup and the rest have made quite a difference already. I assume I have you to thank for saving my life."

"We were caught by surprise like you were by the storm," replied the older man. "I've never seen one come up so fast. We were rounding up a herd of goats we had near the river. One of my men was coming back from the river's edge when he stumbled, literally, over you and your friend. We were headed that way looking for him and heard him yelling for help when he found you. By the way, my name is Ibni-amurru."

"A great pleasure to meet you, sir. My name is Kasher. Could you tell me, how much time has passed since the storm began?"

"Another strange thing. I've never seen a sand storm last so long. It started five days ago, and it is just now really calming down."

I had known unconsciously that something was different, but hadn't noticed yet that it was the lack of noise from the wind. Silence can truly be deafening.

"No wonder I was so hungry and thirsty when I woke. Now, please - how is Utanin?"

"We're still worried about him. He hasn't awoken yet, and he has quite a fever. We are pretty good with remedies and we're applying all the herbs we know to use, but so far he hasn't improved."

"I'd like to see him if you don't mind," I said.

"Of course. Let's see if you have the strength to get off that bed."

I lifted up on one elbow, and then sat up all the way.

"No dizziness now. I'll be alright."

"Good. Ruhamah, please accompany Kasher to visit his friend. I have a tremendous amount of work to catch up on now that the wind will allow it. Hopefully we didn't lose too many of the animals."

She led me through the labyrinth that was their home. I began to see what a complex structure it really was. None of the divisions of the rooms joined the outside world directly; they were all buffered by something of an antechamber that went all the way round, partly made from skins and partly from reeds. It served as a buffer from the heat, the outer area noticeably warmer than where I had been. It also buffered the noise from outside.

There was still some wind; nothing like what we had already experienced, but still noticeable now that we were in this outer ring which we used to get from one part of the tent to another. From inside any of the inner rooms, the wind was just a whisper.

Thinking out loud (a bad habit of mine), I said, "A lot of goats got skinned to build this thing!"

Ruhamah giggled, and I was lost to her forever. She had already charmed me, but that little laugh was too much for my already tender heart to ignore.

She went before me into another room, and as I came in, I saw Utanin lying on a low pallet of skins like I had been on myself. He looked peaceful, if a bit pale. His breathing seemed completely normal, but when I talked to him, there was no sign of comprehension.

I had been around dead people, a few. I had helped my father remove bodies from a battlefield near our farm when Nebuchadnezzar had been there making his stand against the rebels in Nippur.

The rebels had had the support of the Assyrians and the Egyptians, but they were no match for the great Babylonian general. While there were losses on both sides, the rebels were almost completely wiped out.

"Good riddance," my father had said. "Most of them were recently brought in from Egypt anyway. Troublemakers all, those Egyptians."

Still, we couldn't leave the bodies to rot in the sun so close to our home and farm. I remembered how they looked.

Utanin looked like he was at least half-way there, but I wasn't ready to bury him just yet. Little did I know how much this man would still figure into my life.

Ruhamah and I talked in low tones at his side for quite a while. I confess it seemed like only minutes, so pleasant was her company to me. In reality we talked for more than two hours. Just as she said something about having some supper, Utanin began to stir. It was at once both encouraging and disturbing. He was groaning, which was a sign of life, but it also showed that he was in pain. Neither of us knew if he was getting better or just working his way out of this life. Either way, it caused a turn in our conversation. We began discussing weightier things like life, death, what comes after…

Ruhamah related things she had learned from her mother. I could hardly believe what I was hearing. She sounded almost exactly like *my* mother, only possibly a little less certain of what she was saying. I expounded my great wisdom, explaining my lack of need of a god of any kind. All of a sudden she shocked me with a comment I wasn't expecting.

"'The moment we believe ourselves invincible, God has a way of showing us the truth about ourselves.'"

"Where did that come from?" I asked, trying to mask the impact the statement had had on me.

"A man named Jeremiah said that once, right here in this tent. I have not been able to shake that thought. It keeps me thinking straight, I believe. It is as important to know our weaknesses as to trust in our strengths, I think."

"I could agree with that to a point," I said. "But I only want to know my weaknesses in order to overcome them."

The way she looked at me was disarming. I don't know if she was displaying concern for me, disdain for what I said or just plain puzzlement, but I had seen the look before in the eyes of my mother. It seemed clear the conversation was over, and she simply dabbed at Utanin's forehead with a damp cloth and proceeded to lead me to the eating area.

Chapter 5

Utanin was recovering well, but he did not seem to be as robust as he was before; according to Kasher, at least. My father was getting more and more anxious about their presence here, even though neither of them had given us a reason for concern. Maybe it was the way Kasher looked at me. That did concern me a bit, but probably not for the same reasons. With me it was a matter of how it made me feel.

He was just so different from all the young men I knew. He was certainly no shepherd. I didn't think I was better than them; it wasn't that. It was just that Kasher was so driven; so focused about what he wanted from his life. He had already told me of his upbringing, and it was, to me, refreshing that someone would want to break out of the family mold. I had never told anyone, but I had such aspirations myself. Nothing radical, I just could not see myself in a goatskin tent for the rest of my life.

More than anything else, I think, was my desire to be around other people. I lived for the times we went to Babylon to participate in the market. There I felt like I was being carried by the flow of a great river; a tide of humanity, ideas and development. Here there were just sheep and goats.

Not that Babylon was perfect. What a cauldron of religions! I don't know how they kept their gods straight, there were so many of them. And it seemed like religion was more of a pretext for individual advancement than anything else. If you belonged to the right religion, if you worshiped at the right temple, you could move up fast. The problem was that the most popular god today could be despised by those in power tomorrow. And what about the truth? If there were so many gods – and I don't believe there are – what sense does it make that they should be in such competition with each other. Surely one of them would have to be superior to the others, and he should be the one always worshiped.

I had not learned as much as I would have liked from my mother about Jehovah. She said - and I believed still – that He was the only true God, the creator of all. Mother told me about all the great things He had done through the years, mostly in favor of His chosen people, the descendants of Abraham. Her family was from a group that had gone with Abraham from Ur of the Chaldees to Haran, a little ways north of Babylon. From there, my mother said, Abraham went to Canaan a few years later. Some of the family stayed behind in Haran; my mother's ancestors included. She said that many of them believed in Jehovah, but the family leaders at that time either didn't believe, or simply didn't think it best to continue on with Abraham.

It had been many generations since all that took place, and much information about God and his operations in the world was lost to us. Once in a while a man of God, a prophet, would come through and speak to all who would hear about Jehovah, but his job was not an easy one in this part of the world. There had been several over the years, but I only met one personally. His name was Jeremiah, and he was different.

"Ruhamah!"

It was Father, and I knew by his tone that there was work ahead for me.

"Ruhamah – Ah, there you are. We have company. Please prepare a meal, but keep it simple. I've heard about this man, and he can be difficult. We want to put on just enough hospitality to keep our reputation in order; and not enough to encourage him to stay too long."

As I looked down the road I saw a man who was probably tall, but the way he walked stooped over made it difficult to say for sure. Even from this distance he looked like someone who had seen too much of the negative side of life and was worn down by it.

I didn't have much time to reflect on the condition of our guest. My mother died when I was ten, and since then I was the only woman in the family. I was only fifteen when Jeremiah first came to visit, but I had played the role of matron for so long that it came natural to me now. I began the preparations that I knew were necessary.

Later, as Father and Jeremiah were resting in front of the tent, I went and sat with them. They were talking religion, and even though they spoke in even and calm tones, I could sense considerable tension in the words that floated between them.

"So you are saying that God is using Babylon to exact His revenge on His own people? How does that fit with those fancy ideas you like to expound about His love and forgiveness?"

My father never claimed to believe in Jehovah, or any other god, but he had listened closely over the years to several men like Jeremiah (if anyone could really be like Jeremiah). He had knowledge of the Hebrew Scriptures that would be envied by many of their scribes.

"I never used the word 'revenge'," replied Jeremiah, his passion never greatly concealed. "I said that Babylon is unwittingly being used by God to chastise us. He does love and forgive, but what kind of father is it that does not correct his children when they stray from the safe path? How are children to know how they should conduct themselves without a parents help?"

"All right, I can accept that to a point; but do you think that Nebuchadnezzar doesn't know what is going on? Assuming you are right about what God is doing, what makes you think that Nebuchadnezzar isn't following God's instructions like others have done in the past? He's a very intelligent man."

"I've been there," answered Jeremiah, "not just in Babylon, but inside the court itself. The king receives me on occasion, as long as I don't push too hard. He is a hard man to read, and I agree with you about his intelligence. I have declared to him several times what I have told you today, but as of yet he cannot bring himself to accept it. He vacillates between giving Jehovah credit for his successes and bragging about how it is he who has built this astonishing kingdom. Mark my words, someday he will go too far and Jehovah's patience will come to an end."

"Nebuchadnezzar will have to die someday, of course, but Babylon is here to stay," said my father.

"You are a student of history and you believe that? How many kingdoms have believed that before? And how many still remain? The same principles apply to governments that apply to individuals. The moment we believe ourselves invincible, God has a way of showing us the truth about ourselves."

The conversation lasted a while longer, but I had cleaning up to do. When I came back to the front of the tent, Father was gone; no doubt taking care of the many necessary evening preparations. There were so many things against which we had to guard the livestock: Wild animals, thieves, even themselves. Sheep are not known for great intelligence or self-preservation mechanisms, and goats aren't a whole lot better. I remembered Mother reading a psalm to me that compared people to sheep. I had to agree that both needed a shepherd to watch out for them.

I sat down where my father had been, and Jeremiah looked at me for a while without speaking. It was a little unnerving at first, but when I took a better look at his eyes I saw he really wasn't looking at me. He seemed lost in thought, and his gaze just seemed to pass my way.

I saw a depth of sadness in those eyes that I had never seen before. It looked as though his heart would break, and I wanted so much to ask him what was wrong, but I didn't dare break his concentration. I didn't understand much about God, but in the days after my mother's death I had spent a lot of time alone, praying, crying, reaching out for comfort that I knew could not come from any human source. What I saw in Jeremiah's face reminded me of that time; and if he was going through anything like what I thought he was, he needed to be alone with his God.

We sat like that for quite a few minutes. I tried not to stare, and I didn't want to get up for fear I would disturb him. Finally his eyes closed. He stayed like that a little longer, and then, with a great sigh, he looked up. As I was still in his line of sight, he looked at me, not a little perplexed at my presence.

"Hello," he began weakly. "How long have you been there?"

"A little while. I didn't want to bother you. I'm sorry if I have."

"Not at all, child; It is I who should apologize for ignoring you. Sometimes it is just too much for me."

"What is, sir, if I may ask? I don't mean to pry into your private thoughts, but you seemed in such agony. Is there anything I can do to help?"

"You are so kind. Thank you, but my distress has no remedy in this world. I hurt for my people. I don't know why God chose me for this task, but I must accept it no matter how painful. I want so much to simply walk away from it all. It is such a weight on me. But I can't."

"Is He so cruel a master?" I asked. "I don't want to think that Jehovah is like all those gods I've heard spoken of in Babylon. They seem to enjoy inflicting pain on their subjects."

"Oh, I could never consider Him to be cruel. Some of us may have to endure more suffering than others, but our own wickedness is the real cause of it all. When He called Father Abraham out of his home in the south, He was showing a special kindness to him and his descendants. We just seem to be very adept at spurning His gifts. He wants to be our helper, and we turn from Him time and time again."

"You see this rod I carry?" he continued. What tree do you suppose it to be from?"

"I'm afraid I'm not too good with such things, sir"

"It is an almond branch. I carry it to remind me of the first vision with which the Lord burdened me. It was just such a branch I saw, and He explained to me that just as the almond is the first to bloom in the spring, His

52

judgment would come soon upon His people. You see that pot boiling yonder? That was the second vision. The one I saw was boiling over, and the liquid spilt out toward the north. God said that was to show me from what direction His chastisement would come. Babylon. Is He cruel to cry out to us to turn around? Is He cruel to send prophets with such clear visions to warn us of our error? Is he not gracious even in His punishment that we are not simply destroyed from the earth for our iniquities? Even now, when so many of the Hebrews are in captivity, His promise stands true. He will not forsake us utterly. We will be restored when the cleansing is complete."

"It seems impossible that a king so great as Nebuchadnezzar could ever be overthrown," I said.

"I didn't say I knew how God would restore His people; just that He promised He would. He has never lied, and I have no reason to believe He ever will. One of the few things that cheers me even while carrying my great burden is trying to imagine how He will perform this particular redemption. I have no doubt it will be amazing; it always is!"

I left Jeremiah to his meditations and went into my room to relax with my music. Mother had left me few things, and the most precious of them to me was the little ten-stringed instrument I played in the evening. She had played it to me every night, and she sang beautiful songs about the love and justice of God.

And peace – that was the idea that touched me most. Even with all his sorrow, Jeremiah seemed to have peace! He trusted Jehovah completely, no matter the circumstances, and that gave him strength to carry on.

Mother had started teaching me how to play and sing shortly before she died, and I continued to play what I knew, and even learned new sounds by experimentation. I would never sleep, no matter how tired I was from the day's work, without singing at least one of Mother's psalms.

Jeremiah slept in the room I had prepared for him: or at least I assume he slept, for when I awoke the next morning to the dawn, he was already gone. I had heard groaning sounds in the night, and I was sure it was him. What a strange and intriguing man.

Chapter 6

Utanin was recovering very well now, but he seemed to have a haunted air about him. He seemed all too aware of how close he had come to departing for good. He just couldn't seem to get excited about mundane things - like making money, for instance - like he used to. This bothered Kasher, but he couldn't quite decide why. Was it because he thought Utanin was somehow less than he was before; or was it that he envied him some new insight?

Utanin's focus had certainly changed, but Kasher's had not. Instead, he had added new ambitions without dismissing any of the old ones. Babylon and the King's Guard were still uppermost on his mind, and the recent ordeal only served to bolster his self-confidence. True, a new interest - and a lovely one at that - had come on the scene, but he was determined not to let anyone or anything deter him from his life's goal. After all, he had survived a near death experience. Wasn't that some kind of sign that great things still lay ahead?

Both men had pitched in to help Ruhamah and her father. It was the least they could do for all their help. The sand storm had been a particularly destructive one, and there was much to be done to restore order. They had been there for almost a month, and everyone knew it was time for them to move on. Everyone except Ruhamah, that is.

"Just a few more days, Kasher, that's all," she said. "There are still a lot of goats missing, and not all the tents are completely repaired yet."

"Ruhamah, I don't think we will find any more of your goats now. If they haven't appeared yet, someone is probably milking them over on the Tigris!"

"That must have been some ride!" chimed in Utanin. "I can just imagine what new gods have been invented by the 'sky watchers.' They'll soon have us bowing down to every four-legged animal that happens to fly past."

"Look, Ruhamah," said Kasher, ignoring for the moment Utanin's nonsense, "if your father says we still owe him for the hospitality, we will absolutely stay as long as he thinks is right. I'll ask him when he comes in, but if he is satisfied with what we've done, we must get on to Babylon."

"But Kasher," she said, "you told me yourself you didn't know exactly how to get an audience with the king or the captain of his Guard. Just what will you do when you get there?"

"I've been meaning to talk to you about that, Kasher," interjected Utanin.

When Utanin had finished revealing his relationship to the king, both Kasher and Ruhamah sat in a stunned silence for a long moment.

"Why didn't you tell me this before?" asked Kasher, a look of amazement still on his face.

"Why should I? You were nothing but a boat hand. Sure, I liked you well enough; but I owed you nothing but a workman's wage. Now, of course, I owe you my life, and that puts things in a different light."

"So... just what form of payment do you have in mind for this debt you now owe?"

"How about an audience with the king? Do you think that would even things up?"

Ruhamah knew she had lost now. There was nothing that she could do or say that would keep Kasher around any longer. When her father came home that night he made it clear that he felt more than recompensed for his help and hospitality. There was no obligation left.

She was surprised at how much her heart ached at the thought of his leaving. She knew she was very fond of him, but when she allowed herself to contemplate never seeing him again, it was more than she could bear.

They were packing to leave the next day. Her father had given them a donkey to carry their few items - mostly food and drink - to take them to Babylon. They didn't need much, not with a direct connection to Nebuchadnezzar himself!

Both Ruhamah and Kasher spent a restless night, Kasher's agitation was doubled; the excitement of finally getting to Babylon was coupled with the feeling of loss for leaving Ruhamah. For her part, Ruhamah was almost as angry with herself for the depth of her feelings as she was perturbed at the reason for them. Why had she allowed herself to feel so strongly about this boy? Sure, he was handsome and witty. But was that enough to make her miserable because he wouldn't stay around?

Apparently it was, because miserable was the right word for the way she felt.

She paced in her room for hours, trying desperately to come up with any reason he should not be so important to her.

He is kind of arrogant.

Then she realized that she was actually impressed with his confident manner. He was such a contradiction. He could be as shy as a mouse around her one moment and as bold as an eagle the next.

He really is a little wild. Why doesn't he just settle down here and make a good life for himself?

Of course, one of the things that so attracted her to him was his brave, almost brazen, way of seeing things. He was going to do something grand with his life, not just something good. That both excited and frightened her.

It's better that he goes; I can't imagine spending my whole life with someone like him anyway.

Of course, that was just what she had been imagining for quite some time; and if he left, that dream was surely over.

Kasher also passed the night without much rest. To say that his heart was pulled in two directions would be to greatly understate the case. He felt as if it had been cut in two with a sword.

How could I let myself get so distracted? I have a plan, and nothing can be allowed to throw me off course. It's my destiny!

He knew full well, however, that something was very different from when he had left home.

It was just a wind storm; a natural weather occurrence.

But that storm, like it or not, changed everything. It brought Ruhamah into his life. He could leave, but he could never be what he was before.

But we make our own destiny, don't we?

As much as he didn't like to admit it, even to himself, he was beginning to see a pattern developing in which he could only control his responses to certain circumstances. It was beginning to look like there was some sort of outside influence, at least in some parts of his life.

All coincidence.

But what a set of coincidences! Not only had the storm brought him to a girl he was sure he would never forget, she also turned out to be a follower of his mother's God.

There was just too much to think about for him to get a good night's sleep, but he forced himself to envision the glorious entry he would have into the Great City tomorrow. He awoke still imagining what it must be like; he must have slept a little after all. Very little, that was for sure. No matter. The excitement of the day would sustain him.

The dawn was blue, but not the blue of a clear sky. A cool haze covered everything, bringing visibility down to just a few paces. The air seemed filled with dust, something Kasher was not accustomed to back home, but he had seen it a couple of times since the boat incident. Ruhamah had said it was very common there. Kasher even had trouble making out the ropes tying down the tents out on the edge of the compound. They left without fanfare, the haze seeming to dampen the sounds they made as they headed out. The whole scene made it seem to have all been a dream. In his own personal haze from lack of sleep, Kasher even entertained the idea that it really had all been a dream; a dream from which he was only now emerging.

They had only gone a short way when he finally got the nerve to look behind him. He could still make out the main tent - only just - and he was sure he saw Ruhamah's head ducking back inside.

Chapter 7

The journey to Babylon started without conversation. There was no boat loading to do; we walked beside a donkey now, carrying just what we needed to reach the city. There simply wasn't anything to talk about. I kept my own counsel, but wondered about so many things. I knew now of Utanin's history with Nebuchadnezzar, but how would things be between them after so many changes. Growing up with a prince is one thing, but asking favors of the most powerful king in the world... that is something else entirely. We walked in silence as the sun began to burn away the morning haze.

The sky, when it peeked out from behind the haze through ragged holes, was a blue so soft it almost looked white. There was almost no wind, and the day promised heat.

Finally, my curiosity got the better of me, and I began asking Utanin questions about the details of our upcoming time in Babylon.

"I don't really know, Kasher." he answered after I blurted out a string of queries. "I haven't seen him for quite some time, it's true, but I have had dealings with him since he became king. He is a hard man at times, but he is very human, even if some of his followers think him a god. From my talks with him, I believe he has his feet firmly on the ground at most times. There was this one time, though, when I thought he might be going over the edge – giving in to the praise heaped upon him by some religious types. I never heard him say that he was a god, but I saw in his eyes… Well, anyway, I think we will be well received by him. I have advised him from time to time on boat and river matters. It might take some time though. Kings can be a little busy."

"As long as I'm in Babylon, I can wait as long as necessary!"

The morning passed without much more conversation. About noon we stopped at an oasis for a meal. We were not alone by any means. It was obviously a popular stop; a trader's crossroads. There were several caravans, evidently representing a great deal of wealth. I made comment to Utanin about that fact, and wondered aloud to him how secure they were as they transported their wares.

"Well, they are always heavily armed, and they are not foolish enough to sleep with both eyes closed," he responded. "If they sleep at all."

He told me we would not be traveling again for a few hours. The heat was simply more than we needed to endure. I, of course could not sit still. The great city was almost in sight, and I was stopped almost in its shadow!

I decided to nose around the oasis, hoping to get a feel for how things were done in Babylon. I wasn't sure how many people I would be able to understand, and there were some whose tongues bore no resemblance at all to mine. A large majority, though, were obviously Mesopotamians, and though they might have had a slightly different dialect, or at least an accent that seemed odd to me, I could communicate well enough with them.

My physical training had given me plenty of strength, but I knew I would need more than that to secure a place in the king's guard. I had never even been in a fist-fight, let alone a battle. I had talked to as many veterans of Nebuchadnezzar's wars as I could find, but there weren't that many in and around Nippur. Still, I never thought it would be too complicated to fight a battle. It seemed like a natural thing for anyone who was strong enough to handle it. Reality decided it was about time to make itself known.

I had been conversing with a group of lean men who looked like they could fight - and probably had. When they learned of my ambition, they began telling stories of the 'old days'; of the great, manly feeling of fighting and winning; of the spoils of battle; of returning home a hero. They explained that since Nebuchadnezzar had established himself so thoroughly, wars were a thing of the past. They themselves had no choice but to find work guarding caravans from marauders. "Everyone has to make a living!"

Just then there was what seemed like a general stir among the various groups. People were looking to the west and talking loud, nervousness showing in their voices and gestures. As my companions and I followed their gazes, we saw a great cloud of dust in that direction; still a long ways off, but it seemed to be growing.

Oh no, I thought, *not another sand storm!*

Just then Utanin found me. I guess he read my mind, because he said, "Not a storm this time. There's no wind, and the sky is still as clear as can be. It must be riders, but it has to be a lot of them to make that much dust."

My three companions concurred, and started gathering their belongings. As they moved away, I asked where they were going. One of them turned to answer, never pausing in his stride.

"Away; and fast. We're not equipped to stop something like this."

I turned to Utanin. "Are they coming to attack the merchants?" I asked.

"I really don't know, Kasher, but I understand how these men must think so. At least they can't afford not to. Most of these men would be destitute if they lost their caravan loads. I don't know what they will do since their protectors are running away. I'm sure they couldn't get far enough away to make any difference. Whoever is coming there is traveling light to be able to move fast enough to create so much dust!"

"What do you think we should do?" As I asked the question, I saw in Utanin's eyes something like I saw that day on the river when the wind started up. He seemed to be remembering something; maybe even that event. It did nearly kill him. I supposed he would never completely be free of it.

Right now it seemed to transfix him. He stopped speaking and made no move to do anything, just standing there looking at the dust as it grew bigger and bigger. There were small black spots visible now from time to time at the base of that confusion. The riders were getting closer.

I grabbed Utanin, trying to shake him out of his stupor. He responded, but weakly. I saw I would have to make a decision for us.

"Utanin, these men have to stay and either bargain or fight for their livelihood. We don't. Assuming the riders stop here, even if it is just to refresh themselves, we could be a long ways toward Babylon before they catch up to us, if that is where they are heading."

He mumbled something about the heat, but I knew if we were going to act, it had to be right away. I ran back to our stores and found the water bags we carried. I fought my way to the water hole, crowded now with panic-stricken faces. My strength came in handy at this point; and, even though I felt a little guilty about it, my instinct for survival caused me to work very hard at getting to the front.

The water bags now full, I found Utanin right where I had left him and began dragging him out to the north side of the oasis. The water hole itself was not very big, but the spring that fed it was obviously large as the vegetation extended about two hundred paces all around it. In all the confusion of people it took us several minutes to shoulder our way out to the edge. There were others already headed out that way; small groups, sometimes individuals alone, but no large caravans. Those could not be moved so quickly. I felt for them. I was sure they were going to lose something. I hoped it would only be some of their goods. I believed it might be their lives.

Our Donkey seemed to sense the tension. At first he pulled against us, trying to stay where he was. Once persuaded to move forward, it was all I could do to hold him back. It didn't help that we were being passed almost constantly by camels and horses, the ones without large burdens making good time in their flight towards Babylon. We all three felt swept up in the panic, but I knew we needed to pace ourselves in all this heat. The city still was not in view and I did not know how far we really had to go.

Utanin seemed to be better now. We didn't discuss what was going on; wasting breath did not seem really wise at this point. But he was acting clear-headed, and he was obviously as determined as I was to get to safety.

We went on for what seemed a long time. Glancing back, often, we saw that the exodus had thinned a lot. Most of those who would flee were doing so, and many of those had gone on ahead of us. There was a fairly large number more or less parallel to us, mostly comprised of groups similar to ours. As we were moving north, and the dust cloud was coming from the west, we had it pretty much in our peripheral vision all the time. Thankfully, it seemed determined to go directly to the oasis. How much time that gave us we didn't know, but we were determined to make the most of it.

The heat was merciless, and I found myself trying to imagine what it must be like to travel like the "dust-makers" were under these conditions. I imagined that must be what makes the difference between simply a strong man and a soldier; as by now it appeared they must be the latter. To endure under adverse conditions would take more than muscle. I wondered if I had the discipline, the determination, the inner strength. Was any cause big enough in my mind for me to give myself totally to it?

Right now the cause was survival. I had no idea who the dusty riders were, but no one seemed to think they were anything but trouble. Our only thought was to reach Babylon, and hope we would find protection there.

After what seemed like hours of pushing forward, Utanin nearly collapsed. I knew we had to stop, and I brought him in close to the donkey for support. We all three drank greedily, parched as we were by the heat. As I looked behind us, I saw that the dust cloud was much smaller, drifting back now to the west. The riders had stopped. As best I could tell, they had made it to the oasis, which would explain their stopping.

As soon as I could get Utanin moving again we started off, still very anxious about the situation. One of the small groups moving parallel to us moved in closer. I was wary, but there really wasn't a lot I could do if they were hostile. One of them (he had the bearing of a clan leader) spoke to me.

"How is your friend there?"

"He is weak from some earlier trials. He really wasn't ready for this kind of pace. I think he'll be alright for a while longer. Do you know how much farther it is to Babylon?"

"See that set of three hills ahead of us?" he asked.

I looked, and could make them out fairly plainly, although they were still about a two hour walk ahead. I nodded, and he continued.

"The city is just beyond them, specifically on the backside of the largest one. There is a gate there, and if we make that before they have to close it, we should be alright."

"Do you know who those riders are?" I asked, trying to keep any fear out of my voice.

"Not for sure, but there has been a lot of talk lately about a group of renegade Egyptians who want to put Nebuchadnezzar in his place. They don't represent the king of Egypt; he has been pretty well subdued by

Nebuchadnezzar. From what I've heard they aren't powerful enough to overthrow him, but they can sure be a troubling force for this kingdom. If it is them, we don't want to get caught out here by them. I've never seen them in action, but they have a reputation for great cruelty. The stories are of slow torture; just for their entertainment."

If I had needed any encouragement to speed, I now had it. Even Utanin seemed to begin to really understand the situation, and his gait quickened with that realization.

Another hour's walk did not seem to bring the hills any closer. I knew that was just a false impression. I had seen already how deceptive the distances were in this desert land. Utanin had to stop; he was near the end of his strength. I knew I would have to put him on the donkey before long, but that meant leaving something behind as the animal couldn't carry all our stores and a person. The main thing, of course, was our safety. Anything left behind couldn't compare to that. We drank from our goat-skin water bags. I encouraged Utanin to drink well. The final distance would have to be crossed without stopping to drink again.

As if reading my mind about his riding the donkey, Utanin started going through our cargo, taking bags off the beast.

"Where is it?" he asked, almost desperately. "Where is it?"

"What, Utanin, what are you looking for?"

"I know I put it in one of these smaller bags, but I don't... wait! Here it is: Safe and sound."

He seemed so happy to have found whatever it was that I thought he might kiss it. It was small, small enough that his hand basically hid it from my view. I really wanted to find out what it was, but at that moment I heard a cry go up all around us. Instinctively I looked back toward the oasis; my worst fears were confirmed. The dust cloud was back, bigger than ever, and headed our way.

We left the bags on the ground, and Utanin didn't argue much at all when I started hoisting him onto the donkey's back. I didn't know if a donkey would give us any speed at all, but there didn't seem to be an alternative.

What happened next really surprised me. There was a great deal of confusion all around us, people running and encouraging their beasts of burden to do the same. Something in that excitement got into our little donkey, and he started trotting forward, falling in with the crowd of others. Utanin was hanging on valiantly; it was obviously not a smooth ride. In fact, he was flopping about like a mouse caught in the talons of an eagle - only upside down, of course. I kept up for a while but, as tired as I already was, Utanin and his 'eagle' were outdistancing me at a pretty good pace. I was so intent on Utanin that I was pretty much oblivious to all the others around me. I am sure they were in their own little worlds as well; which is probably why no one but I saw the object fly from Utanin's hand.

As I said before, it wasn't large. What it was, though, was very shiny – reflective in the afternoon sun. I saw where it landed (after a considerable time in the air) and ran to pick it up.

I had little time for examination at that moment, but I saw that it was a small crystal disk. It had been polished to such a point that you could see through it, though with some difficulty. I put it away and pressed on.

I finally gave up on trying to stay with Utanin and concentrated on closing the ground between myself and the city. I was now at the top of the hill, and I actually stopped for a moment when I saw the walls for the first time. Not even all that my fertile imagination had been able to believe about it could compare with what my eyes tried to take in. I didn't have time, of course, to contemplate for long, but I was overwhelmed by the magnitude of it. It was huge.

Though I was having difficulty processing everything, one thing that struck me was the amount of water I was seeing. Before one reached the walls of the city there was what appeared to be a canal that had to be crossed. There were several bridges allowing for that crossing, but, of course, that limited the access to relatively small numbers at a time.

There was also water adjacent to the wall itself. Both of these canals seemed to come from the river on my left, which I knew was the Euphrates.

I began the decent to the plain in which the wall was set. It was still a ways ahead, and with the hill now at my back I couldn't see how far the riders were. As I ran I watched the confusion before me.

There were others around and behind, but my attention was in front. I saw a mob of people, some mounted, some on foot. I could not recognize Utanin or our donkey in all the dust. A substantial group was almost at the gate having crossed the first canal, and I assumed Utanin must be among them. I had not yet seen how the second canal was crossed, and in my haste, I really didn't have time to worry about that detail.

Just as I reached the bottom of the hill, I heard the pounding of hooves from behind me. I was focused on the gate ahead of me, and something strange seemed to be happening there. There was a growing throng gathered in front of it now. It took me a couple of seconds to realize what was happening. The gate had been closed.

Some of those around me seemed to be coming to the same realization, and I saw several men change their course. Instead of running toward the gate, they took a new course parallel to the canal. I immediately saw the wisdom in this and turned sharply to my right. It was an obstacle course, with discarded bags and goods wrapped in skins all over the ground. I jumped what I could, weaved my way around the ones too tall, and ran as fast as my exhausted limbs would carry me. I tried not to look at the riders – in all that confusion I couldn't really make out any detail anyway. I don't know how far I went like that, but eventually I found myself surrounded by several horses. A tall man stepped from between them and hit me in the face with a force that sent me immediately to my knees. From there I must have fallen onto my face, but I don't remember.

Chapter 8

When I woke this time there was no angelic figure awaiting me. As the possibility went through my aching head that I might actually be dead this time, the prospect seemed much worse than the last time. There were figures around me - brutish, loud and foul-smelling. There was a glow as of a fire off to one side. I could actually feel a trace of the heat of it on my cheek. I was once again lying on my back; this time on a hard, dusty surface. There were no words of encouragement, not even words I could understand; just a din of voices.

As my eyes began to clear I could see to my right a man sitting facing me with his legs spread, slouching back in his seat like someone of importance. I noticed there were others around me, mostly lying down as well, though some sat with legs crossed.

As I raised myself up to sit, the important-looking man rose to his feet. He crossed the few open paces from his seat to the edge of my group, and then began picking his way through the people. I now noticed that we were about fifty in number, and I didn't see anyone I recognized.

He seemed to be coming toward me on purpose; and, in fact, he came and stood right before me. I was amazed when I got a good look at him. Not only because of his noble bearing, very unusual in this setting - there was something more. He looked very, very familiar; and yet I knew I had never seen him before.

My surprise turned to absolute shock when he opened his mouth. That he spoke to me in my own tongue, and with a very recognizable accent - that was amazing enough. But there was more. His voice was eerily familiar as well.

"What is your name, son?"

"I am called Kasher," I responded through my surprise and shock. I was determined not to show any fear or to reveal anything about myself other than my name. That I needn't have concerned myself with such things immediately became evident.

"I thought as much. Welcome nephew."

He turned to walk away, beckoning me to follow him. I did my best to lift myself to my feet. Eventually - dizzy from all that had transpired before, my head reeling in a special way from this brief conversation - I managed to follow him through the crowd.

We walked for several minutes through a large encampment. Most of the tents were just hastily thrown up, not much more than a roof and some flaps. The place where I had awoken was in the open, in the middle of all this confusion. Ahead of me now I could see a structure that was obviously much more important than the others.

My uncle (so it seemed he must be) entered the sprawling tent without so much as a glance backwards at me. As his tall figure disappeared through the door I hurried forward. There were guards, one on each side of the door. They started to close in to bar my way inside. At that moment I heard a voice from within. It was the same voice, but it spoke in a different language. It wasn't that it was a different language that surprised me the most. I was almost cowed by the tone and the strength of it. One of the guards reached over quickly to open the veil that served as a door. The other went back to his original position, scrutinizing me in great detail; and not without a strong look of malice on his part. I knew that, even if the important man was really my uncle, I was in enemy territory.

Inside, I marveled at the furnishings. It was certainly not a palace, but for something that had obviously been erected in haste, it definitely was well adorned. It reminded me in a lot of ways of Ruhama's family's tent, but there was an obvious difference in social status given the look of wealth here.

"Come, Kasher," once again in my tongue. "Let us talk."

I saw a seat in front of the man, just slightly to his left. I don't know why I even noticed, but I saw that he had a clear view of the door over my left shoulder when I sat down. After a moment I saw that he had a bow and quiver at his right side. It would have been easy for him to retrieve it if he so needed. I was under the impression that he thought he might. Though he tried to maintain an air of nonchalance, he was obviously nervous. His eyes were never directly on me for long. I suppose he did not consider me to be a threat.

"I am sure you have many questions. Let me give you the short version. I left Nippur when you were very young. I don't suppose your mother ever mentioned me? No? I'm not surprised. I don't even blame her, really. She always said I would die far from home without friend or family around me. Well, friends are hard to come by, but look! Here's family!"

"What is your name, sir," I asked, trying to speak respectfully, but without groveling.

"I am known by my Egyptian name; Nakhti. It means powerful. Your mother calls me Lot. It was the name of one of our ancestors, and it is mine as well. We have a great history, our family; great warriors. I see you are in very good shape yourself. But you travel as a merchant. What's your story then?"

"I had no knowledge of this warrior heritage you speak of, but there has always been something in me that pulled toward a soldier's life," replied Kasher. "I suppose my real calling came clear to me when Nebuchadnezzar came through Nippur on his campaign. I decided to join him as soon as I was old enough."

"Well, that might pose something of a problem," said Nakhti. "You see, I am here as part of a plan to overthrow your great king. This force that you see is only the beginning!"

"No offence, uncle, but what do you think a group of this size can do against the whole army of Babylon?"

"Against the whole army? Probably not much. You're young, Kasher, and obviously inexperienced at the art of warfare. There is a master plan in effect, and this is just one phase of it; a small one, but very important. I really don't think we should discuss this further. You already said you have an allegiance to Nebuchadnezzar."

"But why, Uncle? What is it about Nebuchadnezzar that you are against?"

"As I said, you are young. Some day you will understand the way of politics and power. I have nothing against Nebuchadnezzar as a person. In fact, I learned much from him several years ago. You remember when he came through Nippur? I had already started in the direction that has brought me to what you are seeing today. You didn't know me, but I was around. Your mother was ashamed of me, and so I wasn't welcome in your home."

"I had assembled a group of fighting men and we were positioning ourselves to be dominant in that area. Nebuchadnezzar came to see me before he quelled the Farmer Rebellion. He asked me to join him. I couldn't bring myself to fight against those people I knew from childhood, but I saw which way the wind was blowing. I offered to stay away while he did what he had to do there, and then join him afterwards for other campaigns. And that's what I did! I had the "wisdom of a fox," Nebuchadnezzar liked to say. He drew from that, as well as my understanding (from first-hand experience) of simple peoples, to further develop what had already become a fairly efficient general's mind. So I spent the next few years with him, working closely in the planning and execution of his military endeavors. We were very successful."

"Then why are you fighting against him now?"

"As I said, you have much to learn about the way things work. Your dedication to a man seems like a noble thing; but, in reality, he is just a man. What about me? Am I not a man, too? What makes his cause the right one? Why should his word be law over me?"

"But Uncle, there must be rulers and subjects, don't you agree? Otherwise all we have is chaos!"

"Kasher, throughout history great men have risen at critical moments. Yes, there must be order, but why should the authority come because of one's birthright?

What if there is someone more capable to rule? Nebuchadnezzar's father, Nabopolassar, was a great man. He ruled firmly but fairly. His son, however, is arrogant. Nabopolassar earned his right to rule. He was judged by those around him as worthy to follow. I admit that Nebuchadnezzar did quit himself well as a general. To me, his greatest strength was his ability to judge the character of others and choose the right people to occupy the right positions. I imagine he still works that way, and he will not be an easy victim if he does. But if it is really those others who have the knowledge and wisdom to do the job, why is *he* the ruler?"

"You would rule yourself, wouldn't you, Uncle?"

"I am where I am because other men see qualities in me they admire and respect. If that extends itself to more authority someday, it seems to me I haven't the right to refuse. In the meantime, there is much to be done. Nebuchadnezzar would dominate the whole world if he could. I believe he is trying. We won't sit by and watch that happen."

"Who is 'we,' Uncle?"

"I can't really get into it very much with you, Kasher. Frankly, I don't know how much I can trust you yet. Suffice it to say there are quite a lot of us who want small kingdoms with their own autonomy instead of a tyrant who tries to rule over all. That is simply unacceptable to anyone who thinks for himself. Authority must be given, not taken."

"There was talk back at the oasis about Egyptians, and you yourself told me you have an Egyptian name. There seems to be a connection," I said, feeling a little bolder.

"Well, I didn't expect a nephew of mine to be stupid, and you obviously are not. I can't keep you from making observations - unless I have you killed - but I would appreciate it if you didn't pry too far. It might make it necessary for me to do something drastic, and I really don't want it to come to that. I would prefer to send you home to your mother in one piece!"

I think I grew up a lot at that very moment. I saw so many things with a clarity I had never experienced. Family questions made more sense. Events of which I had been mostly ignorant I now saw were shaping the world in which I lived. I began questioning in my own mind for the first time in years some assumptions I had made. I suppose that is what maturing really is.

My uncle was a very busy man; so, after our conversation (which ended with him extracting a promise from me not to interfere with their campaign), I was left pretty much alone to wander the encampment. My first impulse was to try to leave, but the perimeter was well guarded. As I approached some of the guard stations I was greeted with pleasantries (obviously word was out as to who I was, or rather who my uncle was) but also with stern warnings if I seemed to be headed out.

After determining my low chance of escape (which didn't take very long) I decided to try to see as much of the city walls as possible from within the encampment. The day was wearing away quickly; just enough light remained to see them, and they were closer than I would have thought. Exactly how far the encampment was from them I couldn't make out in the dim light, but it wouldn't have taken a runner very long to get to them.

Once again I was struck with the enormity of those walls. I had heard much about them, but seeing them was different. We were close to what appeared to be a corner of the city's outline. To our right, east, there seemed to be no end to it in sight. I realized that was partly because of the fading light, but, nevertheless, the wall went a long, long ways in that direction.

I found a location with food being distributed. It was set up close to one of the fires, and everyone it seemed, captives and captors alike, were served from huge pots. I made my way into the mix and was rewarded with a large bowl of cooked grain with a heavy meat broth poured over it. I hadn't eaten since the oasis – even then very little - and I felt my strength return as I made my way to the bottom of the bowl. I remember thinking how many times I had complained about things my mother had cooked for us. How ridiculous that seemed now.

A very short man, somewhat older than I, sat next to me as I ate. We struck up a conversation, and I learned that he was a captive too.

"My name is Kartan," he told me. "I have been in this camp almost since it was established. I was traveling in a small caravan, and we had the bad luck to intersect with this group as we were all arriving at the great city. This cook saw that I had cooking utensils and decided I should be his assistant. I can't really complain. I get first chance at the food this way."

"I'm Kasher. I was headed for Babylon with a friend. I want to join Nebuchadnezzar's army."

"You're certainly big enough for it," replied Kartan. "Your present situation doesn't seem very conducive to your goal, though, does it?"

I'm afraid not," I answered. "I probably could have an opportunity with this band, but that would mean fighting against the man I have always desired to serve! Well, there's nothing to do for now but wait and see how things play out. Life is proving to be a strange thing."

"That it is my young friend; that it is," said Kartan with a sigh. "Still, it looks like fate has brought us together, and I think we might be of mutual use to each other. Your strength and my connections... could be a good combination indeed!"

Drowsiness started to take me shortly after finishing our walk. It had been a very, very long day and it was already dark. I excused myself from Kartan and headed for the area where my uncle had found me unconscious. By the light of the campfires I saw people beginning to settle in for the night. Soldiers either disappeared into tents (I even saw women waiting for some of them), or they had skins into which they rolled themselves. The latter reminded me of my mother rolling honey and dates into bread dough to make a treat for us. I had never complained about that.

It seemed to me now that I had complained about a lot of things back in Nippur that would now be ignored at worst; appreciated at best.

I lay down on the ground in the middle of the area. No one there had anything to sleep on but the ground, and only a few had some sort of covering - a cloak or an extra garment. The night grew quite cold. Sleep came without much delay but it was not particularly restful. My thoughts were swirling about in my head at great speed. Many of them were in the form of dreams of home, mixed with all of the traumatic events that I had experienced since leaving. One thing kept running in and out of my thoughts; "The moment we believe ourselves invincible, God has a way of showing us the truth about ourselves." Was that what was happening to me? I awoke almost as tired as I had been the night before.

I passed that day alone and unmolested. I used the time to try to get a feel for the camp and surrounding areas. We were just north of a body of water, a canal. As I approached it, I noticed a lush garden ending right at its bank.

I heard Kartan's voice from behind me. "You like my garden?"

I turned to see a man obviously pleased with his handiwork.

"It's very nice. I never expected anything like this here. How long have you been here?"

"Almost two months now. I'm not privy to all the war plans, but I hear plenty. Seems we are waiting for some other generals who are joining Nakhti in the overthrow of Babylon."

"Attempted overthrow you mean," I retorted, probably with more emphasis than was necessary – or wise. I really didn't know Kartan well yet. From what little I had seen he seemed loyal to Nakhti. I resolved not to speak so hastily in the future, especially given my present situation.

"Of course; 'attempted'. Nothing is ever certain until we see it accomplished; but I have great confidence in Nakhti's ability to lead. My only doubt is if he can bring so many factions together into a unified force. That will be his real test of leadership ability."

It seemed my lack of loyalty to my uncle had escaped being detected for now, so I quickly changed the subject.

"This garden is truly amazing," I said. And I meant it. "You did all this in just two months?"

"Some say this canal has magical power, but I like to think I had something to do with it," he replied.

The garden really was a wonder. Just from the perspective of size, it was amazing. It followed the canal for about a thousand cubits, working its way away from the water for about half that distance.

The size was impressive, but it also had a quality about it that was pleasing to look at. Everything was extremely well ordered and cared for with just the right amount of clear space to allow the gardeners to move between the plants without causing them damage. And there were, I now saw, several working the garden at various places along the length of it.

"So this is why we eat so well?"

"Yes, it really is. The security of our camp makes it easy to make sure we have such a strong garden. We eat a lot of what we are producing, and we even have enough to take to the market in Babylon once in a while."

"You mean Babylon is buying from the enemy?"

"Well, it would be very hard for them to know exactly where each merchant comes from in the busy marketplace. Besides, I was selling there long before Nakhti and his men came along."

"So why have you sided with Nakhti?"

"At first I just happened to be passing through when they set up camp, and I was constrained into duty for them. But I have come to respect them; especially Nakhti. He seems like a good man, a great leader, and I think his position is correct. Now my trips to Babylon to sell our produce allow me to serve in another way. I am Nakhti's eyes and ears in Babylon."

We talked a while longer, and then walked to the east, following the canal. Kartan pointed out features of the land around us as we went. He pointed to a village that we could see well out from the camp, telling me that he was born there.

"What about your family? Do they know you are here?" I asked.

"I have no family. My parents and my wife were all victims of a raid about six months ago. Right in the shadow of the great city! And no one did anything to stop it. It's like Nakhti says, Nebuchadnezzar has lost control of his kingdom, and should step down from the throne."

Night was coming on, and I was ready for some rest. As soon as I ate my supper I found a quiet place and fell fast asleep.

It was to a cacophony that I awoke. The confusion in my head yielded slowly but surely to the knowledge of early morning light; and of fighting somewhere nearby. Two men, obviously captives like me, were on the ground fighting over something. Whatever it was, it was small. One of the men apparently had it clasped in his hand, and it was small enough to remain mostly hidden there. The group attending the spectacle was growing, and I made my way cautiously towards it. I now recognized one of the men from the oasis. He had been one of those dispensing his sage advice to all who would listen. Now he was no different from the rest of us. I made a mental note that captivity was a great leveler.

Our captors had simply been watching, obviously enjoying the moment of entertainment. Finally a man of obvious authority stepped into the makeshift arena and grabbed each man by his clothing, right behind the neck.

As he tried to pull them apart it became evident that neither of them was willing to relinquish his claim on the article. He commanded two other soldiers to help him, and they were able – just – to get the men separated.

The man in charge (the other soldiers were referring to him as Captain) took possession of the man who was clutching the object in his hand and proceeded to pry that hand open and take it from him. As he stared at it he let out a cry of disgust.

"It's a rock! A pretty rock to be sure, but just a rock! You two look like you want to kill each other; and for this?"

He began walking away, rock in hand, shaking his head in disbelief. He had only gone a few paces when the man who had held the rock before broke loose and ran toward him, screaming like a madman.

The captain had apparently had enough by now, and in a movement that I can only describe as a flash, he had a sword in his hand. It seemed to come from nowhere, but was now pointed right at the midsection of the onrushing man. There was no time for any more adjustments, even if the captain had been inclined to make them – and it did not appear that he was. The sword buried itself to the hilt in the man's stomach; most of its blade now protruding from the man's back, gleaming in the morning sun. I don't know why, but that gleam made me remember the disk Utanin had lost on his wild ride to Babylon. I felt for it in a fold of my clothing, and there it was. I looked away from the dying man: looked at the object that the captain had dropped in the confusion. It was another disk just like the one I carried.

The stricken man fell to his knees, and the captain drew back his sword. I had seen sword wounds before on men already dead, but this was a new and awful experience. The sucking sound the sword made coming out of the man made me feel faint. As soon as it exited his stomach there was blood pouring from both the front and the rear wounds. The man made a twisting movement as he fell, and I saw he was reaching for the disk lying by the captain's left foot. He did not have enough strength left in him to reach it, but I saw the same desire for it that I had seen in Utanin's face. What were these seemingly unimportant rocks?

The other man who had been involved in the fight was intently scanning the area where his adversary had fallen with his eyes. He did not have much time for his search, though, as he was already being forcefully taken away by the two soldiers. At last he seemed to decide he would not get what he wanted by force and, reluctantly, was led away.

The captain shouted, "Does anyone claim this body?"

There was no response, so he proceeded to call for volunteers to take the dead man away. I stepped forward with as much restraint as I could muster. I wanted a chance to get to the other disk, but I didn't want to be too obvious.

No one else moved toward the body, and so the captain grabbed another prisoner to help me. He instructed us to take it to the perimeter closest to the city wall. We were to arrange for one of the guards to accompany us out of the camp to bury it.

I positioned myself so that as I bent to lift the body my hand was close to the disk. The captain seemed to have forgotten all about it. He was already hurrying away as though he needed to be somewhere else.

I managed to get the disk without (I hoped) being seen. No one still on the scene seemed to have any idea what the fight had been about, and the other fighter was out of sight. I tucked the disk away with the other one and proceeded with the disposal of the body as we had been ordered.

We were instructed where to bury the body, and the makeshift cemetery was at the western edge of our encampment. As we approached our destination I saw for the first time that "we" were not alone. Just beyond the graveyard, there were a half dozen armed men whom I presumed to be the perimeter guard. They looked tough enough, and even though they were interested in what was going on beyond our area, they did not seem to lose sight of the boundary itself. That these were well-trained sentries I could tell. I watched them with no little interest as we went about our unpleasant task. I noticed that there was always at least one (not always the same one, though) looking in our direction. In fact, after a short while I saw that all directions seemed to be within the gaze of at least one of them at all times. I was impressed.

We finished covering the unfortunate loser of the stone disk. As we caught our breath from the exertion and the extreme heat I began noticing the activities beyond the sentries. It looked like some sort of market, but not like any I had ever seen.

There seemed to be no order of any kind. I could see goods being moved throughout the area; goats and other livestock, carts with what looked to be fruits and vegetables in them, others which shone with the reflection of what I thought must have been weapons. And there were people in chains.

I had known of slavery from my childhood; I had even known a few slaves in Nippur. The ones I knew of were slaves because of a debt they owed. This was different. People were being bought and sold here. I suddenly felt cold, despite the midday sun.

I approached the sentries with little hope that I would be allowed to venture into the marketplace. Just as I got there someone tapped me on the back. I turned to see my diminutive friend from the night before.

"A special way to wake up, yes?" He said with a sly smile.

"You were there for the fight, I take it," I replied flatly.

"Yes, I was there. I also saw interest in your eyes when the rock came into play. What is it to you?"

"I don't know yet, but it was apparently important enough to die for, so I plan to find out... in time."

"Can I see it?" he asked.

I searched his face for signs. He seemed to be merely curious, so I decided to take a chance. Maybe he would know something that would help me discover the meaning and importance of these disks. I only showed him the one from the fight, though. No sense giving away everything right away.

"I have heard," he said, turning the disk over and over in his extended hand, "of a device that, it is said, uses disks like this. I don't even know if the stories are true, but it has been rumored that they give special sight into the heavens. It seems our two friends believed it to be true. I am not given to superstition myself. Still, there is something special about this disk. Look how it is carefully cut, not deep enough to hold anything, yet obviously shaped like a very shallow bowl. I don't think

I've seen anything so smoothly cut, either. Polished, as though ground on a wheel like a sword, perhaps."

As Kartan handed the disk back to me I noticed something. As I was lifting it from his palm, I noticed I could see through the disk at some point. I asked him to hold his hand there for a moment and I experimented moving the disk up and down over his outstretched hand, slowly, observing as I did so.

"Look, Kartan," I exclaimed. "It makes your hand look bigger when I hold it at a certain distance."

"Yes, I see that. So it does affect what you see, at least at a certain distance. There's no way, of course, that you could hold it close enough to the sky to magnify that though!"

In my mind I was already thinking of ways to use the two disks together, but I felt I had gone far enough with my new friend for now, and decided to end that discussion.

As I put the disk away I said, "You mentioned you had connections. What does that mean exactly?"

"Well for one thing, there's the market you were so intent upon. As a cook's assistant, I have access to that area; with a guard, of course. Would you like to go with me? I was headed there now to get supplies."

I accepted the invitation readily. It sounded good to get outside of this prison, and I had to admit the market was intriguing.

I did not have a pass like Kartan, but his connections were becoming apparent. He spoke to one of the guards who, after looking me over carefully, simply led the way into the market area with Kartan and me close behind.

It was unlike any market I had ever seen. The basic elements were there; fruits and meats and breads. But there was so much more! Besides the weaponry, which I had already seen from a distance, and the slaves in chains, there were things that surprised me even more.

"Why is there so much gold and precious stones?" I asked Kartan as we waded through the stalls. "Aren't they afraid of being robbed?"

"This is the safest kind of market," he answered. "It looks like chaos, but there is an incredible amount of control by your uncle's army."

I blanched at this declaration of my kinship with Nakhti, but kept my mouth shut, not wanting to give anything away.

"Yes, I have already heard who you are, and if I ever need to use that, be sure I will. I am a good person, but I am a survivor. Anyway, your uncle does not tolerate indiscipline. He is a fair man, but he is a strong leader. Not the kind who shouts commands from within the safety of his palace like the great Nebuchadnezzar. No, Nakhti likes to control things himself."

And, so, another conflict insinuated itself into my concept of great leadership. I knew that Nebuchadnezzar was a great general as prince, but what about now as king? Was Kartan right in saying he was not a great leader; that he kept himself hidden in the safety of his palace, allowing others to fight and die for him? And was that wrong in itself? Maybe that is how it should be. Maybe my uncle would never achieve such heights because he would himself be killed in battle before he could?

My attention returned to the market. The noise was amazing. The animals sounded like they knew they would be slaughtered upon leaving this place. The vendors would not be outdone. They somehow made themselves heard above the din of the beasts, obviously competing with each other to sell their wares. They all spoke the same language: It was not exactly the same as mine but I could understand much of what was being said. Utanin had told me that in Babylon the tongue of choice was Aramaic. I made a quick mental note to study the subject as soon as practical. It seemed it would be prudent to learn several dialects, focusing on this one. It shouldn't be too hard since I was already hearing a lot of words that were part of my language as well.

As I was settling this matter in my head, I was looking, but not seeing. It was easy to lose oneself in the chaos of such a place, but I shook myself back to reality and took another look around. What I saw next shocked me to my very core.

Chapter 9

I willed myself not to accept what I was seeing, but to no avail.

There, among so many women shackled together - some crying softly, some screaming at their captors, some stoically awaiting the next cruelty that life would bring them - there, as calm as though sitting in her own home, was Ruhamah!

Her eyes slowly lifted, as though some unseen hand was lifting her chin for her, until her gaze met mine.

I must have been a frightening sight with my mouth hanging open, my eyes wide in disbelief. To see a mass of humanity in that condition was hard, but after a little time it took on an air of semi-normality. It was reality, and there was nothing I could do about it. Better to accept it and move on. But someone I knew; someone I had grown very fond of, hoping to see her again! Not like this! It couldn't be.

I did not feel like much of a savior figure as I made my way to her. I stumbled more than walked in her direction. I could hardly breathe, and I had no idea what to say, let alone what to do!

She seemed oblivious to my plight, continuing to sit placidly, as if nothing were wrong. She smiled as I neared, and it was only then that I saw how weak she really was. That smile seemed to cost her a great deal, but it energized and focused me.

"Ruhamah!" I intended it to be a yell but it came out so weak I wondered if she had even heard it. Her smile drooped, but I could see now that it was because of fatigue, not because she was no longer glad to see me.

As I approached her a mountain of a man stepped in my path. He said something that I did not understand, but his tone was menacing. I moved to go around him but he was obviously not going to allow that. His size was daunting enough, but the dagger that appeared in his left hand completed the threat.

Without thinking, I started screaming at him. He was obviously as ignorant of my language as I was of his, but he had no difficulty seeing I meant to get past him and to the women. And he was there to thwart that at all cost.

After a standoff that seemed to last forever, another man appeared at his side. He was much smaller, and had the same overeager look as most of the vendors there. He immediately started trying to calm the situation, talking to me in a dialect I could understand fairly well.

"There, there, my boy," he said with what I could only describe as false friendliness, "everything will be alright. Let's find out what you are after and do some business!"

I mumbled something that even I had difficulty understanding. Then I remembered Ruhamah's weak smile and my resolve returned, this time with calm determination. Ruhamah had to be saved.

In my second attempt at speaking I made myself understood, explaining that she was a friend, and must be released. The small man must have understood, judging from the fact that he was now doubled over with laughter.

The big man was obviously puzzled by all that was happening, so I supposed that he must not have understood what we were saying. I wondered if I could use that to my advantage somehow; but it seemed unlikely. His master could clearly converse in both languages, and so had a great advantage over me. My decision to learn languages was reinforced. There was power to be had in communication skills. Right now I had to lean on the abilities I did have.

I gave serious thought to a direct approach - moving the big one out of the way and freeing Ruhamah by force. I had considerable confidence in my strength, but the dagger in his hand changed the odds dramatically. I was willing to be hurt attempting to free her, but I could not do something rash that might leave Ruhamah without any help. I would need another plan.

"Sir," I said to the vendor, with much more calmness in my voice than I was feeling. "One of the ladies - just there - should not be there. She is a dear friend of mine, and I know her family. They are incapable of warring with anyone, so I know she cannot be a legitimate captive. Please, let me take her and leave you to your business."

"A 'legitimate captive'?" Who gave you the right to determine that? She is in my possession, and that makes it legitimate to me!"

"What can I do, then, to convince you to release her?" I asked, trying to mask my desperation.

"Well, you can do the same as any other man here who wants to 'release' one of my girls. You can pay up!"

With absolutely no possibility of coming up with any money, I stalled for time by asking, "How much."

"Since she is such a dear friend of yours, and since I am such a compassionate man, I will give you the same price as my regular customers: Three thousand dinars."

My mind raced. It could have been any amount and I still wouldn't have been able to pay it. The only things I had that might be worth something were the two stones. I reached for them to see if they might get Ruhamah released, but before I could bring them out into the light of the hot desert sun, I felt a tug at my sleeve. I turned to see the broadly smiling face of Kartan.

I had completely forgotten about him in the confusion, but now that he was there I wondered where he had been during this whole exchange. I had been working at this for several minutes at least. Maybe he could come up with some money for Ruhamah's freedom!

"Kartan, I am so glad to see you! I desperately need some money. I will do anything to pay you back. You see, one of the captive women is a friend of mine, and I must get her released!"

His smile did not leave but it changed from amusement to irony.

"Surely you don't think I have any money of my own in my situation. And if I go back to camp with a woman instead of food I am sure I will be relieved of both her and my head!"

My despair returned, and I wondered if his smile was nothing but 'the pleasure of seeing me in this predicament. Suddenly he grabbed my arm and started pulling me away from the two men.

"Over here," he whispered. "I may have a solution for you!"

"If it doesn't include three thousand dinars it probably won't be of much help," I replied, almost ready to give in to my despair. I was already trying to envision myself walking away and leaving Ruhamah in that place. I could not allow it!

"Kasher, look over there; to your right, beyond the stall with the goats."

It was my uncle.

If anyone could help it would be him. But, would he?

I had to try.

I tried to approach without too much fanfare, but he saw me coming.

"Uncle, I need to speak with you, please."

"I know, Kasher. I was following the proceedings from over here and I think I got the basic idea. You found a girl who needs your help! Unfortunately for both of you, you're not in much of a position to keep a woman right now. You need to leave that alone for the time being."

"No, uncle, you don't understand! I know that girl! Her family saved me from a sandstorm a short while ago. I owe them my life! And now she is a prisoner. Can you help me?"

"I could, of course. But I'm not sure it would be the best course of action. I can have a word with the vendor – make sure he treats her well - and I can pressure him to sell her to someone decent. That's about all I know to do!"

"Uncle, please. She is very important to me. We believe she is even a distant relative. She has Abraham in her lineage, just like us!"

"How do you know about Abraham? Has your mother been filling your head with those Hebrew stories? You need to be careful with that. Those people are dangerous. They think they are the only ones who know any truth."

"I know," I said. "Mother is a bit of a dreamer; but the fact remains that this girl is family! Won't you do something to save her?"

Nakhti pondered the matter for a few moments. I was losing hope when suddenly his eyes opened wide. I would come to know that expression well in the next few months.

"I will buy her myself," he said. "I think she could indeed be very useful to me."

"I'm not sure she would be any better off like that than how she is now," I retorted, half under my breath.

The force of his palm striking my cheek would have toppled most men. Even as strong as I was, I was forced back a couple of steps. As soon as I regained my balance I prepared for a fight. Before I could move there were armed men all around me, weapons drawn. I had not even noticed them before; and yet, now, I could see they were all soldiers.

My uncle parted them like a crocodile through swamp grass. His look was intense, and as he approached me I felt real fear.

"You come to me for help and then show me disrespect! How dare you presume to know me, or how I would treat someone? If I do buy your friend, be assured it will be the best situation she could possibly hope for at this junction."

"I'm sorry, uncle. I should have kept my peace. I will try to be more respectful. Please do help her - in spite of me!"

"As I started to say, she might be of real use to me. But if this is going to happen, I need to establish some things between you and me. What I have in mind is using her as a contact within Babylon itself. I already have someone who can come and go freely, but he is not privy to many details of the court. A pretty girl might have better luck at that."

"Yes, uncle that sounds like a great plan!" I knew I was being over enthusiastic, but I was grasping for any arm of help that might extend to me.

"Alright, Kasher, but you have to make some decisions as well before I commit to this. Come over here and let's talk."

He led me away from the ring of soldiers that I had formed with my stupidity. We walked a few paces from them, but we were never more than a couple of quick steps away from at least one of them. We walked slowly as the "Strong One" laid out his conditions to me.

"Six months allegiance to me," he began. "Unquestioning loyalty; absolute obedience. That is your first payment for the girl's release."

"I seem to have no choice, uncle. I would have her freed. But you understand what a conflict this is for me, don't you? I will be the enemy of the king I have purposed to serve."

"I will make you this concession, Kasher. I will not obligate you to fight against Babylon directly during those six months. Afterwards, no matter what, you are free to pursue your own destiny. You have my word. Do you accept?"

"I do, uncle. What will I be doing during this time?"

"At first, you will be my servant. You will do everything I command you to, and everything my steward commands as well. You will not be much more than a common slave; with one exception. You will be present at many of my strategy meetings. I hope you will learn much from those moments. It will be up to you to take advantage of them or not. Until I say otherwise, you will be silent in the meetings. I will explain to my captains why you are there and there will be no trouble from them about it, I assure you. They are always respectful of me. I have earned it."

"Uncle, you want me to hear of all your plans, even knowing that I might be against you later?"

"Ah, you see, Kasher, my plans only extend to the next six months. The world we live in is so volatile none of us knows what conditions we will find in the near future. Besides, I hope by then to have convinced you that you should be with me of your own free will."

"So, let me try to understand all of this," I said. "I serve you for six months, Ruhamah is bought out of the slave market to work for you, and she will be protected. Do I have the details right?"

I almost flinched in anticipation of another slap across the face for adding the part about Ruhamah being protected, but I had to have that assurance. Instead of a buffeting, Nakhti gave a quiet laugh, indicating that he had heard and acknowledged that condition, and said, "That about covers it, I suppose."

With great relief I turned to go back toward the place where Ruhamah was being held. I hurried, worrying that in that short interval she might have been sold to someone else. To my delight she was still on the same place. She seemed even more tired than before. I realized she must have thought my efforts were unfruitful, and was resigned to her fate once again. Such cruelty, to think you will be freed only to have that hope pulled back away from you. I was almost in tears thinking about how she must be feeling, but my joy at knowing I was to save her after all lifted my spirits. When I approached this time, no one impeded me.

"Ruhamah," I called. "I'm back. And I've found help."

She didn't respond or even look up. I reached her, and took her arm gently. She tried to pull away but didn't even have the strength for that. Finally she looked up, puzzlement making her look half mad.

"Ruhamah, come on! You're free! You're going with me!"

I saw the understanding start to come to the surface, and finally, with a lot of help from me, she stood to her feet. The huge man that had barred my way to her at first was suddenly at our side with keys in his hand. I understood what that meant, and made a space for him to reach the ankle iron on her foot. He was much gentler than I expected, taking care that he did not hurt her as he went about his job. He was much nimbler of hand than I would have believed, too.

When he stood up, we faced each other. I pointed to my chest and said, "Kasher."

He pointed to his, and responded with what sounded to me like "Ludim."

He turned and walked back to his master who was now talking to Nakhti. We moved closer and I started listening to their conversation.

"Oh, my master, I had no idea it was your nephew asking for the girl. I would have given her over without hesitation had I known. Now, take her with my compliments."

"You know better than that, you old vulture," answered Nakhti. "You will be paid, and paid the proper price. I will not be in your debt. No sane person would. Now, how much did you ask of the boy for her?"

"Master, I said a number, but it was a bargainer's amount! It was never to be a final price. Do not humble me to say it."

"Say it you will, and get on with it. I don't have time or patience for your market games!"

"I said three thousand dinars, but we are men! We know that a common slave girl could never be sold for that amount. I am sure she is worth two thousand, but I could not require that of the great Nakhti."

"The money will be in your hand by nightfall. Be sure that this business is finished, and that I now own the girl!" My uncle seemed to be talking louder than normal, and it seemed that he wanted everyone to know of the transaction. I couldn't help wondering why, but I was learning that my uncle was no ordinary man. Whatever he did had been well thought out, or, if there was not time for that, his actions and words would come from the vast stores of knowledge and wisdom that served him well in a crisis.

He saw us as he turned away from the vendor. He came over to us, and instructed me to get Ruhamah to his tent as soon as possible. He left a soldier to escort us, but it hardly seemed necessary since everyone now knew she belonged to Nakhti. No one would bother us. No doubt the reason for his loud proclamations just before was to insure her safety. No one would dare mistreat a possession of the great Egyptian captain.

We walked for a short time in silence; her pace was slow, and after only a few minutes she nearly collapsed. I caught her in time to prevent her hitting the ground, but she was in no condition to walk farther at that moment. I helped her to the shade of a large rock, lowering her gently to the sand. The soldier guarding us acted as though he would complain, but instead kept his distance and waited.

"I'm sorry Kasher. I'm just so tired."

I had a skin of water, and I helped her drink from it. I wanted to ask so many questions, but I decided it would be better to wait until she was ready to talk. The only thing I said was, "You're going to be alright now; don't worry. We will go at your pace."

In truth, I was not in any hurry right now. It was all I could ask for to be next to her. I felt like I was being given an opportunity to repay the kindness she and her family had shown me. I was also, I believed, being given another opportunity to have her in my life.

As soon as she was able we continued on past the perimeter guards. No one showed any signs of surprise at our presence, so I was sure they had been alerted to the situation.

The sun was beginning to sit low on the horizon, and with the cooler temperatures Ruhamah seemed to gain strength to continue. She looked up at me at one moment, and was able to give a small smile. Weak as it was, it sparked a huge glow in my heart. For the first time in quite a while I felt like things were going to be alright.

We reached my uncle's tent just as the sun disappeared from sight. A guard at the door said, "I will take her from here." I watched as they passed through the door, then turned away with so many emotions alive in me I couldn't think. I made my way to my sleeping area and collapsed into a sleep that brought little rest. I dreamed alternately of a peaceful life with Ruhamah at my side and of seeing her still in chains. I woke several times, startled by some event I was dreaming.

I must have finally found enough peace to sleep soundly because I was awakened by a rough voice calling my name. I opened my eyes to see an already bright sky, and the face of one of my uncle's men. He gave me a light kick and muttered something about my presence being required. I followed him, trying to clear my head as I went, to Nakhti's tent door.

Without the slightest ceremony, I was ushered into the main room of the tent. Already the captains were assembled around a design that had been scratched into the dirt floor. There was no sign of Ruhamah, which did not really surprise me. Even so, I couldn't help being disappointed.

"Come near, Kasher," my uncle called upon seeing me.

I saw in the ground what must have been a representation of the walls of Babylon. There were lines drawn in various places that did not seem to be part of the map. In fact, one of the captains was, at that moment, drawing one himself as he conversed with a couple of the others.

My uncle continued talking to me as I approached. He came apart from the group with another man, one I did not recognize.

"This is Enusat. He will be your instructor in the ways of warfare during the time you are with us. If you ever become half the warrior he is, you will be feared by men."

It wasn't so much his size that grasped my attention, though he was a big man. It was the absolute power that seemed to be poised to spring from him at any moment.

I spent the next ten days in intensive battle training. Enusat was my teacher, my enemy, my ideal, my worst nightmare - my ticket to army life. He saw in me, I believe, a lot of potential. At one point he told me that he was enjoying training me. Almost none of his other trainees had been in such good physical condition when entrusted to him, and that had presented an obstacle that was absent in me.

Occasionally I would see Ruhamah going from one tent to another, always in the company of several other women. There was never an opportunity for us to talk, but she seemed to be very much recovered from her ordeal.

On the morning of the eleventh day I was greeted by Enusat as usual, but this time he led me to my uncle's tent instead of to the training area.

"Come, Kasher; take a look at our battle situation," Nakhti said as I entered the main hall. There on the ground was the same diagram I had seen the last time there; the map of Babylon.

I knew nothing of the actual layout of the city, and my uncle, presuming that to be the case began explaining it to me.

"We are here," he said, pointing to the south side of a long wall which extended from a corner in the southwest, moving in a north-easterly direction. I immediately recognized that the section of wall I had seen was but a tiny piece of what Babylon was. For the first time I really began to understand something of the massiveness of the city. I had expected grandeur: but this?

Nakhti continued with his explanation.

"From here where we are, the outer wall extends basically due north from the corner to our left. All of the water around us comes from the Euphrates. You probably saw the river itself from the market place last week, Kasher."

I nodded, not wanting him to know how unobservant I had been. My attention had been arrested in another direction soon after arriving at that place.

"The river forms a formidable boundary along that western wall, and yet Nebuchadnezzar isn't satisfied with the protection there. He is building a new wall that will extend for about two thousand cubits beyond the river. The river will end up flowing through the city with this expansion. If it is defensible, it will give them a source of water in time of siege. The other aspect I find intriguing is that what he seems to be building is a sort of buffer zone; one that can be given up at some point without risking the loss of the major part of the city."

What I saw in my uncle's face I can only describe as admiration. Grudging, perhaps; but admiration nevertheless.

"It is said that the idea of the expansion came from that Hebrew, Belteshazzar," said Enusat.

"If you ask me, he's the one running Babylon, not Nebuchadnezzar," another of the captains added.

"Well," said Nakhti, "if nothing else, the king knows when he has someone he can trust. That is a mark of leadership, in my opinion."

"Are you going over to him, too?" Enusat asked.

"You know I don't think he is as great as everyone says he is, and that I don't think he is the right person to rule Babylon; but I never want to get to the point where I can't see someone's strengths as well as weaknesses. That would be foolish and dangerous. Besides," a smile creeping onto his face, "I chose you men, didn't I? Was that not a sign of a good leader?"

The men all had a laugh at that, and I learned a lesson about dealing with different points of view. I knew that if I remembered that lesson it would be helpful to me.

I ventured a question. "Who is this Belteshazzar?"

My uncle explained to me how Belteshazzar and others had been taken in a raid on the city of Jerusalem several years before. They were followers of Jehovah, but seemed to accept their new roles as Babylonians. Apparently, a few of them were the best the Hebrews had to offer and so, after some testing, they were given positions in the king's court.

"Belteshazzar, and perhaps others like him, will be key in any overthrow attempt. It remains to be seen if their allegiance is to the king, or the kingdom. Or maybe they are just playing along until they themselves have the chance to take over. I just don't know yet," he added. "And we need to find out. Didn't you say that that girl I bought was a Hebrew?"

"That's what she told me," I answered. "At least that she believed in their God. I don't know if being a Hebrew is more religion or nationality."

One of the other captains jumped into the conversation at that point. "That is a question a lot of people would like answered. And for that, if nothing else, I think we would be wise not to trust them very far. After all, who is arrogant enough to say their god is the only one? All the other religions have several gods. They might say one is more important, or more powerful, but I don't trust people who are 'always right'!"

"Be that as it may," said Nakhti, we will have to keep these Hebrews in mind in all we do. Whether or not they have the 'only' true god, they are, as a rule, an intelligent and determined people. Just look at where this Belteshazzar is today!"

"And since we must have them in mind," he continued, "and since this new girl is one of them, I think it is time for a plan that gets her to him so she can inform us better as to what is going on. I still can't understand why Nebuchadnezzar doesn't come out of the city, especially with threats all around him. His people must be worried."

The plan began to form with input from several of the captains. It was decided to be too risky for her to go alone; a woman would not travel that way – it was too dangerous, and would therefore be likely to raise suspicions. I immediately offered to accompany her, but Nakhti, with a short, amused sounding grunt, explained why that would not happen.

"No, Kasher. Each of you is leverage for me concerning the other. Our relationship is not built on trust, but fear. Fear of what might happen to you if she doesn't do as she is told, and vice versa. The two of you will not be out of my sight at the same time for as long as our arrangement lasts. But maybe you can recommend someone. A soldier would probably be found out, and you have been around the others of our camp for a while now. Anyone come to mind?"

"There is one man, Kartan," I answered. "He is a gardener and cook, and he makes trips into Babylon on occasion. He seems a serious enough man. Maybe he could escort Ruhamah."

"Go and get him, Kasher" Nakhti said.

I knew where he would be at this time of day, and I ran to the garden, not wanting to irritate my uncle with delays. As I suspected, Kartan was there, tending to his plants.

He saw me running toward him and stopped what he was doing.

"What's the rush, boy? Are we going to battle or something?"

"Not yet," I replied. "Nakhti wants you to go to Babylon on a spying mission for him. He has a plan to get information through Ruhamah."

"Ruhamah? Is that the girl from the slave trader? How can she help?"

"I'll let my uncle explain. He wants to see you right away."

We hurried back to the tent, and were ushered in by the guard. Nakhti led us both to the diagram of the city. He had obviously been thinking the plan through as I was going for Kartan. He explained Kartan's part of the mission, only mentioning Ruhamah as being in his care on the way to and into the city.

I felt my heart jump as he told one of the guards, "bring the girl."

Our eyes met for a moment as she entered the room. I saw an encouraging smile on her face for just a brief moment. It was enough. Nakhti asked her if she spoke Aramaic. To my surprise she said that she did. My uncle began explaining his plan to her, in our own language, and we all listened with interest.

"Everyone of importance you will deal with will speak Aramaic, whether as their first tongue or not, so you have a good advantage there. You are to go with Kartan as far as the marketplace. There you will leave him as soon as it can be done without notice. There is so much commotion in that place no one will probably pay any attention to whether you are there or not, but you must make sure of it. Both of you," he said, turning now to give Kartan a look that said it all.

I was surprised, and relieved, that Ruhamah said nothing, just nodding once in a while. I didn't want her to take any chances of getting on Nakhti's bad side. I couldn't imagine having her sent away now.

"Now," continued my uncle, turning back to Ruhamah, "The rest of your task is quite simple. Get as close as you can to a man called Belteshazzar. He seems to be running things in Babylon these days. I have been made to understand that you are a worshipper of the god Jehovah, is that right?"

"Yes sir, I am."

"Good. It seems that our friend, Belteshazzar, is one also. The story goes that he was taken from Jerusalem by Nebuchadnezzar, along with a group of other young men. Somehow he has managed to gain a position of importance in the kingdom. My hope is that your common religion will help you get near him. Get as near as you can. Hopefully you will find a way to speak directly with him, but, if not, try to get to his inner circle of advisors. I need credible information about the king. He hasn't been seen in public for quite some time. Some say he is ill; others that he has simply gotten lazy, leaving the difficult decisions to others – like Belteshazzar. We need to know what is really going on!"

Without a pause, he continued, "In case it enters your mind that this might be your chance to escape from here, you need to understand that Kasher will be here with me the whole time. If you expect to see him again (and I think you want to) then you will find your way back to the market and Kartan by the morning of the second day after leaving him. Any more would surely raise suspicion about his being there as his produce will either be sold or rotted. If he is not there when you get back you will still have to find your way back here with your information. If I do not see your pretty face within the space of seven days, this young man you obviously care for, will die. Yes, Kasher," turning now to look at me. "I would do it. Some things are that important, and I believe in what I am doing."

"I understand, sir, and I respect you for it," I responded. "Could I just have a short word with Ruhamah before she goes? I promise there will be no trickery."

"Very well. You can go into that room there. Be back here in ten minutes. You will be watched but not listened to."

As soon as we got into the other room Ruhamah embraced me and said, rapidly, "I won't let you down,

Kasher. I will make it back, and with the information Nakhti wants!"

"I know, Ruhamah. I'm not worried about that. Just take care you don't run into trouble. I wish I could go with you, but my uncle doesn't trust me that far yet. With good reason since I am still loyal to the king."

"But Kasher, what if he is right about Nebuchadnezzar? What if he has turned the kingdom over to other men to run? What if that is what I find out when I go there?"

"Then I will have to reconsider; but we don't know anything yet. The main thing is that you get back here safely. My uncle has offered me my freedom at the end of six months' time if you and I help him in this matter. It's not that long, and then we can go where we want and get on with our lives!"

"'We', Kasher? What are you saying?"

The guard at the door began making noises to get our attention.

"Our time is up, Ruhamah, but we will have plenty of time to talk about the future when you get back. You are going to prove to him that we can be trusted, and I believe he will then give us more freedom. Be safe!"

Chapter 10

Kartan was used to this work and so needed no real orientation from my uncle. Ruhamah had been to the Babylon market, but the business that took her there now was very foreign to her.

"Just act like everyone else does in the market. We will set up a ruse for you to leave me after a few hours of selling from our cart."

"I'm not concerned about that part; it's when I go off on my own that I don't know what I will be into," Ruhamah replied.

"What I was told was to explain to you what area you should work your way into. I can do that, but once there, you have to figure out how to get Nakhti's information on your own. I have no contacts in the world you need to penetrate."

Kartan explained how the market was actually a buffer for the king's safety. "It is in the area between the inner and outer walls, and the gate we will go through is the only one open on market day. The inner gates are well guarded, and only people with a good reason are allowed in."

"How will I get through then?"

"That has been taken care of. We have some information about the layout of the inner city, and, through careful planning, we have arranged lodging and employment for one of our people not far from the palace. Word has been sent for him to watch for you at the inner gate and escort you in with him. The excuse will be the amount of goods he has bought from us - they being too large for one person to carry - and since I can't leave the cart, you have to go with him to help. After that, you really are on your own."

Though she had been there before, Ruhamah was still impressed with the massive walls. They were about three hundred cubits high, impressive indeed, but what really made them stand out was their thickness.

After passing through the outer wall without incident they were able to get a place fairly close to the inner gate to set up shop. Kartan had to keep some produce back for the ruse as he had a reputation for good stuff. Not only did he need some to send in with Ruhamah, he also needed to sell for at least two days.

Finally the time came, and Ruhamah disappeared through the gate as planned.

There was no time to take it all in as the man led her down the wide avenue, much wider than the gate itself. Although no one would have paid any special attention to her (inner city or no, it was still market day, with all its chaos) she was still afraid to seem out of place by looking around and gawking. It was an effort, though. It was all so new and grand!

Her guide helped her in to his home and offered her some food and drink. She accepted gratefully, and then asked to be allowed to get on with her task. The time deadline weighed heavily on her and she had no idea how long it would take her to get some important information.

"I understand you are to try to get close to Belteshazzar," the man stated. She had not asked the man's name, and he had not introduced himself. Apparently both felt it was better that way.

"Yes. Do you know if he lives in the palace?"

"I have been told he has a small house within the palace compound. That is really all I know. I have seen him on several occasions, normally reading a royal decree or something, but that has always been from the temple steps."

"I must be off. Can you please point me in the right direction?"

As they stepped out the front door of his house he pointed back to the avenue that had brought them to the street on which he lived.

"Go back there, and instead of going back to your left, go right. You will be following yet another high wall on your right; one that marks the boundary of the palace compound. Follow it to the next gate. You won't be allowed to enter, but in that area, outside the compound, are the houses of people who deal with government matters. I'm told the king likes to have them close by. I suppose that is where you will need to try to establish contact. You are welcome to come back here in the evenings. My wife lives here with me so there will be no problem with appearances."

Like the great avenue she was entering, again Ruhamah's eyes were wide. She tried not to be too conspicuous but she really had to look around in amazement.

To her right was a wall, not much smaller than the others she had passed through to get there. She could not get a feel for their thickness from her perspective on the street. To her left were smaller streets, filled with houses, chaotically spreading away from the avenue. The houses were all pretty much alike; two or three stories, square, with a flat roof surrounded by a parapet. As she looked between some of the houses (there wasn't much room separating them) she was finally able to get a view beyond them. There, still quite a ways off, she could see the opposite side of the river. The side closest to her was not visible as the embankments were quite deep and steep leading down to the water. She could only see a small portion of the river at a time, and could not make out much detail. Wisdom dictated she not stay too long staring. She moved on, trying to take in what she could, still trying to formulate a good story that would explain her presence near the palace.

She began to notice a change in the houses. It was subtle at first, but even before the size changed much there was a difference in what she could only describe as 'attitude'. There was more adornment, gradually, in the architecture, and in the spaces surrounding the houses. That space seemed to be growing also; the difference so small at first that it was almost undetectable. By the time she caught sight of the palace gate, almost a half hour later, she was looking at a completely different class of houses than when she had started her walk.

The gate was the most ornate thing she had ever seen. There were blue clay tiles all over it and the wall to either side, top to bottom. At regular intervals there were inlays of some sort, beginning just above the reach of a tall man. From the look of them she believed they must be gold. Moving as close as she felt comfortable to do, she was able at last to see they resembled clouds; golden clouds.

A voice from behind her was calling out, but she was not paying attention. All of a sudden a hand touched her lightly on the shoulder. Turning, fear in her wide eyes, she saw a familiar face.

"It *is* you, Ruhamah! I hardly believed it could be, but there you are!"

"Utanin! You frightened me half to death! I didn't think I knew anyone here, and then a hand on my shoulder..."

"I am so sorry, my dear," he continued, genuinely contrite. "I had to know if it was you. Is Kasher with you?"

"No, I am truly alone... or was until you showed up."

"Come, we must talk. My humble home is just down this road. Come!"

There really was nothing for it but to go with him. To refuse would surely raise suspicion; and maybe he could even be of help with her task.

"Just a bit further. There, that next house."

The 'humble home' he had referred to was one of the finest she had seen to this point. The walls were sand colored, trimmed with the same shade of blue she had seen on the palace gate. There was no gold, but there were small figures in the blue, themselves the same natural sandy look of the rest of the walls. She looked with interest at the figures as they approached the front door.

"Not my doing, that. They were already there when I was installed here. Apparently the place belonged to a

Chaldean of some stature before. They tell me those figures are things they (the Chaldeans) see in the sky. The night sky to be exact. Forms they see in the stars. I don't mind them being there. They make good decoration, even though they hold no meaning to me."

He ushered her into the house and went through to the back, muttering something about making herself comfortable as he went. She understood him to say he would be right back, so she didn't follow him, just stood waiting.

Utanin returned with a pitcher and two clay cups. "Don't have many people in, so all I have is bit of must for now. We'll get some food brought in shortly."

"Oh, please, Utanin, don't make a fuss. I won't be able to stay long anyway. I brought food from the market for a client myself, and I will have to start back before it gets late. But please, tell me how you came to this situation!"

Utanin explained what he remembered of the day he and Kasher separated outside the walls of the city. "Have you no news from him?" he asked.

"Yes, I do! He is in an army camp just outside the city wall. He is a captive, but seems to be well treated."

"Oh! How I would love to see that boy now. He saved my life twice. An army camp you say? But you were able to speak with him?"

Not sure how much she should reveal, Ruhamah decided to redirect the conversation back to Utanin's story as quickly as she could.

"Yes, I talked to him. The man I am working for, a farmer, sells his produce to that army as well as here in the city. I believe we will be going back there when we leave Babylon. Tell me the rest of your story! I am sure Kasher will want to hear it."

Utanin started, by means of explanation, with his history with Nebuchadnezzar. After telling her about that, he showed her a tattoo he had on his left forearm.

"I haven't seen the king, yet, but one of his men examined us as we came in, fleeing as we were from someone. They later told me it had been a part of the 'Army of Jerusalem'; supposedly in league with Egypt to take over Babylon. Anyway, this official saw my mark, and recognized it as the same as the one the king has, and in the same place. Since then I have been placed in this house with anything I want just a request away; and basically ignored! When I found you I was doing what I have been doing every day since I came here; going to the palace gate, asking to speak with the king. No matter how often I show the tattoo, and tell them my relationship with Nebuchadnezzar, I am sent away."

"I have only been here a day now," Ruhamah responded, "but already I hear rumors. Some say the king is ill. Others, that he has locked himself in the palace compound, turning over the affairs of state to another. I believe his name is Belteshazzar."

"Ah. That name I have also been hearing. The Hebrew, they call him. I think I saw him once speaking to a group of Babylon's important men. They were on the steps of the temple of Marduk, a place where many big decisions are made. I really don't know much about him, but he definitely has a lot of power in the kingdom, that's for sure."

"Can't you talk to him?" Ruhamah asked.

I've tried, but he won't grant me an audience either. I suppose I shouldn't complain. I am being well taken care of. I just don't like being in the dark."

Ruhamah decided to take advantage of what she perceived to be the opportune moment to find out more.

"So, do you think the king is incapacitated, scared, or maybe even dead?"

"I truly don't know, Ruhamah. I wish I did. We were so close back then when we were young. I admired him as a man, but loved him as a brother. I hope he is alright. Ruhamah, would you go with me, just for a little while to the gate area? Maybe together we can find out more than I have been able to do alone."

Trying to hide her excitement about his idea, she calmly said, "We can try, if you think it could help."

"Your religious heritage combined with my personal connection to the king might just be the combination needed," he answered. "I hope I am not asking too much of you."

"No, Utanin. You know how much Kasher admires Nebuchadnezzar. If I could take news of the king back to him I am sure he would be grateful."

A few minutes later they were back in front of the palace gate. They stood for several minutes observing the people who entered and exited. Ruhamah was watching Utanin's face for any sign of recognition and almost missed seeing the man as he turned right out of the gate. There was no mistaking him. She ran to catch up with him. Utanin, as soon as he recovered from the shock of her sudden departure, made his way as quickly as he could to follow her.

By the time he caught up to her she was past the man, turning to get his attention. Utanin noticed her eagerness, but decided it was because she had seen someone she knew. Still, a doubt began to form in the back of his mind: what exactly was she doing here?

"Ruhamah, What a surprise to see you here!" said the man she had been chasing after.

"Oh, Jeremiah; I'm so glad to see you!"

Utanin came upon them at this point and Ruhamah said, "Jeremiah, this is Utanin, a friend. Do you have a little time to spare? Utanin, do you mind if he comes with us back to your house?"

Both men agreed to her suggestion. Utanin was happy that someone who had just left the palace grounds would speak to him, and Jeremiah said he had just finished meeting with the court and would welcome some refreshment.

At Utanin's house they ate fruit brought in by a servant. He explained that the house had come with a small staff who took care of whatever he needed. After several minutes of pleasantries, Ruhamah decided it was time to find out if Jeremiah could (and would) help her.

"Jeremiah, there are so many rumors flying around about the king. What do you know about him at this time?"

"It is odd," he began. "I have met the king on several other visits to the city, but this time I have not been allowed in his presence. Even Daniel seems closed to talking about him right now."

"Daniel? Who is that?" she asked.

"If you have heard of him, you probably know him as Belteshazzar. That is his Babylonian name, a 'servant of Bel'. I cannot call him that as neither he nor I would ever serve that idol. His name is Daniel, 'God is my judge' - the real God, Jehovah."

He paused as if in deep thought for a long moment, and then proceeded.

"Daniel seems to be running things, and that in itself is not unusual. He has been the First Minister since shortly after being brought here by Nebuchadnezzar. He was supposed to be in training for three years before a decision was made as to his usefulness to the kingdom, but Nebuchadnezzar saw what he needed to in just a few months, and promoted him to his present position. I wasn't here then, but I know the Chaldeans well enough to believe they were not (and I'm sure still are not) happy about it. The difference now is that the king has always been involved in the decision-making process before. He lets his ministers do their job, but keeps a close eye on those decisions, asserting himself as king at times. Right now he is completely missing from the process."

"The king is a personal friend of mine," inserted Utanin. "If he is ill or something I would appreciate it if you could tell me."

"I wish I could, sir; I truly do. I wasn't at court very long this time, but I did not see any sign of him."

The conversation turned to more mundane matters. Utanin called again for the servant who brought them some cool drinks. After finishing their refreshment, Ruhamah declared that she needed to start back, and Jeremiah rose to accompany her.

Utanin saw them to the door. "Please tell Kasher of my present estate when you see him. And if, sometime, you can get me word about Nebuchadnezzar; I would be truly grateful."

As the two of them made their way back to the main avenue, Ruhamah opened up to Jeremiah about her real situation. After her explanation, Jeremiah looked her in the eyes and said, "We need to try to find out more. Kasher's life may depend on it. Let's head back to the gate and see if I can get another entrance. Maybe I can ask for you to accompany me, as my servant. If you don't mind that role of course."

"I would do almost anything to help Kasher," she said, her eyes on the ground in front of her. Jeremiah said nothing for another of his long pauses. Ruhamah finally looked up at him. He was looking down at her, and his gaze made her feel that someone really did care about her. It was as if he was feeling what she was. He would help; she was sure of that now.

They reached the gate, and Jeremiah went directly to the guard in charge. He was recognized immediately, and, after a brief word of explanation from him, Ruhamah was allowed to enter with him.

The gate was just the beginning of a series of rooms and courtyards they had to go through, at least one guard questioning them at each stage, before they finally reached a set of enormous stone steps leading up at least the height of five tall men, culminating in a great porch with huge columns holding up the roof.

"Welcome to the palace of Nebuchadnezzar," said Jeremiah.

At one end of the porch there was a large marble table. There were several men around it, and one man sitting behind it. Jeremiah led the way toward it. Ruhamah followed, doing her best to act natural in a place that was anything but natural to her experience.

The man behind the table stood as they came near. He was not particularly tall; not terribly muscular; not remarkably handsome. Ruhamah thought him to be about as 'normal' as anyone could be. He addressed himself to

Jeremiah in a simple, yet respectful way, and there was something in his voice that transcended anything in his looks. Without speaking loudly, he commanded attention.

"Dear prophet of the Lord, you are back so soon. I hope all is well."

"Yes, Daniel. Jehovah continues to flood my heart with His peace."

Ruhamah felt lightheaded. She was standing before a man who was at least the second most powerful man in this kingdom; a kingdom that was probably the greatest in the world. It was almost too much for her to assimilate. And yet, when Daniel looked at her, she saw the same kind of compassion she had just seen from Jeremiah.

"And who is this young lady, Jeremiah?"

"A daughter of Zion, sir. Her name is Ruhamah, and she is assisting me at the moment.

"You are a Hebrew, then?" Daniel asked her.

Ruhamah struggled to find her voice for what to her seemed like minutes, though it was, in reality, just a short pause before she spoke.

"Yes, sir, I am a believer in Jehovah, though not from The Land."

"Welcome, then, sister. You come in good company, and I trust you find more of it in our presence."

Daniel made a low bow to her and she felt her face go completely flush. She had no idea how she should respond, but Daniel turned immediately back to Jeremiah and continued his discussion with him.

"I know you would not have returned if it were not very important to do so, so if you could give me just a few moments to conclude a matter here, you will have my undivided attention."

Jeremiah and Ruhamah stepped back several paces, and Daniel returned to the men at the table.

"I didn't have an opportunity to ask before, but how is your father?" Jeremiah asked in a hushed tone.

Ruhamah lowered her head. "He was killed a few weeks ago, with all of his servants. I was taken for the slave market. I didn't want Utanin to know all of this. It was Kasher who saved me from the market. Or rather his uncle; the leader of the men who are assembled outside the city."

She began to cry quietly. Jeremiah waited for her to continue speaking. She felt as if she could, and should.

"Oh, Jeremiah, I am part of a deception! I was sent here to find out the status of the king and report back to Kasher's uncle. If I don't return in the next few days Kasher will be killed!"

"Calm yourself, Ruhamah. The Lord will show us the way. I have already heard from Him since we met today and all will be well. Daniel will help us, but we must be honest with him. He is Jehovah's servant."

True to his word, Daniel came over to them after just a short time, the other men now making their way down those massive steps to the courtyard below.

"Come," said Daniel. "Let's step inside where we can be more comfortable."

They stepped into a great hall. Everything was simple, yet there was a special elegance to it. Pottery vases formed the main decoration, placed either on the floor or on small tables at irregular intervals. There were paintings here and there on the wall, but there was much open wall and floor space to the room. The principle characteristic of it was its size. It was huge. Daniel noticed the interest Ruhamah was showing in the hall and so he turned to her to comment.

"My apologies, I forget how imposing this place can be to someone who is seeing it for the first time. This room is used for any state function that will be attended by large groups; mostly banquets. It is designed to remind the attendees of the grandeur of Babylon. I think it serves its purpose well."

"It certainly says 'grandeur' to me!" answered Ruhamah. "I could never have dreamed of a room so large."

"Come," continued Daniel. "Let's go somewhere a little less distracting."

He led them into a chamber at one side of the great hall, closing the door behind them. While it was not small, it was certainly less daunting than where they had come from, and Ruhamah was able to relax a bit. This room had more decoration including some cedar couches. Daniel sat on one and indicated that Ruhamah should sit across from him on another.

"Now, sister, we can speak openly here. I assume that the matter which brings Jeremiah here has to do with you as you are the new element to this situation. How can I be of help?"

Her voice trembling, Ruhamah began to tell her story, beginning with the sand storm that brought Kasher into her life and finishing by a plea for forgiveness for coming to Babylon as a spy. Her voice trailed off in tears as she said, "I just didn't know what else I could do, and now Kasher will surely…"

"Your name suits you well, I think, sister. In the Hebrew tongue it means 'compassion'. Do not fear. You are in no danger from me, and neither is your friend."

"But, sir, the only way that Kasher will not be killed is if I give a report to his uncle. What can I possibly tell him?"

"The truth! Tell him you saw me but not the king! That should satisfy his need for information."

"But won't that embolden him to go ahead with his attack on the city?"

"Perhaps, but that could happen anyway. Besides, I am not concerned about that."

"But I would be the cause of the attack. I would be repaying your kindness with betrayal," Ruhamah continued. "There are so many rumors about the king: his health, both physical and spiritual, his will and ability to lead…"

"Do not concern yourself with that, child. Tell him the rumors – I am sure he has heard them already. You cannot confirm or deny any of them still! You must do what you must to save your friend. Anyone would do the same in your situation. You can truthfully tell him that the city is strong – I believe you have seen that for yourself. Besides, your report will not ultimately decide whether an attack will be made. There are many other things involved, not the least of which is the fact that our God is with us, even if it does not seem so at times. Just last night I had a dream. I did not understand it until now."

"In my dream there was a plant that rose up in the middle of a field. I say a field, but it was nothing but dust, except for the plant that came up in its midst. It was a tree of some sort, and at the top of it, though it was a very small tree at the beginning of the dream, there was a single white flower."

"As the dream progressed, the tree grew taller, always with the one white flower at its top. When it reached a certain height I began to be able to see below the surface of the field. I saw that just at the point of the roots of the tree there was a pool of water flowing under the earth. Everywhere else was dry."

"Gradually some pods of some sort began falling from the tree – one here, two there, etc. Some of them landed close by the tree, and I could see them begin to extend roots into the ground. Their roots found their way to the pool and they began to grow. A few had a white flower, but not all."

"Other pods landed farther away from the tree. Their roots tried to find water, but they were too far from the pool, so they withered and died quickly."

"I believe you, Ruhamah, are the white flower on the first tree. Jehovah has placed you as a beacon to a large family. Those who look to you for example, those who stay close to you, will find the strength they need. Others will invariably choose other paths, paths that will lead to their destruction."

"So you see, the Lord is not finished with you yet. Take heart; go back and complete your mission in the knowledge that all will be well."

"I believe you will come again to my presence, and know that you are always welcome. The field in my dream – I'm not certain - but I believe it to be Babylon. If some day you arrive at the palace gate, tell the guard to send word to me that the 'white flower' requests to see me."

After exchanging pleasantries, giving Ruhamah time to dry her eyes, Daniel led them out through the hall and onto the palace porch. They said their goodbyes there, and Jeremiah and Ruhamah retraced there steps back to the gate. Once outside, Jeremiah took his leave of her.

"I must go back to Jerusalem. The Lord revealed it to me yesterday. There are dire moments coming to the Holy City. The people must be warned."

"Thank you, Jeremiah, for all your support. Will I see you again soon?"

"I don't know how soon it will be, but I believe our paths will continue to cross for years to come. Go in peace, sister."

Chapter 11

Kasher saw the cart coming back from the city and could see that Ruhamah was with it. He ran to the edge of the camp where they would enter.

At that same moment there was another group of arrivals, coming from the eastern edge of the camp. As Kasher, Ruhamah and Kartan came together, they turned to face the other group. To be sure, it was a much more exciting entrance for those present than the simple return of a couple of traders with an empty cart. Even so, Nakhti was paying close attention to both events. He instructed, briefly, one of his captains who then headed towards the three of them. Nakhti himself moved toward the other arrivals.

The captain who came towards the little group simply told them to follow him. They did so to a shade close to Nakhti's tent. There they waited as Nakhti greeted the newcomers.

There were about ten or so of them; all men, all mounted. The one who had been leading them was apparently just that: Their leader. He was the biggest man Kasher had ever seen. Nakhti was not small, though a bit shorter than Kasher, and this man towered over his uncle. It was only after a moment of watching that he realized that the men following the leader were huge too. It was just that, beside him, they did not seem so large. As they began to mingle with the men of the camp it became obvious that there was no one here to match them for size.

Seeing Kasher's mouth hanging open at the sight, Kartan moved close to him and said, "I see you've never seen a Philistine before."

"I've heard stories, but it's all so different in person," Kasher replied, his eyes still firmly fixed on those men. "The only person even close to that size I've seen was at the slave market – and he wasn't as big as these men. And it's not just their height," he continued. "They are built like oxen!"

Ruhamah chimed in at this point. "My mother told me a story about a shepherd boy in Israel who killed a Philistine giant and then became king. I didn't know they were all giants!"

"My mother told me the same story," but I always assumed it was a fable." Kasher said. "Maybe there was something to it after all!"

The group – Nakhti, some of his captains and the Philistines – passed very near to them as they headed for Nakhti's tent. Kasher tried not to stare as they came by, but the last man in the group looked right at him as he passed by. Seeing the expression on Kasher's face he gave him a smile – or something resembling a smile. Not familiar with their culture, Kasher could only read it as a sneer of disdain. He decided he would need to know more about this people. They could factor in his life someday.

The Philistines were shown in, but Nakhti left them as they entered and made his way to where the others were waiting.

"I'm glad to see you back safely," he said, addressing himself to Ruhamah. "I need to know what you found out in the city. It will probably have bearing on what I am about to discuss with those men inside."

Stuttering at first, not knowing which side of all these complicated issues she should be on, she told Nakhti about seeing Daniel, using his Babylonian name. "I had a conversation with him," she said, lowering her eyes.

"You spoke with Belteshazzar? How did you manage that?"

"I met a friend of Kasher's, a man named Utanin, who apparently grew up with Nebuchadnezzar. He helped me find an old family friend of mine who is close to Belteshazzar. He got me in to see him."

Kasher could not contain himself. "You saw Utanin? How was he?"

"We will get to that soon enough, Kasher," scolded his uncle. "We have matters of much greater importance to deal with right now. Ruhamah, what did Belteshazzar say?"

"We talked about all the different rumors: That the king is dead, insane; maybe just fearful. He would not confirm or deny any of them. He said the city is strong, and that is what I saw as well."

"You say the city is strong," Nakhti pressed. "But in what way? Of course it is a great and wealthy city, but what of the leadership?"

"All I can say is that Belteshazzar seemed to truly be in charge of the government operations. When I first arrived he was in a conference with a group of men who appeared to be city elders. He was obviously leading the meeting and they all listened to him when he spoke. No one could, or at least would, say anything about the king."

Nakhti questioned her for a while longer, mostly about the current layout of the areas she had seen. Finally, after what seemed like ages to Kasher, he sent her away. Kasher followed her toward the door of her tent.

"Kasher!" It was Nakhti.

"Yes, Uncle." His heart sank. Would he never get a moment with Ruhamah?

A slight knowing smile was all Nakhti he could allow at such a tense moment. "Ten minutes. Then I want you back here."

Kasher ran to catch up with Ruhamah. He would make the most of those few minutes.

She was being led toward the women's tent by a guard as Kasher rushed in her direction. The guard started to protest when Kasher called for them to stop, but apparently thought better of it. *Best not to provoke Nakhti,* he thought. He stood to one side as they embraced and started talking nervously. It crossed Kasher's mind, briefly, that he really should take advantage of his relationship to the leader of this band at every opportunity. When it was not possible; well, he would know that easily enough.

The two young people tried to make the most of their few minutes together. They both knew this experience had changed them. To each one, the overriding concern had been the wellbeing of the other. They were at a new level. They spoke excitedly in the shade her tent cast.

"You saw Utanin!" Kasher blurted out after a few moments. He is well, then?"

"Yes, Kasher. He seems perfectly fine physically. But he is frustrated by the lack of information about the king, and he seems like a caged animal. He has a nice cage, though, servants and all. I'm sure you know all about his friendship with Nebuchadnezzar."

"Yes, but we can't let anyone here know. It could be used in ways dangerous to us, Utanin – maybe even the king."

Kasher looked over at the guard but he seemed not to be interested in their conversation. His curiosity was almost too much to bear, but he knew they had to be discreet.

Men were streaming into Nakhti's tent and Kasher knew it was time for him to go. He embraced Ruhamah and whispered in her ear, "I'm so glad you came back safely. I have never cared about anyone to this degree before. It's a little frightening, but I think it's worth getting used to."

That provoked the reaction he was hoping for. As they pulled away, he saw the smile he remembered from his time in her father's tent.

Nakhti acknowledged his presence with a small nod as he took a place at the back of the room. The room was crowded, and the size of the Philistines didn't help in that area.

The noise was almost unbearable as different groups vied to make themselves heard. Kasher was surprised by his uncle's posture in the face of this confusion. He was simply standing, arms folded across his chest, seemingly waiting for something to happen. It didn't take too long.

Kasher moved back and forth as much as he could to keep Nakhti in sight, finding narrow passages of vision between the massive bodies of the Philistines. He wanted to see how his uncle would handle this situation. At one point he looked to his left and gently lifted his chin in that direction. The corners of his mouth seemed to rise slightly as he put his fingers in his ears. Kasher didn't follow his example immediately, but, very soon, saw the wisdom of his actions.

A noise began to fill the room. It started small; almost a groan. As soon as he heard the sound Kasher covered his ears, understanding that Nakhti would not be plugging his for a sound as low as this. Something else was surely on the way.

If one could see sound this one would have looked like a trumpet. The groan began to expand, almost imperceptibly at first. The tone never changed, but the intensity grew as smoothly and as surely as the length of a trumpet. The other noises in the room began subsiding, not all at once, but seemingly in consonance with the expansion of the groan. Those who were talking the loudest were the last to stop, finally recognizing that something was going on.

The sound reached its climax with no change in tone, or, really, in any substantial way except for volume. And it was really loud. Kasher could barely tolerate it with his ears covered. Some were bending over in a vain attempt to escape the power of that note. One could safely say that all who were trapped in that small space with that powerful noise were now quiet and focused. Kasher wormed his way forward in the group enough to get a glimpse of the source of the noise before it was put away. It was one of the Philistines who had been playing it (if that is what you would call making that noise), and he was now putting an object in a cedar box. He saw, briefly, that the instrument resembled a wide cone. It did not seem to be made of bone like all the horns he had ever seen. This had a reddish tint to it, and was covered in small bumps.

The sound, mercifully, did not fade away as it had come. All at once, it was just gone; except for the considerable residue of ringing left in everyone's heads. Nakhti did not hesitate at all to seize the moment.

"Now that I have your attention, we may begin. I hope you all enjoyed the musical moment. The Philistines seem to use objects from the sea whenever possible, and that was the famous 'Gaza Horn': Very effective."

"Let me state as strongly as I can that there must be order in this meeting, and I am that order. If you wish to speak address me and be recognized – but not yet! I have a few things I need to say here at the beginning. Be patient, and there will be time for all to have their say in good time."

"Yesterday I was approached by the delegation from Gaza," he continued, "with concerns about the length of time we have been in waiting mode. I understand the concern. I too am a man of action: A soldier. I am also the man who has assembled this threat against Nebuchadnezzar. Each faction has its reasons for wanting to overthrow him, and we have all compromised in some way to be able to work together. I am realistic enough to know there are some among us who would like nothing better than to take control of this operation from me. The only thing I ask is that you be man enough to confront me directly. Intrigue is for politicians and others too weak to fight for themselves."

A few glances were cast about the room at those remarks, and Kasher noticed most of them were directed to a certain man to his left. Nothing was said, but Kasher noted the man for future reference. He was average in height. In fact, there was little to distinguish him in Kasher's mind. That is, until he turned to his right, facing him.

He wore a light hood; not unusual amongst soldiers. It did not cover his face, or even the whole of his head. Above his eyes Kasher saw the most remarkable scar. It wasn't necessarily darker or more oddly shaped than other scars he had seen. What really made it unique was its location. It ran all the way from the top of his nose to the end of his rather pronounced forehead. It was as if he had taken an axe to the head and survived. He would not be easily forgotten.

"Right, then: I have obtained some information from within Babylon," Nakhti spoke firmly, but without yelling. It was the voice of authority.

"My sources have confirmed that the Hebrew is in full control of the operations of the city. No one has been able to confirm anything about Nebuchadnezzar himself. I believe the time is almost right to attack."

"Almost?" The voice came from within the group, but space was made for him to move to the forefront of the room. Kasher had not seen him before, but recognized a leader when he saw one. His clothes showed nothing, but his demeanor and voice were enough to know he was a man to be reckoned with.

"Yes, Nassir, almost – Wait! Let me finish! The situation in the city might be right, but we are not yet coordinated enough to perform a successful attack."

"Maybe you aren't," countered the man Nakhti had identified as Nassir, "but we are. This city is rightfully ours already! The Chaldeans are interlopers, and we will have them out!"

"We all know the history of Babylon," interjected the Philistine leader, his voice as big as he was. "We have already come to an agreement about the Assyrian claim to the city, as you well know. As you also know, you are not strong enough to defeat Nebuchadnezzar on your own. None of us are. Whether we like it or not Nebuchadnezzar has a large army, very dedicated to him, and the will of much of the people up and down the rivers is still on his side. Even among us there are differing reasons for wanting him dethroned. The main thing we all have in common, besides our desire for that, is that we need each other if we are going to make it happen."

As Kasher heard the huge man speak he thought about how wrong perceptions can be. He spoke in what Kasher had discovered was called Aramaic, albeit with a strong, harsh accent. The language had many similarities to Kasher's own. Nakhti had told him that most of the languages of the region could be traced back to Aramaic, and so as he listened he understood much. Given his accent, Kasher didn't believe the Philistine's native language was in the same family. By his physical appearance – not just his size, but also his dress and general demeanor – Kasher had thought the giant was nothing but a raging beast, fit only for battle. Yet he had spoken with considerable eloquence, limited as he was to a foreign tongue, and had made very clear, rational points. Another lesson he would be wise not to forget. He had heard his father say many times, "He is a fool who knows only what he thinks he knows." Kasher had had an illustration of that today.

The discussion, though, was far from over. For the next hour or so much of what he heard was bickering about each groups place in the siege and subsequent attack. From this 'discussion' he learned that there were several groups represented there. He tried to memorize the name of each group and as many of their people present as he could. Mainly he worked on remembering the names and faces of the leaders, if they were actually present.

Amongst Nakhti's own men there were factions. The most obvious one (and Kasher had seen it clearly during his time there) was the group of Egyptians. The force itself represented Egypt but was made up of soldiers from several different tribes; their leader, Nakhti being a good example. The 'real' Egyptians were relatively few in number; maybe forty in all. They could usually be seen together and were distinguishable by, among other things, their dress. Once, when I was closer to them than I really wanted to be, I noticed that some, at least, of them had dark, black eyes. They tended to lighter colors, worn closer to the body that most of the others. Their allegiance was to Nakhti but they had a hierarchy among themselves, a man named Sin-Ra the obvious leader of their group.

There were several Assyrians, Nassir obviously leading this delegation. Whether he was the actual leader of their army Kasher was not able to determine, but he was obviously a man of considerable authority.

He found out that the Philistines referred to themselves as 'the People of the Five Cities'. Their spokesman was known in the discussion by the name

'Seren'. A small group – there were only six of them – frightened him in a different way from the rest. They spoke little, but they were watching everyone else intently. There was something about them; again, more than just size. Kasher couldn't put his finger on it, but they concerned him.

One of Nakhti's men, Minkabh, that Kasher knew fairly well by now, had made his way to be by him. He let him know, speaking in low tones, that he was there at his uncle's direction.

"If you have questions, just ask me. Nakhti wants you informed."

"Those three over there. The ones who look so devious. Who are they?"

"I see you have some discernment. Nakhti said so. Those men are Edomites. They are some of the sneakiest, most distrustful people you will ever meet. Never turn your back on them."

"If they are so bad, why are they tolerated?"

"Your uncle is a wise man. The Edomites are no longer a large or powerful group. They are like jackals. They hang around waiting to take advantage of a situation. Nakhti thinks it wiser to keep them close so they can't sneak up on us at a critical moment and cause us trouble. They have accepted his leadership – no doubt thinking they will gain whether we win or lose. This way Nakhti not only knows where they are at all times, he actually places them where he wants to keep them out of mischief."

There were, he was told, Ammonites, Moabites and Phoenicians present. Each group had been given instructions for the siege and for the attack. It was all well-organized. The meeting seemed to threaten their unity of purpose.

One man stood alone. It was the man with the scar. Kasher asked about him and was informed that he represented the 'Army of Jerusalem'.

"They are much less an army than a band of thugs. Not as sneaky as the Edomite 'jackals': Much more open in their meanness. Nakhti tolerates them, but just barely."

"They claim," he continued, "to represent the Jewish people. We all know that is not true. They have a sizeable following in Israel, but they are far from being in charge. So, they wreak havoc in an attempt to destabilize even their own country in hopes they will step into the void when it comes."

"They are, by the way, the ones who chased you as you arrived at the city. They misjudged their location, and so herded you and your fellow travelers right to us. At that point they saw they would not be able to plunder as much as they thought and pretty much broke off the attack."

"Not before I was knocked unconscious," Kasher complained. "Still, I suppose it would have been much worse to be at their mercy."

"Much worse indeed," replied Minkabh. "The Hebrews are generally a fair-minded people, in my experience. But there is always a faction, almost anywhere, which tends to cruelty and domination. These are vicious men."

The discussions went on for a long time. Nakhti somehow maintained overall control. Kasher was very impressed that he seemed to use just the right tone of voice and choice of words in every situation. There were moments that seemed to spiral out of control, but the chaos never lasted very long. Nakhti showed himself a true leader, not just a warrior. Kasher's admiration was grudging, given his desire to serve Nebuchadnezzar; but the admiration was nevertheless real.

During one of the more animated discussions Kasher saw the 'jackals' shift position. They eased their way to be next to the man from Jerusalem. He called the move to Minkabh attention.

"Very observant, Kasher. And an important observation. I will inform Nakhti after the meeting. No possible good can come from an alliance between those two groups. We had to use all of our powers of persuasion to get them involved together in this endeavor. They are historically mortal enemies so they must really want something if they are willing to get so friendly with each other."

The meeting ended abruptly. Kasher neither heard nor saw anything that signaled, in his mind, an end to discussions, but it was definitely over. Doors were opened into various antechambers, all leading to an exit on one side or other of the great tent. Minkabh and Kasher waited for the crowd to clear and then went to talk to Nakhti.

He was standing quietly where he had been during the whole meeting. As the last of the delegates filed out he seemed to relax. A real change came over him, just for a moment, but in that moment Kasher saw a very tired man. He guessed the fatigue was more than just physical. If Minkabh noticed, he said nothing about it. Nakhti recovered quickly as he saw them approaching.

There was an awkward silence, so Kasher said, "I didn't hear a final agreement, Uncle. What's next?"

"I was able to get everyone to agree to wait three more weeks. After that, if there is no attack, I think it is implied that this alliance will fall apart."

Chapter 12

Kasher spent the next days continuing his military training. Here, he was not the only strong man, but he still stood out as being in very good physical condition. He also took the opportunity to learn more about the Aramaic language, Ruhamah serving as his tutor. He certainly didn't mind spending time with her.

He found Aramaic to be relatively easy for him. As Nakhti had said, there were a great many similarities between it and his native dialect. Their structures were basically the same, so his main task was to learn new vocabulary. He was a good student: at least to the degree he could keep his mind on the subject of the language. The hardest part was when he had to mimic Ruhamah's formation of a sound that his old language didn't use. Paying that much attention to her mouth was a real distraction for him. Somehow he still managed to learn a good bit of the language.

Ruhamah, for her part, was enjoying the time with Kasher. She had deep feelings for him, but was still somewhat afraid of letting those feelings take over. She used their time together to try to know more about him. Her belief in Jehovah was real and important to her, so she brought that subject up often.

They had had over a week now for these conversations, becoming more and more comfortable with each other.

They were talking early one morning.

"One of my big problems with the religions," Kasher said, hoping he was not taking it far enough to offend her, "is the lack of freedom they impose on their believers. Anytime someone talks to me about their god I'm presented with a list of things I *must* do, and another of things I *can't* do. I value my freedom."

"Still," Ruhamah responded, "you surely can't deny that there are things belonging to a world we don't see: the supernatural, if you will."

"Convince me," said Kasher, using the Aramaic vocabulary he had learned that day.

Ruhamah smiled and responded in Aramaic, "I can't convince you. But I think you know it's true, deep down. Everyone at least questions where they came from and where they are going. And as for what one can and cannot do, what I know about Jehovah doesn't lead me to believe that is most important to Him. He created us, and He wants us to know and love Him as He loves us."

"Slipping back into their native tongue, Kasher leaned in close to her and said, "I still believe my future will find me in Babylon. Some things have changed in my mind, though. Now I mostly want to know with whom I am going – the *where* I can figure out as I go."

Their talk was cut short as a crowd of people moved toward the side of the camp closest to the city. They were swept up in the movement, asking as they went what was happening. No one seemed to know much, but they heard that the gate directly in front of them had opened for the first time since the day Kasher had arrived.

People were spread across the canal that formed the northern boundary of the camp. As I looked down the line I saw Nakhti arrive, and room was made for him to get to the front. He looked as puzzled as the rest of us.

We watched the gate for some time. After what seemed like hours, but was surely only a matter of a few minutes, there was movement there.

A great, lumbering machine poked its head through the gate. There were two rows of oxen at its front, three abreast, and what they were pulling seemed to be built of wooden beams. The men leading the oxen were dwarfed by the animals. Their heads barely reached the backs of the beasts. They took them right into the canal that ran alongside the wall. As the oxen entered the water their handlers moved back and onto the platform they were pulling, encouraging the forward progress of the oxen with goads. The water reached the animal's chins, but no higher. They continued forward, climbing out the other side without ever changing their speed. The wood they were pulling was drawn until it reached both banks comfortably. As the people of the encampment watched the water drip from the great beasts it became clear what had been placed there. It was a bridge.

There was much mumbling about the meaning of what they were witnessing. It grew in volume until it reminded Kasher of the wind during the sand storm. It died suddenly as more movement appeared at the gate; a team of mules this time. They pulled a wagon.

The oxen having been removed from their yokes, the mule-wagon came across the bridge and travelled about half the distance from the gate to our position. Several men jumped down and began taking things from the wagon. As they watched, they assembled a small but very ornate tent.

The tent was decorated with what appeared to be gold at each of its seams. A breeze blew back one of the flaps before it could be secured and two great wooden chairs were visible. There appeared to be nothing else inside. A banner flew above the tent. Kasher thought he could make out the shape of a lion – golden, on a background of deep blue. Someone whispered, "its Nebuchadnezzar's standard: Ishtar's lion!"

The crew of men mounted the wagon again and drove it back through the gate. No one spoke this time. The silence was more disconcerting than any noise could have been at that moment.

And then he appeared. A tall man, dressed in flowing white robes striped vertically with blue and gold. He wore some sort of helmet; impossible to see clearly from this distance.

He was mounted on a huge steed. Kasher allowed himself a brief thought; the horses the Philistines rode looked small in comparison to this animal. It was of the most pure white he had ever seen on a beast. It almost seemed as if it had been painted! Every part of it was white: even the mane and tail. And it was massive.

Kasher wondered if the sounds of awe he was hearing were for the man or the horse. It dawned on him that the impression was not easily separated into parts.

He knew who it was. He looked much different now, but it was he. The last time Kasher had seen Nebuchadnezzar he was covered in sweat and grime from travels and battles. Even so, it was the same man.

He rode slowly, deliberately out of the gate and across the bridge toward the tent that had been set up.

There were two men with him, one on either side, walking in pace with the horse. There was only one word to describe the tiny procession; regal.

Kasher pried his eyes off of Nebuchadnezzar long enough to analyze the other two men. The one on his left wore a white tunic which contrasted greatly with the darkness of his skin. He was very large, and, at least from this distance, looked every bit the warrior. He was empty-handed, as was his companion on the other side.

It would be a great understatement to say that the man on Nebuchadnezzar's right was not so dark. In fact, he was as white of skin as anyone Kasher had ever seen. The effect of the paleness of his skin was accented by his general demeanor. Even at this pedantic pace he had to shuffle forward now and again to keep up. If Nebuchadnezzar and his steed were power, this man was weakness.

On they came, just the three of them. No one from the camp moved. It would be safe to say that everyone was captivated by the scene. Of course, when anyone could take their eyes away from it, they were looking to Nakhti to see his response. There was none. He simply stood where he was and waited.

If someone thought about the possibility of attacking the king in this moment of vulnerability, no one gave the thought voice. There was practically no noise coming from this assembly: it was just too overwhelming.

When they reached the tent Nebuchadnezzar dismounted without ceremony. He stood and faced the encampment, hands on his hips. Kasher could just make out some detail of his face at this distance. He stood for a moment thus and then spoke to his two companions.

The dark man moved to the tent and proceeded to open the sides of it to the view of Nakhti's camp. At the same time, Nebuchadnezzar opened his robes to reveal a simple garment underneath. The message was obvious to Kasher – no weapons.

At another word from the king the pale man started walking in the direction of the encampment. He headed straight for the closest bridge. Nakhti was just there.

Kasher worked his way closer to his uncle's position, hoping to hear something. Nakhti, Minkabh and Enusat met the man in the middle of the bridge. Kasher had gotten close enough to hear the man's proclamation.

His voice was apparently the strongest thing about him. It rang out with great clarity and enough force for much of the assembled crowd to hear.

"Nebuchadnezzar, chosen servant of the knower of thoughts and declarer of truths, the great god Nabu, invites the Egyptian champion, the mighty Nakhti, to be his honored guest for a conversation regarding the future of Babylon and Babylonia. Will you accompany me?"

His manner of speaking confused Kasher. He spoke Aramaic, that was certain, and he had an accent he had never heard before. But that wasn't the most notable thing. It was the way he formed the words. There was almost a whistle in his exhalation; not enough to mask the words – they remained clearly pronounced through the whistle.

It was hard, though, for Kasher to concentrate on his words. His mind wanted to fixate on the whistle.

Nakhti and his men pulled back a bit from the man and consulted together. After a short talk, Minkabh responded to the herald, "The king has brought two men.

Does he invite our great leader to come thus accompanied?"

"He does. He only requires that all three come as he is: unarmed."

There was another conversation between the three men. Kasher noticed that it was a bit more animated than the first. He could imagine some disagreement on the part of the other two about Nakhti placing himself in such danger. Finally there was calm. Minkabh spoke again.

"It will be so. Be it known to you and these witnesses that if there is any trickery, our men are ready to respond with the swiftness of a bolt of lightning. If Nakhti is in danger, so is your king."

This he said loudly, with the immediate effect that Nakhti's men headed back to the camp for their weaponry.

"Your warning is unnecessary, but anticipated. Your terms are understood. Please, leave your weapons and follow me."

"I require a moment only to give orders to my men. I do not wish anything to happen out of confusion," said Nakhti, already turning to speak with Minkabh and Enusat.

Nebuchadnezzar's servant was obviously put out by this delay, but there was nothing he could do. He folded his boney arms across his chest and looked at the ground. Kasher noticed he was mumbling under his breath, and then saw him reach into his cloak with his right hand.

A cry stuck in Kasher's throat as he tried to call out for his uncle to look back at the man. He moved in their general direction but it was too far and his way too blocked by people to have made a difference.

148

The man's hand came out, and to Kasher's relief it did not grip a weapon. Instead, the man held a small, green stone. He continued mumbling, and Kasher assumed it was some sort of religious object.

In the meantime, Nakhti had given instructions to some of his captains, and they were organizing their men into two groups – one at each bridge.

Kasher noticed that the Egyptians had assembled themselves at the back of one of the formations. They seemed to be watching Sin-Ra, as if they awaited his reaction to what was going on. As Kasher considered what this might mean, Nakhti, accompanied by Minkabh and Enusat, moved across the bridge, following the frail, white messenger.

If the crowd assembled thought the wait for them to reach the tent was long, they soon realized what delay really was. As Nakhti arrived at the tent, Minkabh and Enusat were escorted by their guide to a place on the encampment side of the tent. There they, along with Nebuchadnezzar's two servants, sat on the ground as Nakhti entered the tent.

No one knew what to expect, but certainly no one anticipated the wait that then began. Nakhti had entered the tent just before noon. Two hours later (when there was at last some activity) the crowd was still on its feet. As it turned out, the movement was only that Nebuchadnezzar's servants had brought out some food. The darker servant entered the tent briefly, taking in food for the two leaders in conference. Then they shared what was left with Nakhti's men. Except for the soldiers, who remained where they had been assembled, the crowd took this as a sign that no conclusion was likely any time soon.

Some sat where they were. Others went for food. No one took their eyes off the tent for very long.

Through the heat of the desert day they waited. There was no breeze. It was as if even the air was also holding its breath in anticipation.

Marking the passing of that amazing day, shades of color already tinged the horizon when at last something happened out there.

All four men outside moved to the main door of the tent. Nebuchadnezzar exited first, then Nakhti. The two great men stepped toward the waiting encampment a few paces, separating themselves from the other men. And then it happened.

Chapter 13

The six years of my reign have been hard on me. Sometimes I even long for the days when I was a general: when I only had to obey my father's orders. There was much responsibility then, but nothing like this. Now I am to be obeyed. But what if I am wrong? I can destroy all that has been handed down to me in a moment of weakness, indecisiveness or bad judgment. It weighs heavily on me.

I miss my father. He was taken before I could learn all I needed to from him. He was a strong man, in more ways than one.

He told me often that we were the new Babylonians; wisdom of the gods, strength and learning, religion and human ability joined in a new and important way.

Knowledge of our origins have been obscured for years now to most of the world; even to most of those closest to the throne. Nabopolassar made sure I was instructed in matters of Chaldean history and culture. I knew, however, that my father was not fully representative of that culture. Their priests were ever present in our world, but it was an uncomfortable alliance that we had with them. We felt we needed them, but we did not really trust them.

They seemed, to me, to think themselves superior to all: even the king. At nearly every turn they had interfered with my father's reign. Yet, he endured them. And now I was doing the same.

It wasn't so much a direct fear of them; I didn't believe in much of what they said. They claimed a special relationship with the gods, but I didn't see much sign of that. There were moments that made me wonder: prophecies that seemed to come true, manifestations that appeared supernatural, etc.

What troubled me most about them was the hold they had on so many. Father warned me on several occasions that to cross the Chaldeans was to invite the displeasure of the people, or at least a large segment of our kingdom. I was finding this to be true in my time as king. We are a superstitious people, we Babylonians. Even the most cynical among us seem to want to keep on the good side of the Chaldeans. Just in case.

The discovery we made on the day I received the "Scepter of Princes" took some wind out of their sails. They have been much more manageable since then, though they are still a constant concern.

When I left Utanin that day I was ushered into a council of all of the powerful men of the kingdom. The heads of the Chaldeans were among them. They were especially smug that day. I learned later that they had negotiated many powerful things from my father for their approval of my ascension to my new position.

What happened next allowed us to renegotiate.

The final phase of the ceremony was a procession to the tower called Etemenanki. I had been taught from very early on the origins of the tower and its significance to us.

Built, it was held by our people, by the great hunter and warrior Nimrod, the tower had been a marvel just in size; it had dwarfed all the buildings in the city, even the massive palace my father and I have occupied.

Of course, the height of the tower was impressive when it was still standing. It was built, according to the Chaldeans, as a platform for seeing right into the throne room of the gods. The base was almost as wide as the tower was said to have been high.

My father had built the temple of Marduk here in this square, just a short walk from the base of Etemenanki.

I knew something strange was happening long before we reached the base of the tower. It was no more than a feeling, but it was a strong one.

The world in which I had grown up was filled with mysticism. If I had to describe the Chaldeans, that one word would be my choice. Although I did not understand much of what they did and said, there was always an air of the supernatural in them. That much was not hidden. They invoked the names of gods at every turn, claiming themselves to be their spokesmen and their seers.

They saw what others did not: an easy thing to claim, but not as easy to prove. The proofs were fairly abundant, though. They were constantly displaying their powers publicly, sometimes by interpreting dreams, other times with what they called, "signs". These might consist of conjuring fire, clouds or even rain. Sometimes it was in the form of a curse; they often seemed to come to pass, though not always.

The people were afraid of them.

I myself had seen enough from them to wonder at their mystical powers. I wondered even more at the hold they had on our people.

As we arrived at the base of Etemenanki I was summoned to stand before my father. A Chaldean priest was at his side, and next to him was our most revered god: Marduk.

Marduk: He of the fifty names. One of my tutors (a skeptic in matters of religion) had explained to me that our chief deity had undergone many changes over the millennia. Even so he had long been, in all of his manifestations, the number one god of the Babylonians.

I had learned of the great "Marduk Prophecy", given, it was said, by the great god himself. He desired, the prophecy detailed, to travel to other kingdoms to spread his fame as the chief of all the gods. This he did. An outsider to the story might conclude that he was merely stolen by invaders of Babylon and successive cities, his "travels" thus effected. But the Chaldeans insisted that this was all within his divine plan.

When Marduk left Babylon, he left behind two things: a great famine, and a prophecy of his return.

The famine eventually subsided, but the prophecy was not yet to be fulfilled. Many years later, as the prophecy had told, a savior arose from among the people of Babylon. He, as was destined for him by the prophecy, restored Babylon to greatness and brought back to the great city the very god that stood before me on this august day.

This deliverer was my namesake; Nebuchadnezzar I. I had been informed many times over, by my father and my tutors, that I had been named for him because of a new prophecy, one told to my father upon my birth by a

Chaldean seer. There were elements of the prophecy that had been kept from me so far. I was told "what I needed to know for now". I wondered if this ceremony today would reveal more; maybe even all!

It was the priest who actually held the scepter, not my father. I was commanded to kneel before Marduk. The priest spoke for quite a while in a very strange language, then switched to Aramaic. He began by revealing the rest of the prophecy.

"The continuation of the words of our lord Bel-Marduk," he began. There was a lot of flowery religious talk that seemed completely wasteful to me, but that was how these things were done. I was destined to be king one day, so I knew I would have to put up with a great deal of this.

"...and we know that the second Nebuchadnezzar shall continue the great work begun by the first; to wit, the restoration of all the glory due the god Marduk, his subject gods and his mighty stronghold Babylon."

"You are chosen, mighty prince; you are presented the unique honor of Supreme Defender of that beloved first-born of Marduk, Nabu; possessor of all wisdom. You are his champion, his beloved, his favored. With the presentation of this scepter I declare you to be *Bakhat Nasar*, fated to be the incarnation of Nebuchadnezzar I; he who gained this same renown becoming the embodiment of the great hunter, warrior, builder of mighty Babylon: Nimrod."

I had been instructed, of course, in the legends surrounding that name. Nimrod was said to be, among many other things, the founder of this city and the architect of this massive tower. To hear his name in this context was unsettling. What could I possibly have to do with Nimrod?

There was little I could do at this moment but accept the scepter. I had so many questions... but I was Nabopolasser's son; his successor; heir to the throne of Babylon. My own will was not an issue. I was Nebuchadnezzar II.

I rose to my feet in order to receive the scepter. The Chaldean instructed me to train my eyes on Marduk as I did so. He pronounced the words of dedication for me to repeat:

"I will defend... the name of mighty Marduk... his right as sovereign over all things... the right of his great son..."

The words kept coming - and I suppose I kept repeating them as no one ever said otherwise - but soon after the vows began I ceased to know if I was talking or not.

As the words faded into the background I saw a transformation come over the statue of Marduk.

It was a gradual change; I didn't believe it was actually happening at first. Surely the stress of the situation was causing me to see things that weren't there. But instead of the statue going back to normal, it continued to change, becoming more and more like a real person. And then it spoke to me.

The voice was unlike anything I had ever heard. Even now, so many years later, that voice returns to speak to me. Sometimes I feel like I will go mad when I hear it. That, of course, is not an option for me. Not then; certainly not now.

On that first day I suspected some trickery by the Chaldeans. It was some trick; that was for sure. Only, as the statue continued to change and talk to me, it became apparent this was not the work of mere humans. I became a believer in the gods at that moment.

It spoke harshly at first. I have no idea what it said in those first few moments, but it certainly had my attention. Then the tone calmed, and there actually seemed to be a tenderness to it that surprised me. The first word I understood was my own name.

"Nebuchadnezzar," it said, "you are truly my chosen vessel. You have great glory awaiting you, and I will ensure that glory. There is also great responsibility. You will usher in the next great era of my influence among the world of mortals."

I wanted to speak - to ask all the questions that were flooding my mind - but no sound would leave my mouth.

All that had been present at the beginning of the ceremony was no more than a swirl of color. Behind Marduk (by this time I had accepted that it was really him), it was as if night had fallen; but a night as I have never seen before or since. Some of my despair now, when I hear his voice, seems to me to come from a longing for that night sky. A longing that cannot be satisfied.

It was beautiful. It was like the real night sky, but so much more. It was brighter, and yet still dark. There were stars that were much larger than any I had seen. There were at least three moons visible. In that confused state there might have been more; I can never be sure. More frustration! I have tried to recreate that moment in my mind I have tried so hard. I have spent countless hours remembering, and yet the memory is always incomplete, and I fear my quest for it will drive me mad. That, of course, is not an option for me. Not then; certainly not now.

I have been chided by several of my ministers for what they see as a lack of concentration at certain moments. They are not very forgiving when these moments come as they are working through affairs of state with me. But I cannot control when it happens. Nor can I ignore it, though I have tried.

I learned very early not to try to ignore Marduk when he speaks. He has some unpleasant ways of getting my attention.

The headaches are almost unbearable, but as soon as I give him my undivided attention, they cease.

The messages vary. There are specifics that are given to me at important moments. The same ministers who are irritated by my lapses are always very impressed when I come back to them with the counsel I receive from Marduk. He has made it clear I am to take credit for it all. No one is to know that Marduk speaks to me.

That first day - the first instructions – they are repeated every time. Somehow I don't think I will forget them. The tower must be rebuilt.

He began giving me some fairly detailed instructions about how the tower was to be built. I wasn't understanding all of it, but as these details are repeated, I understand more and more. Then Marduk instructed me to probe the side of his statue for an object. He said it was engraved with some symbols that would be key to a great secret, one concerning the tower.

I started toward the statue, my head clearing as I moved forward. The priest made as if to stop me, but I gave him a look that he read correctly; he was not to interfere with what I was doing. He backed away, a look of fear in his eyes.

I reached the statue, and felt around its left side. Just as Marduk had said, I found a tile tablet stuck into it there. It was as though it was made as a part of the statue, and its presence was not obvious. In fact, I would never have known it was there by observation. Feeling along its edge I found a small indentation, just enough to insert a fingernail. It required almost no effort to remove the tablet.

It was extremely thin – almost impossibly so. I had never seen anything like it before, and I couldn't imagine the process that could create something that thin out of clay.

As soon as he recovered from the shock, the priest asked me how I knew about the tile. I was still not thinking well from the ordeal and almost told him of the whole conversation I had just had with the god. I decided that would not be to our best advantage; Father's and mine. I called him to one side, not wanting everyone present to hear.

The priest took a step backwards as I said, "I have a special sight. The gods reveal things to me in ways you cannot understand."

From that moment forward, I was treated differently by the Chaldeans.

The ceremony was over. Most of the attendees left the square. In short time only my father and I and the heads of the Chaldeans were left. They gathered around me, obviously desiring to know about the new information I now possessed.

I was staring down into my hand at the piece of tile. I felt the others crowding in around me to see it, but I didn't pay them much mind. I was studying the symbols engraved on the tile.

I had never seen this kind of writing (if that was what it was; it seemed to be). I was familiar with several forms of writing having been exposed to them in my studies. This was similar to Aramaic, but with sharper lines. It was enough different to keep me from understanding what was written. One of the Chaldeans, however, recognized it immediately.

"It is the ancient writing," he said in a hushed, reverent tone. His pronouncement was met by utter silence; from my father and me because of our ignorance of what he was talking about; from the Chaldeans from some great respect for what they were seeing. They actually fell to their knees before this message.

When they finally recovered (Nabopolassar and I watched them in amazement until they stood back up), their leader demanded that the one who had made the declaration give a translation. Evidently they were not all versed in this "ancient" tongue.

Even he, after considerable time studying the characters, was not very clear on their meaning. That it had something to do with the tower he could ascertain, but there was more. He would need help from someone who knew more than he.

Also, there was the question of the missing piece.

A good-sized piece of the upper left-hand corner, almost half the tile from appearances, was broken off. Words were cut in two. Sentences were left incomplete.

The high priest made to take the tile from my hands, but I would not allow it. He grew visibly angry with me, but my father backed up my determination to keep it. "If you want to study this writing you will do it with Nebuchadnezzar present. Leave us now."

They left reluctantly, their power over us greatly diminished by what had just transpired. I watched them move away slowly, glancing back over their shoulders as if the king might change his mind.

We waited until all of them were well gone, and then Father sent away our servants. In just a few moments time the square went from a place of great ceremony to only having two people in it. The air seemed charged with something. I felt as though I was hearing a buzzing sound, but when I concentrated on it, it disappeared.

We sat on a step at Etemenanki's base.

"I won't ask you to tell me everything that just happened," he said, his voice low but clear. "Obviously you had a very moving experience. Just let me ask you this; how did you know about the tile"

"Father, I don't know if you will believe me – I'm not sure I completely believe it myself – but Marduk spoke to me. The statue came to life and told me, among other things, where to find the tile."

"Among other things? Nebuchadnezzar, you reached for the tile almost as soon as you finished repeating the oath. There wasn't time for more than that."

"I don't know what I can tell you, Father. It seemed like Marduk was talking to me for several minutes, though I have to admit I lost track of time."

"Alright, don't worry about that right now. I certainly don't know enough about the gods to say how something like this should work. Right now we need to get back to the palace and find a safe place for that message."

We walked back to the palace compound in silence. The king had commanded his personal guards to keep some distance from us as we walked, but to keep others away from us as well. Neither of us spoke until we were inside again.

Even then, we spoke little. I know I was still overwhelmed by what had happened, and Nabopolassar seemed to still be trying to understand everything. Eventually we started debating where to keep the tile, finally deciding upon a hidden hole in the floor of the great room. The hole was something I had made myself. I kept memorabilia in it, and only now did I make my father aware of it.

"If you have kept it secret from me," he said, "I suppose it is fairly secure."

"Yes, father. I believe it to be safe even though it is in a public place- possibly more so because of that. No one would think something was hidden here."

"Please don't be angry. I have not hidden anything from you. It was just a place to keep some things that are special to me. See, some of mother's jewels; trinkets really, just things I remember her wearing."

My mother had died during my ninth year. She succumbed to some sort of fever; the Chaldeans claimed it was a curse on my father for not giving them more say in the affairs of the kingdom.

"Don't worry about it, Nebuchadnezzar. I'm glad we have a place ready-made to keep this thing in. Here, let's put this table over it as well. That will hide it even better from sight."

Time went by, and I was able to forget about the tile for some periods of time. Once in a while, though, those priests would come asking to see it. Father had instructed me to let them, but it always galled me. They acted like they had a right to it; but it was mine!

They were never able to come to a consensus about what it said. Once in a while one of them would arrogantly declare its meaning, but the chief priest was no fool. He would send them in one at a time without allowing them to consult together. Whenever their translations were contradictory (and they always were) he would call in a new batch of translators and start over. Word got around: when a new group started translating, the old group disappeared from Babylon. There was much speculation as to their disposition, but all we really knew was that they were not around anymore.

The visits of the translators became rarer. It seemed the pool of translators was shrinking fast. Some were disappearing; others seemed to conveniently forget what they knew of the ancient language. In any event, I was pleased they were leaving me alone about it.

Marduk, on the other hand, did not.

His visits were the other reminder I had about the tile. I dared (finally, after several of his visits) to ask him to translate it for me.

"After all, you want me to follow its instructions. I can't do that until I know what it says! Just tell me and I will try to get started with it."

"That is not how I have decreed it!" Marduk countered. "Yours is to obey my voice. You will arrange for the translation and then complete the work!"

The first time this kind of exchange happened, I was amazed that I was not consumed by fire or something. What was I thinking? Arguing with a god?

But I was not consumed. In fact, the dialog became a bit more civil after that. Emboldened, I began challenging Marduk on bigger and bigger things as time went by. I won't say we became friends, but an uneasy alliance began to grow between us.

For one thing, we both despised the Chaldeans. That caught me by surprise when it became clear.

"But they're *your* priests!"

"So *they* say. I never gave them that right or privilege. They are simply arrogant enough to assume that role."

"But why do you allow it?" I asked.

"They help me… unwittingly."

I suspected that he didn't actually know the language himself. Odd that a god might be so handicapped, and I didn't know it for sure, but I had my suspicions. I kept them to myself, though. He was still a god, after all.

Belteshazzar alone knows the reason for my "bad moments"; the one I have just come out of lasting for almost a year. Though we serve different gods, Belteshazzar is loyal to Babylon. He says it is the will of Jehovah. Whatever his motivation, he understands that Babylon must continue; and that I, Nebuchadnezzar, must be her king.

I told him I was troubled by Marduk, but I withheld from him the knowledge of the tile.

He spoke one day about the tongue his people spoke. I knew they spoke Hebrew, and I had heard it spoken from time to time. This day he mentioned his belief that Hebrew, or at least an ancient form of it, was the first language of man; given by Jehovah Himself to the first fathers.

I said nothing about it then, but filed the information away for use at a later time. Maybe Belteshazzar could help me decipher the message.

Years later, I still consult with Belteshazzar about many things, including the Egyptian situation. We know, of course, that it is much more complex than just another conflict with Egypt. Our supremacy over them was established at Carchemish, when I was still a prince. No, this is much more complex, involving many more enemies. We call it the Egyptian conflict primarily because of Nakhti. And he is key to any resolution of the problem. That is why I must speak with him personally. Belteshazzar agrees. Now that this latest crisis has left my mind, I am blessed of the gods to have him around, especially when the madness comes over me. This has been the worst so far, but my mind is clear now, and Belteshazzar and I agree. It's time to go face to face with Nakhti.

Chapter 14

All four men outside moved to the main door of the tent. Nebuchadnezzar exited first, then Nakhti. The two great men stepped toward the waiting encampment a few paces, separating themselves from the other men. And then it happened.

The two men faced each other. The pale man handed Nebuchadnezzar a scepter which he held in his right hand. Nakhti knelt before him.

The noise that erupted came from everywhere at once, and it seemed to Kasher to somehow include every type of sound a human voice can make, all at the same time.

There were cheers, groans and cries of anger. These sounds did not all come from within the camp. A large group of people had assembled on the ramparts of the city, and all he could discern from that quarter was jubilation.

Around Kasher; well, that was a different story. There was cheering to be sure, but there were others who were obviously very angry. Then there were those who had been making a good living off the situation: artisans, traders, prostitutes; hangers-on of all sorts that assemble whenever there is a conflict. These were bewailing their bad fortune. The siege was ended.

Kasher divided his attention between the bridges and the edges, to the left and right of him, of the assembled crowd.

At the bridges there were heated discussions, and they were being handled deftly at the points of the swords in the hands of Nakhti's men stationed there.

To the edges, several groups were headed; moving with great purpose. Kasher recognized the men he had come to know as fringe elements; they were the ones leaving.

In the middle ground between the two bridges, a small distance back from the main crowd, the Philistines stood in a tight group. Although they were not talking much, they seemed to be trying to decide what course of action to take. As he observed them, one of the Edomites approached their group.

Watching his movements reminded Kasher of Minkabh's description of them: Jackals. The Edomite moved in beside the edge of the group almost unnoticed. He was actually able to begin a conversation with the closest Philistine to him with what seemed an amazing naturalness.

Soon, however, he was fully acknowledged by the whole group. Kasher decided to move closer.

"Can't you see? We have all been betrayed!" It was the Philistine closest to the 'jackal' who spoke.

Kasher noted that it was also the one who had sneered at him during their first encounter.

Seren shot back, "Hold your tongue! You think you are ready to lead already? Your father only sent you as an observer. I alone choose our allegiances!"

Hands reached for swords, but none were drawn. Instead, the younger Philistine turned quickly away from the group. He rapidly strode a few paces in the direction of the western edge of the camp, the Edomite by his side.

Turning he said, "We'll see who is the 'observer' and who the warrior! My father did not send me to be your dog, but to 'observe' you; to see if you are worthy to be followed. You are not, and that is what my father will learn from me."

Seren and the other Philistines started in his direction, but were cut off immediately by the other Edomites and the Assyrians. I noticed, in the middle of that group, the man with the scar.

As Seren stopped, glaring at the group assembled before him, he began speaking quietly (at least for him) in the beginning, his voice rising in volume as he spoke; a crescendo which terminated in a roar reminiscent of a lion who has taken its prey.

"Very well, Krona. Go and tell your father what you have observed here. Tell him that I trust Nakhti and that my men trust me. Gaza will be allied with Babylon, and you and your family will be removed from the face of the earth!"

Some in the opposing group moved as if they would attack at this declaration, but another voice boomed from within the pack. It was the man with the scar.

He simply said, "Not now!" and they all backed down. A moment later they joined the group leaving the camp.

Kasher watched as they moved to the western edge, formed by the river. They followed the water south until they came to the bridge there which allowed them to continue their trek westward.

Following their movements drew his eye to another group. This one was moving due south. There were a few horses, but most of this band rode camels. Kasher recognized this group as the Egyptians. Only now did he begin to think of how this news would be received in Egypt. Nakhti was *their* champion *against* Nebuchadnezzar. Now he was with Babylon.

Chapter 15

We spent several days preparing to leave this desert camp. Ruhamah and I were finally allowed time alone, and we made the most of it.

The days were filled with activity but the evenings afforded us time to talk. We spoke of our pasts and our dreams for the future. That we were in love no one would have doubted.

On the second night, I told her so.

"Ruhamah, you must know how I feel about you."

"If it is how I feel about you, Kasher, it is called love."

We embraced for a long time, afraid (at least I) to speak and destroy the emotion of that moment. Finally I pushed her gently away.

"You must know also that my plans have not changed. If you would be with me there will be sacrifice, especially at first. A soldier's life is not easily reconciled with a family."

"I understand, Kasher. I would never ask you to be anything but what you are. If you will have me, I will be a soldier's wife."

She had tears in her eyes and I pulled her to me again; mostly so she wouldn't see mine. I had never known such joy!

We talked the rest of the night away, only sleeping a few hours before the new day started. Just the simple fact of the sun rising comforted me. It was as if the night before had been a dream until I could look at Ruhamah's face in the sunlight. The greater radiance was hers, and I could finally believe fully that she was mine.

Another day of preparation. I was anxious to finally enter the great city, but not like before. I had new purpose, without abandoning the old.

"Kasher! Kasher, it *is* you!"

I heard the cries before I saw him running toward me, his arms stretched wide. I had no idea how he had come out to our position, but there he was.

"Utanin!

The preparations could not stop, but they were now filled with renewing a friendship. If we had grown close through our trials, we were even closer for having been separated. There was a bond between the three of us that transcended any I had known. Not stronger than family, but as strong, in a different way.

Ruhamah apologized to him for her deceit during her trip to the city.

"Think nothing of it," he told her. "You did what you had to under the circumstances."

Sometime about noonday, Nakhti came to us. I had not had the chance to speak with him since that moment he declared his allegiance to Nebuchadnezzar. To say he had been busy since then would be a ridiculous understatement.

"So, nephew, it appears we have landed on the same side of this conflict after all."

I presented him to Utanin, careful to show him respect as my military leader.

"Kasher. If you accept, I would have you in my unit. The king has given the option to those who have been with me to serve under me still; provided they swear allegiance to him as sovereign, of course. I don't think that part will be a difficulty for you. The only question is whether or not you will serve with me. If not, I will respect your decision. I am sure I could get you a posting with Nebuchadnezzar's army in another unit if you prefer, but I would like to have you with me."

I knew that I would have to serve in the regular army for a while before applying to the Palace Guard. I had seen enough of my uncle to know what kind of man he was, and I respected him greatly. I could think of nothing better than serving under him at this time, and I told him so.

"Just one thing, Uncle. Would I be too presumptuous to ask what changed your mind about Nebuchadnezzar?"

"Not at all, Kasher. I think that is a reasonable request. I can't tell you everything, but the time I spent with the king revealed to me what kind of man he really is. The simple fact that he came out himself to talk with me convinced me of his sincerity and his courage. In the tent, he listened to my reasons for coming against him with great interest. I can tell you he didn't like some of what I said, but nevertheless listened with an open mind. Some things he explained to my satisfaction. Some things he actually accepted as error on his part – particularly impressive coming from a king.

He agreed with me that there should be more autonomy for cities within the kingdom. Some things we never agreed on, but they were minor, and we both decided they were not worth going to war over. On balance, I found a man I can follow."

"What about his absence from public eye," asked Ruhamah? "A lot of people, yourself included, made that a point of distrust."

"He said he had gone through a severe illness, but that he was fully recovered and able to lead again. He made a point of praising those who maintained the kingdom in his absence. I find it a mark of greatness to know whom to place in positions of responsibility. After all, he chose me!"

"What sort of unit are you to lead, and what title do you now own," I asked.

"As to the unit, you will have to wait to hear that from the king himself. Your final decision to be in it or not will be reserved to you for that moment. As to myself, I am now Captain of the army of the Chaldeans. It is a new group that I am to form and command. I have the choice of men; of those who have already served under me and of those in Nebuchadnezzar's army. We will have some special functions. I do not know all of them yet, and I'm not at liberty to discuss what I do know about that."

"I would like very much to serve under you, sir," Kasher said.

We talked for a few more minutes; then Nakhti excused himself to get back to the great task at hand. He said, "We will move into Babylon tomorrow."

The rest of the day was chaotic, but a certain order began to take shape. The sizeable group that would accompany Nakhti into the city moved closer and closer to the bridges where all of this had started, Nakhti and Minkabh organizing them into functional bands. There was always a formidable perimeter guard in place. Those who were not part of the army, along with those few of Nakhti's men who decided not to stay with him, began assembling at the southern extremity of the camp, near Kartan's fields. Seeing them there made me think of him, and, as I hadn't talked to him for a while, I decided to look for him. Ruhamah came with me.

As we approached, I saw Enusat. I had really enjoyed the combat training he gave me, and I went over to him to tell him so.

"Thank you, Kasher. I wish all the soldiers I have trained were as apt as you; and as pleasant to be around. I wish you well in your next venture. Are you going with Nakhti?"

"Yes, sir, I am. I suppose we will be serving together in Babylon."

"No, I won't be going. I've had enough adventure for three men. It's time for me to settle down a bit. I have a wife and children in Haran I haven't seen for a long time. It's time for me to be there. That's why I'm down here with this lot. We're forming a caravan south."

"I wish you all the best," said Kasher. These people are lucky to have you as their leader. Be safe!"

We left Enusat to see if we could find Kartan. It didn't take long. Even under these circumstances, he was still working in his dirt.

"Kartan! It's over," Kasher called out. "We can move on now. On to Babylon."

"Hello Kasher; Ruhamah. I'm glad you came. I hoped I would have a chance to tell you goodbye."

"What do you mean goodbye? We're going into the city now," Kasher responded.

174

"I've been thinking about something. This camp has developed quickly into a settlement. My gardens are absolutely flourishing. I can't imagine subjecting myself to the confines of those great walls. I am going to help start a town here, right in the shadow of Babylon."

Kasher started to argue, but Ruhamah cut him off.

"Look around you, Kasher. He's right! This place has real potential. But Kartan, you said 'help' start the town. It sounds like you are not alone in this endeavor."

"I've been preparing for this moment for quite a while. I wasn't sure what the final outcome would be, but it was obvious that things could not continue like they were for much longer. I began talking with some people from the market crowd. Some of them were also interested in slowing down; tired of travelling after armies."

Kasher decided Ruhamah was right not to argue the point and began looking around the garden area. It was as if he was seeing the development there for the first time.

There were houses now – small, to be sure, but houses nonetheless. He remembered when he had first gone there, not that long ago. There had been some small shacks, nothing more. They had obviously been built up to hold more than just a few farm implements now. As his gaze continued to move from spot to spot in the area, he now noticed that there were quite a lot of people near each of those small houses. One in particular caught his eye.

"Is that the brute from the market? The one I almost had to fight to get to Ruhamah?"

"Ludim; yes. There's much more to him than meets the eye, I've learned."

"And there's already much that meets the eye!" said Ruhamah, a wry smile forming at the corners of her mouth.

They all had a short chuckle at that, and then Kartan said, "I have found him to be very bright, and very eager to help. With the little I have been able to understand (his language is one of the most unusual I have ever heard) he has convinced me he's a good man to have around."

"When he first approached me about joining our little group, he explained (the slave trader translating for us) that he was a man without a home. He seems to believe he has a shot at a new beginning here with us."

Ruhamah spoke up, "He was always very gentle when he guarded us. I believed he was doing that job reluctantly."

"He certainly gives you some security," added Kasher.

They talked for a short while longer, and then Ruhamah said, "We had better get back to camp, Kasher. It's getting late, and your uncle will be concerned."

They said their good-byes, but Kasher sensed there would be more contact between them. "After all," he said, "we will still be neighbors."

The night was filled with the noise of preparation. It would be a big change for everyone involved. Kasher reflected on the fact that he had only been there a short time, but it seemed like he was leaving something behind. His uncle commented that he had matured a lot during his time in the camp, and Kasher knew it was true. Maybe that was what he was leaving behind: the child he had been.

In the morning, clarions were sounded, coinciding with the appearance of the morning sun. As Kasher washed his face, he noticed that a good number of Nakhti's men were already dressed and standing guard around the camp.

Dressing hurriedly, he presented himself before his uncle. Nakhti looked preoccupied.

"What's wrong, sir?"

"Nothing specific, Kasher, I just won't rest until we are safely inside the city walls. Some of those who left us are pretty angry with my decision, and it wouldn't surprise me if they attack us as we move into Babylon. I have set a guard, and we will proceed with our eyes open."

"Is there anything I can do to help?" asked Kasher.

"Yes. You will come with me at the front of the group. When we arrive at the gate we will establish a safety corridor for the others to pass through. Stay close to me and keep your eyes and ears open. Situations like this can change very quickly."

Final preparations were made and they set out. There was no sign of trouble as they approached the massive gate. The sentries waited for them to organize their lines, one on either side of the entrance. Then the great doors swung open.

Almost immediately, a cry went up from the rampart. Everyone looked up and saw they were pointing to the west. Nothing could be seen there, so whatever was causing such an outcry must be coming from around the corner that began just a few cubits from the gate. Kasher took one quick glance at the entrance and was pleased to see that their people were flooding through. Still, there were a lot of people, animals and goods to get through there yet.

He looked back to see horsemen rounding the corner. They were making a wide arc, evidently so they would not themselves be taken by surprise by Nakhti's men. Kasher recognized several members of the shouting horde.

He was posted almost at the opening of the gate. The battle began back where their lines ended. By this time, everyone not involved in the security force was at least well within the corridor. Kasher saw a couple of their men fall. Those at that initial position had little chance of escape, but they did not run or hide.

Nakhti began barking orders. Each man was to hold his position until everyone of our group was past him, then take their place in an ever growing line perpendicular to the city wall. Without further instruction, that line began to take on a "V" shape, increasing the depth of the protection. We were still losing men, but at a slower rate now. The injured were brought into the corridor as soon as humanly possible, then carried or assisted by anyone who had a free hand into the city.

As the line spread sideways Kasher found himself closer and closer to the fighting. He was equipped with a sword and shield. Thankfully, there did not appear to be archers in the attacking group. Neither did Nakhti's army have any of their own, but suddenly a shower of arrows began to rain down upon their enemies from the top of the wall. The flow of the battle turned decidedly.

It was not over entirely, though. Some of the attackers were already locked in combat with Nakhti's men; some still mounted; others now on foot. It would have been irresponsible for the archers to try to shoot into the close fighting.

Kasher found himself face to face with the man with the scarred face.

The shock of that deep purple line in the man's forehead almost caused him to stop fighting. It was the first time he had got a good look at it. Now he was face on with the man, and the distance between them was getting smaller by the second as the captain of the army of Jerusalem pressed his attack.

The attacker paused for a split second; possibly saving Kasher's life, distracted as he was by the man's appearance. The scar-faced man's pause was to look quickly around him, assessing the battle situation. Anyone watching from the periphery would have recognized immediately that it was all but over, the new Babylonians having won with the aid of their colleagues inside. Recognition of this fact flickered on the Hebrew's face, but he was not willing to simply run away.

He made one more attack. Both men were holding their swords in their right hands. This thrust was unusual, however. It came from very high up, and, slashing downward, pinned Kasher's sword against his leg.

The man fell full into Kasher, both their swords useless for the moment. As he drove the back of his right shoulder into Kasher's side, the man with the scar spun with amazing speed, dropping his sword and ending with his back to Kasher. Before he knew what was going on the man had thrust his right arm under Kasher's left arm pit. The next thing he knew he was on the ground, on his back, several paces outside of the line of soldiers.

The scar-faced man was already on top of him, a dagger in his hand. Just as he was about to drive it into

Kasher's heart, the head of an arrow appeared in the middle of his chest, almost reaching Kasher's chest as well. The scar that had been so prominent due to its deep purple color turned white, and there was a look of rage in his eyes for just a moment. Then he fell forward toward Kasher.

How ironic, he thought, would it be to die pierced by the same arrow that had saved him from his attacker. With considerable effort, he was able to push the man off of him. Jumping to his feet, he ran to his uncle's side. They were the last two to go through the gate, and it closed quickly, leaving them suddenly in a new world.

The noise of battle ended abruptly. The soldier's hearts were still racing from the fight, and a few of them still turned this way and that, as if expecting a renewed attack. Of course, it did not come, and they slowly began to breathe normally, the tension draining from their faces like rain cascading down a rock face.

Kasher sought, and found, Ruhamah. No words were necessary as they held each other.

Finally, she said simply, "Welcome to Babylon, Kasher."

Chapter 16

As I look back on those first few weeks and months it seems like I started a whole new life by stumbling through those gates.

We were cared for in a makeshift tent city for a few days while other accommodations were procured. The soldiers who did not have family members with them were taken to their quarters on the third day. We were told that they would all be in the same place. Our little army was intended to be a special unit under my uncle's command. Whether by word from Nakhti or just because of an assumption about Ruhamah and myself, I was not taken – to my great relief.

On the fourth day, as we waited for more word of where we were to be lodged, the single men were brought back. They told us they had been ordered to assemble with the rest of us.

They were not there long before we saw a contingent headed our way. The first things we saw were magnificent horses, ridden by men in equally magnificent robes. Their helmets and swords identified them as soldiers.

As they drew close, they parted ranks. A hand from beside me jerked me to my knees. I had frozen at the sight of the king appearing so suddenly and so close. His horse (it could only be the same one he had ridden when he came out to talk with Nakhti, so brilliantly white it was) continued directly toward me. Only afterwards did I realize that it was because I had been next to my uncle at the time. In fact, it had been his hand pulling me to my knees.

Still unaware of why it was happening so near to me, I watched as the king dismounted. I could actually feel the breath of his horse on my head.

My head spun with the realization of his nearness - even more as I saw he was coming directly at me.

It was his own voice that shook me from my stunned state.

"Have your men arise, Nakhti. We have much to discuss. I would have them all understand what I expect from them."

Realizing it was to my uncle he had come calmed me somewhat, but I was still in awe. To complicate my situation even more, Nakhti said, "Great Nebuchadnezzar, allow me to introduce my nephew, Kasher. He has come all the way from Nippur to join your forces. In fact, he would have been here sooner if I hadn't waylaid him."

The king looked me over carefully before responding.

"Welcome, Kasher. May I inquire as to why you wish this?"

My mouth felt as dry as when I had been beneath the sand on the river bank. My head felt as voided as a gourd prepared for dipping water. I stammered for a moment, then somehow managed to regain a little composure.

"If it please the king, I have been an admirer since I was a child. I saw you at the end of the Nippur campaign and have been dedicated to you ever since."

"We must speak more of this dedication in the near future," replied Nebuchadnezzar. "For now, we have pressing matters. Let me say, however, that I am grateful to have you with me."

The men were assembled and Nebuchadnezzar said a few words of gratitude to them all. Then he presented the captain of his host,

"This is Muldan. He is your military leader. Know that I have full trust in him. He will now explain your function here in the kingdom of light."

Nebuchadnezzar stepped back to his horse and mounted unassisted. Just as quickly, he wheeled his horse around and left at a gallop. It all happened so quickly that none of us had time to bow, let alone kneel.

Muldan was a man of some age; not huge, but not small either. The life he most surely had lived had, as surely, aged him prematurely. His face had the hard quality of a man who has seen terrible things. I was surprised, then, when he spoke. His voice was firm, but not at all harsh or even loud. The pitch of it was much higher than I ever would have expected, bordering on effeminate. Looking at him, I could not imagine anyone accusing of that.

"Many of you have already seen how complicated it is to secure a large kingdom," he began as we moved close in around him to hear. "It is one thing to protect a city against enemies. It is entirely another to maintain allegiances."

"Your force will be unlike any conventional army. You will be ready to move at a moment's notice. One minute you will be living a fairly normal life, and the next you will be expected to move with the speed of the dessert wind to take care of a matter that only you, the king and I will know of. You shall be known as the 'Samma Ruach' - the Poison Wind."

"Because of the special nature of this force, it will be manned entirely by volunteers. The king has decided that your type of experience – and, especially, the leadership that you already have in place – qualify you for this honor. If any one of you does not want to be involved in this, however, you have one – and only one – opportunity to inform me of that decision at the end of this meeting. After that, you will only leave by decree of the king, should that be his good pleasure."

"I said it is an honor for you to be chosen; and so it is. The king is bestowing upon Nakhti and his men a great responsibility. They will be expected to show absolute loyalty to him. No dissent will be tolerated."

"Along with this great responsibility will also come great reward. As your methods will be fluid, so will your opportunities be. A normal soldier in Nebuchadnezzar's army can expect a regular pay. You will not be required to turn over the rewards of your operations to the crown, such is the trust the king is placing in you. The only accounting you will be required to make is of accomplishment. That, of course, is what is being expected of you."

"Nakhti has been instructed to use what he needs of the spoils to continue your operations. The rest will be paid out to his men as he thinks correct.'

Utanin showed up the same day our unit was commissioned. He invited Ruhamah and me to share his home, and Nakhti agreed with the arrangement. We (Ruhamah and I) lived in separate wings of the house for about three months.

During that time, even with all the rigorous training I was going through, we found time to deepen our relationship.

One warm afternoon I was released early from duties. It was just as well since my thoughts were not on my work that day. My group leader had said so, and I feared he would cause me some trouble with my uncle, but he seemed to understand what was going on with me and simply said, "Go clear up your distraction and come back when you are ready to fight again."

As I came through the door of Utanin's house, I heard music; I had not heard that there before.

I remembered the sound well, however, having heard it only once before.

It was coming from our wing of the house; a beautiful melody in an equally beautiful tone. Ruhamah had not sung around me since I found her in the market that day. I waited, listening intently, for some time, fearful of interrupting a moment that might be profoundly personal to her.

There was a pause; not an ending to be sure. The music faded into the air in a way I was unfamiliar with, but I felt the moment deep in my soul. Ruhamah had sung (more said than sung, really, a musical sound, but not in the normal sense) the single word, "*Selah*", and the word hung in the air as the chord that accompanied it on the instrument lingered just a second longer. Somehow I knew there was meant to be more music forthcoming.

Still, I could keep my presence secret no longer. I called gently, trying desperately not to change the mood, "Ruhamah."

She did not answer me immediately, but I heard her moving to come out to the main room to join me. The movement seem to be a continuation of the music still.

"Kasher! You're home earlier than I expected."

She was flush, as if caught doing something wrong.

"We had a light day of training today. Please don't be angry - or embarrassed! That was a wonderful reception."

Ruhamah blushed at the comment, but I was not through.

"I haven't heard you sing for a long time. You still sound like an angel."

"Oh, Kasher, you go too far. What little music I know is only for my own enjoyment."

"I hope you won't deprive me of it. I wouldn't dream of spoiling your special moments of privacy, but I would love it if you could share your gift with me sometimes."

"Of course, Kasher. I didn't mean for you to think I would be selfish about it. It's just that sometimes I need to sing, and sometimes alone. It reminds of my parents, and so it saddens me, but it also reminds me of all the good moments I had with them. Father never sang, but he loved to listen to my mother; and, later, to me. Yes, Kasher, I will be glad to share my music with you if you wish it."

"With all my heart, I do. Ruhamah, speaking of sharing things, we have so much in common. I have been thinking about it a lot lately, and - well - I would like to share everything with you. I love you, Ruhamah, and I want you to be my wife!"

Ruhamah let out a little gasp, which frightened my heart up into my throat. I don't know what I was expecting, but that noise was not it.

She composed herself quickly and said, "I'm sorry, Kasher, that just came out! It was just such a surprise to me."

"A pleasant one, I hope!"

"Very pleasant, just very unexpected."

"Well," I continued, "now that the initial shock is over..."

Ruhamah looked at me directly with a look I had never seen on her, or anyone else's, face before. I thought I saw love, but that might have been wishfulness on my part. The other elements of her look were hard for me to decipher. It seemed I was seeing concern, fear and longing all at the same time. To my delight, I did not see repulsion or rejection. At least, that was my hope.

Finally, she spoke.

"Kasher, I love you."

I waited breathlessly for the word "but". I finally exhaled when I realized it wasn't coming.

"I love you with all my heart, Kasher, and I want to marry you."

I could have run the length of the Euphrates at that moment, I was so excited. Then, as if falling from the sky, details began to invade my thoughts.

"I don't even know how it is done," I exclaimed. "You have no parents to prepare for a wedding, and mine are far away. How can we get married?"

"Calm down, Kasher. We have good friends that I am sure will help us with whatever details have to be worked out."

"Friends - of course. Another detail. We don't know if Utanin will let us live here if we are married."

"I don't see why not. He invited us to live here in the first place. Why should it matter to him if we get married?"

Well, for one thing, he might not want a bunch of children running around his house."

"Children! Wow, Kasher, you are really thinking ahead!"

"We will have them, won't we?" I asked, fairly confident I knew the answer.

"If Jehovah wills it, yes we will have children, but that will take a little time, and by then we can know Utanin's mind on the subject. Kasher, I would like for us to speak with Jeremiah about our union. He is a wise man, even trusted by Daniel."

"Trusted by whom?"

"Daniel. You probably know him as Belteshazar, Nebuchadnezzar's counselor."

"Oh, the Hebrew! Well if Jeremiah is counselor to the counselor to the king, we should be able to trust his advice. Do you know where to find him?"

She said she did, and soon, through the contacts she made during her previous trip into the city, she set up a time for us to speak. Basically his counsel was to accept a simple government decree of marriage, which could be performed by any one of a number of the kings lawyers scattered around Babylon for the purpose of handling small matters of law that did not require the direct attention of the throne.

During our conversation he seemed to drift off at one point, talking, it seemed, to himself. There was something about *one day these things being done as they should be, back in the land, under the proper priesthood.* When he came back to us he simply said, "Just avoid the

Chaldean priests. Their ceremonies are full of invocations upon their gods. You don't want that kind of trouble."

As it turned out, Utanin gave us the house. I argued with him that he shouldn't give up something so nice, but he assured me that he had just been offered a new position at court, and that this new posting required him to live in the royal compound.

That was just over six years ago now. Our second son, Kishin, was born three years ago. Our first, Utanin, is almost five.

Utanin (the boat captain) did in fact receive a royal commission. We have had a few opportunities to talk since he moved into the royal compound. Now he heads a project that will bring about a system of river transportation into, out of and within the city.

The new walls expanding the city beyond the banks of the Euphrates are nearly finished, and Utanin has devised a method for the flow of merchandise on the river. It is as simple as it is ingenious, allowing the flow of merchandise to continue into and out of the city while maintaining a high level of security where the river comes through the walls.

There were two basic problems with a simple gate over the river. First, the water levels in and around Babylon are subject to large changes. The great city is close enough to the mountains to really feel the effects of the melting snows in the spring. Summertime is so dry that the rivers drop dramatically. There were already several canals for irrigation, like the one Kartan was using (with great success) at the settlement outside the city walls. Those were sufficient for agriculture, but did not help much with transportation issues. A normal gate could not compensate for such drastic differences. At high water it would be difficult to open; at low water it would not deter anyone from entering through it.

The other complication was that any normal device would not eliminate a threat that came from underwater. If a gate only lowered to about water level, what would prevent someone from swimming under it?

The answer started with the creation of a huge lake on the north side of the city. I had reminded Utanin of a similar solution in Nippur. It was made to funnel down to the size of the entrance. That allowed for control of the water level. All of the other problems will be simplified by this detail, and Utanin is working tirelessly on resolving them.

One day I remembered the shiny disk I had found when it escaped his flailing hand that day in the desert. He had never mentioned it, but his eyes lit up when he learned that I had it.

"I assumed it was lost forever! I am pleased you found it."

For some reason – I know not what – I did not tell him about the other one.

"It is yours, of course, Utanin. I carried it on my person all the time until we moved into your house. It is there now, well hidden. I will bring it to you this evening."

"No, Kasher, I want you to keep it."

"But I saw how important it was to you. You must surely want it back."

"I would have before; but I think now it is better off in your hands now.

I have been away from home some; a small rebellion here, a peasant revolt there. Our little band has been able to fulfill Nebuchadnezzar's wishes; sometimes alone, often in coordination with the 'official' army. Peace has been kept in our kingdom, and expansion, wisely, has been carried out at a careful pace. In these years since I came to Babylon, even Egypt has been calm. Until now.

Chapter 17

Nakhti informed us this morning that there was an incursion to the south. Apparently, Susa, to the east of Nippur was taken a few weeks ago; word had only reached the capital yesterday. The Babylonian contingent there had been completely wiped out in an overwhelming attack. No one was expecting it. It seems the Egyptians had risked a desert crossing, complicated at any time, but made even more treacherous now in the spring.

Springtime is the time of the greatest rains, even in the desert. That might seem a good thing, since deserts are so dry, but heavy rain can cause floods that seem to come from nowhere.

I had seen that phenomenon first hand on one of our military actions. We were sent to deal with a Philistine problem last spring – Seren flexing his muscles - and the troublemakers had fled south. We followed for a while, but it was as if the giants were opening great rivers behind them as they fled, and we were cut off time and again, sometimes losing men or beasts in the flooding. Finally, we gave up the chase, content with the fact that they had been put in disarray and were out of our hair for a while.

Now we were at once both impressed and dismayed that the Egyptians had braved the great expanse of Arabia in springtime. As Nakhti explained our orders we understood, even before he said it, that this would be a formidable foe.

The information that had come to my uncle was disturbing. I was not prepared for the next part of our briefing.

"We understand that they are now moving on Nippur," he said. "We will be moving as rapidly as possible in hopes that we can get there before they take the city; or, if we are too late for that, maybe we can keep them from settling in - destabilize their takeover."

I had not given much thought to my family for quite some time, to my shame. To say I had been busy would be an understatement, and most of our military efforts had been to the north, away from my home. Neither of those excuses brought me any comfort as I thought of my family being invaded by the Egyptians.

Nippur was very loyal to Nebuchadnezzar these days. The pharaoh would surely know that. I hoped with all my heart we would be in time to stop the takeover. If not, there could be many casualties.

We were all dismissed to make any final preparations necessary for our departure. We were always in an advanced state of preparedness; such had this become our way of life.

Ruhamah greeted me at the door; first a kiss, then, knowingly, she went to the alcove where we kept my travel gear. As she turned to hand my bag to me, a shadow came over her face.

"What's wrong, Kasher?" she asked in a worried tone.

"This one is different," I replied. "We're on our way to Nippur."

"I understand. I know you will do your best to take care of your family there. Just remember, Kasher; you have a new family here who needs you too."

I smiled. She had a way of bringing everything into focus in a few short words.

I grabbed the boys and hugged them, then kissed Ruhamah hard on the mouth, turned, and went out the door.

Most of our band was already assembled at the gate when I got there, the group leaders organizing for our departure.

Muldan was there. He often saw us off on our campaigns, normal enough for the captain of Nebuchadnezzar's army. He waited patiently as the last of our men joined the travel formation. When all was ready, he spoke.

"This is not a rebellion or a minor incursion," be began sternly. "This is the latest, and in recent times the most blatant, act of war by the Egyptians against Babylon and Babylonia. As such, it must be dealt with quickly and decisively. You are just the spearhead in our campaign to throw the Egyptians back across the desert."

"The situation in Nippur will have to be evaluated, and a plan constructed and carried out based on what we find there. We have precious little information at this moment. No word has come to us from Nippur for several days. It seems likely, therefore, that the city is taken, our garrison killed or imprisoned, the populace sequestered."

"You must move fast to analyze the situation. I will be going with you to coordinate all the various forces we will no doubt need to utilize. Nakhti is still in command of your function. I am always his commander; the only difference this time is that I will, of necessity, be with you at the battle site. Please do not take this as a lack of confidence on my part in you. I am counting on you to give me the tools I need to direct the whole of our army against these attackers."

With that he mounted his horse and positioned himself next to Nakhti. The order was given, and the gate opened to allow us on our way.

The next day and a half was a blur. There was no time to reacquaint myself with the parts of the journey I had already experienced, let alone to try and take in all that was new to me. Basically, I saw sand and the river, with a town or settlement in the distance on occasion.

We rested for three hours in the hottest part of the first day. It seemed that Nakhti knew where every tree was on the way to Nippur, and I was glad of the shade.

We crossed two canals on our way; once again, Nakhti did not hesitate in the least about where to cross, and, either they were easy to cross at any point, or my uncle knew the right spots.

Before noon the second day, the walls of Nippur were in sight. I was shocked that my original journey had taken so long now that I saw the direct route. Of course a group of mounted men, trained to travel fast and light, bore no resemblance to any part of my original travels to Babylon.

We stopped in a small settlement on the canal of Birdu which ran into the moat along the northern edge of the city. The Euphrates was on our right, making up the protective barrier on the city's west. Looking past it I could just make out the market I had gone through as I left for Babylon that day, between the Euphrates and the parallel canal we left on. We could see the city walls slightly above us in the distance, and we were close enough to make out movement on the wall, but not so close as to be able to recognize individual features. To them we would probably look like any other small caravan looking to avoid the noon heat. One thing we could easily ascertain even from this distance: the gates were shut fast and no one was going in or coming out.

We did exactly what would be expected of us; avoid the heat. There was a trader with several tents set up. Some served food and drinks while others had bed rolls spread out through them. Nakhti advised us all to rest and replenish. He did not need to tell us why.

I drank some cool must made from pomegranate, and then looked into a place to take a short nap. The first sleeping tent I stuck my head into was full.

There was one more tent, but it had been placed a little distance from the main area. I had no idea why until I was almost at the door. The noises from inside let me know immediately the purpose of the tent, and it was not a place I would get any rest. I recalled seeing those slave women along the shore on my first journey to Babylon. I shuddered as I remembered how close Ruhamah came to being subjected to that life. No matter how much I might yearn for female companionship, I knew there was no way I could ever be part of that degradation.

As I moved away from the tent I saw Muldan entering it. Apparently the rumors were false. I remembered Nakhti telling me how dedicated Muldan was to the army and Nebuchadnezzar. I understood how he might not have time for a family.

Looking toward the canal I saw a small stand of palms. There were several men there resting, some in quiet conversation, others fast asleep. I saw there was room for several more in that shade and made my way there.

I found a place away from any conversation and lay down to rest.

There were a few men at the site who were not a part of our group. They seemed to pay is little or no attention. We traveled light, and our weaponry was always stored out of sight in packs, as if it was merchandise we could be selling. No doubt there was a hard look to us, but that could be said of most travelers in this area. One had to be hard to ply a living in the desert.

For some reason, I was having a hard time getting to sleep. It wasn't that I was uncomfortable. There was a nice patch of thick grass under the tree. And, besides, I was accustomed by now to sleeping in all sorts of conditions. A breeze mingled the sweet smell of dates with that of the grass under me and the water in the canal. It was all very conducive to a good nap. But my time as a soldier had done what it does to us all; honing certain senses that people living a normal life don't require to the same degree. I felt I was being watched.

I slowly, carefully, rolled onto my left side to get a look at the two men who were talking in low tones beneath another tree, farther down toward the water. It was the direction from which my unease was emanating.

Feigning sleep, I looked through nearly closed eyelids. Another thing this life had taught me was patience. I stayed very still, allowing my brain to decipher what my eyes were struggling to bring in.

It only took a few moments. I recognized the man who was looking my way.

It was the 'jackal' who had confronted the Philistine leader, Seren, after Nakhti had declared his allegiance to Babylon. My mind worked for his name and finally retrieved it: Krona.

The question now was, what was he doing here? Was it mere coincidence that he showed up at the same place and time as us? Did he recognize me? It seemed so, from the way he was watching me, but it could be I was just the closest member of our band to him right now. In any case, his presence was cause for concern. He had already shown himself to be hot-headed, and he was certainly no friend to Nebuchadnezzar.

As I surreptitiously observed him I noticed that he was not actually looking at me, but rather past me to a group under another tree. That group included my uncle and Muldan.

I tried to hear what Krona and his companion were saying. They spoke softly most of the time, but once in a while one of them would become more animated, raising his voice slightly – enough for me to hear.

I recognized the language they were speaking. Since arriving in Babylon, I have purposed to learn something of other languages. My Aramaic was now quite passable. I had even learned some Hebrew from Ruhamah and Jeremiah. Nakhti had, reluctantly, given in to my many requests for him to teach me Egyptian ("I really don't have time for this, Kasher. Besides, you'll never need it!"). Though I could not understand everything the two men were saying, they were definitely speaking Egyptian.

Suddenly, Krona stood and gathered his belongings. He tried to act casual, but he moved with purpose.

He made his way to a horse that was tethered a short distance from where he had been reclining, mounted, and left; again, trying to disguise the urgency that I knew he was feeling.

Krona made his way along the canal, heading west. If he continued in that direction I knew he would reach the Euphrates, probably in a few minutes time.

Trying not to seem too obvious to the man he left behind, I stretched and rose. I feigned drowsiness as I made my way up to where Nakhti and Muldan sat.

They were sitting quietly at the moment, each seemingly in his own thoughts.

As I approached, Nakhti motioned me to sit. His face showed concern as he saw the same on mine.

"Something wrong?"

"I´m not sure, but I think I just saw something important."

After telling my story, Muldan began questioning me.

"Are you sure about the identity of the man?"

"Yes, sir. I have no doubt it was Krona."

"We know about Krona. He has become an ever increasing nuisance to the kingdom. He represents the most unstable of the Edomite families, and doesn't seem to mind who he aligns with as long as they can further his goals: primarily to control all of the Sinai."

"You say he went west?" interjected Nakhti,

"Yes, sir. Along the canal towards the Euphrates."

"Kasher," it was Muldan who spoke now. "I think you have just given us the information we have been searching for. Rumors have abounded that a group of Edomites and Philistines, possibly with the aid of the Army of Jerusalem, were in league with Egypt, and that taking Susa and Nippur was part of an orchestrated move to defeat, or at least deplete, the Babylonian army."

"Your uncle and I have been trying to figure out their strategy. It looks to me like Krona was here waiting for our advance party to inevitably arrive, and, now that we're here, he's off to inform the others of that fact."

"What do you think they will do now?" I asked.

"I never doubted there would be an attack from without the city of Nippur. We needed to know from what direction they would come. Our forces are ready to leave Babylon. Now we will split them into two contingents. One group can come directly, as the enemy obviously thinks they will come"

"We have two other groups prepared; lighter, quicker forces. One is waiting just to our north in case of an attack from that direction. We sent the smallest group there because it seemed the least likely place. They would have had to circle all the way around Nippur to get into position, but we couldn't count out that possibility."

"Now we can bring them in to help with the attack on the city. We have another troop along the Euphrates. They will be mobilized as soon as our rider can get to them, and they will try to cut the Edomites off before they can attack the flank or the rear of our main force. With a little luck, they could catch them as they are crossing the river. That would give our force a real edge. Good work, Kasher."

Muldan left to get his message on its way. Nakhti turned to me.

"Kasher, we still need to find out the strength of the enemy inside the city. Now that we are prepared for them I don't expect much trouble from the Edomites, but we have no idea what is really going on in Nippur."

"You and I," he continued, "are the most familiar with Nippur of anyone in our band. I want you to help me get into the city and get the information we need."

Chapter 18

We waited for the sun to show signs of resting beneath the horizon, and then Nakhti and I, accompanied by two other men, started walking down the canal. It intersected, a short ways ahead, another smaller canal that ran down to the Euphrates. We could have crossed it easily, but turning to follow it wasn't suspicious either, and so we did.

After about an hour, moving slowly, we had reached another group of tents. We were hopeful that four men, still dressed as travelling merchants, would arouse no great suspicion; neither there, nor on the city walls.

The sun was setting as we approached this makeshift camp. As I looked about me, I realized that I had seen similar encampments on my trip toward Babylon. The water was higher now, and so things looked different from that day when I last saw Nippur.

We paid for some hospitality; a bit of must of questionable origin and some stale dates. As we lounged, trying to see everything around us without being obvious about it, a parade of young women strolled past us. This time I knew what they were there for.

A few of them looked frightened. Those were the ones who seemed in better condition. It made sense when

I thought it through. They were new. The others just looked tired. They were obviously fed well enough, but there was no life in them.

Nakhti leaned in toward me and said in a hushed voice, "Do not make a scene about this right now. We have a bigger wrong to right at the moment."

"I know," I whispered back. I had learned already that there are good things that must sacrificed to other, more pressing, things

The other soldiers we had brought with us were talking to some of the women. Nakhti said nothing, and I followed his lead. It would help us seem normal to any who might be observing. I hoped that they wouldn't take it too far. I needn't have worried; they were professional soldiers, and they came and lounged with us after just a few moments conversation with the women.

The owners of our temporary resting spot got the message that we were not going to spend a lot of money. There were a few more traders about, so they left us to try their luck with them. Thus we were able, finally, to speak with a certain amount of privacy.

Looking discreetly at the walls of the city I suddenly realized that we were just above the point I had passed when I left with Utanin. The water was much higher now, but I could see the wooden water gate set in the city wall. There was something about it that seemed important, but I could not remember what it was.

Nakhti was talking, "...and I'm convinced there is a large contingent of Egyptians inside. As Kasher and I know firsthand, Nippur has very well designed walls, which have historically been able to repel..."

"Nakhti!" I interrupted, "Forgive me, but I just remembered something that should get us inside. From there, we might be able to get the gates open; at least some of them."

"Of course, Kasher, that would be ideal, but what is this way in you've just remembered?"

"That wooden gate; there in the wall. It has a small door in it. You can't see it now for the level of the water, but in the dry season it is visible above the water line. If we could get through that unseen there is a chance we could move about unnoticed – maybe even get to the gates!"

The last part, about getting to the gates, had only come to me as I was thinking through the idea of what to do once inside the city.

"Are you sure about that door, Kasher?"

"Yes, absolutely. Utanin told be how it was used during sieges to bring food into the city. It was also used by an enemy long ago to gain entrance to the city and take it. It must be our answer!"

"How far below the water line do you think it is?""I studied the gate for some time; then answered, "I would say it is at least the height of a man below the surface. That would mean it would be well out of sight from anyone on the wall."

"True," Nakhti said thoughtfully, "but it would also be very hard to get at. I've never been very good at breathing under water. It's certainly worth considering, though I don't see how we could do it."

We fell into a contemplative silence. The heat of the day had transformed into a pleasant coolness. A moderate breeze accentuated the effect.

My gaze wandered from the gate to the canal and back again. Something gnawed at my memory, but I couldn't bring it out.

A noise caught my attention down at the water's edge. A small animal of some kind was working its way through the rushes.

I looked up the canal, towards Babylon, remembering the journey that had taken me there. The calmness of the first part of the trip: the panic of the storm...

The storm!

"I have an idea!" I blurted out, louder than I had intended. I looked around to see if anyone outside of our group had taken notice. It did not seem that they had, so I continued, trying to speak lower now.

"Remember I told you how I was able to save Utanin and me from the sand storm? We were breathing through hollow reeds. We could do the same at the water gate!"

Nakhti mulled over the idea. I knew him well enough now to know he needed a few moments of silence to weigh the merits of an idea. He was quick and decisive in battle, but preparations were done with a deliberation that often seemed excessive to me.

I have to admit, though, I had seen the wisdom of such prolonged consideration at times. Many a battle had been obviously influenced our way by these 'Nakhti moments', as we called them.

Finally, he spoke.

"The reeds would have to be very long."

I had also been using the pause to try to anticipate his questions or objections.
"Not necessarily. I think we would have to go at night anyway to avoid detection, and we could use the reeds to get to the gate, then hold our breath, go under, and come up again to breathe when we need to. We would be right

against the gate, so no one from above could see us. We just need the reeds to get us there."

Another silence. Mercifully, this one did not last as long.

"You understand how risky this is, Kasher. And once inside, the risk grows even more."

"Can you see another way, Uncle? I can't, and my family is in there."

Another of Nakhti's 'ways' came into effect at that moment. When he was through deliberating, the great general was a man of instant action.

He stood abruptly, then, apparently remembering the need for stealth, he slowly moved toward the water's edge.

Bending to the water in a nonchalant way Nakhti broke off several of the reeds growing there. Just as casually, he made his way back to where we were seated. Joining us again, he began his examination of the reeds.

As I had told him, they were hollow. He played with them as though he were a child. I had never seen him so intrigued before.

"Uncle, have you never seen this before?"

"I have never been much for swimming." He answered. "Or for travel by boat," he continued. "The truth is; I am afraid of water!"

There was a stunned silence: this great warrior; none of would have believed him afraid of anything. None of us wanted to make much of it either.

"Alright, now you know. And, of course, your plan requires me to submerge myself in the stuff for long periods of time."

"Nakhti," (It was one of the soldiers we had brought with us.) "I would be glad to go in your place. I have a lot of experience in the water."

"Thank you for your willingness, but I know it has to be me. Kasher and I are the only ones in our entire band who know the layout and operations of Nippur. No; I have to do it."

We lapsed back into a silence. Nakhti continued playing with the reeds. It was time to rest, but I sensed that none of us was relaxed enough to sleep well just yet. Each remained for a while with his own thoughts until, finally, we started drifting off to sleep right where we reclined.

The following morning we made our way back to the main camp. Nakhti and I went directly to Muldan to make our report. We went into a tent and began discussing the plans.

Nakhti and I drew a map of Nippur in the dirt floor, each of us correcting anything that did not seem right. After several minutes, we were in agreement about the city's layout.

Muldan spoke. "So you think you can move about inside once you have gained entrance through the gate?"

No one bothered to bring up the obvious: we had no certainty we could find the gate underwater, let alone get it open and get through to the other side. There seemed no other way, so we left that part of the plan as decided.

"Kasher and I know our way around in there, as you can see from the map. It is very helpful to me to see it here, to refresh my memory, but I can see most of it in my mind. We both spent our youth in and around the city."

"I remember," I added, "how we used to make a game of figuring out how the gates were opened and closed. Once, on a dare, I actually closed one of the smaller gates, this one here. I think we could get a couple of them open. What difference would that make to the battle plan?" I asked.

"A lot of difference. We could position our troops to attack at those two gates and, the gods willing, gain entrance. At that point we could get the other gates open and flood the city with our men. All of the gate mechanisms will be guarded, of course."

"Yes," said Nakhti, "but there should only be one, two guards at the most at them. Surely no one expects an infiltration."

"I hope you are right, Nakhti. Time will tell. One more detail. The fact that both of you are from here is good in one way, but what if someone recognizes you?"

"That's a good point, sir." Nakhti began, "I hadn't considered that."

"But our people will be glad to see us," I interjected, without thinking it through.

"And in their jubilation they might give you away!"

He was right, of course. I could just imagine my mother's reaction if she saw me.

"Disguises are in order then. Something that will be expected, and so ignored," said Muldan.

We all thought for a while. Finally an idea occurred to me.

"How many Egyptian troops do you think are in there?" I asked of Muldan.

"A lot; the reports that we think are the most reliable put their strength at six to eight thousand."

"That many men would require a lot of provisions, especially water," I said.

"I think I see where you are going, but continue," Nakhti said.

"You speak perfect Egyptian, Uncle, so you should be able to blend in well, especially at night. What if you were to pretend to be drawing water from our entry area? I could be a local pressed into service for that same purpose."

"That makes sense, Kasher," Muldan interjected. "That would give you a reason to be near the water. If you're caught coming out, you might even get away with a story about falling in, but I wouldn't want to test that theory."

"We would need some water baskets and a poles," I went on, thinking aloud. "Now that you mention coming out of the water, how hard will that be?"

"We may need a ladder," said Nakhti. "This is starting to sound complicated."

"Complicated it may be, but I don't see another way at this point," said Muldan. "I will not order you two to do this, though. We were caught by surprise, underestimating the will of Egypt to get a toehold here in Babylonia. We can wait them out if we have to, but I don't think it would be best for us. Nakhti, you know the Egyptian's way of thinking and acting. What do you think would be the result of waiting a while?"

"Pharaoh is patient. He learned a lot from Carchemish. He knows the strength and will of those who fight for Nebuchadnezzar. I don't think we will see any more direct attempts at takeover until he has gained much ground gradually."

"Also, he is a very good coordinator. He probably intends to take cities in a circle around Babylon, allowing him to strike from various angles at once. No, Muldan, we must not wait. It would be to their advantage, not ours."

"If Kasher and I fail, you may have little choice but to try and siege the town, but that would be a difficult and costly option. Our best plan is still for us to get those gates open and trust the might of our army to gain back the city. We will do it. We must."

I nodded my agreement. Thinking of my family in there during a long siege was not a pleasant thought.

We began preparing materials right away, calmly, so as not to arouse suspicion. The water baskets were easy enough to find, and no one would think anything odd about their purchase. A staff was procured so that I could carry them on my shoulders; a common practice.

The ladder was another matter. We finally had to make one. There were materials available, and it we didn't exactly need a piece of art, so 'sturdy' was the word for the project.

We built it inside of a tent so that it wouldn't draw attention. There was nothing to climb in close range to us but some date palms, and ladders were not normally used to climb those.

We weren't even sure how long it should be. If it was too short, our egress from the water could be complicated. If too long, it might be noticed. If we were not involved in such an important operation, our discussions about the ladder might have elicited considerable laughter as we imagined what could go wrong. As it was, something going wrong probably meant our death and the failure of the operation. That knowledge tempered the mirth considerably.

Finally, we decided upon a length that we hoped was within an acceptable range. I turned to one of the men who had been helping build it and said, "If we live through this, we'll have plenty of time to laugh about it. I'm sure there will be good stories to tell."

He smiled, patted my shoulder, and turned to go out of the tent. I saw movement around Muldan and made my way there. It was a courier, and he was being ushered into a tent with Muldan and Nakhti. I went straight in. In that moment the realization hit me of how far I had progressed in my career. No one questioned that I should be in that meeting.

As I came in, the courier was explaining, with no small amount of exuberance, how the attack at the river had gone.

As we had hoped, the main body of the enemy's force there had been caught in the very act of crossing the river. Completely unaware of our knowledge of their presence they were sent into complete chaos. The few that had already emerged from the water were slaughtered immediately, causing great indecision in the others. Some tried, in vain, to fight their way forward; but the transition from water to land, along with the readiness of the welcoming party on the shore, made that option completely disastrous. About a third turned and fled back into the desert. We lost absolutely no soldiers in the affair.

The commander of that group was moving his men slowly in our direction and awaited further instructions.

We decided to wait one more night to plan the details well. Also, Muldan had reports that both sets of his troops needed another day to all be in position for the attack.

I found a place where I could be alone and lay down. Sleep did not come easy. I had seen many battles in the last few years, but this one was different. I was responsible for a large part of this plan. That weighed heavily on me. Also, the fact that my family was involved made it especially personal. I couldn't stop wondering what their fate would be if we failed. Would my sisters, and even maybe my mother, be sold into slavery? What little contact I had had with Egyptians did not lead me to believe they were a particularly barbaric people, but I had already see that, in any group, there were always a few selfish individuals who crossed the lines of decency with frightening ease. My family could not become spoils of war.

I spent a lot of time looking at the sky. I dozed from time to time, but mostly I observed the celestial bodies, so distant, and yet seemingly almost within reach in the clear desert air.

When I judged the time to be approximately the hour we intended to start our underwater journey, I took notice of the moon. It was about one quarter of its fullness. It seemed to me to be ideal for what we planned; enough light for us not to have to operate in total blindness, but not so much as would make us easy to see. Its position was very good for our approach as well. It would be behind anyone on the wall, and, at close range, would actually illuminate the inside of the wall, leaving the outer part very dark by contrast.

By the time of our planned attack, an hour later, the moon had swung more to the east. I had been waiting to see this as it would influence which of the gates were best to attack. By attacking the north and south gates I believed we would have the moon's light as much to our favor as possible.

The next morning, Nakhti accepted my analysis. We would open one gate to the north, and another to the south; almost directly opposite each other. We explained to Muldan all that was between the two points, returning to our map in the tent floor to add details. On the north side was a small temple; small, but located very close to the gate at that point. Our troops would not need to get inside it, but it would make good cover from which to attack.

The south side was more complicated. There was a lot of open space. We decided that our own elite force would join the part of the army that entered there to strengthen that effort. We had a lot of practice improvising cover in open areas. Nakhti dispatched Minkabh immediately to join the southern contingent and explain the plan and help them understand what would be expected of them.

Muldan would lead the northern group personally. The biggest need in that arena was for speed. Outside the city, they would have to cross a large area of open ground to reach the wall. Any delay in their approach would allow those inside to prepare for the attack.

Both attacks would benefit, in one way, from the fact that we would engage in the dark. Certainly it was a help in surprising the enemy, but a logistic nightmare just the same. We planned the attack for two hours before sunrise. That would still allow us deep darkness to begin; and, hopefully, daylight in which to finish the job.

We decided that I would open a south gate, a fairly obscure entrance known as the 'gate of the unclean women'. I had no idea what that name represented, but I knew its location well enough. It faced the Euphrates as it curled around two sides of the city before turning back southward, and it contained a drawbridge for crossing it. Nakhti would open the Ekur gate in the northeast. We gathered materials from which to make a torch for signaling. We carefully wrapped those materials in three layers of skins, each swathed in fat. Hopefully, that would keep them dry while we were in the water, and any fat that remained would be helpful with the fire. If the torches didn't work we would have to try and improvise.

The signal was to come from immediately above the gate, and it was to consist of waving the flame madly back and forth, something that would not happen under normal circumstances, and, so, could not be easily confused.

Word of these plans was dispatched to the respective leaders, now to the north and south of Nippur.

I made my way back to the tent where we had been making our preparations. Nakhti and Muldan were still there going over a few details. They spoke with a calm that I admired, but I suspected it masked their real emotions at this moment.

A plan was needed to get the ladder to the other camp without raising suspicion. The answer came in an unusual way. We were outside, resting, while we thought the problem through. Minkabh had joined us. He would be the leader of the army of the Chaldeans until Nakhti was reunited with them inside Nippur. It was Minkabh who saw the solution.

"Look, there – up the river. That camel is dragging a load of some kind. I've seen that on occasion, but not very much lately. Anyway, that is the answer!"

"I see it! You're right," said Nakhti. We can use the ladder as a frame for just such a load. Let's do a bit of trading, shall we?"

There were merchants enough around us to make our task fairly simple. We bought skins that were tanned and ready to be made into tents and clothing. Some of the more supple of them we kept out for the water-proofing of the fire making materials. By early afternoon, we were all set.

The four of us who would be moving out for this mission - the same four that were at the other camp the day before; Nakhti, me, and the two other soldiers who would relay the news back of our success (failure we would be able to report ourselves) settled down under a good shade and tried to rest. Tonight would be special.

Chapter 19

Our movements were deliberately slow, masking a deep and intense nervousness. Four men packing a couple of camels with wares should not be cause for much alarm. The late hour might cause someone to pause, but likely for no more than a moment. With the rivers and canals to guide, night travel, though unusual, was not unheard of. A casual observer would likely assume we meant to travel only a short distance, and had decided to avoid the heat of the day. They would be mostly correct. The following day portended to be very hot indeed.

We positioned one of the camels directly in front of the tent that housed our makeshift ladder so that we could attach it, already covered by some of the skins we had bought, without much visible movement. None of us were particularly knowledgeable about camels, but we thought we should be able to handle it. As it turned out, we had to call for help. It seems camels get very nervous if forced into close proximity to large things like houses or tents. In our attempt at not calling attention to ourselves, we almost created a spectacle.

Three of us were holding the animal the best we could as it tried to break away. It wasn't making too much noise just yet, but it was obvious that was about to change. Nakhti had gone to find the man who was in charge of our beasts of burden, hopeful that he could sort out our dilemma. He did.

Immediately upon seeing the situation he took the camel's reins and led it away from the tent. As soon as they were just a few paces away, the camel calmed down completely. We decided our little expedition needed a fifth man.

With his help, we got the load attached to the camel with no trouble. We tied the rest of our gear on the ladder, and then hefted a pack onto the other camel with other items.

When we arrived at the forward encampment, we moved immediately to the river edge, unloading right there. It was beginning to get dark and as we carefully scanned our proximity we did not notice anyone paying us any special attention. Our camel man took them up the bank and tied them to a tree. As we had decided, he stayed with them, making himself comfortable there on the ground for the night.

The rest of us started opening some of our bundles, as if to prepare our bed rolls. We built a small fire as the darkness deepened.

To make sure we were truly convincing we stretched out as if to sleep. The bundles we had unrolled had been prepared for this ruse; they also contained the supplies we needed for our next adventure.

There was obviously no sleeping to be done. We waited, each with his own thoughts, for the appointed time. I used the hours for my normal pastime; trying to see as much as possible of what the night wanted to tell me.

As usual when he was visible to me, my gaze was drawn to Orion. Ever since Pul had told me stories about the mighty hunter I believed there was something special about him: something that would affect me personally.

In Babylon I had heard more stories about Orion; conflicting stories, but with certain common elements. Almost all of the stories involved a great warrior returning from somewhere. Some said he was Nebuchadnezzar and that he was the reincarnation of the great Nimrod. I did not have a well-formed theology, but the idea of someone coming back from the dead did not fit with what I knew of death. As a soldier I had become well acquainted with the final journey. It seemed to me to be exactly that: final.

As I pondered these great questions, my eyes on Orion, I saw it again.

For only the second time, I saw the flash of light just below Orion's belt. This time I was sure.

It lasted a few seconds, much longer than the first time. I had time to analyze it even. It was red. Not just the reddish glow that comes from some stars, but a real, deep red.

After it was gone, I could not take my eyes off the spot. But gone it was, as completely as if it had never been. I felt a longing that defied description. And for what – a flash of light in the night sky? And yet, I couldn't shake it.

After quite a few minutes of staring into that now empty place, I came to a new sensation. I felt a calm come over me, and it seemed to me that I had been given a sign that all would be well in the coming hours.

A sign? From whom? I had no answers for that, but the sense of it was very real to me.

I don't know how long I lay there in that state, but all at once I looked to the moon. It was time.

We were such a cohesive team by this point that we all started moving at about the same time. Possibly one of us moved first, provoking the others into action, but, if so, it would have been impossible to say who was the trigger.

The other two men helped Nakhti and I store our equipment on our bodies. We had planned and rehearsed all of this several times. The dark was not a complication.

They were to see us off, then make their way back to Muldan with the news. The plan necessitated an assumption of accomplishment.

I had worked with Nakhti on the use of the reeds; I being the one with some experience. We had even gone in the canal (albeit for a short time) just the night before. When I finally was able to convince him of the need to hold his nose while breathing through the reed, he was able to manage to stay under for a while.

We both had to fight off feelings of panic: it just isn't natural to breathe with your head under water. Tonight we could not afford any such distractions. Tonight we had to be completely focused.

We slid silently into the water. We did not need to be submerged at this point. No one could see us until we were much closer to the wall.

We stopped in unison as we approached the corner of the city wall. Both of us sensed that we were as close as we should get before hiding ourselves beneath the cool darkness. Carefully, we brought out the reeds we had prepared for the occasion. Neither of us made as much as a ripple as we began breathing through them. If Nakhti had any difficulties they were not evident. He swam as though he had done it all his life. We had needed no verbal communication as we came. There was no chance of it now.

As we had planned, we stayed in physical contact at all times; shoulder to shoulder as much as possible. We heard nothing from outside the water, but it would have to be a loud noise if we were to hear it. That kind of noise would not be good news.

Slowly, we moved forward until we could touch the corner of the wall; then, farther down, the wooden gate. We could now safely bring our heads above water. As I had calculated, the moon's light was blocked by the inside of the wall, and it would have taken a miracle for anyone it notice us in the darkness of wood and water.

Our first task here was to find the middle of the gate. On the boat trip out I had seen that the door was located there.

That accomplished, it was time to find and open the door. We had decided that I was to make the first attempt at it. Nakhti would remain stationary, and I would go straight down and straight back up again so we could keep track of our positioning.

I had to hold my breath for this job. I inhaled deeply and handed my reed to Nakhti. He knew what that meant.

I was my usual, optimistic, confident self, so I went down with my pry bar in hand, ready to get that door open as soon as I reached it.

I didn't even find the door, let alone get it open. I was convinced that I had gone deep enough, and, for just a moment, I contemplated a lateral move, believing we had missed the middle of the gate somehow. I fought the urge and dove deeper. Being a soldier had taught me the importance of sticking to a plan. What I hadn't counted on was how hard it was in the dark to determine how deep I had gone.

My hesitation left me little air to investigate a deeper option, so I resurfaced. I was craving air at this point, but I knew I had to break the water as quietly as possible, so I willed myself to rise slowly.

I had no reference point to tell me how close I was to the surface. I was on the verge of panicking and shooting up to find the precious air. I started thinking I had gone too deep to recover safely, especially at a rate slow enough to come up quietly.

Just as I was about to give in to my panic, I felt my head touch the surface. A moment later I was taking in a slow, deep breath, trying not to gasp as I did so.

At this point we really had no alternative to vocal communication. Nakhti whispered the question, and I explained what had happened. That was all that was necessary, and we hoped no one had heard.

Without hesitation, Nakhti handed me the two reeds. I could barely discern when he was actually gone from the surface, but I was left alone, one hand on the gate.

It seemed like several minutes before I felt him coming up alongside me. If he had experienced the same sensation I had he showed no sign of it.

"It is sealed with pitch, very tight," he whispered. "We will take turns digging it out.

I handed him the reeds, more a means of communication now than a necessity. Obviously, I had not gone deep enough on my first attempt, but we were at the right spot. I took in as much air as I could and started down.

I found the door much quicker than I expected. I now had a better feel for the depth, and I had simply

221

miscalculated before in my haste. I felt for the edge and started working at the pitch sealant. It was old and hard, but I was able to make some progress.

With just about enough air to reach the surface again I decided to try to pry the door open. A little movement encouraged me, and I almost forgot that I needed air. I pried some more, but my lungs finally got the message to my head that I couldn't wait any longer.

The trip to the surface was agony. I expelled air in short bursts as I went, and by the time my head came into the open again, I could not keep myself from a quick intake of air. It sounded like thunder to me in the stillness of the night.

Immediately, Nakhti handed me my reed: but just mine. As his head went under the water I understood. He was not going down to the door now. This was our contingency if we were afraid of being found out. As I placed the reed in my mouth I heard a noise at the top of the wall.

Clenching the reeds in our teeth, we used one hand to hold our nose. With the other hand we pulled ourselves below the surface.

We held onto the wall to keep us under. The fact that it was wood at this point was a great help. We clung to edges of boards with fingers made strong from training and battle.

Looking up, we saw the light of a torch. Logically, I knew the possibility of our being seen was very remote. The light from the torch would reflect off the surface of the water. All that would be visible were the two thin reeds, and in that weak light, they were not likely to be seen. But that was logic. My heart was racing as I looked into the face of the two guards peering over the wall right at our position.

One slip, one small movement, and all could be lost.

We watched as the light, still hanging over the wall, moved down the wall. It had a calming effect, but we still could not afford any movement. Finally, it disappeared.

Still we waited. There was no room for rashness now. As I clung there, I knew that my judgment had been poor. My desire to finish the job quickly had almost cost us the whole operation. I could not allow myself any more such mistakes. Too much was at stake.

Nakhti started to the surface and I followed his lead. Nothing was said; there was no need. He simply handed me his reed, took a deep breath, and went down with his pry bar at the ready. He surfaced after a moment, and I handed back the reeds.

I didn't count how many times we went back down there. We had to go as many times as necessary to get that door open. Each time I went, I was able to get more movement, but I didn't outstay my air anymore.

Finally, Nakhti surfaced, took a few breaths and took hold of my arm instead of handing me the reeds. This was the predetermined signal that we should both go down – Nakhti believed we could get the door out now.

I stowed the reed in a strap on my back made just for that purpose. We looked into each other face, breathed in unison, and went under. We went down hand in hand so that we could coordinate our work. As we reached the door, Nakhti took my hand (the one with the pry bar in it) and guided my bar to a spot on the edge of the door. Together we got the bar in place in the gap. Then he was gone. Very soon I felt movement on the door as his pry bar started its work, and I knew it was time for mine to join in.

The door moved out, but not all the way. There was no way to judge its thickness, so when we needed more air, we surfaced.

It turned out to be quite thick, and we had to repeat the process several time, but, finally, the door came free.

I had a frightening thought just as it did so. My other emotion was of irritation at myself for not considering this thought at an earlier time. What if the door floated to the surface and made a great noise?

Considering this possibility, I reached for the door as it came free. I was not convinced I would be able to hold it down very well if it wanted to surface. It was a large door, thicker that we had anticipated.

I needn't have worried. Looking back I should have known that it would be both waterlogged from so much time there and heavy from its banding and pitching. It sank slowly to the bottom as soon as it was clear.

We made our way back to the surface for one more breath. Before diving again we checked all our gear. There was no backtracking from here.

Nakhti descended silently. I waited a moment before following. The opening was fairly large, but we weren't going to go through together.

I slid through the doorway without hesitation.

Chapter 20

As I came out the other side I was surprised how much I could see. I clearly made out Nakhti's form ahead and in front of me. He was still swimming forward. We thought it might not seem normal, pretending to be water bearers as we were, to be right at the wall, so we had agreed to move down the waterway for whatever time our breath held out; barring any surprises, of course.

I was tired from all the effort of getting this far, but I had taken on board a good amount of air and was maintaining my position behind Nakhti.

As we swam, I discovered why I could see so well. Primarily, it was due to the moon's light. I felt a bit foolish at being surprised by this as I had been the one to point it out during the planning.

But there was more. The city was fairly well lit; normal, I suppose, under the circumstances. It was not terribly prudent, though. It would give an edge to attackers (like us) who would take advantage of the darkness.

I was happy to see that there were no torches close to the water. Nakhti made a seemingly effortless exit onto the bank. We had left the ladder behind where we entered the water, hoping it would not be necessary. I was very happy we would not need to return for it.

I followed him up onto the bank, turning as Nakhti had into a sitting position as soon as I was clear of the water. Our feet were hanging into the cool liquid, but we hoped that would not seem to strange if anyone noticed us.

To our great joy - and increasing confidence - no one was near our landing spot. So far, we had not been noticed. I hoped that moving through the city would be so easy.

Still sitting, we began opening our bundles. Careful not to make any big movements we wrapped ourselves in coats we had brought, hiding our wet clothes - sparse though they were - from detection. The wooden pole we had each strapped to our backs we had taken off just as we exited the water, placing them on the ground. From our packs we took two large water skins a piece. Now we began filling them, alternating storing the other items we had brought in large pockets sown especially into the coats for the purpose.

Still no one seemed to notice us. Between the light question and the lack of vigilance we were experiencing I began to believe this was not a well prepared army. I mentioned something like that to Nakhti, no longer afraid to speak as that would be normally expected behavior.

"You may be right," he said. "But never take that for granted, no matter what the indications. Also, unpreparedness in these areas does not necessarily mean they can't or won't fight."

Wise words, as always, from my mentor. I did well to bear them in mind this night; his analysis turned out to be very accurate.

Our water bottles filled and hanging from the poles we made our way away from the water. There were few houses right in this spot, but our plan was to hide in plain sight. After a few minutes walking toward the center of the city, we came to a crossroad. Nakhti was unsure in the dark about our exact position. He had been gone from Nippur for as long time. Even in the dark, I knew where we were.

I was able to direct him in his direction, towards the northeast wall as we had planned. We went our separate ways without ceremony. Each of us knew what we had to do; there was no more need or desire to talk it out.

I had to walk along the canal for a short way until I came to a bridge that would allow me to cross over. We had decided to both exit the canal on the same side, but now we were moving in opposite directions.

After the bridge, I wound my way down a dirt road. There were increasingly more houses as I went, all of them looking alike in the dark. Once in a while I would pass someone going the other way, but no one questioned my presence.

I could now make out the south wall ahead of me. I stopped alongside one of the houses and emptied the water from the skins I carried. That way they would be lighter; not that they bothered me at their present weight, but I could be free of them more quickly if I needed to. Besides, I was now moving towards water instead of away from it. Any necessary ruse now would be that I was going to fill the skins at the inside moat below the south wall.

As I turned from my task I found myself face to face with a man. Given the closeness he had chosen for our encounter, I had no difficulty discerning who it was.

"Pul!"

The word came out faster and louder than I wanted, but my surprise was complete. Looking around it didn't seem that anyone had taken notice. I turned my attention back to my old master of the stars.

"Kasher. I should have guessed you would be a part of this."

"What do you mean; a part of what?"

He glanced around now to see if anyone was watching. There was no one in sight.

"I saw an omen in the sky tonight; a sign from Nimrod himself. He is back."

"I saw a light in Orion's girdle. Is that what you are referring to?"

"Yes, Kasher. Orion is what the Great Hunter is called by the Chaldeans, but he really represents Nimrod, and that sign means he is back!"

"But why did you say I had something to do with it? You can't possibly know why I am even here."

"True, I don't know what brought you here, but I have always known you would have a part in the fulfillment of the prophecies. There was something about you; and you can't deny your fascination with the stars. Something, or someone, is calling to you through them. I am not surprised you are here now."

"You must be here," he continued, "to help usher in the new kingdom, with Nimrod himself on the throne."

"But Pul, he has been dead for a long time."

"Yes, but he has returned: reborn. You are here on a mission, yes?"

At this point I made a huge mistake. From that time forward I assumed much less about allegiances. Even when it involved people I thought I knew well. My mother's words soon proved to bare all the marks of true wisdom; "Speak little and listen much. This is the way of safety and learning."

Unfortunately, I did not remember that advice at that moment.

"Yes, Pul, We are taking back the city for Nebuchadnezzar."

I suppose I can blame the darkness for the fact that I did not notice any reaction in his face at my declaration. I thought he hesitated a bit before responding, but I didn't think that terribly odd, given the circumstances.

"So, my young warrior; what is your part in this great drama?"

I explained to him the job before me. He seemed genuinely excited about the task, and offered to help me with it.

"I am known among the invaders. Since you have been gone, I have risen to a position of minor importance here in the city. I have been used by them to calm our people, avoiding conflict during this time of occupation. Come, you can be seen accompanying me to the wall. You no longer need your disguise."

I left the water skins where we had been conversing, but I kept the staff, using it now as a walking stick.

"You won't need that, Kasher. You won't be challenged as long as you are with me."

"We don't know yet what will happen when I try to get the gate open. I will keep this just in case."

I began to worry a little at his suggestion that I leave the staff behind. I wasn't sure anything was wrong, but I was more wary than before. As we walked toward the wall my anxiety increased; not so much because of the task ahead, but more by the way Pul was questioning me about the whole operation. I decided not to reveal all that

I knew, telling him I was not informed of the plan as a whole; just my part in it.

I stayed very close to him as he approached the guards at the wall. I didn't want to doubt him, but something didn't seem quite right.

He spoke a few words of Egyptian to them. Based on my lessons from Nakhti, his pronunciation was not very good. I understood most of what he said, and I didn't hear anything that sounded threatening to me or my plan. We made our way to the wall.

We walked past more soldiers; and, sure enough, none of them questioned us about being there. A few even acknowledged Pul as we passed by.

We walked right up to the mechanism that lifted and lowered the drawbridge. I was familiar with it from childhood days. There was always a guard posted, even in peacetime, as much to keep anyone from hurting themselves as anything else. My curiosity had caused me to study the way the gate opened and closed back then. It was really quite simple.

The door (bridge) itself was hinged on the floor of the gate opening. Another piece of wood braced, with metal, was placed above the drawbridge, parallel to it when the bridge was lowered across the moat. It (the upper door) extended inward and outward of the gate, balanced slightly to the outside, making its normal position that of open.

To close the bridge, there was a box built into the inside edge of this delicately balanced upper door. Sand was shoveled into it to bring that back edge down, lifting the actual door (attached by ropes) in the process. To open the door again, a trap door in the sand box was opened, allowing the sand to escape and the bridge to return to its natural (open) position.

We had made our way to the upper door, now vertical and creating a second layer of protection against attack at that point. The inner door was secured by ropes; a good indication they were not thinking of using that gate any time soon.

As I approached the final guard, the one charged with maintaining the security of that mechanism, I felt, rather than saw, Pul hang back. Something was wrong; I could sense it.

A shout from behind me confirmed my fears.

At that same moment, Nakhti was going through a complication of his own.

He had emptied his water skins just as I, but these guards were not pleased with his idea of refilling them so close to their watch. They sent him away before he could get anywhere near the gate.

There were houses nearby, so Nakhti went behind one of them without being seen. Carefully, he removed his heavy clothing, lay his water skins down and started back toward the closest guard. Staff in hand, he came behind him without making a sound. The staff was around his neck before the guard knew anyone was there. One quick pull of those strong arms, and he was dead.

Still silent, Nakhti pulled the man, still standing, behind the closest house. There he took his clothes, hiding the body in a shallow pool.

The rest was easy for him. He began working his way from guard to guard, whispering (in perfect Egyptian) to each of them of some officer that wanted to see them. He told them he had been sent to take their place. The placement of these soldiers was such that no one noticed the others leaving. After about twenty minutes of this, Nakhti found himself guarding the drawbridge mechanism.

There was some confusion as, one by the men returned to their posts. As they discussed what had just happened, small arguments ensued. Soon, however, embarrassment over what appeared to be bad communication took over, and the men fell into a sullen silence.

The problem element was the man he had replaced last; the one right at the gate. That he had taken care of as well, telling the man that his captain had singled him out for a reward: "He said you should take the rest of your shift off," Nakhti told him.

Back at the south wall I was not having it so easy. Pul had sounded the alarm against me. There was nothing for it but to fight these men head on.

The good news was that the posts were separated by a considerable distance, with only a few small patrols going between them. The bad news was that I was going to have to fight about fifteen armed men.

I turned to face them. They had gathered into a fighting group between my position and the wall. Everything I had ever trained for came together in that moment. I would defeat them. My king was depending on me. My family needed me.

They came with a confidence normal in the face of numeric superiority. They were not counting on the confidence that I had in my own abilities as a fighter.

Before they were ready to strike, I was already upon the front three men, swinging my staff like a whirlwind with a speed that caught each of them on the head, removing them from the combat. My attack also had a huge effect on the rest of them.

Organization was gone. So was their confidence. I waded into them without hesitation, mowing them down as they slowly tried to reach for weapons they did not think they would even need.

The two at the rear had enough time before I got to them to have their swords out. They lasted a little longer than the others, but not much.

As I finished with the last two I saw light out of the corner of my eye. Turning, I saw the signal fire at the north gate. Nakhti had succeeded.

There was no time for me to revel in my victory. I was behind schedule. The attacks needed to occur as close to each other as possible in time if they were going to have their full effect.

I turned back toward the gate at a run. The balanced device was now unmanned, and I tore the bottom of the sand box open as soon as I reached it. It didn't move.

I felt my heart rise into my throat. How could I have mistaken how the simple mechanism worked?

I cast about frantically to see what I was missing. I grabbed at the edge of the door, thinking it might just need a helping hand. It was then that my hand went around the rope.

In my haste, I had forgotten the door was tied down – an effective precaution as it turned out. I released both ropes in a fury of anxiety and momentary self-loathing.

The internal end started moving upward immediately. The balance was almost perfect, so it rose smoothly: slowly.

My next task was to reach the top of the wall and signal to the hidden troops that the door was open. I was unopposed in this as well, but I had quite a lot of stairs to climb once I reached them. By the time I got to the top, the drawbridge was fully open.

I pulled out the rag I had that was soaked with something flammable. Tying the rag onto the end of my staff I used the flint and rock I had been provided to get it burning. Just as I began waving my flaming banner above the parapet, two things happened simultaneously.

I heard, more than saw, our men leave their waiting place. The moonlight was where we had calculated it would be, leaving them in the deep dark of the wall's shadow. Any attack upon them would have to rely on sheer luck for success.

The second thing was that I could see the door starting to close.

As I ran toward the inside edge of the wall I could see someone was on the upper door, his weight taking it back down to the closed position. I couldn't make out his face, but I recognized the slight, tall form of Pul.

Already he had tried to keep me from my plan. I had lost track of him in all the fighting, but he could not be allowed to win now.

The door had already reached about a forty-five degree angle. Pul was perched on the top of the sand box, giving it the benefit of all his weight, such as it was. Our men would be nearing the outer door now. If they were caught there instead of making it inside before the enemy rallied, they would be in trouble. By design, there was no cover for a long ways out from the wall.

Precious time would be lost if I chose to run back down the stairs to confront Pul. By that time, some of the

Egyptians could have arrived to keep me from getting the door back open. I made a quick decision. I jumped for it.

The top edge of the swing wall was now well above the level of the wall. It would only get higher.

I hit the face of the door and thought I had failed. With no time to think, I reached as high as I could. With relief, I felt my fingers curl around the top edge. In a flash, I was up and over.

I had aimed for the middle of the door, laterally, when I jumped. That meant that my flight over the top put me right where I wanted to be: falling straight down onto Pul.

He never saw me coming. I landed directly on him, knocking the wind out of me, and rendering Pul unconscious. I twisted to fall off the door, and, with my rapidly waning strength, I dragged Pul with me, my hands grasping the collar of his garment.

I lay, gasping, in the dirt, unable to rise. I was able to see, however, that the door was once again opening.

Moments later, someone shouted my name. I called out as loudly as I could - still fighting for air - and I was heard for my effort.

Minkabh came and stood over me. His gaze went to Pul, still lying on the ground. Between gasps, I explained that he had been a friend of my family, but had played the traitor. Two of our soldiers immediately drug him away.

On the other side of town things seemed to be going according to plan. Muldan and his men were able to enter almost before the guards knew what was happening, and they were quickly dispatched.

Just to the east was the tower. Known to both Nakhti and I, it had been chosen as a key location to take. If necessary, we could climb it and fight from a privileged position. Most of Muldan's men were moved to the base of the tower, encountering very little resistance as they went.

In Babylon, I had seen the great tower of Nimrod, dedicated to the god Marduk. It was ancient, and had been partially destroyed when Marduk-baladan had taken Babylon from the Assyrians. At that time the tower was in honor of the goddess Ishtar, and she was, for him, a rival to Marduk. He lost the city to the Assyrians again, before the present ruling family came in. They rededicated the tower to Ishtar, but never seemed to get around to rebuilding it.

Nabopolassar wanted the favor of all the gods of the land. When he took Babylon back from Assyria, he continued the worship of their gods; adding in the Chaldean deities for good measure. His son Nebuchadnezzar seemed to be following that tradition, and, lately, had set his men to the work of rebuilding the tower.

This one, in Nippur, was much like it. It was dedicated to Enlil and had been for as long as anyone could remember.

I believed it was good politics to let people worship their own gods. It made for a much more peaceful land, and I considered Nebuchadnezzar very wise in this policy. After all, those gods really didn't exist, did they?

In our discussions before the attack on Nippur, there was talk about this tower. Neither Nakhti nor I had studied it (or the one in Babylon) close up. As we went through our troops to see if anyone else had any special knowledge about them, we were surprised that there seemed to be a great shroud of mystery covering these massive structures. No one could give us any helpful information.

The present battle would have gone much better for the Babylonians had we known more about the tower.

The soldiers spread around the tower, claiming it as their first real prize of the battle. A quick look was all that was needed to see that no one was on it. They turned their attentions to the logical direction from which an attack would emanate; away from the tower.

There was a lull; a small victory had been won. The men began setting up a logistical base from which they could continue their conquest of the city; a few moments to rest, knowing that there would be more fighting.

It came much sooner that they expected; and from a place they thought impossible.

With a collective shout, Egyptians poured from the tower onto the backs of the Babylonians. Nearly half of that contingent was killed in a matter of seconds, so great was the surprise.

Nakhti had taken his leave of Muldan and was headed to our position, eager to be with his own men. He hadn't gotten far when he heard the din behind him. Turning, he saw what was happening, though he still could not understand how it had happened.

As he ran toward the tower he began encountering Babylonian soldiers in flight. No one could blame them, really; such was the shock of the surprise attack. He began shouting orders at them, gradually working them into a unit that he could lead. Once they were minimally organized, they started back into the fray.

Emotions are funny things. They can change shape without losing intensity.

Confusion and panic had been replaced by rage and determination.

There was no time – or will, really, either – to form a battle plan. They waded into combat, looking for Egyptians to kill.

Those Babylonian soldiers who had not fled, but had survived by being shielded by the men closest to the tower, were now turned, weapons in hand, engaging the enemy. The Egyptians were now slowed because of having to step over and on the bodies of the fallen Babylonians. Even so, Nebuchadnezzar's men were faltering – until they saw Nakhti and his new unit arrive. They couldn't know that the men who were now encouraging them so much had, moments ago, been fleeing the battlefield.

A shout started at the point where Nakhti entered the battle and spread around the tower. They shouted his name and faced the enemy, determination replacing desperation.

The Egyptians soon discovered that the same tower that had allowed them such an advantage in the beginning was now reducing their fighting space dramatically. They literally had their backs to the wall. Some were able to retreat up the stairs: most did not have stairs to climb, and the top of the wall was too high to reach.

In a normal battle, some might have been given mercy from the Babylonians. This was not a normal battle. Having to step over the dead bodies of their comrades did not incline them to leniency. Every enemy soldier they could get a sword to was cut down without a thought.

Chapter 21

Their defeat at the tower broke the Egyptians' back. Most of the others spread around the city surrendered as soon as they heard the news. After a few skirmishes, the battle was over.

I was informed of the battle and summoned to the base of the tower by a messenger. Muldan gave us what details he knew about the battle. No one yet knew how the Egyptians had appeared.

As soldiers began identifying and organizing the dead, Muldan, Nakhti and I began climbing the steps of the tower. We took a force of about twenty men with us. Apparently, quite a number of Egyptians had escaped up the stairs, only to disappear right away.

We found several inscriptions explaining the purpose of the tower; something I had completely ignored when I lived here. Some sections were dedicated to the worship of the goddess Inanna.

Before we reached the first landing Muldan was at our side. We were surprised, but there was no conversation. The set of his jaw said all we needed to know.

Our weapons at the ready, we searched each level for a hiding place. There were seven levels in all, and I, for one, was not looking forward to the task, not knowing what we would find, or when.

We didn't have to go far for our first clue. We found a huge door on the first level leading to a wide corridor.

The door was ingeniously disguised as a part of the stone structure. A wooden door, it slid on a track that allowed for it to move forward as it closed so that it did not stick out or in from the rest of the wall. It was plastered on the outside and colored the same as the rock structure. If we hadn't been looking so intently we might have passed it by unnoticed.

Sliding the door open, we saw immediately that the corridor led all the way to the other side of the tower. There were ribbons of light coming through the edges of the door at the other end. There was room for at least four men to enter abreast, but we were seasoned soldiers; not likely to be caught in a dangerous formation.

As we entered cautiously, Nakhti and I took the lead, and the others immediately took up positions that allowed for visibility in all directions.

At the halfway point we discovered another door on the right hand wall. It was much simpler, swinging inward on hinges, but it was about the same width as the hallway we were in.

It was open just a little.

I gave it a shove with my foot and then stood back a pace. Nothing. No light of any kind. None of us were eager to stick our heads into that darkness. I turned to see that word had already been spread to the rear of the contingent, and I saw four men head back toward the door we had entered. I knew they were going for torches. These were Nakhti's men – they did not need minute instruction when the next step was obvious.

It would have been almost impossible for anyone to mount an attack against in our present battle pose, but being inside this huge structure made me uneasy anyway. It seemed like we were waiting a long time, but I knew it would take a bit to find and light enough torches for us. Even so, I couldn't help thinking that our enemies could be getting farther and farther away while we waited.

Finally, I heard the sound of running on the stone walkway we had followed coming here. Suddenly the space we were in was lit up, revealing nothing new, but easing my sense of dread nevertheless.

Torches handed from man to man reached us at the front, and we began probing the new area inside this door. We were very glad we had waited.

The light revealed that the floor ended just inside the door. Below, there was a landing, just over the distance of a man's height, and only wide enough for one person to stand on, then a gaping hole the entire width of the corridor. We could not see the bottom.

Beyond the hole the floor started again at the same level. The gap from where we stood to there was more than anyone could span by leaping. Our torches revealed a wooden bridge on the other side. Obviously, the escapees had used it and then pulled it over behind them. Nakhti sent word down the line for our men to arrange a similar device to carry us across. More waiting.

We decided there was no reason to wait inside the hallway so we came out into the air, dousing our torches to preserve them for later use.

By now daylight was fading, but as we thought about and discussed our next task we concluded that it didn't make much difference to what we had to do. We would be in the dark anyway.

Just at sunset a group of our men, along with some locals from the town, came bringing a ramp for us to use. I recognized some of the townsmen, and realized that in all the confusion of the battle I had not taken time to find out about my family. I asked one of the men if he knew anything.

"Your mother is fine, Kasher; your sisters, too. A number of us got together a few years ago and built a shelter in case of attack. Most of our women and children had time to escape there before the Egyptians attacked. The men stayed back and defended the city as long as we could, but we finally had to surrender. Several men died keeping the secret of the hiding place. More would have been killed if you hadn't come when you did. They were determined to find them. I'm sorry to tell you that your father was one of those killed. They tortured him to find out the location of the women and children, but he wouldn't talk – none of the men would. They saved many lives."

The news was bitter-sweet: my father was dead, but he died a hero.

"Thank you for telling me," I responded. "Where are the women and children now?"

"They've already come out of hiding. I saw your mother a little while ago. She was tending to your father's body."

"Kasher, go be with your family. They need you," Nakhti said.

I hesitated for a moment, and then said, "No. I have a job to finish. I will go to them when we are done with this."

"We both will, Kasher."

I had forgotten they were his family, too.

Swords drawn, torches lit, we headed back in with our bridge. It was wide enough for two men at least to cross at a time, but at this juncture, Muldan stepped forward.

"I will go first, Nakhti," he said quietly but firmly. "This will be a fearful moment, and the men need to see that their leader does not shrink from fear – not that he is exempt from it, you understand."

The light of the torches revealed a determined face, but there was something else there as well. Looking back I think he might have had a premonition of some sort.

Without another word he jumped down to the platform below us. There was a sort of collective gasp from the rest of us. By torchlight we saw he had landed just fine.

"Hand me the edge of the bridge and I will begin feeding it across to the other side," he commanded, his head just below the floor where we stood.

We did as he said, and he did the job without hesitation. That he was extremely strong for a man of his age was apparent.

Thankfully the men had made the bridge with a little extra length, so we were able to help some until it reached the other side. Then it was up to Muldan to get our end down and in place.

The ledge was precariously narrow for such an operation, and Muldan had to stand to one side of the spot where he would place the board. Just as he was about to set it down, an arrow came up from the abyss.

We heard it more than saw it, but we were all too familiar with the sound.

Muldan looked up at us, and as he did we saw the head of the arrow protruding through the collar of his tunic, jutting upwards next to his chin.

His look was not what I would have expected. He didn't even seem all that surprised. Instead, he set his face with grim determination and said, "Make them pay for this, Nakhti."

"I will, sir," Nakhti replied, raising himself to his full height.

More arrows pierced his body in rapid succession, and Muldan fell into the hole.

After just a moment's hesitation I tossed my torch into the hole. Immediately we saw several things: the space was made curving inward up to the ledge, which explained both why our light would not penetrate down into it and why we couldn't see the attacker (or attackers). It was also quite deep, probably fifteen or so cubits, which surprised me. My torch lay on the ground in the middle of the space. Muldan's lifeless body was a short distance away.

We saw Muldan was not shot until he leaned over the ledge because of the curvature of the walls. Someone else could – would have to – go down onto the ledge to take care of whoever was there. I turned and called for an archer. Several came forward immediately.

For a few moments we discussed a strategy for getting to the enemy. Time was not on our side, so we had to decide quickly.

Without asking permission I reached for a bow from one of the archer. He relented without protest. I never knew if it was out of relief or respect for me, but I was grateful.

"What are you doing?" Nakhti asked.

Without responding to him I reached over the shoulder of the archer sand removed three arrows. Nakhti began to rebuke me, but before he could say very much I was over the side.

"You don't even know how many there are!" Nakhti grunted.

"I am about to find out!" I smiled my response back up to him.

I knew Nakhti well enough to know he would not call me back. This was something he would have done if he had gotten to it before me.

I lay prone on the ledge, careful not to allow any part of my body stick over. Slowly, I moved the side of my head closer to the edge.

The first thing I saw was movement. A flash of something whizzed by my head. Someone down there was ready, and the nearness of the arrow as it went past my head told me this was no amateur.

That brief moment when I saw into the hole had registered a couple of important things. I was almost certain there was only one person, and that had to be good news. The other thing was that the wall did not go farther back in down there than it did up here, giving the assailant a small space from which to work – and in which to hide. I decided on a plan that would require cooperation and no small amount of courage.

I spoke to Nakhti in hushed tones, in case the enemy below could understand our speech.

After explaining what I had learned I said, "Send down four more archers. We will attack in force."

Quietly the three men joined me on the ledge. I explained what I had in mind.

"We will do this in three stages, each coming immediately following the last. There can be no delay between them or we will surely fail. First, you two (pointing to the men farthest from me, one on either side) will begin firing into the opposite wall, down below the ledge level. With any luck, we can actually hit the attacker with a ricochet. In any case, it should serve to distract his attention. As soon as the second arrow flies, I will run as fast as I can across the bridge. That should cause him some confusion and give you other two enough time to reach out over the ledge and shoot him."

"Obviously, there is a considerable risk for three of us. If either the two of you I have tasked with the kill are not willing to take that risk, tell me now, and I will replace you."

They were true soldiers. There was no hesitation, just as I had expected.

Before I could even position myself at the bridge they all had their arrows notched and ready. I looked left and right, then nodded.

I heard 'twang, twang, twang, and I was off as fast as I could move. As I reached the other side I realized I hadn't felt anything sharp entering my body. I hadn't even been aware of any projectiles whizzing by me as I ran. I hoped that that impression was correct.

I kept running until I was in the shadows, throwing myself to the floor before turning back toward the hole.

I saw immediately the attacker below; his bow now on the ground; a perplexed look on his face. He was still standing, supporting his back against the wall. I watched as he slowly slipped to a sitting position. His eyes told me he was no longer a threat.

Looking up to the ledge I saw that all the archers were smiling.

I motioned for them to come across the bridge to me. As soon as they cleared the ledge, others were taking their places, Nakhti in the lead.

Two men were posted at the doorway and two others on the ledge. The rest came across the bridge, and we started working our way forward.

Almost imperceptible at first, the floor sloped downward. As we went, it got steeper, finally ramping down in a very obvious way.

After a bit we came to a sharp bend to the left. It continued until we had reversed direction, still heading downward. There was light in front of us now. We were obviously headed for the archer's hole.

We began calling out to the sentries we had left behind. None of us wanted to surprise them. They responded, and we were able to move forward into the opening.

Some of the men took a moment to lay Muldan's body out in a dignified fashion. The rest of us were examining this odd room we were now in.

The opening we had just come through was almost impossible to see from the doorway above because of the slope of the wall. There did not seem to be another opening. Had we come to a dead end? And if so, where had the Egyptians gone to?

The room was plenty big enough for all of us to be in comfortably. We had ample room to move and to investigate the walls and floor for an opening, which we did. There didn't seem to be one.

The walls were completely smooth; so much so they actually seemed polished. There was no paint on them, but the light of our torches glared off their brilliant whiteness. This place had obviously been built a long time ago, and the tower was built on this white rock. We couldn't see if all the foundation was of the same rock, but everything we had seen certainly was.

We continued searching for an exit: tapping, beating, trying to dig into the rock. At one point Nakhti ordered everyone to be still and quiet. Then he ordered the sentries at the doorway to close the door. He stood in the center of the room and held his torch above his head.

There was a slight inclination of his torch's flame in the direction of the passageway we had followed here. He moved slowly back in that direction. The flame bent just a little farther that way when he reached the opening.

I followed him back into the tunnel. I was astounded when we reached the bend. There, on the floor, in plain sight, was a door.

"We were all so intent on getting to the source of the light when we rounded this turn, that we didn't see something so obvious," I said. "That needs to be a lesson for the rest of this adventure."

Nakhti just nodded and grunted. We both knelt to examine the hatch.

It wasn't hard to open. Seeing how long it had taken us to get to it, someone fleeing through it would have a good amount of time to get away anyway. I was beginning to think we would not catch them.

"They haven't gotten away, Kasher," Nakhti said, seeming to read my thoughts. "We have men stationed all around the city – even in the outer settlements. No

Egyptians have left the area. They are hiding somewhere, and I believe that somewhere is through here."

Shining a light into the opening we saw that it went almost vertically down, with only a slight curvature in one direction, like a sort of slide. We could not see the end of it, so we were going to have to make another leap into the unknown.

I started to go, but Nakhti caught my arm.

"Not this time, son. I need you to see this to the end."

I backed away, and another man took my place. He went through the opening without hesitation; sword in one hand, torch in the other.

After a short pause he called back for us to follow him.

"Now you can go, Kasher."

One by one we went down the ramp, each of us shouting back a signal for the next man as soon as the way was clear.

The slide ended in a large room.

Standing, we saw a vast, empty chamber. There was some light, but very little, and it entered the room in a very odd way. The roof was a very high dome, and there were tiny holes piercing through, placed at the edges of the ceiling; thin beams of light (presumable sunlight) slicing through the semi-darkness to form patterns on the floor. On one side there were two larger holes. From this distance they looked to be smaller than my fist. Immediately below them on the floor was a short pedestal, no more than half a cubit high.

As we entered cautiously, we saw - in that pale, eerie light - several doors in the walls of the round room. The ceiling appeared solid, so we were not concerned about

250

an attack from above. Nakhti gave silent orders, and his men began spreading around the room investigating.

I allowed my eyes to adjust to the room's light, looking away from any of the thin beams for a few seconds. Then, with a sudden twist of my head, I looked at the area of the larger holes.

I could only see the roof around the holes for a moment - before the brightness of the light coming denied my eyes the ability to see anything but the holes themselves - but in that moment I saw that those two holes were the eyes of a figure painted there. It looked like an owl.

Remembering the surprises we had already encountered since entering the tower, I decided to look in less obvious places than the others.

There was really nothing remarkable about the room apart from the fact that it seemed to be cut out of the same type of rock as the tunnel. As I worked my way slowly around the walls, I spied what seemed to be a vertical slit about eye level. It was almost invisible due, in the first place, to its thinness. It was also located in such a way that the poor lighting of the chamber did not shine on it.

I began feeling my way around its edges. Eventually (with no small trepidation), I began probing into the slit with the tips of my fingers.

As my finger reached the bottom of the opening, I recoiled as I felt something sharp. Recovering, I touched it again. It wasn't as sharp as I had thought; not enough to cut me, for certainly. I pulled a knife from my belt and began working at it, careful not to damage whatever it was.

A piece of clay tile emerged. It was almost as thin as papyrus, but it was definitely clay.

As I called softly to Nakhti, I noticed the jagged edge; no doubt the sharpness I had felt. I was not surprised to see it had broken. More surprising was that it could ever have been made!

There were small characters on it – some sort of writing. There was, in fact, quite a lot of writing on it. I did not recognize the script even though it was not completely dissimilar to my own language. I had already learned that different languages had a lot in common with each other. I wondered if that commonality meant there was an original source from which they had all sprung.

As Nakhti examined the writing over my shoulder he said something that seemed to fit well with my thoughts. "I think this is in the 'Ancient Language'."

"Can you read it?" I whispered.

"I was taught some of it as a child, but I wouldn't be able to decipher all of this, even if it were a complete text. There is one interesting word, though. Right here, in this corner. It appears that one word was scratched out – rather crudely – and another written over it. It says, 'Nimrod'."

Chapter 22

I'm tired of this stupid tower idea.

Father says there will be a great revelation from the heavens when it is completed, but I think he has chosen the wrong god to follow.

What do I really think this is all about? An old man trying to make sure he's not forgotten here when he has passed to the other world.

'Nimrod, the mighty hunter!'

It's already emblazoned on everything he owns, from city gates to the doors of the palace.

"Erech!"

There's no confusing that booming voice. Some people consider *him* to be a god. I think it is the power of his voice.

"Yes, father."

"Erech, your brother says you tried to get him to reveal the location of the instruction plate again. Even if he knew where it was, he wouldn't tell you."

Asshur, my twin brother, and I had been walking down parallel roads for some time now, ever since I chose to follow a god other than my father's. Always looking for more approval from the Mighty Hunter, Asshur was completely dedicated to Ishtar.

"I hate to do this, son, but you have worked against me for the last time. You need to leave my city at once."

I was shocked into silence. I had always been a thorn in my father's side – he didn't know half the story – but I never expected him to take such a harsh attitude. Even now I wouldn't let myself believe he would send me away from Nimrud.

"Father, what could I possibly have done for you to be this angry?"

There had been tense moments between us before and I had always been able to talk my way out of his ire. The look on his face caused me to doubt. Could he really send his baby boy away in anger?

"I knew you were against the tower, and I even had my suspicions you might be working to delay construction. But now I have been given proof that you are deliberately sabotaging my great work! You will be provided for, but you must go somewhere where we will no longer be in conflict."

"You're serious, Father? What have you been told? I assure you it is mere…"

"Silence!" he boomed, louder than I think I had ever heard. "You will not talk your way out of this one, Erech. I know what you are!"

"Keep quiet, boy. He can't know you are serving me. That is not what he is talking about. He knows about the sabotage, but he does not know the reason."

I wondered if Enlil was right, or if he simply wanted more time to find out himself. I had realized, quite a while ago really, that these gods did not know everything. They were powerful alright. Enlil had shown himself the most powerful and the most ruthless of them all, to me. But there were things he did not know. Some

254

things got past him. I believed this might be one of them. Nimrod might know I was serving a rival to his god.

Still, Enlil might be right. I could see no good purpose in revealing the fact if it was not yet known.

"Father, I don't know what you have heard, but you have obviously been misinformed. There was a time, sure, when I resented the tower. I didn't like it consuming all your time and attention. But I'm over all that now. I understand your need to build a monument to your great name."

"If that is all you see, you have not listened to anything I have said," continued Nimrod, his voice now strangely quiet. Did I detect a note of sadness in it? That was not something I could ever remember coming from the great man.

"No, Father. I remember all the talks: Seth passed the message of the stars down to Noah; Cush, your father, learned from Ishtar the 'Old Truth' about the message, something your cousin, Aram, a follower of Jehovah changed to suit his beliefs; Ishtar made the sacred Tablet of Destinies with the instructions engraved on it for the construction of the tower; Ishtar only reveals to you their meaning one phase at a time; The tower will prove the validity and power of the 'Old Truth', making Ishtar the chief goddess for all time."

"You heard, but you do not believe – no! Do not say any more! One of those you tried to corrupt to serve your purpose has told me all. You have purposed to thwart my project. You have rejected me and my goddess."

"There is a camel train waiting for you at the south gate. Go to it – now! And never be seen here again. I have given order that you are to be killed if you return."

Nimrod turned away, his head high, but it was obviously with great effort.

"*I have located the tablet. Tell Nimrod you need to get some things from the palace.*"

"I need some things from the palace."

"Be quick. You must leave today."

I ran to the palace. Daylight was already fading and I knew I needed to get some distance between myself and the city of Nimrod. He was not a man of idle words. The sentence of death was indeed upon me.

As I entered the main portico, Enlil began to lead me into parts of the palace I knew nothing about.

Nimrod was not a man to do things in a small way. The palace was enormous, with wings going in every direction imaginable.

I wound in and out of seemingly endless corridors until the voice told me to stop. I was in front of a statue; a representation of Ishtar with a lion's body.

"*Slide the statue to the left.*"

Doing so opened a shallow space below where the statue had sat. It that space was a clay tablet with writing on it.

I lifted it gently. It was very light, and I didn't want to break something that Enlil obviously held so dear. Holding in my left hand I used my right to slide the statue back into position.

"*We will leave a different way – it will be quicker.*"

Following his direction I turned to my left. There was an open door just a few paces ahead.

As I reached the door I was prevented from going through it by a figure who appeared out of nowhere. He had me by the arm before I could avoid him, and we spun together back into the corridor.

It was Asshur. I wanted to shout at Enlil for not warning me about him!

Asshur was screaming at me and pulling at the tablet. As we fought over it, it broke; one piece in my hand, and a slightly larger one in his.

With my free hand I landed a sharp blow to Asshur's temple. He went down hard. I reached for the other piece of the tablet, but he was still conscious and had a crocodile's grip on it. Frustrated, I turned to run.

I bolted for the door. Enlil was screaming in my ear, but my father's warning was louder at this moment. If I were caught like this, I would be killed for sure.

I could only hope that Asshur would be unconscious by now, or at least that I had made it difficult for him to get up. If he got to Nimrod before I got out of the city, I had no chance. I was convinced my loyal men would be at the camels and would fight for me if necessary; if I could get there in time.

I don't remember the run for the gate very well, but it seemed that Enlil did at least get one thing right. The door I came out of was very close to the gate where my caravan was waiting. I started shouting instructions as soon as I saw the first of my men.

It was probably as much their understanding of my father's ruthlessness that caused them not to question my pleas for speed as anything else. Whatever the reason, we were underway with no delay.

It was getting late, but there was no way we were stopping. We traveled all through the night. I had decided we would go south, but I didn't have any more than that to go on. To the north was mountainous, and I wanted to stay close to the life-sustaining rivers; so south it was.

At one point we lost the river, our reference for the journey.

Some of the men were familiar with the stars and were able to assure me we were headed in more or less the right direction. I was still very afraid. I could just imagine us accidentally heading back into the waiting wrath of my father.

I hadn't heard from Enlil since we left. I supposed he was angry with me now as well.

I started to shiver, partly from the cold, but the shock of everything that was happening was also starting to set in.

I was riding on a small wagon pulled by two mules. Off to my right I saw a flutter of movement. I ducked instinctively, pulling my cloak over my head.

Nothing happened. When I dared to look out I saw, perched on the yoke between the mules, a huge owl.

Even in the darkness I could see that the owl was pure white, something I had never seen before. There was a sheen to it that made it almost seem to glow.

It extended its right wing, just slightly. I adjusted the wagon a little in that direction; my left. I knew I was being ridiculous, but I had nothing else at this point. The owl was in charge.

The change in direction was the first of many, all subtle. The others never even noticed.

As the rays of the morning began to present themselves, I saw a small settlement ahead of us, on the banks a river. I recognized it as the Tigris.

The owl was gone. I never noticed it leave, but I was convinced it had brought us here on purpose.

We camped at daybreak; not unusual this time of year as the sun would soon be unbearable. We kept a respectful distance from the settlement so no one would be bothered by our presence.

I awoke after a few hours, the sun high in the sky. I had slept well knowing my men would have sentries out at all times. I was not expecting this event, but I had assembled a good group of soldiers knowing I would eventually need them one way or another.

There was no activity to be seen, so I slept again; not as well now - probably because of the heat.

In the late afternoon, I was roused by the sound of someone calling to me. It was Hulen, my captain. I had visitors.

"Welcome, great king!"

I had never been addressed thus before, but I accepted the title as if I heard it every day.

The man who had spoken had an air of one who told others what to do. There was deviousness in his eyes as well. He would bear watching closely.

"Please forgive our intrusion, my lord. We were weary from a long night's journey. We do not wish to cause you any difficulty," I said. The full truth of my situation was not for one such as him: at least not yet.

"You do us honor by sojourning here, my king. We would serve you in any way necessary."

"You name, friend?" By dropping the title 'lord' I was trying to see how far he was willing to let me assume the title he had so easily bestowed upon me.

"I am called Eber, my lord. Of the line of Shem, recently coming to this place because of - shall we say - misunderstandings with my brethren."

I needed to continue our journey as quickly as possible. I believed Nimrod when he said I was free to go, but I didn't trust Erech at this point; especially after the festivities accompanying my departure.

Father had provisioned us fairly well, but at some point we would need alliances for protection and trade. Based on his comments, I wondered if Eber was supplied enough to be of any use; not to even speak of his trustworthiness. I simply didn't know him.

"I have already been informed, my king, as to your person. Your captain has enlightened me concerning your pilgrimage to begin a new kingdom in the south."

I was very pleased with Hulen at that moment. He had shown a keen sense of loyalty and a great ability to protect me with that story. He was a wise man.

Eber continued, "As I said, we came here a short time ago, and as such we have no real ties here. Perhaps we could join your quest? I can promise you absolute loyalty. My band on its own would not be very safe travelling to new lands, but in your service, we would all be gain from increased safety."

"How do you know you can trust me, friend? We have only just met."

"Yes, my lord, but are you not the son of the great Nimrod?"

"Indeed. Very well, then, how do I know I can trust you?"

"If it please the king, we would entertain you and all your men this evening. I believe that by tomorrow's dawning we will have proven our loyalty."

"Let me have a word with my captain before I answer you. If we are to accept, you will receive my emissary in one hour's time. Good-day, Eber."

He was a man who understood the ways of diplomacy, and so he retired from my presence bowing his way to his waiting camel.

I called for Hulen to get his understanding of the question.

"My men have been watching the settlement since we arrived," he said in response to my queries. "There are only about twenty men of soldiering age and condition. They look capable, but we need not fear they could overwhelm our ninety-plus band. I can post men around the festivities discreetly, and we would all go armed and alert. It would be a great help to find an ally so early in our move, don't you think?"

"Of course, Hulen, but they must be proven. Very well, we will go as you say."

The Shemites had a reputation for being somewhat reserved. Some called it arrogance. Shem himself, they said, was the favorite of his father, and that favoritism caused a rift between the three clans.

This particular band of Shemites did not live up, however, to the reputation for calmness.

No sooner had we arrived in their encampment than we were regaled with loud music, and women dancing around a huge fire. Some sort of drink was being passed around. When it got to me, I took a whiff. Just the smell of it was strong enough to make your head spin. I took a small drink to be polite and quickly passed it along.

Eber was ebullient. He was not being particularly crude (not yet, at least), but his spirit was soaring above the party, mingling with the sparks from the fire. He danced with one after another of the women, seemingly tireless as he sprinted around them in a fury. I had never seen such a display, and didn't really know how to interpret it. I could only assume this was normal for him.

Another man, about the same age as Eber came to my side and began speaking over the din of the trumpets and drums.

"He gets carried away when he has had too much beer. He's harmless, though. Makes the occasional pass at a woman he shouldn't, but as soon as he is rebuked he leaves her alone."

"Beer. That was that foul liquid that came my way?"

"Your first experience with Nikasi's magic, eh? She's the goddess who showed us mortals how to make it."

His smile was infectious, and I liked his way. I decided to trust him; at least a little.

"Yes, my first. It is fermented, of that I am sure, but it is nothing like wine! Even vinegar is less abusive!"

He laughed loud enough to call the attention of several of my men; even over the noise of the party. They reacted by moving in my direction, hands reaching for weapons.

I held up my hand to reassure them, and they retreated. I was glad they were so attentive, but I didn't feel threatened.

"Your name, sir, if I may," I asked of my new friend.

"Gamesh, my lord. At your service."

"And what, may I ask, is your function in this little band?"

"I am, primarily, a chronicler, sire. I lend a hand at whatever needs doing - as do we all - but Eber has big plans for our 'little band'. He wants the story to be told throughout time. He says that will be his immortality, having others read about him."

His talk of big plans unnerved me a bit. But it could be a positive thing for us, Eber's ambition; as long as I could keep mine just one place above his in the order of our priorities and outcome. It would be a tense partnership to be sure, not unlike that of a lion and a jackal. I had to be sure I would always be the lion.

The merriment lasted well into the night. There was food, music, dance and much conversation. My principal soldiers did not partake of any of it. They were very disciplined and knew their business. Some of them stayed at the perimeter, alternately facing inward and outward from the settlement. Others mingled within the area of festivities, seemingly involved in the party, but I knew they were not inebriated. They were alert for any problem that might arise.

Several had been stationed near me, never moving from their positions. I noticed some of them being enticed by pretty girls. They gave them some attention, but always without giving up their stations.

Hulen had been at my side the entire time, and I turned to him.

"So, what is your assessment? I asked him.

"I think there is potential for an alliance, my lord. True soldiers are few among them but they seem to know how to stay well supplied; if this party is any indication at least. In any case, there is great value in simply increasing our numbers. It makes an attack less likely."

"So you think we should ask them to join us?"

"Only with a clear understanding of our preeminence. That shouldn't be too hard. They need us more than we need them."

"Agreed," I said, thoughtfully. I was still thinking about my conversation with Gamesh. The fact that I was

Nimrod's son was not enough to guarantee my position any more. I had left those days behind at the tower.

The night wore on. I was anxious to put the city of Nimrod farther behind us, but if this alliance was to be made, I would have to be patient. We had scouts watching back along the path we had come, and we would be warned in good time of any approaching danger.

Hulen took me by the arm and led me to a circle of men, very animated about whatever they were looking at. There was a small earthen mound just to one side of them which we mounted to be able to see inside the circle.

We looked down upon a huge scorpion and a camel spider circling each other, searching for an opportunity to strike.

I was impressed by their patience. The scorpion's tail was poised to strike, and the spider was crouched as it moved, looking for the best moment to pounce. This went on for a long time until, finally, the spider got a little too close, and the scorpion launched its deadly tail with incredible speed.

I thought the grim spectacle was over, but we were to be treated to a still starker picture of the cruelty of this world.

The spider, with the scorpion's stinger still imbedded in its back, managed to somehow get its front legs on the scorpion, and, before succumbing to the venom, bit down on its head with all its might. The two creatures lay dead or dying within moments.

As I stood there contemplating the cruelty of fate these animals had suffered – a conflict which left no victor - I could not help making a comparison to my brother and me.

The show had apparently not had the same effect on my host. He tugged at my arm once again, this time pulling me towards the central bonfire. I noticed immediately the presence of quite a few women there.

It was a distraction; a nice one, to be sure, as there were none travelling with us. Still, distractions are not conducive to clear thought; and I, above all my men, needed to be thinking clearly at this time. There were several advances from lovely young ladies but I resisted the temptation.

One of them in particular really caught my eye. It was as if the light from the fire was reflected in her eyes. Once, when she came near me, I saw that her eyes were green. Not like grass; paler, but without losing any strength. When she turned away from me (I confess I watched those eyes until they were no longer visible to me) I saw the fire dance in them once again. The red of the flames on that green made an unforgettable impression.

I allowed myself to indulge in the food that was made available, but drank the beer carefully, sipping enough not to offend my hosts (they were very proud of their beer) but not enough for my senses to be affected. I knew my men were doing the same.

It was well into the night when we made our way back to our camp. Eber had halfheartedly insisted we stay longer, but it was obvious to everyone when the festivities were ended.

The next day we kept to ourselves until late in the afternoon. I gathered Hulen and other lesser leaders of our band, and we discussed the situation that had presented itself to us. We were all in agreement that we would be well served to have Eber and his clan with us.

We were also unanimous in our opinion that he was not to be trusted implicitly. With the proper measure of caution, we were convinced we could gain from this alliance.

In a move designed to accentuate my elevated position in this venture I decided not to go to Eber myself with the offer. Hulen would be my emissary. He left camp as the sun sank low into the desert sand.

As I waited for his return I saw movement out of the corner of my eye. Turning my head, I saw something flying toward my tent out of the setting sun.

I had not mentioned the owl event of the other night to anyone. I wasn't sure if it was a dream, a hallucination or if it was in fact real. I felt a chill as I recognized the figure coming towards me as an owl – the same owl, I believed, with all my heart.

In those few, quickly passing moments before the owl got close I felt an icy chill in my spine. How could I expect to know that it was the same owl? But, there it was; I knew it was the same one.

I was frozen where I sat. The owl landed directly in front of me, almost near enough for me to touch. It looked like an ordinary owl, but there was something very different about it that its appearance alone didn't reveal.

Our eyes met, and I heard a voice. It didn't seem to come from the owl, and yet it did. There was no logical explanation, but I was being spoken to.

"We've spent so much time together; talking, planning; working on our mutual future. And yet you don't even recognize me when I take a visible form. I'm disappointed, Erech."

It was Enlil! I knew the voice, though it sounded different now. I said as much.

"Yes, you see, when you took up my cause (to the point of defying your father and his worship of Ishtar) you increased my power. I have new abilities; physical ones even. It would have been much more if we had gotten the whole tablet, but even that piece that broke off holds great influence."

"But you're an *owl!*"

"For now, yes. When our work is done, I will finally be able to take on human form. The owl suits me for the present. I needed a host with certain characteristics. Flying is very helpful."

The owl fluttered its wings, giving me a start.

"I must go now. Continue your journey to the south tomorrow morning. I will find you in the next few days. I must conduct a search in this area before I rejoin you."

With that the owl was gone, flying back the way it had come. The experience left me drained of all energy.

I sat there, just staring into the sunset.

A voice shook me from my trance. Turning to look behind me I saw Hulen walking toward me.

"Is everything alright, my king? You look troubled."

I cleared my throat and tried to seem like all was normal. "Yes, Hulen; thank you. I seem to have dozed off. The sunset is so peaceful it must have lulled me to sleep. How did the talk with Eber go?" I asked, eager to change the subject. I was pretty sure of the answer.

"They are ready to move with us on short notice, sire. I took the liberty of saying we would depart in the morning. Of course, if that is not your wish…"

"No, that is perfect, Hulen. Thank you for your service. We should prepare!"

I rose and started organizing my personal belongings. Hulen took the cue and went to inform the men.

In the morning, my men and I were greeted by a caravan ready to travel. There was an obvious and impressive order to it.

Eber was not at the lead, but was behind four armed men mounted on horses; he, himself, was astride a camel, a handler holder the reigns.

The camel was made to kneel and Eber descended with the grace of a king. I began to worry when his four horsemen parted their mounts and lowered their heads at his passing. Such pomp! Would there be a challenge to my leadership from this man?

My worries abated when Eber approached. He stopped several paces from my position and went down on one knee, his head low.

This was done in sight of all his people, and the intent was clear to anyone watching. Eber, and all he commanded, was mine.

We followed the river southward for three days without making camp. We would travel through the night and rest for a few hours during the day's heat. If any of Eber's group was troubled by our pace or travel method they kept it to themselves. There were (amazingly, now that we had women and children with us) no delays. When I declared it was time to move on, everyone was ready.

At the end of our morning trek on the fourth day we encountered a place that was too good to simply pass by.

None of us knew anything about this area. I suppose we should have expected something like we were now seeing, but it seemed to take us all by surprise.

It was a city – or at least it had been one sometime in the past. There were walls encircling an area of considerable size. They looked as though they had been eaten away from the top. They were certainly too low to be of any real defensive use, but they had been built well, and so stood in spite of their mistreatment.

I had no doubt about what had happened to them. My father had a close relationship with his grandfather, Ham until his death a few years ago. Ham's father, Noah, almost outlived him, and my father knew him also, but only casually.

These walls had survived the great flood.

We entered the city cautiously, but there was no movement other than the odd jackal or crow darting between the other ruins that were left.

Walking around the inside of the walls I found an inscription cut into one of the blocks. It must have been deeply etched, I thought, to have survived the flood. There was only one word I could really make out. It said, 'Babil'.

"This is it!" I declared to Hulen. "Our new home. It is called, 'Babil!"

Chapter 23

The next few months were spent rebuilding the basic structure of the city. It was much too large for the number of people, so we concentrated on a certain area.

Within the outer city walls were several divisions still discernible. One in particular, at about the center of the city, had walls almost as good as the outer ones. I decided to make that our starting point.

Besides the practical reasons, this area had some sort of draw for me that I couldn't completely understand. There was a large foundation at one edge of the enclosure. Only the foundation itself remained, and I wondered what it might have been.

I thought of my father's palace, but this was very unlike it. The palace I knew was a sprawling affair: there were wings going in every direction it seemed, many times joined by open courtyards. I couldn't imagine a square base like the one before me relating to that.

I surmised it must be a palace. I began having dreams almost every night in which Enlil came to me (always in the form of an owl now). He instructed me to build on that foundation and to make that construction a priority.

I fought the idea for several weeks. I wanted my people to respect me, and putting a place of worship ahead of their own safety and comfort did not sound like the best way to do it to me. One night I said as much to the owl in my dreams.

"Erech, you need to understand your place in the grand scheme of things," Enlil began. You are now a king in your own right, having assumed your position apart from your father's kingdom. The world is in transition. The Flood left a vacuum for dominion. You mortal kings come and go. Without my help, the best you can hope for is to be remembered for your wisdom, or daring; maybe even both. But then you are gone. I, on the other hand will still be around! So you see, how you think is not nearly as important as what I tell you. This will be a great tower in my honor. Now, GO BUILD MY TEMPLE!"

As the last words were uttered, the owl's face (indeed, his whole self) was momentarily transformed. What I glimpsed, just for a moment, was a terrifying being, something I could never have imagined on my own.

I saw a rage that I cannot describe, yet I had the impression that rage was not directed totally at me. It seemed the principal emotion coming my way was one of irritation, much as one might have towards a child who couldn't understand an adult concept. I had to confess that I felt a bit like that child. Some pieces of the puzzle that was Enlil (and other gods, too, for that matter) seemed to be coming together in my mind, but it was a laborious process. This last revelation of himself to me caused me to believe I knew something more about him.

That rage – almost directed at no one, yet so powerful and all-consuming: that seemed to be his reality. All the rest was manipulation; an attempt to right some perceived wrong.

I did not respond to his outburst, partly out of fear; but there was more. I was waiting to see where all this would lead.

Did he say tower?

The owl was silent for a long moment. Then he spoke, much calmer now.

"Do you understand, Erech, that I am a god?"

"Yes, of course I do."

"You probably don't know this, but there is, in our realm a spiritual struggle going on that parallels your mortal world. We gods can be very beneficial to you mortal kings, but our help is not without cost. If you would truly be great, dedicate yourself to my cause."

"May I ask what your cause really is?" I asked, fearing another burst of anger, but unable to contain my curiosity at this point.

The owl's feather's remained unruffled this time. He spoke evenly, but with great force and conviction.

"I shall overthrow first Marduk, then Lucifer, and then Jehovah himself. I will become the King of kings, the Lord of lords; the God above all gods."

This was indeed a revelation to me. I knew of several gods, but I assumed (as in fact I had been taught) that they were all working more or less together. I had never heard that they were in any sort of rivalry.

"You are young," he continued, seeming to sense my confusion, "and you come from a time when much has changed. Before the flood, things were much clearer. Each of the gods had men through whom they influenced world events. I have had my kings; men who saw how much I had to offer if they would be used by me."

"Then Jehovah brought the rains. Everyone loyal to me, and to the other gods, was wiped from the face of the earth. He has tried to stop us before, but we don't go down easily."

"The flood complicated things, but I see it as an opportunity. We all hate Jehovah. He has always expected absolute obedience to him and his plans. The flood showed how weak Marduk really is in comparison to him. It is my time to rise up. I will be the Exalted One! And you have the opportunity to be my king."

The tone in his voice left no room for doubt. He was not saying "my king" as a subject. He meant mine in the sense of possession. I was more afraid of him than I had ever been, but I felt that few choices were now left to my volition. I began to believe there was no turning back.

Finally, after several moments of pure mental agony, I regained enough composure to ask a question. I mustered up as much bluster as I could and said, "So, what do I have to gain from this arrangement?"

I fought to not step back a pace, but I feared some sort of retaliation at my impertinence. Instead, the owl spoke in a most kind tone.

"Why do you think all these people have gathered around you? Does it really appear so random to you? Do you not see that I have been assembling my troops since before I revealed myself to you? You are part of a grand plan."

"You will be *Zaluti*, the champion; part man and part god; immortal. You will lead a coalition of humans; leaders in their own right, they will still bow to you. You will make *Umman Manda*, the host of Manda (my royal seat) a reality!

"My world, Erech, is the next - and last - one you will have to deal with. We gods have always lived in the realm of spiritual things, entering and exiting your world

273

as we will. Your time as a mortal will end someday, and you would do well to look to your position in the afterlife. I can help you with that. I'm already there, after all."

"I can offer you power on earth; and, if you serve me well, I can actually make you completely a god at the end of your earthly sojourn. Does that not interest you, Kasher?"

"A god?" I asked, incredulously. One can be *made* a god? I thought gods were eternal – no beginning, no end."

"Jehovah claims that condition for himself, but no one else has that much audacity. Most of the gods you have heard about are either offspring of us major gods or humans we have transformed in the afterlife."

"And you are saying there is a conflict for dominance in your realm?"

"Absolutely! One I intend to win."

The temple was being built. Enlil communicated to me the plans as we went. At the same time, he seemed dependent on me for some of the planning. He said we had to proceed, in part at least, based on things written on the piece I had broken off the Tablet of Destinies in the struggle with my brother.

The irony did not escape me. What had driven me out of the city of Nimrod was the conflict with my father and brother over their tower, and now I was building one just like it.

It seems that, first of all, the part I got explained some important details pertaining to a certain type of construction. The second revelation it brought was that, apparently, gods couldn't read; at least not the writing on that tablet!

Enlil would never give me any explanation. He simply commanded me to read it to him, and we followed its instructions. I wasn't brave enough to try and use that information against him; not yet at least. He was a god, after all.

I was able to decipher enough from my piece of the tablet to understand the basic dimensions of the temple we were to build. I was able to read clearly the size and orientation of the base: exactly like the one we had found in the compound.

I had no idea where all this information went back to, but there was an obvious connection to the past. Enlil either didn't know himself or simply didn't want me to know. He refused to even discuss it with me.

My god became irritable even as we worked on a temple for him. After about two months, he appeared to me at the end of a long work day. His owl face showed no emotion but I had come to know him well enough to tell from his posture that something was wrong.

I was tired; exhausted even, from these long weeks of temple construction combined with trying to organize Babil into something that resembled a city. I was in no mood for a divine temper tantrum, and I almost said so as he appeared before me.

Something made me hesitate, and I waited for him to speak. What I heard was more frustration than anger. He actually sounded tired as well. I wondered if gods got tired.

"It appears there's not enough information on our fragment to tell us how to complete the tower, is that correct, Erech?"

"That's right. We have some basic measurements, starting with the base, and we have been able to extrapolate from that some of the other levels. We will not be able to get detailed information about the rest of the tower from it.

"I was able to understand most of what was required for the internal part of the tower, and that which I did understand has been completed, with a small touch added by me."

"What are you talking about, Erech? You dare to deviate from the instructions?"

"It's not really a deviation – more like an artistic addition, changing no functionality. On the domed ceiling of the first level there are small holes drilled, according to the instructions, leading to the outside. Two of them inspired me to make them the eyes of an owl, which I had etched into the plaster. I thought you would be pleased."

"Very well. That does not seem to alter anything crucial. I wish the rest of the construction could proceed as easily as that."

"But it's your temple. You can have it however you want it!"

"If only that were true, Erech. What you don't understand is that this tower, like the one your father is building, is not just aesthetic – it has a very important function that it cannot perform unless it is built correctly."

"What function is that? If we know that we can try to get it accomplished."

"You cannot know its function. I don't even know all of it, and only if completely constructed according to the pattern can all be seen clearly. So far, it has not been done. The base you found here was an ancient attempt, but Jehovah put an end to it like he has so many great things. I must have the rest of the tablet!"

He was gone. Enlil didn't reappear for a long time. I wondered if he had given up, but that seemed unlikely given his passion for the tower. What was the power these constructions had over men and gods? Whatever it was, I was relieved not to have to think about mine, at least for the present. I put it as far out of my mind as I possibly could and set about rebuilding the city.

Enlil was not forgotten, however. A king needs to be connected to a deity, after all. How can a mere mortal hope to lead and protect his people?

Regular worship of Enlil was begun as soon as there was a sense of stability in our new city. The tower had reached its seventh level. We had no instruction as to how it was to be used, but I knew how important religion was to people, so I ordered a modest altar built in front of it.

I appointed Gamesh, Eber's chronicler, to be our first high priest. His charisma was without question and he had proven a loyal subject.

I had no intention of letting him, or any other priest, gain too much power over the people, so I remained involved in the worship process personally.

No one but me had heard the owl talk, but several people had seen us together, and they no doubt saw me talking to him. I couldn't tell them that our god had abandoned us, so I had an owl captured, and I communed with it on a daily basis, high upon the seventh story of the tower. I was a little concerned that Enlil might take offence, but there was still no word from him.

I commissioned a man to create two identical owl sculptures. These I had placed facing each other on either side of the altar. In the back of my mind it seemed I had seen a drawing of just such a configuration; not with owls, but some sort of winged beings. In any case, it looked very religious.

I decided that being king should have some personal benefits, so I declared that Enlil had proclaimed me his direct representative on earth, and that he would direct me as to the development of our religion.

The gods are notoriously sensual in nature, so why shouldn't a god's representative be? If I was to faithfully represent Enlil, there would have to be women involved in our worship.

I had married earlier that year, a marriage that sealed an alliance with a powerful tribal leader who came our way from a nearby town. My new wife, Ornah was pleasant enough, but I was a king! Surely a king should have access to more than one woman.

The girl with the green eyes (one of Eber's daughters, it turned out) had been on my mind for quite a while. I went to talk with him.

"Eber, I would like to offer your family a prominent role in the new worship scheme. Enlil has indicated he would like for Khala to be our high priestess."

"We are indeed honored by this word, my king. Might I be permitted to ask what her duties would be?"

"Certainly, my old friend. She would attend to the maintenance of the altar area and any future worship instruments Enlil commands to be included. She would have an easy life; well taken care of, I assure you. She would also be dedicated to the ritual mating with me, representing Enlil's union with Ishtar. I promise I would be kind to her, but she would have to be dedicated, sexually, only to that function."

"The prestige you offer is impossible for me to refuse, sire. It shall be done as Enlill directs."

I ordered a small but very ornate and comfortable house to be built against the wall of the inner compound. The front door of it faced the altar and the tower beyond.

On the day of its completion, I went personally to Eber's house to fetch Khala. She appeared instantly when her father called for her. Without conversation, Eber took her hand and placed it in mine.

Her face was covered with a veil, so I could not read her expression. I was excited as I thought of lying with her, but I hoped it would be more than just a duty for her. I had enough experience to know how much more pleasure was derived from the act when both parties were glad participants.

I had ordered an assembly before the altar, and there, at my instruction, Gamish, our new high priest, declared that Enlil would consecrate the new house by consummating his union with his consort Ishtar. The people had already been instructed as to what that would mean.

I had not ordered my wife to be present, but I saw she was in the processional way created by the crowd, leading from the altar to the priestess' house. As we passed by her, she bowed dutifully. I did not see any hint of anger in her, and I thought myself lucky to have a wife like her.

We disappeared into the house alone, Khala and I. There was a luxurious bed in the middle of the entry room. Two doors led off that room, one to our left, the other to the back of the house.

A small table, against the wall on the right, held a small incense pot, and it was emitting a tiny wisp of smoke. The effect was felt in two senses at once. The odor was sweet and bitter at the same time. There was not enough of it to be overpowering, just as the visual effect was minimal but very real at the same time.

There were tapestries on the walls; kingly stuff, mostly. Great hunting scenes and royal processions were woven into what appeared to be flaxen rugs.

In each corner of the room was an oil lamp, each of them the same shade of green as Khala's eyes. They were lit, and it dawned on me that there were no windows, at least not in this room. The lighting from the lamps was as perfect as I could imagine for the purpose of the room.

There were clothes laid out on the bed, obviously for my priestess. She also understood, and bent gracefully to retrieve them. She made her way to the door at the back and went through it, pulling the curtain closed behind her.

I just stood where I was. I had always enjoyed spending time with a woman, but this was a special moment. Someone had gone to great lengths to make this moment entirely about one thing.

I wondered, again, how Khala would react to all of this. I knew as soon as she reappeared through the doorway. She was mine in every sense of the word.

I slept late the next morning. Throughout the night Enlil and Ishtar grew very close to one another, but I awoke alone.

I dressed slowly, partly to see if Khala would come in to see me before I left the house. She did not. I was disappointed, but realized it was probably the best way to establish our new relationship. We were not going to live

280

together as man and wife. We had accomplished what had been decreed.

Later that day, I found the man I had put in charge of building the sacred house.

"Who took care of the furnishing of it?" I asked.

"Your wife, sire - I understood you had sent her."

I hadn't, and this news was a shock to me. I tried not to show it as I asked, "did she say anything while she was there?"

"It's interesting you should ask that, sire. One of my men told me about overhearing a conversation she had with one of her attendants while they were decorating the house. The girl asked her if she didn't mind doing it, considering the house's purpose."

"And what did she say?"

"She said, 'I am the wife of a king. I expect to be the wife of a great king someday. The path to greatness requires sacrifice."

Three years had passed since I last spoke with the owl. The city was well advanced now; almost comfortable.

The new conditions had attracted other people to the city. Most were Shemites, like Eber and his clan. They were sometimes hesitant to kneel before a Hamite king, but the combination of Eber's presence, combined with the fact that Babil was, by far, the most developed population center for a long ways in any direction, caused many to join us. There had been no major trouble, and my position as sovereign was gaining strength steadily.

My army had not grown much in our time here. Still, we had not suffered any security problems so far.

Neither Hulen nor I felt comfortable enough with the Shemites to have them armed in our presence. Occasionally a small Hamite band would come to us, and, as often as possible, their able-bodied men would be included in the army. None of the others seemed to mind – probably glad not to have to serve that way themselves.

And then everything changed.

I was awakened abruptly in the early morning by Hulen, accompanied by several of his soldiers.

"There is only one course of action, sire. We must flee."

I was quickly brought up to speed, and I thought I must still be asleep and having an incredibly bad dream.

"You're sure – it's my brother?"

"Yes, sire. There is no doubt. And the army he has with him... we wouldn't stand a chance, sire."

"But our citizens! The *Umman Manda!* Surely they will join us to save their homes."

"We can try to mobilize them, my lord, but even if they are with us, they aren't soldiers! There's no time to train them, and their loyalty may not be as strong as we would hope."

"How much time before an attack is upon us?" I asked.

"We estimate they will be in position to attack, or at least lay siege, the day after tomorrow."

"Then we will talk to the people before we make any final decision. Let me dress, and we will go out to them."

"May my men at least begin preparations while we talk?" asked Hulen.

"Just make sure they are discreet. I don't want any panic."

We quickly assembled the leaders of the city. It became clear very early that they would not fight.

As I left them I was disgusted and deflated. Everything I had worked for these past few years would be lost to me.

I had to be practical, this I knew; so I summoned up as much courage as I could still find and spoke with Hulen about preparations.

As we were talking, we were interrupted. It was Eber, with Gamesh at his side.

"Sire, my people are not willing to try to fight off your brother's forces, but they would go with you, and I think we can convince some of the others to join us."

I looked at Gamesh who smiled broadly at me.

"You will need a priest, my lord… and a chronicler!"

I couldn't help but smile with him.

"Very well, but you must get them ready quickly! We can't afford to wait beyond tomorrow morning. Gamesh, a word alone, if you please."

"Gamesh, I need to speak to you about your daughter."

"You speak of the high priestess, my lord?"

"Yes, Gamesh; Khala. I need to ask her a difficult thing."

"My lord, you need not ask of her – or anyone – anything. She is yours to command, as we all are."

"But she is your daughter."

"No more, my lord. She is your high priestess; nothing more."

While everyone else was busy bundling their possessions I went to the house.

"You've been informed?"

"I have, my king, and I am ready."

"I have a request to make of you, Khala. I feel awful asking it of you, but I believe it is necessary."

"If Enlil commands, I must obey."

"Khala, I have told no one of this, but I believe you should know. Enlil left off communicating with me quite a while ago – even before I brought you here."

"Then I serve you alone, my king. In truth, it is how it has always been. I am yours completely, and it pleases me beyond explanation that I am."

"Your words make my request even harder to make. Please, Khala, know that you are very special to me, and that what I ask is so that one day we may be together in an even greater way."

"I am yours, my king. A request is a command to be obeyed, no matter what it is or for what reason."

"Khala, I can't reveal myself to anyone else like I am doing with you right now. And I must do so, because I could not leave any doubt in your mind. I care for you too much to do that."

"This attack has shown me just how weak I really am. I have been able to make it on my own to a certain level of power, but if I am to ever be truly great, I must have a god on my side. I need Enlil back with me."

"He left me because we could not finish his temple according to all that was given as to its construction. There is a tablet, passed down from some god in the past, with directions on how these towers are to be built. I have a small piece of it; my brother has the rest. I am convinced he is here to try to get the part I have, and, if I am right, he will be bringing his piece of the tablet with him, no doubt intending to finish my tower when he puts the tablet back together."

"How can I help, my lord?"

"I need you to stay behind. I need you to convince my brother that you are dedicated to the gods, not to me. Then, when you have his trust, I need you to get me his part of the tablet, and bring it to me. Only when I have the entire Tablet of Destinies will Enlil return to us, and you and I can be together forever."

Chapter 24

I was unsure if our safe departure from Babil was due to our swift action or just because my brother's true and final aim was to take the city from me. Whatever the reason, we did not seem to be pursued.

About half of the people stayed. Most of those who came with us I had no reason to trust, but they came thinking it was in their best interests, so they could still be useful.

We followed the Euphrates southward. Our progress was slow due to our numbers, the amount of goods we carried and concerns for our safety.

As we travelled, small to medium-sized groups of people joined us. We were careful about who we let in. I had not been outside the city much for a long time, but I had heard the reports of lawlessness going on in the region. I understood the desire of these joining us to be a part of a large party, and the larger we got, the safer I felt.

At the end of the fourth day's journey we came to the edge of something unlike anything I had ever seen. The river was to our right, but now there was water in front of us as well.

Water, but not a river, or even a lake exactly. There were reeds growing all through this body of water, as far as we could see in front of us. The edges of it extended a long way to our left and mingled with the river bank to our right.

The area we had crossed on our approach to this reed swamp was a fairly level piece of ground, a couple of cubits higher than the water level, and covering an area about three times the size of Babil.

As we could not proceed directly forward I decided we would make camp where we were.

After consulting with my military leaders, and several of the other leaders of the tribes with travelling with us I decreed we would begin to build a new city on this spot.

Hulen assured me that we had not been followed at all since leaving Babil. We would, of course, be vigilant against an attack from my brother or anyone else, but this seemed as safe a place as any we were likely to find. The river on one side would give some protection, and the swamp would serve as a natural barrier against intruders. At least that's what we thought.

Tired from travel, we slept soundly that night. Hulen had men posted at our perimeters and no one was terribly worried we would be attacked.

We were not attacked, but we awoke to a surprise.

I was approached at daybreak by a large and loud group of men from our group. They had been robbed in the night.

Hulen was there in the mix, trying to restore calm. It was obvious they would only listen to me, and even that was not an easy thing to accomplish. In time I was able to extract some more information, and it was distressing.

"I had a strong perimeter guard everywhere but at the edge of the swamp, sire. I had men there, but not a lot as

I was convinced it offered safety in and of itself! It appears I was wrong."

There were jeers from the assembly, and some started calling for discipline against Hulen. I quieted them once more and addressed myself to them and their concerns.

"An error was made, but let's be fair. None of us believed a threat would come from the reeds. Hulen! Figure this out without delay!"

His solution was to increase the guard at the swamp, but to do so subtly in an attempt to lure in the thieves. His plan worked perfectly.

The middle of the night found us heading toward a commotion at the edge of the reeds. When I arrived I had to force my way through the already assembled crowd. As word spread forward through the throng, way was made for me to pass so that I finally ended up in the middle of the confusion.

A squad of ten or twelve soldiers had their swords drawn and pressed into the bellies of four men.

At least they seemed to be men. A quick assessment of them left me with some doubts until one of the soldiers, seeing my arrival, reached forward and pulled something off the head of one of the prisoners.

Until he did so, I could not make out many features of these prisoners that would lead me to believe they were human. Mostly, what I saw was reeds!

The soldier had taken off what turned out to be a sort of headdress. It was made of short reeds, the top part with green leaves. The rest of their bodies were covered by reeds lashed to them. I approached the one who was now uncovered, and asked him who he was.

Silence.

The soldier made to strike him, but I staid his hand. I continued questioning the reed-man. There was no answer forthcoming. I leaned in to him and stared deeply into his eyes. I saw two things: understanding and determination.

"So, my friend, you do know what I am saying, but you will not talk to me. That's alright, but this thieving must end, and, what has already been taken must be returned. If you can make that happen, I think we can live in peace with each other."

He cocked his head slightly to one side, and the thinnest of smiles appeared on his lips.

"Release this one and bring the others to the center of the camp," I said. Turning to the crowd I proclaimed, "Now we sleep! Let us see what the morning brings."

I turned to see the swamp man putting on his head gear. Without a word or gesture he took three quick, graceful (I could not see how, dressed as he was) steps and disappeared into the swamp.

The following morning, all the items stolen were lying just where he had disappeared. I ordered the other prisoners unceremoniously released, and they left just as the other had. I believed we had made a large step forward in establishing ourselves in this new place – much more than any armed conflict could have achieved.

Days turned into weeks; weeks into months. We were all so busy with the new that the old no longer seemed very important. Once in a while a sentry would report that he believed he had seen a scouting party from Babil, but there was never any confirmation. And even if it were true it would not be an unusual thing. We ourselves had watchers at Babil and other communities as a matter of course.

And then one night, the past came knocking at our door in a very vivid way.

Hulen himself was doing the knocking, at my personal door at least. I went out to him and the scene before me I could not have anticipated.

There, between two other soldiers, was a woman. The most emaciated human being I had ever laid eyes on. Her head was down, but much of her pitiful body was visible through the rags of the robe she wore.

"What, Hulen? Why is this poor creature brought before me?"

Without a word he reached down and lifted her head so I could see her face. She was almost unrecognizable so sunken were her features, but there was no doubt about her identity.

It was Khala.

I called for my servants who immediately took charge of here care. I waited anxiously for a few minutes for them to get her into a bed and see to her comfort. When I could hold back no longer, I went to her side.

"Khala, what has happened to you?"

I could see more of her devastation now in good light, and it filled me with horror. It seemed impossible that she could be alive in this condition.

She seemed too weak to speak, but she mustered up enough strength to point to a bag that was tied to her girdle. It was an odd shaped affair, long and wide, but not deep. In my despair at what I was seeing I could not imagine what might be in it. When I opened it, a gasp came involuntarily from my throat.

It was the other part of the Tablet of Destinies.

I stayed at Khala's side until she died two days later. All efforts to help her failed. My wife actually took over the task of trying to get nourishment into her, but she was too far gone.

She spoke briefly on three occasions. I wanted to hear words of love, some indication that she would do all she could to survive to be with me! She was more practical, using those hard-fought moments to provide me with helpful information.

I learned from her that my father had died. Asshur had built himself a large empire in a short time; several new cities had been erected by him and his vassals. I surmised that he must have tried to do too much too quickly, as Khala also related that he was chased from Nimrud by a coalition of local kings.

Asshur had concluded that the part of the tablet he possessed, along with what I had already constructed, was sufficient for building a tower good enough for Ishtar's worship, and had decided to finish the project in Babil. That explained why he hadn't come after me. Apparently he had almost finished his tower work when Khala stole his part of the tablet and disappeared.

At one point she said, "Our child...", then fell into a deep sleep, never to speak again.

On the third morning after her arrival she was gone from this world. I had fallen asleep on my knees beside her. When I awoke I kissed her cold forehead, closed her beautiful green eyes, and went outside.

There was a mist hovering just above the ground; a common occurrence here on the shores of the reed swamp. I stood facing the swamp, two kinds of moisture mingling in my eyes.

A movement on my left – a bird flying in the direction of the tower we were building. I made my way to its base and looked up. Through the mist and tears I saw it; the hazy figure of an owl.

"My name is Gamesh, but I write under the name of Gilgamesh."

"My master, Eber, has successfully taken over the city of Erech, which he has renamed Uruk."

"Erech, son of Nimrod, did not know it, but we were always under the protection of the great god of wind, water and creation, Enki. Now this city is his, Eber his king, and I his high priest."

"We have successfully fooled the other son of Nimrod now, and by the time he discovers our duplicity, we should have enough strength to keep the city."

"I presented myself to our former lord as a chronicler; and so I am. Enki has related to me the true stories of antiquity: the creation of man, the flood etc. And I have chronicled them meticulously for all mankind."

"There are other versions of these events; mostly proffered by the followers of Jehovah. But the world will see the truth in my writings – I am sure of it!"

"He promises to reveal more as time goes by, and my fame grows as I serve his purpose."

"He also has promised to reveal future events, and such revelations will bring me much power. Perhaps I will be king one day. Certainly I have secured great help for the afterlife at Enki's side."

"Erech, you ask? He has moved on once again. He claims to have Enlil to his aid, but so far all I have seen from him has been weakness. He works hard, building

city after city, but to what end? He is never able to hold them for himself."

"I know not of his fate since he left here. Some say he did not go far, and he was able to convince a large group to accompany him still. Perhaps his next city will finally be his place of rest."

Enlil assures me that our losing the city of Erech does not mean Enki is stronger than he. I have my doubts, but there doesn't seem to be any way for me to change my allegiance now; I have walked this path too long now.

The swamp people have become my staunch allies, but they did not have the military power to prevent Eber's takeover. They are still with me, though.

Leaving the city I had named for myself, we followed the edge of the swamp away from the Euphrates. The swamp people followed along with us - always in the reeds – as we travelled. Most people would not even know they were there, but I had gotten to know them intimately, and I now recognized the subtle distinction between a knoll covered with reeds and a person dressed in them.

After our first encounter with these people I had become fascinated by them. I spent almost all my free time at the edge of the swamp, hoping for a glimpse.

It took some time, but my persistence was rewarded. At first, I would turn at a noise and find a basket of fish behind me. Their speed and stealth were remarkable. When I saw this was going to be a ritual, I began leaving some dates as payment.

This went on for several days. Sometimes there would be a pot of milk – not goat or sheep to be sure, something different; smoother, with lots of cream.

Finally, there was personal contact. I turned at the usual rustling of reeds expecting to find a basket or a pot. Instead, there was the man I had spoken to about the thieving and released. He was alone, and he was not wearing reeds.

It shouldn't have been such a surprise, but I flinched visibly when he spoke.

"You come with me, see my home."

His speech was rudimentary, but perfectly understandable.

"I would like that very much," I replied, "but it will have to be tomorrow. I am alone here now, and I am king of this city. My absence would cause great alarm. Please, meet me here tomorrow at this time and I will accompany you to your home."

Without a word he disappeared into the swamp. I had no idea if he would come again or not, but I was thrilled with the contact that I had finally made. I would be here waiting for him tomorrow, and I truly hoped he would return.

"Absolutely not, sire! It is out of the question! You shouldn't even have been there by yourself."

I had assembled the leaders of the city to explain what I was about to do.

"Surely, Hulen, you do not pretend to tell your king what he will or will not do!" I was genuinely irritated by his impudence, but I also knew he had the interests of the kingdom at heart. In his place, I probably would have said the same thing, but I was not to be deterred.

"Of course, your majesty," his face red with both anger and shame now, "It's just that, as you well know, I have dedicated my whole life to your service and protection, and I do not intend to stop now. It is simply too dangerous, especially alone. You must not!"

"Oh, but I shall, my dear friend; I shall."

"Think of the kingdom, sire! What would this city be if you were taken from it?"

"Don't be so dramatic, Hulen. If they wanted to kill or kidnap me they have had plenty of opportunities already. You have seen how they appear and disappear from within the reeds. It is amazing!"

"Even more reason for you not to go, sire. They can evade us at will – they have proven that."

"Yes, but they have done me no harm even though they could have. Even their first sins against us were of a nonviolent sort. I truly believe they are a gentle folk. Now, wait... No, do not speak. Let me explain my plan in its entirety. I have drafted a document placing you in charge of everything in my absence. You will have my seal, and surely no one will challenge that. The document also states that you are to succeed me as king if my death is confirmed."

The entire room erupted into chaos at this. It took me several minutes to calm everyone down. Then I spoke again.

"I have decided it. As you know, I have no heir to this point, and no one can dispute Hulen's abilities. I will return; but so that everyone can be tranquil about my time away, the document is signed and sealed and binding. Pray to Enlil and all the other gods that I may have safety. I go."

I spent about two weeks with the swamp people, I think. I lost all track of time as soon as I entered that mystical world.

The day I left, I went down by the edge of the marsh and sat down at the place my new friend and I had agreed upon. I didn't have long to wait.

Only now did I really consider some of the practical implications of stepping off into the reeds. The first thing that came to my mind, now that the time was at hand, was how one actually moved about in such conditions.

Smiling reassuringly, my friend motioned for me to follow him. We stepped into the water.

There were patches of fog in some places; not everywhere, and it hung low to the water's surface, creating an otherworldly effect.

It was not deep at the edge; only about ankle deep. We waded – he quickly and silently, I splashing and thrashing – in until we had water to about our knees. There, tied to a stand of reeds, was a boat.

It was made of wood, and I wondered where the wood had come from, but it mattered little at the moment. Without a word, or even a glance backward, he was in it.

It had happened so quickly that I did not know how he had gotten in. I hadn't even noticed the boat tilt with his weight.

When I finally made it to the side of the boat I saw a peculiar thing. It was to be the beginning of many surprises this world had to offer me.

At the side of the boat, almost invisible, was a floating mat. I say almost invisible because it was floating, attached to the side of the boat, but below the actual surface of the water.

My host seemed surprised by my hesitation. He leaned my way and said, "step on it."

I hoisted one foot up to the level of the mat, still very tentative, and placed it on the mat.

As I pondered the event later I realized how foolish it had been to even worry about the mat. I was only standing in knee-deep water. But there was something about the act that was beyond my experience that I was actually afraid to do so.

As it turned out, the mat sank about two palms down in the water with my weight. When I finally realized what I was going on, I saw that I could now step into the boat without any effort.

Without another word, my friend hauled the mat into the boat, picked up a long pole and began pushing us farther into the swamp.

I tried to start a conversation, but for the first hour or so he would not speak. The air seemed heavy, as if creating a barrier for sound even if one did want to talk. The silence was beyond anything I had ever experienced. I felt as though my ears were plugged up. Even the pole moving in and out of the water seemed to be silenced somehow.

Finally he stopped his work with the pole and turned to face me.

"Don't talk close to the 'outside'. You already see how we take from out, quiet."

"Yes, I see that. May I ask your name?"

"I am Ma'soren. We are called Ma'adan, 'people of delightful place' and I am one chief."

"There are more chiefs?" I asked, not sure I had understood his true meaning.

"Yes, six tribe. Six chief."

At that he opened a basket. It contained some of the cheese I had come to enjoy so much and some hard, heavy bread. Accepting his lead, I ate in silence.

After we ate, he resumed pushing the boat. I thought about asking if I could help, but I had no idea of the way. Everything I saw looked exactly the same.

After a couple more hours I saw something different ahead of us. It was not very different, but after so much time seeing the same scenery, one small change was enough to catch my eye.

As we got closer, I saw that there was a structure sitting out of the water. Before I could even recognize it was there we had beached on a small island.

Ma'soren jumped off the bow of the boat immediately, a rope in his hand. He tied it to something I couldn't see and then gestured for me to follow him.

Once out of the boat, I got a good look at what I thought must have been a house. It was not like any I had ever seen - a recurring theme here in the land of the Ma'adan.

It was a tall building – probably twenty cubits high. The walls were vertical until about two-thirds of the way up where they arched inwards until meeting in a ridge that ran the length of the building. It was about twice as long as it was wide, about fifteen by thirty cubits.

The material of its construction was completely unidentifiable to me. There was a plaster of some sort covering everything, but unlike any I had ever seen. It wasn't exactly shiny, but it had a certain sheen to it that was not like I was used to.

Ma'soren must have seen my intrigue, and, stepping to the wall proclaimed, "Dung!"

He took me inside the building and I saw that it was a storehouse. I inspected the construction more closely and discovered that the basic frame was made from reeds. Over the framework, visible on the inside, were woven reed mats. These were covered (on the outside only) by a plaster of dung mixed with mud and straw.

I wondered what produced the dung, but I was reluctant to ask. I didn't have to wait long for the revelation, however.

Ma'soren took me to the end of the building where we found cheeses being cured. There was a door at that end as well, and we stepped back out of the building.

As soon as we were out I saw the beasts. They had been hidden from view at the other end, but now I saw them clearly. At least some of them I could see clearly. Others, farther away, were only distinguishable at times as the fogs swirled in and out of the open areas. They were large cattle with great, wide horns. They were in water up to their knees - or sometimes even their bellies – either chewing their cud or dipping their massive heads below the water's surface in search of more cud-producing material.

"They are water buffalos," Ma'soren explained. I had never seen an animal like that before so I was glad for the explanation.

There were, here, many small islands stretching off into the distance. It was plain to see why the water buffalos did not graze on the dry land of the islands: they were completely cleared of any vegetation. Most of the islands I could see had one solitary building on them, very similar to the one we had just exited.

As I stood taking in this unfamiliar scene I saw movement to my right. It was Ma'soren poling the boat around to this side of the island. I hadn't even realized he was gone!

He motioned for me to join him on the boat, and when I did I noticed he had brought some things from the storehouse: several cheeses, some of the ubiquitous reed mats, of varying sizes, and two more poles. These were different from the one he used to propel the boat; they were about the same length, but thinner, culminating at one end in a trident.

"We catch fish! Not to day, though. Almost dark."

We poled for another few minutes before beaching on another island. Here there was a much larger structure; higher as well as wider and longer. It was obviously well cared for. There were even a few decorations surrounding the wide front door; symbols I didn't recognize, designed with reeds and inset in the plaster.

"Temple; my tribe," my host explained.

With no more comment, we rounded the temple, going to the rear of it where we found a house much like most we had seen.

The front door opened, and a woman appeared.

I couldn't have said what her age was. She looked at once a child and a woman who had already lived through many trying years. In her own way, I found her attractive, not really understanding why.

She spoke, and I realized where her true beauty was; at least for me. Her eyes were the most alive part of her face. They were of a different hue that anyone else I knew. They were basically a light, sandy color, but there was a hint of green in them that reminded me of Khala.

"There is food ready," she said simply.

Even this simple statement seemed to bring even more expression to her eyes. They seemed to smile, without any cooperation from her mouth.

We passed through the door unceremoniously. Ma'soren moved directly to a low table set in the middle of the room we were in. He motioned for me to be seated opposite him.

We dined on a rich plate of rice with fish, accompanied by some more of the hard, brown bread and some of that delicious, creamy buffalo cheese. We washed our meal down with fermented milk.

When we had finished eating, Ma'soren's wife called to the room behind us. Four children appeared, their ages ranging from about three to twelve. They all had their mother's eyes.

I was presented to them by their father as a chief of a great tribe outside the marsh. Their eyes were as wide with wonderment as mine must have been as I had experienced this new world earlier today. Now, I was the different one, and that put things into a new perspective for me.

For the next few days I was introduced to the details that made this exotic world function. Ma'soren never showed any sense of awe of my person. He apparently considered us to be equals. For some reason, that never bothered me with him. It seemed like the most natural way of things, at least here in the marsh.

There were several meetings with other tribal chiefs; sometimes individually, sometimes in groups. The same familiarity was evident among them as Ma'soren practiced with me.

The relationship of a chieftain to his subjects was at the same time clearly demarcated and blurred by task sharing. The chief was chief, and his word was to be obeyed without question or delay. Even so, there did not exist the kind of lord/peasant hierarchy that I was accustomed to in my world.

We all fished, farmed rice and patched plaster together; king and commoner together.

I was introduced to their religion. They had an attitude about it that was, in some ways, different from those I was used to. Ma'ason himself did not show great enthusiasm for their god, but his wife was very involved in the tribe's worship. My curiosity led me to question her about the god they serve.

"His name is Ma'own. He is a great serpent. We do not fear him as long as we do what 'They' show us."

Who are 'They', and how do they show you things?"

"The good wind, bad wind, good rain, bad rain, water tallness, many fish or few fish, good milk, bad milk… these are the big things."

Her language abilities were better than her husband's. I guessed that was because of her religious activity.

"These things," she continued, "say is Ma'own smile or frown. If smile, more good. If frown, bad… very bad. Many things turn over; not working things that did work."

"We have a word for times like that," I said. "It's called, 'Chaos. It describes my god pretty well also. He is known as 'the god of the winds'."

"Ma'own serpent of 'Chaos'!" she said, obviously enjoying her new word.

As I analyzed the figures on the front of the temple I began to see a pattern.

There was a creature involved, that was evident, but it looked more like a dragon than a serpent to me.

Whatever it was, it seemed to be causing some serious mayhem, if I was interpreting correctly.

I asked her what her own name was.

"Nippur. We call the whole world 'Ur'. Nip is our word for 'daughter'.

My time with these people flew past. One day, Ma'soren nodded to his boat, and I got in like I had every other day. We did not fish, however, and he poled us in silence, just as he had the day I came in here with him.

Late in the afternoon, he tied the boat to a bundle of reeds and pointed for me to step out (on the same reed mat as before). As soon as my feet touched the mud beneath the water, he pushed the boat away from me and, without a word or gesture, was gone.

I couldn't see the dry land, but guessing its direction was easy. Pushing through fog pockets, I simply waded in the opposite direction from where the boat had headed when it left. In just a few paces, I was back in my city – exactly where I had left it.

From that time forward, I went once a week to that spot. There was always a basket, and I began trying to be inventive with the gifts I left. It brought a smile to my face sometimes imagining their reactions to things they knew nothing of. They never showed themselves again, though.

Not in the city called Erech, anyway.

Chapter 25

Eber had made a secret pact with my brother. I had no idea when it had happened, but somehow he got enough help to take over the city I had named for myself.

When we fled Erech City, we followed the edge of the swamp to the northeast. It was the only logical direction in which to go, but I also was reluctant to be very far away from that world that had become so important to me.

The Ma'adan followed alongside us, staying just inside the marsh. Once, some of our scouts reported that we had been pursued from behind. Hulen had dispatched a squad to begin a repelling maneuver against them. What they found at our rear were the bodies of soldiers, stripped of everything they had carried. In the midst of the bodies was a tall reed stuck in the ground. There was no doubt about any part of the message.

After a few days' travel we found a new spot on which to build. I still had the whole tablet, so Enlil was always with us. The others only thought I was keeping a pet owl, and he and I decided that image was a good one to maintain.

We now had some experience at these things, and as soon as we had basic dwelling places (made, now, from reeds covered with plaster), we began work on the tower.

As in the other places we had been, local tribes were pleased to accept the protection of a king and his subjects. As they joined us, we became a city once again. Without explanation to anyone, I decided to name the city 'Nippur'.

The two pieces of the tablet were kept under careful guard. I had them kept separately as an added precaution. As often as necessary I would join them and read instructions for the building.

As the end of the tablet came closer, the tower rose higher. One day, with only a little over a line to go to the end, I came across the words, "Insert the eyes of Orion. They only fit two holes."

Nothing more; no explanation about what these eyes were. I read on to the end of the instructions and saw more references to the eyes, but nothing that helped me understand what they were or where to find them.

At that moment, Enlil appeared.

"You look perplexed, *Zaluti*."

I hadn't heard that name for quite a while. It revived feelings within me, desires that I could not have explained to anyone if asked. I was destined to greatness, and the name brought back the assurance of that.

For a brief moment, I thought about deceiving him. Obviously the tower would be finished with or without the 'eyes', whatever they were. But I could not imagine not getting this one hundred percent right. Whatever the true function of this tower was, I had invested too much not to see it.

"The tablet, right here, speaks of 'the eyes of Orion'. I have no idea what they are."

"What does it say they are to be used for?"

"It only says they are to be placed in certain holes in the ceiling of the lowest chamber. Then there are some numbers. I don't what they mean."

"Speak to the swamp man. He will get you the 'eyes'.

With that the owl flew away; an irritating habit of his. I suppose gods don't have to worry much about politeness.

I went straightway to the edge of the marsh. I had brought a basket with me with, among other items, a note stating I needed to talk to Ma'soren. I wasn't sure if he could read, but his wife surely could. At any rate, I decided to call out to him and see if he was close by.

My cries were answered by the appearance of a man in very short time. It was not Ma'soren, but I gave him the message for his chief. Apparently the Ma'adan were watching us. I was comforted by the thought.

The next day I met Ma'soren at the usual place. He handed me a wooden box; strange, as anything that had come from the march before was either in something woven from reeds or a clay vessel of some sort.

"Wife tell me long ago man bring box to Ma'adan land. He die soon, but say box from god, have eyes of Orion in. We keep in temple long time, pray. You need now so take."

I thanked him and renewed my promise to always be his friend. With the look I now understood was his best manifestation of happiness (the small smile, barely discernible in one corner of his mouth), he disappeared back into the reeds.

Enlil was nowhere to be found for the next four days. I was nearly in a state of panic.

I was certain we were rapidly approaching the culmination of all these years' work, and now I was stopped cold. I read and reread the tablet, and nothing there helped me have any idea what to do next.

After all the pushing and prodding Enlil had done to get to this point; where was he now? It was only because of him that I had placed any importance on the tower. He was the one who wanted it!

If I had dedicated myself to our city defenses, either at Babil or at Erech, I might have been able to hold out against my brother. I might be working on building an empire instead of a stupid tower!

By the end of the third day I was ready to forget all about it. There might yet be time to secure this city if we moved on to other projects now.

I decided to marry again. My wife had given me no heir, but there had been no time for worrying about that, what with building towers and fleeing to start over. I discussed the problem with my wife. Ornah was very practical about such matters.

"You should have several more wives. Surely one of them will be blessed of the gods."

So it was decided. I left the selection to her, and at noon the next day I wedded four lovely young ladies.

There was never an heir forthcoming, neither make nor female. I always remembered that Khala had spoken those words: 'our child'. If not for that, I would have been sure that the problem lay with me, not my wives. How, I wondered, could I have a child with her and never with any other? If I did indeed have one.

Ornah never brought it up again. She was very open about her opinion that a king with several wives looked powerful and rich. It never really seemed to be about an heir for her.

I suppose I can be forgiven for not thinking things through better. The tower: always the tower!

Even as I was preparing for my wedding night (one of my new wives would be sent to me each of the following four nights; sent by Ornah, of course) Enlil came back.

"Where have you been?" I fairly shouted at him, forgetting for a moment the fact that he was a god.

Oddly, he did not upbraid me for my disrespect. He simply began explaining the need for his absence.

"As you know, the tablet does not give details about the use of Orion's eyes. I have been at a council of the gods – some of them at least – and, with some alliances made, I have the information we need."

This news made me forget everything else that was going on. We were finally going to finish the project. Whatever power this tower had to offer would now belong to Enlil, and I was his king.

He led me through the only door on the ground floor of the tower. We proceeded down into the underground chamber. There we studied, once again, the placement of those holes in the domed ceiling.

They were placed around the edges of the ceiling, where that level was exposed to the sky.

"There," said Enlil. "Those two you have made into eyes for the owl. That is where Orion's eyes go. First, we must place a mirror here on this pedestal. The numbers at the end of the tablet will tell us the angle of placement for the mirror, and, then, the calculations we must make as the beams of light rise up to strike the ceiling."

"What will all this tell us?" I asked, my voice almost a whisper from the solemnity of what we were doing.

"It will show us, from the heavens, how Jehovah can finally be defeated. It predicts the coming of His Son.

Something that must be prevented at all cost. Imagine our power if we are the ones to accomplish this! Even Marduk will have to bow to me! I will be the most high god!"

He continued in a state of euphoria like I had never witnessed before.

"Marduk thought he was great when Lucifer led the rebellion. He was the first to side with him, and so became his right hand. We followed Lucifer because he was so successful at defying Jehovah. It has to be said that his work in Eden was spectacular! But what has he done since then? How foolish to lead men into open hedonism! Where was the old subtlety he's so famous for in that? Was anyone really surprised by the flood? How foolish he and Marduk looked as people were so deep in their self-love they didn't even listen to Jehovah's prophet. More weakness on Jehovah's part - warning them. He really has a soft spot for you humans. It will prove His downfall, mark my word!"

"But now it is my time! I will show them both! They will see true power in *Umman Manda!*"

At that, Enlil led the way back up to the ground level. I was excited and terrified at the same time. That something huge was about to happen I had no doubt. Just what this day would bring I could not begin to understand.

As it turns out, neither could Enlil.

"Place the eyes, Erech!"

But before I could, it happened.

It started with a noise like thunder. Unlike thunder, it continued building and building without ever fading out.

309

In the midst of the cacophony a voice could be distinguished occasionally, and I surmised (correctly as it turned out) that the noise was human in origin.

I turned toward the door, the eyes still in my hands. It burst open, letting the noise reach inside in its fullest expression. It was deafening.

In the doorway stood Hulen. The look in his eyes was something I never would have expected to see from this seasoned warrior. It was sheer panic.

He was filling the doorway with his body. It was obviously a struggle for him to keep that position. He was strong – possibly the strongest man I knew, but there was a force buffeting his body that he would not be able to restrain for long.

With one great effort, he managed to close the door behind him, bolting it in place.

"Your majesty!" he gasped. "Something horrible has happened. I can't explain everything, but, all of a sudden, Japhethites were speaking one language, Hamites another; and we could not understand them, nor they us. Chaos broke out. Each group seems to think it is because of hatred from the other groups, and that each is plotting to take over. You must hide! To the basement – hurry! This mob will kill anyone in their path."

My mind was reeling. I knew he was right about the course of action, but I couldn't think straight.

I turned around and saw the owl lying on the floor. It didn't exactly look dead; it was as if it had never been alive!

A crash behind me brought me back to reality. I turned to see the door explode into pieces. In the next instant, Hulen had the head of a spear projecting through his neck. As he began to fall I saw his mouth form the word, "run."

Run I did. I closed the door behind me as I made my way down the stairs to the nether chamber. I knew it wouldn't hold for long, but I needed all the time I could get to try to escape.

The instructions for the tower had included a hidden exit. I knew it well. I had thought it a bit ridiculous at the time, building a means of escape from a monument to a god, but I was happy for it now.

The tablet had not specified where this escape route should lead to, and so I had taken the initiative of building a tunnel from here to a place at the edge of the marsh. As the chamber and the swamp were both below the level of the city it was a fairly level floor.

The door was hidden within some designs on the wall. I fumbled with the mechanism that opened it; my hands were shaking like a camel trying to shed flies. Finally, it swung wide enough for me to enter.

I had placed a torch and flint to light it just inside the door, and I took the time to do so before closing the door, knowing I would have difficulty doing it in the dark. Just as I pulled the door shut and pulled down the beam that secured it, I heard the shouting getting louder as the mob pushed its way down the steps. Their enthusiasm probably saved me since they hindered each other's progress in their eagerness. I could only hope they had not seen – and would not see – the door. In any case, I wasn't about to stick around to find out.

It seemed an eternity until I finally reached the other end of the tunnel. I hadn't remembered it being so long, but I was glad now that it was. When I exited, I wanted to be far from the confusion I was fleeing.

I was also relieved that no one came after me into the tunnel. I began thinking I might survive this ordeal.

Survive: for what? Another city lost… where could I possibly go from here?

I brushed away most of my thoughts of that kind; I could consider them another day. There were two thoughts I could not brush aside so easily. All of this was down to my brother, Asshur, and Enlil.

Coming to the door, I hesitated, listening for any noise on the other side. I heard nothing so, very carefully, I eased the door open and stepped outside.

The boat I had hidden with Ma'soren's help was there and ready to take me to the next step in my troubled life. I headed into the marsh. I was now very familiar with this world and my journey started well enough.

The silence of the place seemed to demand that I think through where my life would now take me. I had lost everything this time. Grief overtook me, and I wept tears that fueled rage.

I ranted to the sky, defiling the name of Enlil with every hate-filled utterance I could contrive. The shear frustration of that act caused me to fall down exhausted in the bottom of the boat. After a while (I had lost all track of time now), I found enough strength to stand again. I started having trouble thinking of anything but my brother; Enlil being completely out of reach.

I don't remember anything after that until I awoke (how much later I do not know) in this pit where I am now being held.

Chapter 26

Now that Asshur and Erech are gone I can bring my kingdom up to the glory I deserve. I have decided to use my assumed name as my royal title. My heirs will continue the line of Gilgamesh.

I must content myself with this city for now. It had to be renamed, of course, like me. My scouts brought back information of a city on the opposite side of the marshes. They spoke of a great walled city, all painted white. It seems the city is as bright at night as in day due to a royal decree that torches – hundreds of them – be lit all through the dark hours.

Their king named the city Ur which means 'shining' in some language. There is a certain majesty to it all, to be sure, but I won't imitate everything about it. I have decided to play with names a bit, something I have talent for from my years of chronicling. Instead of 'Erech', the city will be called 'Uruk'.

Speaking of the Chronicles, I have had to rewrite them all. Some time after the confusion of the languages, I went back to append them with new stories. To my absolute shock, I was not able to read them. At first I thought the gods had altered them into a new language, but I finally realized that we, in fact were now speaking a different tongue.

I (and probably everyone else) had assumed that the others had changed their languages and we, being the principle and most important people, still spoke what we did before. Only when we read things written before the change do we see that all of us speak something new.

I wonder how much information has been lost to us because of this. I suppose we will never really know.

So, the Chronicles are written again, at least what I have been able to remember so far. I'm sure my memory isn't always exactly accurate, but I know of no other records like them; so if I have changed history a bit, no one will even know!

I've decided that some of my new writings could be a lot more interesting if they were embellished a bit. For example, Erech's wild charge from the swamps, culminating in his brother's death, is not nearly as exciting as the way I told it.

Erech becomes the wild man Enkidu, created by the gods to distract me from extracting my rightful servitude from my people. The gods are foiled in this plan as he and I become great friends (after I tame him) and we work together to build my kingdom without their intervention.

They, (especially Ishtar, whom I spurn as a potential lover) become irate and send The Bull of Heaven (Asshur) to kill us both. We defeat their bull, and they become so angry they take Enkidu away and kill him.

I, two thirds god, one third man, am left alone with the burden of bringing this new kingdom to immortality.

Chapter 27

"That name, Nimrod, keeps coming up lately."

"What do you mean, Kasher. Where have you been hearing it?" Nakhti asked, still looking over my shoulder at the piece of clay tablet I was holding.

"When we invaded Nippur, I encountered Pul. He said he had just had a vision that Nimrod was back – reborn!"

"Pul; sure, why not Pul. Leave it to him to say something completely ridiculous and have coincidence confirm it for him," said Nakhti. There was something difficult to decipher in his voice; not venom exactly, though there was a sharp edge. What I seemed to detect was a tone that communicated a deep sadness of spirit about someone. It seemed to tire him just hearing the name.

"It's just coincidence, Kasher, trust me. This tablet is nothing. 'Nimrod' gets called upon for just about every cause that arises these days – especially from the religious types. They have been claiming for as long as I can remember that he will be back in some form or other. Someone wrote it on a tablet; at least on this broken off piece of the tablet. They even had to scratch out another name to make the tablet say what they wanted! Let's just stay focused on our mission, shall we?"

He was right, of course. There was no reason to think that Pul had some special gift of revelation or something. Sure, I had seen the same thing in Orion that he saw, but he was the one who started me looking at the stars in the first place.

I stuck the tablet piece into my soldier's bag and tried to forget about it for now. We did have important things to do after all.

One of the men had found another way out of this chamber. It was cleverly hidden, but we were now headed into another tunnel, about half the size of those we had come through before, but still tall enough to stand up in. There was nowhere to go but forward, so that's where we went.

That closed-in sensation came over me again. Ever since the near suffocation on the river bank, small areas like this caused me to feel very nervous. I fought off the feeling, remembering the dead we were avenging; especially my father.

We walked for some time, probably a quarter hour, before seeing the next opening. The tunnel had been almost straight, with just a slight bend here and there, like some sort of minute adjustments in direction. What struck me as odd was the lack of incline; the floor was basically level, which surprised me. I would have expected it to either go up or down considering the level we had come from. I couldn't imagine how much work went into building such a thing. What could possibly motivate someone to create something like this?

Finally, after a more pronounced curve than any we had encountered in a long time, there was a faint light ahead of us. Still a fair distance ahead, we could already see that the tunnel widened to about twice its size before ending at a large door.

We halted immediately and prepared ourselves for – what? There was only one way to find out, and we were not in a very advantageous position.

We knew we would be coming out into the open. An ambush was a very likely scenario.

No ambush was forthcoming. Using all our training and experience we maneuvered our way outside in a way that would limit casualties if we were attacked, but we stepped outside without incident.

The door was built into an embankment. The level at the top corresponded, more or less, to ground level back at the tower.

I knew this place vaguely from my childhood, but I had never known of the door or the tunnel. We were standing in a dry lake bed – dry for as long as I could remember.

There was a completely dry band that ran along the bottom of the embankment. Just a few paces further – moving away from the city – the ground began sloping slightly downward. There was still water there, but I knew from my childhood forays into it that it was very shallow.

As a child, I never gave much thought to how it might have been at some time in the past; but now, contemplating the height of the embankment, I believed this must have once held quite a lot more water.

As if reading my thoughts, Nakhti said, "This was once completely under water; a part of the vast marsh that still exists farther in."

At the edge of the water we saw the footprints of the men who were retreating before us. They had, indeed, entered the swamp.

Nakhti commanded some of his men to climb the embankment to get a better view. There was nothing to report; the enemy was not to be seen.

Night was coming on, and we decided to make a camp overlooking the marsh. A messenger was sent to the others back in the city. We didn't know if we would find any of the escapees, but we were not going to set back and let them enjoy a comfortable night around a fire. Any sign of that would surely lead us right to them.

Our own fire was comfortable enough. We were not worried about an attack as we had high ground and plenty of sentries posted to warn us. We settled down to rest.

The moon was still about a quarter full, enough to see fairly well by, but there were a couple of hours, deep in the night, when it was below the horizon. It was during that time that I heard a noise.

I went to the closest sentry, but he said he had heard nothing. I decided to take a walk along the top of the embankment.

I had walked for a couple of minutes, still convinced I had heard something in that direction. Sure enough, there in front of me, a band of men were making their way up the embankment.

I was alone, so I didn't think it wise to make any noise. Instead, I crouched down behind a stand of brush and took note of their numbers and the direction they seemed to be heading.

Just as the last man clambered up the slope, the top edge of the moon peeked above the horizon directly behind me. As it did so, the man at the front of the group turned my way.

I started believing in ghosts when the moonlight revealed the scar that went from the top of his forehead to the top of his nose.

Chapter 28

There was no way I could confront them on my own, and by the time I made it back to our camp with the information they would surely be long gone. I nevertheless woke Nakhti to give him the news. I decided to leave out the part about scar-face. That was my own private complication.

"There were about fifty of them. They must not know we brought only the same number of men with us. Either that or they think we are stronger than they are."

"You're right, of course," said Nakhti. "We certainly couldn't catch them tonight. They are obviously tough men – and dedicated, too – to travel through that marsh at night. We may have a hard time catching up to them. Get some rest, and we will see what we can figure out in the morning."

I was surprised at how easily I fell asleep. I was accustomed now to the soldier's life. I would wake easily at a sound that was out of place, but I could also rest well in short spurts when I knew all was well. There would be no attack on us tonight, so I allowed myself to relax.

The next morning we followed the embankment to the place where our enemies had climbed up. There was plenty to mark that spot, but I was amazed at how quickly their presence was swallowed up once they were at this level.

We tried to follow their trail for a few minutes, but it soon became clear they knew how to evade detection. There was nothing to follow.

"Kasher, where would you go if you were them?"

"I would follow the edge of the marsh, uncle, in case I needed a hiding place again."

"No doubt that is what they are doing. If so, we will not find them here. They have already shown how well they can hide themselves."

We decided to head back into the city. As we approached the wall we saw something hanging from it. As we came closer we realized that it was a body.

It had been hung by the neck. There was nothing covering the face, and I soon saw that it was Pul.

Once inside, I asked leave from Nakhti to find my mother and sisters. He told me to make whatever preparations I needed to quickly as we would have to start back for Babylon on the following day.

It only took about half an hour to find them. We embraced and comforted each other in silence for a while.

It didn't take much talking to persuade my mother that they needed to accompany me to Babylon. My father was dead. Then there was the shame of his friend, the traitor, hanging from the parapet.

Nakhti and I made it our business to see to Muldan's body. I asked my uncle if he had any family.

"Once, a long time ago, he did. He was a simple farmer then, somewhere to the north of Babylon. The Assyrian army was indiscriminate as they made their way to the city, killing everything in their path. Muldan was knocked unconscious during an attack. The rest of his family - father, mother, wife and two small children - all killed without a thought. He has no one now. He will be buried here with honor, killed in the last of many great battles he has fought."

With that over I returned to help my mother and sisters with their preparations for the journey to their new home.

"Kasher, this will be a great change for us, but how do you think your wife will react to such an imposition?"

"I have every confidence that she will accept you completely, Mother. She is so much like you! You are the kindest two people I have ever met."

"I hope we can get along, Kasher. I am thrilled to be able to help her, especially with my grandchildren!"

We spent the evening organizing their belongings. I purchased two camels and a donkey for the trip. There would be some things left behind, but I heard no complaints from my mother or my sisters.

The girls were caught up in it all. They were still very sad, of course, at our father's death, but they couldn't seem to contain their excitement for going to Babylon. It reminded me of the day I had left with Utanin.

We spoke of that day. The girls remembered it, but were not greatly affected by my leaving because they were so young. What they remembered most was Mother's sorrow and concern. As the weeks had turned into years - and all without any word from me - her fears grew until she even allowed for the possibility of the worst having befallen me.

"Father always believed you were alright," said Katurah. My mind wandered away from what she was saying. She was almost ten now, the older of my two sisters. Only now did I take a good look at her. I had been so absorbed in all that was going on that I barely took notice of either of them. It dawned on me that I had always been that way with them, and I took no pride in that knowledge. I would try to do better.

I was amazed at what I saw now. She was still very young, but it was obvious she would be a beautiful woman. I found myself looking from her to my mother, and the similarity was striking.

Kadiah, the younger one, was a very pretty girl, too, but she had much more of her father's features; as did I. As I looked into her eyes I noticed something I had not before. They were green.

"...He said you would be back, and here you are!" she continued, her eyes filled with what looked like admiration for her elder brother. The fact that I looked so much like our father must have been involved in her emotions just now. I vowed to myself that I would fill as much of that void as I could.

About a third of our men were to be left to protect the city. A more permanent garrison would be developed in the near future. Nippur was an important part of the Babylonian Empire. It had never had a great role politically, but it was the seat of much religious activity – which equated to two things primarily: power over the people's minds, and, much more positive in my opinion, written records.

Nakhti decided we would make our way along the canal that flowed through the city. Outside the walls it was known as the Chebar Canal, and it came all the way from the canals surrounding Babylon, emptying into the marsh at the south side of Nippur.

We came together at dawn. It was late in the harvest season, and at this time of year, we could travel through the day without facing scorching heat, and the threat of a sandstorm was low.

"It will be a little farther than going up the Euphrates," he told a group of us as we assembled by the Nergal Gate, with its huge lion's heads towering above each side of the opening. "But keeping the canal on our right flank will allow us to have an unobstructed view of the direction the enemy soldiers escaped to. Having water to our east will make it very difficult for them to sneak up on us, should they decide they want to."

Several other families had asked to join us, and Nakhti had agreed with little hesitation. The only thing he required was that they be known to someone else already in our group. He didn't want any surprises.

A woman came to me just as we were about to leave. Her head was bowed, and so I didn't recognize her at first. Only when she lifted her eyes to speak to me did I realize it was Pul's wife, Tinsa.

"Please, Kasher – may I be allowed to go with you?" she pleaded.

My first inclination was to distrust her; after all, it was her husband who had betrayed me and almost caused the city to be lost to Egypt for good.

She must have seen in my face what I was feeling, and she quickly added, "I cannot change what my husband did, and I am deeply ashamed. It is known by all, and I will have no allies here anymore. Please, I need a patron. I will be no burden. We have no children, and I will do any work that is required of me – only do not leave me here, I beg of you! I will die if you do!"

At that moment my mother, who had been close by and heard the conversation, came over to me.

"Kasher, I know her well. She has never shared your uncle's crazy ideas. Please, allow her to come with us. I will watch out for her."

I nodded my assent and Mother took her by the arm to join the others. A few minutes later, we were on our way.

Chapter 29

The nature of our journey was clear to all of us. As hard as it was for us who were soldiers, we knew we had to move slowly. For my part, I was ready for a slower pace.

I had plenty of time to catch up on the details of my family's life during my absence. The smallest things held importance for me.

They wanted to know all about my time away also. We were so lost in these conversations that we wouldn't have even thought to eat if Nakhti hadn't called a halt for the noon meal.

In the afternoon we talked less. It seemed each of us was mostly meditating on the morning's revelations. An air of melancholy fell over us. I was thinking about my father. How I longed to be able to talk with him as well. I believed the others were involved in similar thoughts.

As the day began to wane, a sight before us drove all other thoughts from our minds.

We came to the green edge of a farm settlement. Palms began taking over the landscape. It was a big area, stretching for a considerable distance before us along the canal.

The green fields themselves weren't what caught our attention.

As we came to the first stand of palms we saw objects hanging in their fronds. They were musical instruments.

I recognized harps, but there were other instruments as well. There was a flute, and something I thought must be a drum of some sort. Other instruments were there also; at least I assumed they must be instruments. I did not know what many of them actually were, but I judged them by the company they were keeping.

As we went farther along, the green area widened. The amount of instruments hanging in the trees grew greatly also until they seemed to be the very branches themselves.

Starting from the riverbank, and moving away from the canal, we began to see houses. They were obviously new; a few years old at most.

We had been climbing slightly as we went. The incline was almost imperceptible, but now we were looking down slightly having reached its peak, such as it was. What I had assumed to be a small village was now revealed to be a city of considerable size.

All of the houses seemed to be new, and they seemed to have all been poured from a mold, so similar were they. They were laid out in a circular manner with a grassy circle at the center. There was no wall or moat.

As we were admiring this view three men came up to Nakhti. I remember wondering just what it was about him they saw that made them so sure he was the leader of this band. They were, of course, correct, however they had arrived at the conclusion.

After a few minutes discussion they took their leave of him, and he began leading us back to where we first encountered trees.

He explained that the men had agreed for us to camp there, so we made our way to the shelter of those musical branches.

After we were well settled in and our area secured, the same three men, accompanied by a few others, joined Nakhti and us at our campfire.

"…We were uprooted – gently enough for the most part - but no one likes losing their home. Nebuchadnezzar's orders were for us to be treated fairly, but the planning was not as it should have been. Many of us wandered from town to town looking for a place to put down roots."

"It was the prophet, Ezekiel," another man took over. "When he first saw this place, he said it was ideal for a new community. There was a small village here in an oasis a short distance from the river, but the people here welcomed us. We learned they were followers of Jehovah also, only they were not descended from Jacob, but Esau. Most Edomites have long since left the true God, but not this group. We found much common ground with them."

"Nebuchadnezzar conceded a limited amount of autonomy to us here, and gave us a Hebrew noble, Mishael (they call him Meshach) to administrate the area around and including this settlement.

A third said, "Ezekiel continued directing people here, and, well, you see the results!"

I had listened with interest, but there was one question that I was dying to hear answered.

"What about the instruments in the trees?"

"We are a very musical people; always have been," said one of them. "A large part of our worship is the singing of the Psalms of David, Moses and others. One day, about a year ago, a caravan stopped here at the oasis.

We try to be accommodating, understanding what it's like to be a pilgrim, and most of our experiences with passing travelers have been positive. This group decided to be antagonistic."

"It started slowly. They were apparently having a difficult time as the backs of their camels were clearly visible as they rode in: no merchandise. I suppose their foul mood was down to that."

"They stayed for several days; unusual, but not normally a problem. The trees and the river provide for most of a traveler's needs. At first they were friendly enough, but then they started coming into the middle of town."

"We have decided not to build a permanent meeting house. Instead, we hold our worship in the green at the center of town when the weather allows. In bad weather, the head of each home conducts prayers and reading in his own house."

"Our visitors began hanging around at worship time. The first day they kept quiet. The next day, things got ugly."

"They started trying to sing with us, which we ignored for a while, but they came drunk, and began to be abusive. One of the elders went to them and asked them to be respectful. They got even louder, but eventually went back to their camp."

"The following day we decided to worship privately in our homes. Our 'guests' were unhappy with our choice. They began dragging people out into the street and mistreating them. We were many more than they, so it didn't last long. We banded together and sent them back to their camp with clear instructions to be on their way early the next morning."

"During all the confusion, they seemed obsessed with our music. They shouted at us to sing the songs of our God."

"Of all the things they did, that seemed to mark us the most deeply. They left, but our worship was never the same after that."

"What you see here is a manifestation of our deep sadness about not being in our own land. We have said we will not sing any more the songs of Zion here in this strange land. This is a reminder that we are not at home."

"Ezekiel came by shortly after the trees had been adorned. I was here then, and I watched as he approached."

"He took one look at the trees, and without a word to anyone, simply sat down with his back to one of them. He stayed there for a whole week, never eating or speaking to anyone. We brought him food and water. He drank the water, though no one ever saw him do it. The food sat untouched until someone else came along to replace it with something fresh."

"I watched him a lot during that week, and twice I personally went to take him his refreshment. As I looked into his eyes up close, I saw he was indeed aware of what was going on around him; not in a trance as I had imagined. But he seemed perplexed by what he saw. I explained to him (as I'm sure others had already done) the significance of placing the instruments in the trees. He ignored my explanation, but his face changed slightly. He looked both sad and irritated for a moment, then he reverted to his observance of the things going on around him"

"It was the end of Sabbath when he finally stirred. I was a small ways off, but I heard his booming voice break the silence of that sunset moment."

"'Jehovah is aware of your plight,' he began. That such a powerful proclamation could emanate from a man so long deprived of food, or even movement, was a shock to all present. 'But the times are determined by his sovereign will. Israel will remain in exile until the appointed time has passed. Let the people understand that it is our sin that has brought us here. Let the people also understand that God will grant a new heart to any and all who turn to him. Israel will yet rejoice, and in her land.'"

"I was close to him as he moved toward the center of the city. Someone gave him fruit to eat, which he did without the slightest pause in his gate. I heard him mutter, 'Jeremiah... he infests the people with his gloom...' and then he was past me."

"So, that is how the instruments came to be in the trees. I won't bore you with the rest of Ezekiel's visit, but there were strange things going on in Chebar for a while longer."

Our camp was unusually quiet that night. There was a somber feeling in the air. We started out again early the next morning.

Chapter 30

We spent a short time with Kartan as we approached Babylon. We all had reasons for wanting to get into the city, but it was refreshing to speak with my old friend for a bit.

"We've named the town 'Kish'. We learned that there was a city by that name just a short way from here that no longer exists."

"The progress you have made is amazing!" I said.

"Kartan is a great leader!"

The voice came from behind me, and, though it sounded familiar, I didn't know who it was until I turned around.

"Ludim! My gigantic friend! It is wonderful to see you. And your speech – I would never have known it was you, speaking Aramaic so clearly."

"He is as smart as he is large, my friend." Kartan sounded genuinely proud of the big man. "Together we have made a place for ourselves."

"I eat your produce regularly, Kartan. I just haven't had opportunity to come speak with you. But your reputation in Babylon is solid," I said.

"You have something of a reputation in Babylon yourself, my young friend. You defend us all in the name of the king, and many know your name; and your deeds."

I introduced my family to them, took some refreshment, chatted a while longer and then we headed for Babylon.

We were met by the same pale man who had accompanied Nebuchadnezzar when he had come out to meet with Nakhti that remarkable day. So much was now as it was because of the events – and the decisions – of that day. This man I had not seen since that day.

"His majesty, lord Nebuchadnezzar, requests the immediate presence of Nakhti and Kasher. Please come with me."

I glanced at Nakhti. I wanted to request time to see my wife and children first, but Nakhti gently shook his head while giving me a knowing look. We had been together for so long now, and through such complicated circumstances, that we seemed in tune with each other's thoughts. He knew what I was thinking, and I knew his silent advice was correct; we would see the king as our first action back in Babylon.

Nakhti gave quick orders to one of his aides to see to the civilians that had accompanied us. My mother had watched all that transpired, and when I looked her way she smiled her understanding. I knew someone would get her to her new home safely, so I smiled back briefly, and then turned to fall in behind my uncle.

There was no talk as we moved purposefully in through the staggered outer and inner gates. When we came to the entrance gate to the royal area, the guards opened for us without hesitation or conversation.

We mounted the great steps, still in silence. I expected to see the king enthroned, possibly at the top of the stairs, but no one met us as we reached their summit.

Without the least ceremony, we passed through an open door at one side of the patio.

Again, no throne scene greeted us. In fact, there was no furniture at all other than some short tables bearing decorated clay vases. Nebuchadnezzar stood at the far end of the room staring out of the wide, open door there.

At the sound of our approach he turned. His face revealed real pleasure at seeing us, but there was a solemn air about him all the same.

"Nakhti: my gratitude to you and your men. The kingdom is much safer because of your actions on our behalf."

I followed Nakhti's lead as he bowed his head slightly to our sovereign. Only then did he reply.

"Our duty, only, my lord. We are grateful for the privilege to serve you and Babylon."

"I heard about Muldan. His sacrifice will not be forgotten. I have given order that his name will be the first mentioned when I am presented to Ishtar at the next solemn ceremony."

I did not know what that meant but it seemed to be a great honor, and I felt good about it. Muldan had died a great warrior and deserved to be remembered.

"Thank you sire," Nakhti's voice revealed genuine sorrow, but his head was high and he spoke with pride. "The men will be pleased."

"These are not times for games, Nakhti. Babylon still faces enemies on all sides. I need the best possible leader to replace Muldan. It must be you, Nakhti. You must be my new commander."

"I am honored, sire, and I pledge my best to you."

"There will be voices raised against my appointment of you; some from those close to the throne. I need you to be as strong facing them as you always are in battle. Can you pledge me that as well, Nakhti? I need your strength on all fronts."

"I am sure you would not make such an appointment without standing fully behind it, sire. I know you to be such a man. With that support, I fear no one, and I make the pledge you require with great pleasure. Great is Babylon" Great is Nebuchadnezzar!"

"Your name shall now be Nebuzaradan," said the king, "for the great god Nabu has given continuation to our vision. You shall command all the forces loyal to me."

"And you, Kasher; your feats have been brought to my attention as well. It seems you and your uncle work well together."

"I have learned much at his side, sire." My mouth was dry. I was more nervous than in pitched battle, so great was my awe of this man.

"I need a good connection between my forces in the field and those who see to the defense of the city. I would have you here, beside me in the palace. Your knowledge of your uncle's ways would be invaluable to me as I assess the state of things without our walls. I will not order it so, and you could not hold a position of leadership in the beginning, but I ask you to consider being part of my Palace Guard."

In light of all that had transpired recently I was given a few days to spend with my family before beginning my training as a palace guard. I confess that they were difficult days for me. I tried to concentrate my attentions on matters at home, but my mind would not let me stop

335

thinking about it: I would finally be able to do what I had worked and sacrificed so long to achieve.

Ruhamah and my mother greeted the news of my new posting favorably, for various reasons. Ruhamah was very happy that I would be staying in Babylon. Mother liked that too, but for her there was the added bonus that, at least in her mind, I would be off the battlefield.

She was right, of course, for the most part, in that my principle duties would put me at the last line of defense for the king himself. What she didn't know (and I didn't bring up) was that I could be called upon to go to battle anytime the king or Nakhti deemed it necessary.

As excited as I was about finally achieving this great goal, I was a bit sad at standing down from my position as a front-line combatant. I had grown into the job, and had come to enjoy it for the most part.

As I had believed they would, the two groups making up my family were getting along very well. Mother and Ruhamah had to practically tear the boys from my sister's arms to have any time with them. My only concern in that area was that they would be spoiled from so much attention; but I had seen both ladies administer discipline, and I trusted they would make good decisions for my sons.

They were so much alike. Their shared beliefs gave them an immediate bond which was strengthened by their shared love of me and our son's.

The fact that the house had two separate wings gave everyone as much privacy as they wanted or needed, which went a long way toward avoiding conflicts. I was very proud of both of my ladies. Ruhamah confided in me that it was almost as if her own mother had returned to her. Mother, always wise, did all she could to keep from giving the impression she was in charge. I was a privileged prince in a peaceful land.

I was able to find a good situation for Tinsa very quickly. I convinced Utanin to hire her as his maid – something he desperately needed from the look of his quarters. It wasn't long before they were married.

The time went by quickly. The moments Ruhamah and I spent alone, exclusively in the evenings because of the circumstances, had taken on a new tone. Before, when I had been away for a while, there was an eruption of combined feelings in our passion: angst mingled with relief; our joy at being together seemed to be at once tempered by the knowledge that we had but little time before the next separation and yet heightened, emotionally and physically, by that knowledge. We now found ourselves in a very different kind of closeness.

I suppose it was the fact that I would come home every day that changed our intimacy, but, whatever the reason, it was decidedly different. It was as if we were, for the first time in a long time, really enjoying each other's company.

It wasn't less passionate; in fact, in some ways there was an even deeper physical element now. Whereas before seemed to be about fulfilling an urgent need, now it was a desire for experiencing each other. We drew very close in those few days.

When the time came to go for my new training, I did so with a calmness I had never known. The combination of many factors had brought me to a new state of mind. I firmly believed I had reached a new level of maturity.

On the day that had been appointed to report for my new posting I approached the royal gate alone. There had been no instruction other than the day and time I was to be there.

The guards opened the gate for me without a word. I was amazed, but I tried not to show it.

When I reached the top of the steps the pale man stepped out from the door through which he had led Nakhti and I a few days before. He stepped forward and said, "Asphenaz."

"Pardon… you said, Asphenaz?"

"My name. You will need to know that now."

Without another word he led the way inside.

The king was not there this time, but I saw two men standing at the far end of the room.

"Welcome Kasher," said the smaller man. He moved toward me, placing one hand on each of my arms. I knew who he was from Ruhamah's description of him. It was the Hebrew, Belteshazzar – the number two man in all Babylon. His greeting did not at all seem contrived, an impression confirmed by his warm smile.

"Thank you, sir." I replied simply.

"I am Belteshazzar, servant of Nebuchadnezzar," he added with a simplicity I would soon come to know was characteristic of him. I had always admired men of power who did not think it necessary to constantly affirm the fact. Turning to the other man he said, "This is Arioch, the captain of the king's palace guard. He will be your military leader and in charge of your military instruction."

Arioch and I greeted one another with a nod.

"You will notice," Arioch began, "that he said I was in charge of your *military* instruction. Your training will include other areas better taught by others than myself. You will learn something about diplomacy; necessary for this position. Belteshazzar himself will instruct in this discipline."

Belteshazzar picked up the conversation at this point: "You will also learn palace decorum. Your teacher in this area will be Asphenaz.

As if on cue, Asphenaz entered the room at that very moment; entered, passed through and exited through the door where he had brought me in, all without saying a word.

All three of us had watched him, and the look on my face must have said everything I was thinking as Arioch gave a short chuckle.

"You'll get used to him," he said, still smiling from the corner of his mouth. "He is unlike anyone else I have ever known."

Belteshazzar looked a bit more serious.

"You will find no one more dedicated to the king than Asphenaz. One day I will tell you his story and you will understand much more about him. For now, suffice it to say that, though he may be a bit rude with people like us, he knows all there is to know about how to behave in the presence of royalty."

"The palace guard is divided into four groups," he continued, "each with an extremely important function. There is, of course, one group always at the king's side for his personal protection. Another group maintains vigil around the walls of the palace compound, including the gates. A third group is tasked with accompanying the messengers. In some ways that detail is the most complicated as there must be physical protection for the king's emissaries along with proper decorum in the presence of royalty. If a messenger is incapacitated, the head of the guard detachment traveling with that particular emissary must take over the duty of delivering the message."

"The fourth is the queen's guard," said Arioch. "You will be tasked with that detail for the time being. Don't think of it as a lesser task. You will soon see that it has its own complications. As time goes by you will, if you are deemed capable, spend time in each of these divisions. It is rare, but sometimes a guard distinguishes himself in one of these areas and is posted permanently to that detail. That decision can only be made by royal decree. For now, you are with the queen, and Asphenaz is your principal guide for this posting."

I wasn't sure if he was still smiling about Asphenaz, or if it was now for a new reason. As he said, I would soon find out about the complications of guarding the queen, and, looking back, I think that was the motive for his sly smile. Either way, I was warming to the man and his way.

Arioch was nearly as tall as me, and I could see that he was not in his position just to keep him active in his old age. Though he was several years older than me, he was as fit as anyone I had encountered in my time in the army. I was glad to be on the same side as him. Who would win a faceoff in battle between the two if us would be difficult to call. I believed his experience might give him an edge.

Just then, Asphenaz came back into the room. This time he came in a straight line to our position. He was silent until the moment he came to an abrupt halt just in front of me.

"The queen has been prepared to receive you. You will come with me."

I glanced at Belteshazzar who gave me nothing in return. When I turned to Arioch, he merely shrugged, smiled (or continued the same smile as before) and said, "I will see you later."

Asphenaz turned on his heel and started for the door in that fast shuffle of his to which I was becoming accustomed. I followed, only now realizing just how fast he was capable of moving. A quick pace of long strides was necessary to keep up. As we passed through the doorway I glanced over my shoulder. I was pretty sure Arioch was laughing.

With no discussion on the way, I was led through several passageways. They were confusing, and I believed that to be by design. It was a good strategy for defending someone.

My training had prepared me to pay close attention to details, and I was fairly certain I had the route we were taking memorized. One last turn placed us before a large door.

The door was closed, but even so I could see that it was formidable. Whoever had designed and built it had security in mind.

There was a scarlet cord hanging against the wall to the right of the door. It disappeared through a small hole in the wall a short distance from the ceiling.

It was only now that I really noticed the ceiling. It was as ornate as the great room from where I had just come was simple. There were figures in the plaster of all sorts of things: animals (many of whom I had never seen), lush vegetation (also foreign to my experience), and fruit – some I recognized; many I did not.

I glanced back down the hallway we had just through which we had come. These images went quite a distance away from our present position, but began fading away at some point, eventually disappearing altogether.

Asphenaz noticed my gaze and began my education concerning Nebuchadnezzar's wife.

"Amytis is from another land," he explained in a matter-of-fact way. "She is used to things that we do not have here in Babylon."

"She has made it clear from the beginning of her time here that she does not feel at home. This has caused quite a lot of friction in the royal marriage. Everyone does everything possible to make her comfortable in hopes that she will be as content as possible. When the queen isn't happy, she upsets the balance between herself and the king. It is our solemn duty to do all we can to maintain as much harmony as possible between our sovereigns."

"Forgive me for asking," I interjected, "but, it sounds like a very complicated marriage. Surely the king can marry whomever he wills?"

"This is a lesson you must learn and never forget, young Kasher. Not even kings can do everything as they like. Nebuchadnezzar has the wellbeing of Babylon to consider – even above his own desires."

"I never thought of it that way," I said. "I have always equated Babylon with Nebuchadnezzar, so his desires are to be the desires of all his subjects."

"That is a very important perspective, to be sure, but we must not be caught up in the fervor of the Chaldeans. They claim deity for the king. I am completely dedicated to him, but I am realistic enough to know that Nebuchadnezzar is only human. His end need not be the end of Babylon. That is his thinking as well, and so he married this particular woman to strengthen the position of the kingdom as well as give the throne continuance through his heir. Our duty is to try to make things work out between the king and queen."

With that he pulled the cord forcefully. A noise sounded on the other side of the door, greatly muffled to our hearing, but, given the obvious thickness of the door, the sound was probably easily heard within.

The door immediately began swinging inward. It took some time to come completely open, and I saw that my assessment of it had been correct. It was almost a cubit thick.

Once open there stood, completely blocking the opening, two of the largest men I had seen since the meeting with the Philistines outside Babylon so long ago. They were taller, at least, than even Ludim.

These were not Philistines; that I knew immediately. Their skin was as black as the bitumen Utanin had used to seal the joints of his boat; skin than fairly gleamed in a beam of sunlight that came upon them from a skylight somewhere in the room. I was fairly sure the one on my left was the one who had accompanied the king as he came out to speak with Nakhti.

I had no doubt they knew who had pulled the cord before opening the door, but their show of dominance was obviously important to them - and to their function. I was left with no question as to their resolve as they stared hard into my eyes.

Asphenaz moved forward as if they were not there, and they moved to either side to accommodate his entrance. I hesitated just a moment, still somewhat intimidated by the scene, and then went in quickly as though the corridor formed by the two brutes might close before I got through.

Once well inside, I saw that we were in a large chamber, lavishly furnished and very well lit. Most of the light was from multiple skylights, but there were enough lampstands to keep the room well illuminated after dark.

The ceiling was a continuation of the one outside, only more elaborate yet. Here there were also great murals on the walls depicting green, forested mountains of a kind I had never seen. Some were even white at their peaks. Beasts, great and small roamed through the scenes in a most natural way. The effect was very pleasing.

To our right was another door as large as the one through which we had just passed. I recognized the strategic placement. Doors at right angles caused a momentary confusion for attackers – sometimes just enough to facilitate an escape to safety. I commented on that fact to my teacher who, though silent, seemed impressed with my understanding of the matter.

There were other guards at either side if the door – just as big, and just as dark of skin. This door was open, and the area inside was partially visible to us from where we stood. I could see several young women inside. They all seemed very busy, but I could not make out the nature of their activity.

We stood waiting for several minutes. Asphenaz pulled something from inside his robe. I saw that it was a green rock like I had seen him with as he waited for Nakhti's answer to the request to talk with Nebuchadnezzar.

He saw me looking, and said, "A precious gem, very common in my land. I hold it at times like this. Waiting makes me nervous, and my stone reminds me of home. That calms me."

I simply nodded my understanding.

All of a sudden, a lone figure appeared in the doorway. With no hesitation queen Amytis had come through and was standing before us.

She was a striking woman; not beautiful by my standards, but so distinctively different in her features from the women I knew that she held a kind of fascination for me.

Her hair was as fair as any I had seen. That was unusual, but not completely unique. Her skin was also very fair; though not nearly so much as Asphenaz'. It was the color of her eyes that most intrigued me. I had seen some people, like my sister, with green eyes. Amytis was the first person I had seen whose eyes were blue.

When she spoke her voice was strong, also unusual for a woman, in my experience. She spoke Aramaic, but her speech was thickly accented, and, even though it did not diminish the strength of her voice, she struggled with the language.

"Who did you bring me now?"

With a low bow, Asphenaz said, "This is Kasher. He will be your personal guard for a while."

"He is young. Can he make me safe?"

"Yes, my queen. He is a soldier of considerable experience, and I think you will find he has a pleasant demeanor as well."

"I hope you are right, Asphenaz. That last one you brought was a disaster. He was crude and rough. No manners for conversation with a queen."

I decided to seize the opportunity and spoke up.

"My queen, I notice you are fond of nature. I presume the decorations depicting animals and plants are because of you."

"You are correct. This place to which I have been dragged is without any natural beauty. I cannot leave my quarters without being sad. All I see is sand!"

"May I ask where you are from? It must be a lovely place if you have tried to recreate it here."

"I am from the north of here. We have all this (she pointed to the murals) and so much more. I miss my lovely land!"

I had made contact with her in a personal way, and I believed that would help me with this assignment. Time would tell.

It was Asphenaz' turn to speak:

"There is still training for you to accomplish before you actually begin your work here, Kasher. Good day, my queen."

With another low bow he turned and moved toward the door. I hadn't heard it close, which surprised me, but as I turned to go (having bowed to the queen myself) I saw it being opened for us.

Outside, I was bursting with questions. To my surprise, Asphenaz stopped just past the door and indulged my curiosity.

"She is from a region known as Armenia, well to our north," he said in response to my first question. "It is an area of great, tall mountains. The white you saw on top of some of them in the paintings is called snow. Apparently the temperatures at the tops of mountains can get quite low, and rain falls in a solid, white form in that cold. That snow turns back into water as the air warms, and Belteshazzar tells me that those snow-covered mountains are the source of our two great rivers."

"When it is not very cold, and down lower from the mountain tops, that region gets a lot of rain. You know how green our fields are along the rivers? The queen has told me that all of her land is that green just from rain and snow. There is more protection and food for animals there, so there are more of them."

"Amytis is the daughter of the king of Media, and this marriage sealed (eight years ago) a pact of cooperation and mutual tolerance between the two nations. It is very important that the marriage works."

"I didn't know the king had been married for so long. Do they have any children?" I asked "There was never any talk of that when I was last here."

"They have a son, Evil-Merodach. He was born seven years ago. From what I have seen (and I see a lot) there will probably not be more."

"Surely Nebuchadnezzar has other wives and concubines."

"He does not. This kingdom is his one true love and passion."

Back in the great room Sirrah, Arioch's second-in-command took over my training.

For the next two weeks I spent several hours a day with him learning the art of fighting in close quarters. There was much discussion of tactics as well, with him and other members of his team. I discovered he was a capable soldier and instructor.

When I was not training with Sirrah I was learning more of how to deal with royalty from Asphenaz. They both seemed satisfied with my progress.

I was placed on a 12 hour shift guarding Amytis at night. There was not much to do but be alert for any danger. I had to fight the tendency to complacency. After all, if anyone could get into the palace compound, through the massive doors of the queens chambers and past those giants at the doors, there seemed little I would be able to add. I passed the time examining every part of those chambers for possible points of infiltration. There were none. The only problem with that was there was no path for escape either, should that ever become necessary.

In the evenings, before the queen retired, the royal prince would be brought to her. I watched them together, and saw a mother who truly loved her child. He was not very pleasant to be around, so I did not try to interact with him. I had never seen so much arrogance in one so young.

After a few days of this I was summoned to speak with Belteshazzar one morning.

"So, Kasher, how are you faring? You have been on a rigorous schedule, and I have not heard any complaints: neither from you nor from your trainers. That is a good sign, I think."

"I believe it goes well, sir. The nights have been long, but I understand well the need for vigilance."

"I would appreciate your analysis of our security of the queen, Have you any observations?"

"The queen's security seems to be airtight. If I may say so, that could be a problem in itself."

"How so?"

"Well, if all the measures intended to keep attackers out were to fail, as unlikely as that appears to be, there is no more to be done. The queen would fall prey to the attackers. My concern is that there is no way for her to flee such an attack."

"I see. I never looked at it that way, but you may have a point. The king's contingencies do not take him into such a dead end. He would not allow it. He will permit protection to a certain point. After that, he will fight himself. The queen's case is much different."

"I will speak of this with Asphenaz and Arioch. Do you have any ideas about how this escape could be made?"

"I have the beginnings of a plan, sir."

"We will discuss this one day, but I must demand that you keep this between us for now. We are experiencing some problems with our security that could, one day, precipitate the need for such measures, and if we implement new measures, they must be kept secret"

"May I ask the nature of the security problems?"

"As you must know, all governments have their spies. We are no exception, and we are getting word from ours of certain groups banding together – historical enemies who seem to find a common cause in destroying Babylon's power. They do not seem strong enough yet to move, but, somehow, they are getting a lot of information that they should not. There is someone, fairly close to the king, who is not loyal."

"You must not know who it is; otherwise you would have taken action."

"We don't know yet, no, but we have mechanisms in place that should yield that information soon. Just be very attentive, and very discreet, Kasher."

"I will, sir."

Chapter 31

My training seemed to go by very quickly. I had very little difficulty learning the new information.

I did learn some new fighting techniques. Most of what I had learned before would still apply, of course, but there were details that were different now. Fighting indoors brought its own set of complications, and my function now was not simply to stay alive and kill the enemy. Now I had to place another person's life as my top priority.

The queen and her son took to me well enough. My guard shift started early in the evening and the royal heir was normally present from the time I arrived until his bedtime a couple of hours later.

How she doted on the child!

One day, a couple of weeks into my time there, she began to converse with me for the first time since our initial meeting.

"Tell me about yourself, Kasher. Do you have a family?"

"Yes, I have a wife and two sons. My mother and two sisters also live with us."

"You have two sons – how old are they?"

"The youngest is four and his brother is six."

"Do you think your wife would approve of the elder son coming to spend time with my Evil-Merodach? He has almost no one of his age to be around. Your son could study with him as well as play. I am sure he would never receive such an education elsewhere."

The thought pleased me – my son educated at court!

"I will speak to her, my queen. Thank you for the invitation."

As the door of conversation had been opened I decided to ask her about her homeland.

"If it is truly anything like the depictions on the walls and ceilings, I should like very much to see it in person one day."

She did not require much prodding to tell of the land she loved and missed so much. She told stories of great hunts she had gone on with her father, riding through forests of trees as tall as any tower.

"There were so many trees, so close one to the other, that at times everything looked the same. They even blocked the sun in some places. I would become frightened thinking we were lost, but my father knew those places intimately, and would always bring us home safely – and always with lots of game for the table."

I began allowing myself to dream about such a place, and those thoughts came together with others as I thought on how to keep the queen contented here in Babylon.

I turned to see Sirrah enter the room where we were. It was the first time I had seen him there. I glanced at Amytis, and she was staring at him with a puzzled look on her face.

"My queen," he bowed slightly as he addressed her, then continued. "My apologies for the intrusion. My name is Sirrah, and I am Arioch's second on command.

Kasher's presence is required elsewhere. I will take his place while he is gone. Kasher, Belteshazzar would see you."

My other two mentors were already there when I arrived.

"Kasher, welcome!" Belteshazzar exclaimed as I entered the room. He seemed genuinely pleased to see me. It was also as if he was totally comfortable with me now, something that I was still trying to get used to. I was moving freely within the ranks of the most powerful people in the world.

"Thank you, sir. How may I be of service?"

"I've been discussing with Asphenaz and Arioch your comments about the lack of escape planning for the queen's quarters."

"Very astute of you, young man," added Asphenaz.

"Do you have any ideas about what might be done?" It was Arioch this time, and he seemed genuinely interested in what I had to say: they all did.

"As you might well imagine," I began, "guarding the queen in the absence of any imminent threat allows one plenty of time to think. I have come up with some ideas, yes. I think I may have a way to accomplish more than one objective at once."

"Sort of like piercing two enemies with one spear thrust, eh," chimed in Arioch.

"Exactly. The queen is discontented with the lack of vegetation here in Babylon. We are used to it, so we are not bothered by it, but she is. The murals and the ceiling decorations have, no doubt, helped to a degree; but they are not alive. I suggest we build the queen some green-covered mountains."

"How would we do that, Kasher," asked Belteshazzar.

"Obviously, the 'mountains' themselves would be artificial. They could be made of brick. I think, if they were tiered just right they could give the impression of having slopes like a hill or mountain, and those tiers could be planted with green vegetation giving the effect of something very different from our normal scenery."

I hurried to continue. "This 'mountain' structure could also figure importantly in my idea for an escape route for the queen. It could be built adjacent to her quarters, and a secret passage built within it leading to a place of escape."

All three men stood silent for what seemed minutes. I feared they thought I had lost my mind with such wild ideas.

Asphenaz fumbled with his green stone as he pondered. "Absolute genius," he said finally.

"I agree," said Arioch.

Belteshazzar simply nodded, his mind obviously moving through the logistics of the idea.

"She could have access to a courtyard surrounding the structure in normal times," he said after a moment, "and secret entrances from there and from inside her quarters into the 'mountains' for safety. It shall be done! Do you have any ideas about the specifics, Kasher?"

"Not concerning the actual construction, sir. I have no particular expertise in that area. But when it comes to the gardening, I know a man who I think would be ideal."

And so the plans began to create something that would become known far and wide – at least the outside part. I recruited Kartan and Ludim for the garden aspect of the project. Before they could actually get to work the massive construction had to be built. I must admit that it went well beyond anything I could have imagined. It took almost a year to complete, and the palace compound had to be enlarged to accommodate it and its surroundings.

During that phase, I petitioned my masters for something very special, and yet, given the current project, something very practical.

"I would like to travel to the queen's homeland and see it for myself. I think it would be of great benefit if Kartan and I could see with our own eyes what we are trying to replicate."

Permission was given, with all provisions necessary at our disposal.

And then Amytis heard about the trip.

I was not privy to the discussions that went on, but after a few days we were informed that our journey would include a diplomatic mission headed by the queen herself.

"Asphenaz and Sirrah will be going with you as well," Belteshazzar told me. "Asphenaz will be a big help to you as I am sure you can imagine. Any whims of the queen will be handled by him. None of us want you to be burdened with matters of royalty on this trip. We do not expect you to take full responsibility for security yet, either, so Sirrah will be in charge of that detail. You are to make sure Kartan gets what he needs to make the new garden a success."

"You will travel up river as far as possible. To reach your destination, you will have to procure whatever transportation you need at that point. You should bring back as much of the queen's favorite vegetation as you can."

Sirrah was brought in for me to speak with. I had experienced an odd feeling about him since the day he appeared in the queen's quarters, but I had no rational basis for it. It hadn't helped that, when I was in the meeting that night, I asked Arioch why Sirrah himself had been my replacement. He seemed surprised, saying that he had simply told him I was to be replaced for the meeting.

"I assumed he would send someone, but I suppose he felt he should handle it himself," he said. A frown passed across his face, but only for a moment, so it seemed not to be a problem.

I tried to push those thoughts from my mind and concentrate on the task at hand. Arioch obviously trusted Sirrah, so I should too.

Belteshazzar gave us two days to prepare for the expedition. After just a few hours the first day I saw I was not needed for the preparations, and so went to spend as much time as I could with my family before leaving.

Things at our home had settled into a comfortable routine. Any fears I had had that the women in my life would get along were long gone. Mother and my sisters respected Ruhamah greatly as a mother and a guardian of the home life. Ruhamah, for her part, loved them deeply and allowed them to fully integrate into our family. I was a blessed man to have such a situation.

I arrived to some unexpected news.

"Kasher, we have been asked to move into the queen's quarters while she is gone and look after Evil-Merodach," Ruhamah blurted out as a greeting.

"We?" I asked.

"All of us. Your mother, your sisters, the boys and I. It seems Utanin and the prince have become fast friends,

355

and the queen does not think the trip would be good for her son at his age, so she wants us to move in and help in her absence."

I knew the boys were getting along well. Utanin was with Evil-Merodach for a large part of every day, either studying or playing. He was a sharp boy and was having no trouble keeping up with the studies.

They were taught basic subjects like reading and writing, but there were specialized classes as well.

In conversations with the queen I had been informed that the king demanded his son receive instruction on religious matters form the Chaldeans. I was reluctant at first for Utanin to attend this, so I sat in on the first session that Utanin went to.

There was a lot of what I considered nonsense in it; this god and that god, etc. But there were other elements of their instruction that I thought might be useful to the boy.

It seems the Chaldeans were very knowledgeable in mathematics; to the point that they were even advancing that discipline; taking known systems into new areas. I found this fascinating and began sitting in whenever I could to learn what they were developing. They were also very concerned with the stars, and that had always held great fascination for me.

What I heard from them was very similar to things Pul had taught me, but they had a much more complete system of names and meanings than he had ever had. If half of what they said was correct, the stars spoke to them.

Both boys seemed fascinated with the sciences the Chaldeans taught them. One day I mentioned it to Ruhamah. She was not entirely pleased.

"You are teaching him your beliefs about Jehovah," I countered. "He surely won't be hurt by hearing what other people believe?"

"I'm afraid he will become confused!" Her lower lip was doing that little quiver that was usually followed by of sobs and tears. "And besides, you always tell him not to believe in any god. What is he going to end up thinking?"

"He will have to choose – like all of us – what he truly believes is right. I don't think it is helpful for anyone to hear only one explanation all the time. He is young now, and doesn't need to have a religion yet. All of us decide which information we think we can count on and what we reject. Neither you nor I – and certainly not the Chaldeans – will ultimately make his mind up about such things. You have told me yourself that Jehovah doesn't force anyone to believe in him. If he makes a good enough case to our son, he may get another follower."

As always, our conversation on this subject had to simply be dropped. We just didn't agree. At least I was able to soften the end of the talk enough that the floodgates didn't open this time. And she didn't object any further to Utanin studying with the prince.

After much preparation, we were finally on our way north. My family members (with the exception of Utanin, of course) were awed by the queen's quarters. They were less in awe of Evil-Merodach. He dismissed their very presence when introduced, but Ruhamah put a brave face on and promised Amytis she would take good care of her son.

We had a difficult time convincing Amytis that we needed to travel simply. Any show of ostentation could bring unwanted attention to us, and that would surely endanger the queen. We were able to outfit what looked like a crate for her with some luxuries inside while maintaining a normal appearance on the outside; and we made it nice enough that, after examining it thoroughly, Amytis relented.

Several of us making the journey were soldiers, and we knew it would be impossible to completely disguise that fact. It was also not unusual for a caravan of boats to have fighting men along for security. The only nod we gave to disguise was to obtain some well-worn clothes that would hide our official status.

To my surprise – and joy – our boat captain was my old friend Utanin.

Chapter 32

The first day brought basically no change in scenery; in fact, if anything, it was more barren than the zone immediately around Babylon.

I hadn't informed myself of all of the details of the trip; just the things that related directly to my mission. Nakhti had drilled into me the benefits of delegation, and, though it went against my natural tendencies, I was trying to follow hi example.

I was very surprised when we stopped on our second day out, right in the middle of the day. Utanin was extremely active as soon as we docked. He still moved pretty fast for a man his age. I decided to leave him to his work, whatever that was, and asked one of the boat hands why we had stopped.

"This is 'the crossing', he said simply, no hint of scorn at my question, but no further explanation either.

"I don't understand... what is 'the crossing'?

A look of surprise crossed his face, and then understanding: "You didn't know about it," he stated succinctly, his face as expressionless as his voice. Later, when he was alone with the other boat hands, I was sure he would have an entertaining story to tell, but he was careful not to offend me, simply going into an explanation of 'the crossing'.

"As I am sure you know, our destination, at least as far as we can go by boat, is the city of Nineveh."

I didn't know, but I nodded for him to continue. He had enough already to keep his mates entertained without my adding to it at this point.

"And, of course," he continued, graciously accepting my nod, "Nineveh is on the Tigris."

I could console myself in the fact that I had never ventured north from Babylon before, but I decided I needed to rethink my leadership style. I needed to know where I was and where I was going, at the minimum.

"Sippur," my informant said, unprovoked, "and on the Tigris side, Opis.

With that he was off to do whatever was his part in getting us from the one river to the other.

It turned out that there was a canal going east from this point, which we entered after waiting our turn behind three other boat caravans. It also turned out that, after about two hours travel, the canal ended.

There, I was treated to yet another surprise. There were great buildings, which I saw quickly were stables for many beasts of burden. There were oxen, asses, camels and mules in abundance, and a fairly large settlement existed there, with all that a small city would normally have on offer. From where I sat on the boat I could see all the various stages of this place's purpose at once. I was able, by the activity, to see that this was a place to unload boats' contents onto the beasts, or onto wagons and sledges pulled by them. The boats themselves were hoisted out of the canal by ropes run through pulleys. I could not see exactly what the process was, but oxen were involved in some way, and a row of devices made from three tall poles each. The boats were subsequently loaded onto wheeled transports. Ahead, lined out in intervals, these boats and their cargoes moved in a straight line, a bit more northerly than the canal had run. The path they took was indented into the surrounding floor.

There was an army garrison, and we were escorted by armed men ("for your own safety") to their fort to await our turn to start the trek between rivers. Those of us who were soldiers did not reveal ourselves to these men, and we were not questioned.

Our turn did not come that day, and we were quartered for the night. The queen managed to continue her farce, and no one seemed to suspect who she really was. At sunrise the next day we were called to help with the last preparations for our trip to the other river.

We moved faster than I would have believed. Anything that could be loaded onto a camel was, and that facilitated the transport of the larger items – including our boats.

Great sledges were laden with our cargo, which wasn't really that much. I worried that someone would find it odd that ten boats carried so little cargo and so many men, but no one seemed to care. As I reasoned it through, I realized that caravans would be heavier or lighter depending on their given situation, so that there was no specific expectation. People needed transportation as well.

I asked one of the cargo handlers why they used sledges at all.

"Why not have everything on wheels?

"Mainly because sledges have no moving parts, and therefore almost never break down. The boats are too heavy, and some cargo is as well, but we use sledges pulled by oxen whenever we can – after the camel and mule packs, of course."

I was surprised by the speed the sledges were able to make. The oxen seemed to be lumbering along, but the distance was covered rather quickly. The thing that really struck me about them was their consistency: they moved at the same speed late in the afternoon as they had done when the crossing began.

There were stations at regular intervals along the route equipped for feeding and lodging. There was always a strong military presence at these locations. Obviously, this was a great temptation for bandits.

We spent the night in one of the facilities, and I decided to speak with some of the soldiers. I could not reveal myself to just anyone, but I felt I could trust these men.

My reveal to them was simple: I showed them the tattoo that I received when we were enlisted in to Nebuchadnezzar's army. Mine was different from theirs, but only in some small details based on unit designations. All tattoos of the realm started with a basic figure, a creature that seemed to be made up of several animals – a lion, a lizard or crocodile, and a bird of some kind (I had always assumed it to be an eagle). We all knew what marks were legitimate, and theirs definitely were.

"This route has been here as long as anyone can remember," one of the men told me. "The two rivers are relatively close to each other at this point."

"Why doesn't the channel reach all the way across?"

"It once did, and not that long ago. About seven years ago, right before I was posted here, the order came to fill in the middle section. At first, everyone thought the idea ridiculous, but now we see what was truly in mind."

"There was no way to have this sort of control," he continued, "with just a continuous waterway. Tomorrow you will see the Enki gate. It marks a line that can be defended, from one side or the other, if need be."

"An attacker coming down the Tigris would have a real fight on his hands trying to get an army across to the Euphrates at this point. The Enki gate is a narrow opening in a great wall running north and south here between the rivers. Even though it is not visible from Babylon itself, it reaches almost to the city, blocking one attack route very effectively. I was told it was the Hebrew who came up with the idea. So far no one has tested its effectiveness, but I am confident it would do what it was designed to."

The next morning dawned hot and dry. There was no vegetation seen, and I mused that that fact in itself would be a deterrent to an army. There was no place to hide, no water to drink, and nothing to eat.

The morning seemed to drag on endlessly. For a man of action like myself this plodding place was maddening. Finally, with the sun directly overhead, we made out a shape in the distance.

The Enki gate was indeed just an opening. It was decorated only slightly; nothing like the gates in Babylon. There was a lone figure near the top of each side; the same one tattooed on my right shoulder.

If the gate was unimpressive, the same could not be said of the walls themselves. It wasn't a question of decoration, but of shear immensity. I thought they were even taller than the walls of Babylon itself, but that was probably an illusion created by their dramatic and sudden appearance in such a barren place, and by the fact that they followed the crest of a ridge. As I had been informed, they did indeed stretch left and right as far as I could see. The passage through the wall was much lower than the ridge, and I remembered that the man I was talking to yesterday had said this was a canal before.

At the gate, there was considerable bureaucratic activity. We were still under orders not to reveal the presence of the queen in our midst, but now Asphenaz stepped forward, taking the chief inspector off to one side for a brief conversation. When they returned, we were allowed on our way, much to the dismay of other groups who had arrived before us, and were still awaiting authorization to move forward.

The other side of the gate was much like what we had seen on the Euphrates side. I decided to talk with Asphenaz for a bit. He had been on the boat with the queen until coming out to deal with the gate passage, and he seemed glad for the fresh air.

"I don't know how much more of that woman's whining I can take!" he declared. I had never seen this side of him. He was always so proper and diplomatic. I was glad he felt he could open up to me that way. Our relationship had grown beyond its strict beginnings, but he was not usually an easy person to converse with. Now, it seemed, the floodgates were opened, and the journey back to diplomacy would have to wait for the tide to slow.

"I realize she is cooped up. So am I! But one must make sacrifices for the good of the realm at times, don't you agree, Kasher? Of course you do. Look at you. Your whole life is dedicated to Babylon, just as mine is, and Daniel, and Arioch. But we are few these days my boy. People just don't seem to understand how important the stability of Babylon is! Not even the queen! She is so concerned for her own comfort that she cannot see her true role in things. If she is found out – if she were to be captured – I won't even try to imagine the ramifications."

I thought about interjecting a thought at that point, but I sensed he was not through and needed to continue the flow for a bit more.

"Loyalty. No one seems to know what that means any more. Commitment to a cause bigger than one's self. That is what Nabopolassar showed me when he came to my village. You probably don't know about my roots, do you Kasher?"

"No, sir. I only know who you are now, and I admire you, especially your dedication to the king."

"He came to our village, Nebuchadnezzar's father did, when I was just ten-years-old. You and I, my friend, are in fact neighbors! My village was one of many scattered through the reeds just outside of Nippur."

I attempted to blink the look away that spontaneously appeared on my face, but it was to no avail.

"Yes, I am Ma'adan. No need to hide your reaction, Kasher, I know all the stories told in Nippur about my people. I don't hold it against you – in fact I don't hold it against the citizens of Nippur now. There was a time, though, when I harbored deep hatred for them. The things they said about us! But I now realize that, along with the fear that is normal when we are confronted with something different (and my people are, indeed, unique), the 'dry people' (as we called you) were worried their children would wander off into the swamps and be lost forever – a real possibility. So I have come to forgive them the stories invented of our love of human flesh and our ability to breathe under water."

"I… I don't know what to say," I stuttered. "When I first saw you, and then met you, I must confess I found you different from anyone else I had met. But now, after knowing you as long as I have, I have pretty much stopped thinking about the differences. You are simply Asphenaz to me."

"I understand perfectly," he assured me. "Imagine what it was like for me when I was brought out of the swamp and everyone was different to me."

"You mentioned Nabopolassar. Was he the one who brought you out?"

"Yes, it was he, but not against my will."

"My parents had been killed in a raid from Ur. Somehow a group of very evil men had found my village and decided they should have what we had. I barely remember the raid. I must have been about three or four at the time, but I do remember my father and other villagers fighting them. At one point my mother got me into a small boat, and began pushing me off the knoll. She waded out as she pushed the boat – I suppose to make sure it had cleared the land completely – and then she tried to climb into it. The last image I have of my mother was of her being dragged backwards away from the boat."

"I don't remember much after that until a year or so later. I was found by a man from another village as he was out fishing. He and his family were kind to me, but they never were able to consider me as one of their own. I tried every way I knew how to please them, thinking they would eventually see me as a son, but they already had three sons and two daughters, and that acceptance just never came."

"Then, one day, we had a very big surprise. The chief of all our tribe showed up unannounced at our village, and he was not alone. The boats that came to shore in front of our house were almost too many to find space along the shoreline."

"The men that came with the chief reminded me of those in my nightmares, but I was too intrigued to be very afraid. I stationed myself near a side door of the warehouse they were in, and I listened as an alliance was formed."

"As I listened, hearing little, and understanding even less, two rough hands grabbed me from behind. I had time for one short yelp before one of the hands released its hold on my arm and clamped down over my mouth. I was able to bite the hand, and then it was my attacker who was yelping!"

"Someday, if you get very close to Nebuchadnezzar, you might even see the scar in the meat of his hand, just back from his left thumb."

"Nebuchadnezzar! You bit the king's hand?"

"Well, to be fair to me, he wasn't king yet. In fact he and I are the same age. He had accompanied his father on that trip and caught me snooping. I couldn't very well be blamed for biting an unknown hand that was trying to take hold of me, now could I?"

I stood, my mouth agape, for several moments, trying to take in what I had just been told.

Asphenaz had not said anymore to this point, and I finally found my voice.

"The man you serve, as one of his closest aides and advisors, you met by biting!"

"Indeed. I was taken prisoner at that point, and the family who had taken me in had no objections. As nice as they had been to me, they were obviously relieved to have one less mouth to feed."

"Alright, so you were taken prisoner. How did you go from that… to this?"

"It didn't take long for my situation to change. In fact it was the next day. I was bound, just my hands, and guarded closely. Nebuchadnezzar walked alongside my guards, his hand bandaged and his anger for me very apparent. I decided to try to smooth over the situation, and started talking to him."

"At first he ignored me, or shot me looks that would have frightened me if I knew what I know now; but I was not intimidated. I had already gotten the best of him."

"I was brought up in the palace; not unlike your son's experience now. It took a while, but Nebuchadnezzar and I worked through our initial antagonism and became good friends. I have grown to respect him as a great man, but I will always consider him my friend."

Our land journey ended unceremoniously. All at once we came to a canal just like on the other side, and, after loading everything and everyone back on the boats, we floated to the Tigris where we turned north again.

We were obviously moving gradually higher in elevation, the ascent of the river becoming more difficult as we went. At certain points along the way there were mules along the shore to pull boats through a particularly steep section. The cost was nominal, so we paid for the service without fear of revealing our true wealth. Most boats we saw were doing the same. Because the terrain was still so similar to ours I began doubting the queen's descriptions of her land. There would have to be a rapid change for it to become as different as she said in such a short time.

The morning of the third day started the same as the first two. We had not encountered any complications thus far. A few caravans dotted the river banks, but nothing about us seemed to stand out to them. They greeted us cordially as fellow travelers and continued on their way. A short way into the morning I noticed two new things.

First, there was another group of boats coming along behind us. I could not make out any details yet, but they were obviously moving a little faster than us as they were gradually making up ground.

The other thing was in front of us. There was a line of mountains, taller than any I had seen, seeming to block our way.

Before we actually reached the beginning of those mountains we came to a large dock area. Utanin led all our boats into an empty section, and we prepared to disembark.

"Welcome to Nineveh," he said.

Looking around I saw much movement, but no sign of an actual city.

Seeing my confusion, he began explaining.

"Once a great city, capital of the Assyrians, Nineveh met its end at the hands of a coalition of Babylonians, Medes, Scythians and Cimmerians, shortly before Nebuchadnezzar came to power. They basically destroyed the city, razing it to the ground. It has not been rebuilt, but the site is well known still as a crossroads between the kingdoms; a fact which keeps trade very much alive here."

"Be especially careful here, because there is trade in more than just merchandise. Nineveh is the place to go for information, political and military, and that is always a dangerous business."

"Belteshazzar instructed me to stay here at the docks and wait for your return. You will need to go into the area known as Nimrud."

"Nimrud," I asked. "As in Nimrod, the ancient warrior?"

"Yes, there was a city founded there by his son and named for him. It was eventually absorbed into the huge city of Nineveh, and is now completely in ruins."

"There is a large, square pillar (impossible to miss) in what was the center of the city. You will be met there by a representative of Amytis' father. He will outfit you and guide you north to her home."

"How will he know we are here?"

"As I said, the trade in information here is big, and it is lucrative. Everyone in the area knows we are here, and probably has learned or deciphered by now who we are. You must take great care."

As we unloaded and bartered for transportation into Nimrud, I kept glancing back down the river. For a while I saw nothing. Then, just as we were about to set out, the boats appeared.

I tried to push them out of my mind. I had no reason to think there was anything sinister about them, but something just didn't seem quite right. I looked around me and could not locate Sirrah. Of course, with so much going on, he could be anywhere, but I was growing more and more suspicious of the man, and his absence at this moment did not help calm me.

We arrived at the pillar without incident. Amytis was finding it harder and harder to maintain her assumed identity. She was close to home, and now, in the presence of her own people, she wanted to again be allowed the ostentation of her position.

"Your highness, please," I admonished. We are still far from your land, and there are doubtless enemies about."

Reluctantly, she agreed not to change her clothes. Her bearing, however, would surely draw attention to her, but there was nothing to be done about that now. All we could do was stay attentive and protect her.

Utanin was right again. The pillar was very easy to locate, and we only had a short wait before the Armenians arrived.

All around the pillar was rubble; remnants of buildings and walls it seemed, in places piled as high as a man's calf.

The Armenians were also trying to maintain a low profile, and were being equally unsuccessful.

As the leader of the band came forward I had to physically impose myself between him and the queen. He was obviously moving to welcome her, and such an act would have been much too conspicuous. I reached out my hand in greeting, a smile on my face. In a voice that would not carry far I said, "Discretion, sir! We must have the queen's protection above any protocol, as important as that is."

A look of understanding came across his face slowly, and his pace slowed. Coming to my outstretched hand he greeted me as one would a fellow merchant.

"Of course, sir, you are quite right. Please accept my apologies. It is difficult not to present oneself to the princess without ceremony; but, of course, her safety is paramount. My name is Hekimian, and I am the captain of my great king, Rusa IV."

I hadn't even noticed at first, but it suddenly dawned on me that we were speaking in Aramaic. I commented on how well our new host spoke it, and that elicited a chuckle from him.

"I should speak Aramaic well," he said. "After all, it is our language!"

I did not feel it was the proper time to go deeper into the matter, but I knew I would have to someday.

By this time Sirrah was at my side, and I introduced first myself and then him, making sure to emphasize his leadership role in our venture.

Plans were discussed, and we were soon ready to travel to a location the Armenians had set up just outside the remnants of the walls of Nineveh.

We did not make it that far.

I heard a small noise that was somehow out of place just to one side. As I turned, armed men came in from all sides.

In the chaos of the first moment of the attack several of our men went down, stricken by swords or lances. As we recovered from the initial shock we forming a protective circle around the queen. One man charged directly in her direction, knocking his own fellow soldiers aside as he came. I jumped between the queen and him as quickly as I could. As I faced this raging figure all my joints went limp. It was the man with the scar.

An evil grimace came over his face, recognition of me seeming to fuel his rage.

So it was true. It was the man I had seen run through with an arrow as he was aiming his sword at my heart; the same one I had thought a spirit back in Nippur. Yet, here he was, intent upon finishing what he had started at the gate of Babylon.

My mind would not allow me to accept that he was real. Suddenly, a blade tore open the flesh on his arm. He was less than three paces form me when it happened, and the blood that spurted out was very real.

He did not stop, nor even slow his attack for a second, but rushed on still at me; and, ultimately, at the queen.

If I had had time to think it through, I would have been grateful to whomever it was that had cut him. Though it did not slow him, it woke me to action. My sword came up just as his was driving for the final plunge into my chest.

The fighting all around became so much background noise. Nothing else mattered but to stop this fiend. His determination was no less than mine, and we clashed repeatedly.

Somewhere in the fight between us a lull occurred, both of us having spent much energy already. As we paused, briefly, he spat in my direction.

"Your fighting skills have improved since our last encounter," he shouted over the din, "but not nearly enough to get you through this battle. Last time you had help! Where is your archer now?"

Just at that moment, something struck him on the back of the head. He went down in a heap.

As he did so, another figure came into my view. It was Ludim, my huge friend from the slave market. He stared down at the fallen man, a large stone in his massive hand. Another stone, just having been deployed, lay beside the unconscious (or dead) man with the scar.

As I smiled my gratitude to him, a strange look came over his face. He had not moved at all, but, suddenly, with a big crash he fell forward to the ground.

Behind him, bloody sword still in his hand, was Sirrah.

Anger replaced my shock, and I closed the ground between Sirrah and myself in long bounds. The speed of my attack astonished everyone who witnessed it, including myself. Before I really knew what I was doing, I was pulling my sword from his lifeless body.

I had to assess the situation. Mourning and questions would have to wait. The battle was still on.

My assessment did not encourage me. Many of our men, Babylonians and Armenians, lay dead on the ground. I glanced back at Amytis. Hekimian and several others were surrounding her, fighting off those who got close to their circle.

The circle was growing steadily denser until there was a wall of men about six deep around the queen.

As I ran toward them, I noticed they were moving their circle slowly as they fought. A quick analysis told me they were headed for the tower where we had met.

As I joined them I saw that one by one they were slipping through an opening in the tower that I had not even seen. It was a small opening at the level of the ground, only large enough for one man to get through at a time.

The circle became a semi-circle around the face of the tower where the opening was. The queen was now against the tower wall itself.

The group of men tightened as they disappeared. Soon the queen was inside as well.

Hekimian motioned for me to approach. Without a word he reached through the remaining men and grabbed me by the hand, pulling me through them, then through the opening itself.

Passing through the door, I slid downward almost immediately. Hands reached upward to ease my descent.

I understood that the men outside were to hide the existence of the opening. Some of them would, no doubt, give their lives fulfilling that task. Hekimian said as much.

"They will already be away from the tower now, as though they had never been there. Our hope is that our entrance will go unnoticed. In any case, we should move quickly."

'Move where,' I thought. We were inside of a tower. It was only a moment before I realized that this was not completely unfamiliar to me. Torches were lit, and I immediately recognized the space as identical to the one in which Muldan had met his end: we were in the pit from which the archers had shot him in Nippur. As in Nippur, there was an opening into a passageway.

The Armenians had obviously set this escape route up ahead of time in anticipation of something like what had just happened. Torches and flint had been at the ready, and they evidently knew where to go from here.

Looking around me I could see several of our men from Babylon, but many were unaccounted for, including Kartan. I hoped they would be alright, but assumed the worst. We had a job to do, and that was to protect the queen. They would have to fend for themselves.

The sloping corridor led, just as in Nippur, into a great chamber. It was remarkable how similar all this was to the structure there.

With the new information I surmised that the tower we had entered was just one chamber of the original structure; the only thing that was left of a great building just like the one in Nippur and the one under construction in Babylon.

All the talk that I had heard about Nimrod – and here I was in the ruins of one of his cities. I was still unsure of all the connection to Nimrod and these structures, but there was no denying that one existed.

Maybe Pul had been right. Maybe Nimrod was coming back.

For a brief moment I allowed myself to think about a spiritual world; one in which such things would be possible – maybe even normal. But I knew better. There was always an explanation, and in my opinion these buildings were attempts by superstitious people to escape reality. If Nimrod really had lived, he was certainly gone now.

The thing that caused me the most confusion in all this was Nebuchadnezzar's part in it. Was it possible he had really been deceived, or was he just keeping the Chaldeans happy?

My thoughts were cut short as something on the ceiling gleamed in the light of the torches. I called for several of the men to join their torches with mine as I tried to make out what I had seen up there on the vaulted ceiling.

As my eyes became accustomed to the darkness of the place I was able to make out, by torchlight, the figure of an owl, just where it had been in Nippur. The rubble above was doubtless blocking any sunlight from coming through its eyes, but in one of those dark sockets was the source of the gleam.

Even from here, and even in these conditions, I recognized it as a disk like the two I possessed.

I had mine safely stored away in our home. I hadn't even thought about them for a long time, but this one brought back all the memories of how I had come to have them.

I didn't have time to contemplate what all this meant, but I would certainly investigate the connection with the eyes of the owl as soon as I could.

We moved farther into the room, headed for the opening to the tunnel at the other side. There was no noise from behind us, so we believed our ruse must have worked. The queen was much calmer than I would have expected under the circumstances, and she followed Hekimian's instructions without question. For all their lapses of judgment at our original meeting, they were very professional in their protection of Amytis.

I knew now, of course, that their demeanor had not been the cause of the attack. Sirrah was obviously working for someone who wished to harm Babylon. I vowed to myself that I would find out who that was.

There was a side tunnel running off to the right of the one that led out of the great chamber. I did not remember such a route in Nippur. Either it had been well hidden or this one was unique to Nimrud.

We took that way and found ourselves in another room; nothing so grand as the one we had come from, but large enough for all of us to find a place to sit on the floor.

The queen was led to a stool covered with leather and sheepskin toward the back of the room. I had not seen anyone bring it in or set it up, so I presumed it had been ready from before. I was pleased to see Asphenaz at her side. We had not talked much during all of this, but I knew his place was with her, and she would be comforted by his presence.

There was food, too, pulled from a hole on the middle of the floor. It had been covered simply with wood planks as it did not need to be hidden down here. We all ate cheese and some hard bread, drinking a slightly fermented juice of some fruit I did not know.

I watched as the men came through the door, trying to see how many of ours had made it. There weren't many, and that made be both sad and proud, knowing that many of them had given their lives defending Babylon's queen.

We stayed for what seemed like a full day or so. I understood the need to do so, and I had learned the importance of being still at times like this. I had heard Nakhti say many times, 'A good soldier is always alert, but still but takes advantage of opportunities to rest.'

Obviously, we were waiting for the enemy to move on while we caught our breath. I could not imagine what they must have thought when we seemingly vanished from the battle field. Hekimian had told me the entrance we used was completely sealed now.

"I was told Nineveh is the place for information," I began. "I am in need of some right now."

"What is it you need to know, Kasher?"

"I need to know who these men are who attacked us. More importantly, for whom they work. Sirrah was with them, a traitor to his king. I have no doubt now that he has been subverting the kingdom for quite some time now, but which of our enemies did he aide?

"I will find out what I can; but understand, the information may not be complete given the circumstances."

After a little while (time being difficult to judge underground) Hekimian came back.

"They say it is the new *Umman Manda*. Zaluti is back."

He also recounted the results of the battle we had just fought. Our men, Babylonians and Armenians, had fought valiantly, eventually killing well over half of the enemy forces before succumbing or escaping through the door into the tower. The Armenians had a second force just outside of the city which was able, eventually, to push the attackers away. They then went to wait for us at a predetermined meeting place.

The skins supplied for the queen to sit on were stretched out at one point so she could recline on them. I began to admire her calm demeanor in a difficult moment. She appeared to be able to sleep soundly here in this place that was as far from what she was used to as it could be.

I took the opportunity to sleep as well, but before I could really relax my mind went through what I knew about the owl and its eyes.

That there was a connection to Nimrod; that was certain. Utanin had said the Chaldeans would be awed by them, but he had never explained why.

I wondered if Nebuchadnezzar would have an owl like that in his tower. It made sense that he would as so many things were the same between this one, the one in Nippur and what was visible in Babylon…

I woke at the sound of movement around me. My sword was in my hand before I could even think of reaching for it. A gentle voice said, "It's all right Kasher. Only friends here!"

"Kartan! I thought surely you were lost to us."

"You know I'm no soldier, Kasher. I hid when all the fighting started. I recognized one of the Armenians a few minutes ago up above, and he brought me down here."

"I'm so glad you're alright. I'm afraid Ludim wasn't so fortunate. I saw him go down. I presume he is dead."

"I'm afraid so, Kasher. I went to him as quickly as I could, but he was already gone. I will miss the great hulk of a man very much. We have become very close."

I motioned for him to sit next to me, and we were silent for a while. I would miss the big man, too.

"And the man with the scar – the one Ludim hit with a rock. Is he dead?"

"I don't know, Kasher. I saw the whole scene, but in the chaos that came after, I never saw him again. If he died, his body was removed."

Would I ever be free from that man?

The rest of our journey was without major incident. We emerged from hiding in another section of the ruins, and, filtering ourselves out a few at a time, roused no suspicion.

The last of the men came out during the second night after the attack. All of us had been advised of the new meeting place. When we arrived, Hekimian had everything in order for the next leg of our trip.

We left Nineveh, climbing to the top a small ridge. On the other side was the view I had seen from the river. Directly in front of us was a mountain range; rugged, rocky and still as barren as all the land I had seen that was not hard onto a river or canal.

I was happy to see we were actually skirting the range. It might mean a longer walk, but climbing those steep slopes did not seem a smart idea.

Our path was clear enough. Many others had opted for going around, long before we came by here.

The air was hot, but less than before. Even though we were avoiding the steepest part of the mountains, we were still climbing steadily. The first night was one of the coldest I had ever felt. Fires were lit and animal skins were brought out, but still it was cold.

During the second day, we entered into a pass in another range. We were still climbing; now with rocky ridges extending upwards on both sides.

On the fourth day, I noticed we were descending. The slope was very similar to what we had been climbing. Below us was a huge body of water, still a couple days walk I calculated.

"*Parsuwash.*"

It was Hekimian who spoke, now walking beside me.

"We should have plenty to drink soon," I said.

"Not from that lake," he responded. "Parsuwash is a salt lake. Not fit for drinking."

Nakhti had told me of seas that were full of salty water, but I had not seen one before.

"We know where the sweet water is, don't worry. But don't drink from Parsuwash – warn your men. It will make you sick at the very least."

We camped on the northwest side of the lake on the sixth night out from Nineveh in a huge oasis called Dilmagan. It was well farmed, and the inhabitants treated us with kindness. It was obvious they knew who Hekimian was.

We spent two days in this comfortable spot. I was anxious, as always, to move on, but Hekimian had informed me that he had sent scouts ahead to assure our safety as we travelled from here to Amytis' home.

I was already seeing more things for the first time. I had judged the mountains we skirted as being tall, but those to our immediate north had to reach right to the stars.

Some of the tops were white. On the second day there I asked some questions of the Armenians around me, and they directed us to a man they called 'the Chronicler'.

"He is the one to answer your questions fully. It is his function to record all that we see and experience."

I called Kartan over and we were taken to the Chronicler. He was a small man whose age I could not determine. He looked both old and young at the same time to me; and he reminded me a lot of Asphenaz.

"What knowledge do you seek, young gentlemen?"

"We are seeing such mountains for the first time, and I have only heard of the white substance that covers some of them," I answered.

"Snow. The air up there gets very cold. Water can become completely solid in that air, and rain becomes a softer version of it. Why it is white, well, I suppose the gods decreed it."

"It is beautiful," said Kartan, "but the queen spoke of green hills, covered in trees and all sorts of plants. We have yet to see that."

"From here we have about six more days travel before we reach Kafan where King Rusa is presently residing. You will see plenty of green as we near that city, I assure you."

"Chronicler, can you enlighten us as to the nature of this Umman Manda and their leader, Zaluti?" I asked.

"The priests tell us," he began, "that Umman Manda was formed by uniting smaller kingdoms from around this area into a force for unified control. That control was to belong to the god Enlil in his struggle for dominance among the gods. He chose a man (some say it was a son of the demigod Hayk) to lead his earthly host."

"And we are told they are back," I added.

"That is what is being said. I do not know who their leader is, but he will not be easily thwarted. It is said he is part god – possibly immortal already."

My mind went immediately to the man with the horrific scar. I had seen him dead - or at least that was what I thought - and yet here he was again, fighting against Babylon.

"Nebuchadnezzar serves Marduk," I said, thinking aloud.

"He is Enlil's greatest rival, other than Jehovah," said our guide.

"I remember something about one of the men who attacked us in Nineveh. I have already faced him several times in battle. I was told he belongs to the Army of Jerusalem."

The chronicler frowned. "That would normally make him a follower of Jehovah. But those people are known for their lack of faithfulness to their god. It could be this 'army' is in league with the Umman Manda. His presence in Nineveh seems to indicate that."

383

"One more thing, sir." I spoke with hesitation, but I felt it necessary to ask one more question. "I mean no disrespect, but if Umman Manda is from this region, is there any chance Rusa could be with them?"

"Not as long as his daughter and grandson are in Babylon; even if he had any inclination that way – which he does not!" he answered.

I nodded my understanding. His answer made perfect sense.

He excused himself, and I hoped I had not caused any hard feelings. I was happy enough for him to go. I had much to contemplate.

Kartan and I talked well into the night, trying to make sense of all these new pieces of the puzzle. Some things were starting to make sense – some of the alliances and resulting battles. Too much of it was related to the gods for my liking.

"So, Marduk and Enlil are at each other," Kartan said. "And Nebuchadnezzar, being a follower of Marduk, has enemies because they follow Enlil."

"I believe that about sums it up, yes," I interjected. "And here we are in the middle of it all – required to give our lives for our cause. Religion is such a muddle! But I serve Nebuchadnezzar because I believe in him; not his god."

Chapter 33

The following morning we started out again. Our path led us between the north edge of the lake and another mountainous area, then through a pass in those mountains. From there we followed an extremely barren valley, skirting more tall hills at the northern end.

At the end of the second day we came to a small river where we camped for the night. We had seen no one outside of our group since we entered the valley the day before, adding to the desolate feeling. At least here we had running water. That seemed to buoy all our spirits.

The sandy soil we were used to had changed gradually as we progressed. This river was lined with rocks up to the size of a man's hand, and we could see another terrain change just to the other side.

There we began to see bigger rocks, and up the slopes of the hills, boulders the size of a man.

We followed the river eastward for most of the next morning, crossing just after noon. On both sides of us we had tall hills; still rocky, but now there was more vegetation.

"I'm beginning to see what Amytis was talking about," said Kartan. "This far from the river and still green – it truly is a beautiful place."

One of the Armenians walking close by joined in. "If you think this is green, just wait a little longer."

I could not imagine a place greener than this that was not right by running water. The next day brought a totally new perspective.

We came to what appeared to be the very end of a mountain range. The heights before us were unlike anything we had ever seen up close. Our guides turned us into a thicket of wood. A path began to make itself known through the denseness of the trees. Soon, we were enveloped in a cool shade that caused us to shiver – though I don't know if it was only from the change in temperature.

We walked wide-eyed through trees that only got taller and thicker as we went. There was no horizon – only green.

The Armenians were obviously enjoying our amazement as they watched our faces. We didn't mind too much. Besides, there was no way we could keep from reacting that way even if we had wanted to.

Even the sounds were different here. Our footsteps seemed muffled, and yet any conversation seemed louder than normal. The man who had spoken to us the day before came over to us again.

"So, now do you understand?"

"Please tell me," answered Kartan, "that it doesn't get even greener than this. I don't think I could bear it."

"No, this is about the limit – anywhere in the world, I would suppose. Look there!"

With that exclamation he ran to the side of the path and through himself up on a large branch. Looking at the tree we saw it bore fruit, about the size of a pomegranate, and dark red as well.

The Armenian proceeded to pick one and toss it to us. I caught it, and immediately saw that it was not at all like a pomegranate after all.

The skin was smooth, and when I dug a fingernail into it, it oozed a clear liquid; something like a ripe fig.

By this time the man was standing next to us with several of them in his hand. He handed one to Kartan and then took a bite out of one of the others, showing us the white flesh inside.

As he had not died from the eating, we both took big bites out of ours.

"They are called apples, and they are a northern fruit."

"They are delicious, and so refreshing," I said. "They would certainly be welcome in the desert."

The Armenian introduced himself as Armo.

"Sounds like your country is named for you," quipped Kartan.

"In a sense, it is," Armo responded. "I am descended from an ancient leader named Armayis. Some claim he was the son of a god; but I won't ask you to kneel."

"Hekimian said Aramaic is the language of your people. Does that mean it originated here?" I asked him.

"It is our belief that it did. Our stories tell us that Hayk, the giant, brought the language with him in a pouch on his belt when he came from the night sky to begin our people. I'll point him out to you tonight if the sky is clear. He taught it to Aram, whose father was on the Ark. He is our first father."

"What is this 'Ark'? asked Kartan.

"High in those mountains you see in front of us sits a huge boat: Noah's Ark. Noah, along with his wife, three sons and three daughters-in-law, were saved from the destruction the rest of the world experienced; the Great Flood. The ark came to rest on Mount Ararat, just beyond that first ridge there. You have never seen anything like it. The Ark is huge. Noah carried every kind of animal on it, saving them for our use as well."

"Is it still intact?" I asked, truly intrigued by this revelation.

"Mostly. As you are about to see, some parts it have been used for other things."

"What are you talking about?" asked Kartan.

"You'll see when we get to the palace. We should be there in an hour or so."

We talked about the differences and similarities of our experiences as we continued on our way. The terrain got more and more rugged as we went. Finally we made our way up and through a narrow pass. As we came out the other side, the most beautiful valley I had ever seen greeted us.

It was a large valley, hemmed in on all sides by mountains. The ones we had just passed through were the smallest, and the ones at the far end of the valley from us were gigantic, and topped in white.

A lake filled a large portion of the center of the valley, and at the end closest to us there was a settlement.

The central feature of the town was a huge, brown structure. Even from this distance I could see it was different from any I had ever seen.

As we approached the town I could see that the large building had a base of stone – huge slabs of granite. Much of the structure from about half way up the walls was made of wood.

"From the Ark," Armo informed me.

We were escorted, with quite a lot of pomp, into the palace through a massive wooden door.

"The actual door of the Ark."

Inside, Amytis was greeted directly by the king and queen. They were obviously very fond of their daughter, and a great banquet was ready for us in the great hall.

We feasted on meats that I could never have imagined: deer boar and bear were in abundance. I enjoyed the new tastes as much as anything I had ever eaten.

There were several varieties of fowl that were also new to me, as well as fish that I had never seen. Topping everything off were thick, gooey cakes; not completely unlike what I was used to, but the fruits used were different. I recognized apples in quite a few of them, but there were other fruits I did not know.

The next few days were uneventful for me and my men. Asphenaz had stayed in the background until now, and I recognized his great wisdom in this seemingly small detail: He let the fighting men do the fighting and protecting, never interfering. Now it was his time for action. He and the royal court spent the next three days in whatever discussions such people have. We soldiers were accustomed to such lulls, and this was a particularly pleasant place to be stopped.

A lot of our time, mine and Kartan's, was spent in discussions with Armo. He was particularly helpful as we attempted to mentally design the new garden we were planning for Amytis in Babylon.

"When you look at a tree from above, like up in the pass, you don't notice how much the branches hang downward. That might sound like a simple thing, but the perspective you are going to have there in Babylon is

389

always from below. The garden needs to have a sense of things hanging down - like the tree branches - if you want the right look."

We also gazed into the night sky together. I was not surprised when he pointed out the figure of Hayk to me. Hayk, Orion, Nimrod; there were elements of the story that were always there.

When the conferences were ended I spoke with Asphenaz.

"There is a man here, very faithful to our queen, who has great insight into the natural beauty of this place. If he could be convinced to accompany us back to Babylon, I think he would be of great service."

"If he agrees – and his king, also, of course – that would be fine with me, Kasher. I will speak to the king for you. Find the man and know his mind on the matter."

Armo agreed to go back with us, at least for a time. King Rusa was also glad for him to go.

"He said it would be good for Amytis to have an Armenian at her side," Asphenaz told me.

Asphenaz appeared sad as we spoke. I asked him if he wanted to talk about what was troubling him. He seemed glad of the opportunity, and we found a place to speak alone.

"I do not think Amytis has any notion of the troubles her father is facing. Even the fact that he is staying here in this valley is a bad sign. Of course, he just tells her that he is on a respite from the normal pressures of his duties, but I have talked to others in his court that say he has been here for almost a year now."

"I thought this was the capital of the kingdom" I knew Asphenaz would not ridicule me for simple ignorance. I would not have had access to this information.

"No, Kasher, the capital is quite a distance from here, and I have information (reliable, I believe) that it is no longer under his control. I believe he is hiding here from some powerful enemies."

"*Umman Manda?*"

"How do you know about them?"

"Hekimian's chronicler filled us in on some of the local conflicts. Are they behind Rusa's troubles?"

"I believe they are, and I intend to gather a bit more information when we return to Nineveh. This coalition could mean real trouble for Babylon if it goes unchecked. It might even be necessary to rescue Rusa in order to have a strong ally here in the north. As it stands right now, he does not look to be very strong."

Chapter 34

We had lost a large percentage of our men in the attack in Nineveh. I was standing with Asphenaz in the courtyard of the palace when Hekimian came to us.

"There is a contingent of seventy men waiting for you at the city's edge. They will replace your security force on the journey back to Babylon. I guarantee they will follow your orders as long as you are protecting Amytis. Keep our princess safe!" he said, then turned on his heel and was gone.

On the trip back to Nineveh we were attacked by two different bands of men at two different times. They were obviously common thieves, poorly organized and armed, and we had little trouble handling them.

As we approached Nineveh I realized, to my shame, that I had not given any thought to Utanin since we left him there.

Asphenaz had decided we would camp on the outskirts of the city ruins for the night, making our way to the river the following morning. He wanted the opportunity to get current information, and we needed to arrange supplies for the trip down the river.

I asked his leave to go and see about Utanin, and he gave it. I chose some of our best men to accompany him as he moved about the city. I went to the river alone.

It was almost dark by the time I found the river's edge. I saw some of our boats – only four, nothing like what we had come with - as soon as I came close to the docks, but they appeared to be abandoned. A quick check verified that fact, and I began to search the area for some sign of what had happened.

I soon saw a fire a little ways up river. It looked like the kind of fire a traveler would use to cook on, so I headed that direction.

I was met by an armed party of men well before I reached the fire. There were five of them in a semi-circle blocking my path: one had a sword, though it looked like it had seen better days. The others held either daggers or wooden spikes. I believed I could probably take them all, but I was not looking for a fight. I wanted know what had happened to my friend.

"I mean you no harm," I said. "I seek only information."

"What information do you seek?" said the one in the middle. He appeared to be the eldest of the group, but the quickly fading light made it impossible to say for sure.

I had spent so much time with Asphenaz now that I barely noticed his peculiar way of speaking. But this man was only the second person I had ever speak with that whistle in his voice.

"You are Ma'adan," I declared evenly.

The reaction was immediate and strong. All five took a step back and raised their weapons as if in defense.

"Please, do not misunderstand!" I pleaded, my hands held out in front of me to show I was not threatening. "I am a friend of the Ma'adan: at least I have a good friend who is one."

"So it is true what the elder boatman said," the elder man said, still wary. "We believed it to be something he dreamed because of his injuries."

"The elder boatman! He lives?" It could only be Utanin, surely. "Please, take me to him. He is very important to me."

They were not quick to respond, talking amongst themselves for a few moments. Finally the same man spoke.

"Tell us his name – if he is so important to you. And yours. He speaks always one name in his dreams."

"His name is Utanin, and mine is Kasher. We have shared many adventures, and he is as close to me as a family member."

Their mood changed immediately. Their weapons now held carelessly at their side, they approached.

"You have found your friend, Kasher. Come, you need to see him now. I fear his time is very short."

I was relieved that the confrontation was over, but my heart sank as he spoke of Utanin's condition while we made our way towards the campfire.

"We found him in the river. There was debris all about, and dead bodies, too. We were scavenging for anything useful when someone heard a moan coming from under a pile of wood on the shore. I, myself, lifted the wood and found him there, barely alive. Just before he lost consciousness, he said, 'Sirrah.' It meant nothing to us, but we took him to our camp to try to help him. He has been coming and going to and from the next life since then. I fear he will go soon to stay."

Without further conversation they led me back toward the fire that had caught my attention. Around the fire were several tents; not large, but each big enough for a few people to sleep in.

Still without speaking, one of the men went to the front of the center tent and opened the flap. He looked back at me, and I understood I was to enter. As I went inside, he handed me the torch he had been carrying.

The flap closed almost silently, but I felt the air movement it caused. That slight stirring was enough to cause the figure on the floor to stir and moan lightly.

I knelt before Utanin and said his name. He immediately looked in my direction. I had seen death many times, but always as a sudden event. This was death happening; coming on slowly, but no less certain.

"Kasher!" His voice was weak, but the joy in it at seeing me was still intense. "Now I can let go."

"Let go – what do you mean, you old river rat? It's time to go alright, but back to Babylon."

"No Kasher," a thin smile on his face. "I won't see Babylon again in this life. No! Don't speak! I know, and I have accepted this. I am consoled in the fact that you came. My prayer is answered, and I can go in peace."

"What prayer? What are you talking about, Utanin?"

"I never told you – I should have, but I lacked the courage. About a year ago, after Tinsa died, I was very ill. Your wonderful wife and your wonderful mother came to my aid. You were off on a mission when it happened, and by the time you came back, I was well again. Anyway," he said with a weak gesture, as if trying to push on while he still had time, "they kept me at your house and nursed me back to health. Kasher, there was life in that house I had never experienced before. There was peace, even when things did not seem to go well. I was curious - I wanted to know how such peace could exist in the human life. They began to tell me of their God – the true God, Kasher! They explained to me, showed me from their writings, how different Jehovah was from all the gods I had known about. How He hated evil and loved those who chose good. How He was the giver of spiritual life – for the asking! I could not resist such a God. I embraced Him as He is, the one true God."

I was speechless, both because of this revelation, and because I was trying to process what all this had to do with my being here now. Perhaps it was delirium; he was dying, after all.

Mercifully he continued before I could form a question or response.

"I asked Jehovah for the chance to see you before I died… and here you are!"

I found my voice at last. "I'm glad I found you my old friend, but let's not talk of death. We have cheated it before, and we will this time, too."

"No, I am ready for the next great adventure, and it will come very soon. I prayed to get to see you so I could tell you just a few things. Please, let me continue. I am running short of time."

"First, I beg you to ask your wife and your mother about their faith. I know we have lived a long time, you and I, doubting the very existence of things spiritual, but believe me, Kasher, they exist. Even before I learned of Jehovah I was confronted by that reality. Some things I saw and heard could be explained no other way, but for most of my life I preferred to ignore them."

I wanted to interrupt – to debate this ridiculous ranting. But he was growing weaker right before my eyes, and I couldn't go to such a cruel place. I listened, nodding from time to time.

Finally, I did interrupt. There was something I needed to confirm.

"Utanin, the man who found you said you spoke the name of Sirrah. Was it he who did this?"

"I'm afraid so, Kasher. The band of men looked like a mixture of Egyptians, Assyrians and Philistines. As a sword was being pulled out of me, I looked up on the ridge above the river and saw Sirrah and some others talking. They were clearly in charge of what was happening."

"You must get that information back to the king as quickly as possible. May God protect you."

I started to protest, as I had done when my mother said similar things, but Utanin held his hand up to stop me.

Instead I said, "The king will be informed, but Sirrah won't be bothering anyone anymore. I made sure of that. He came for the queen when he was done here."

"Do you still have the eye?"

"The eye?" I feared my friend was losing touch with reality. It made sense given his present condition. "What eye, Utanin?"

"The disk you recovered when I dropped it as we fled to Babylon."

"Ah, that eye. I have never heard it called that, but I think I understand why you would. Yes. I still have it, and another besides."

His voice took on a new strength as he said, "You have two?"

Something about the way he asked the question caused me to feel a chill deep inside me.

"Um, yes, Utanin. I found another disk while I was a captive of Nakhti, before we came into Babylon. And there's another – here in Nimrod, in one of the holes made for them in the ruins of a structure like Etemenanki. Apparently there have been several towers built, or at least partially built, with the same purpose; whatever that is exactly."

My old friend mustered up strength from somewhere and leaned forward to speak a grave warning. "Kasher, you must never let the Chaldeans know you have them both. If you need leverage with them, you can tell them you have one. They will want it desperately, so keep it hidden if you do tell them. But never - never Kasher - let them know you have two."

"What are you talking about, Utanin? Why would they care if I have them?"

"I never discovered the exact use they want them for. You remember how concerned I was about losing mine? I learned - years ago when I was growing up with Nebuchadnezzar - that they were searching for them: two of them. They called them the *eyes of Nimrod;* but, again, I never knew why.

"I found mine in Ur, right before you came on my boat. A friend and I had stumbled onto a fascinating chamber beneath one of the temples there. It was mostly full of documents – cylinders written in several languages. I found a small wooden chest, and it contained only the eye."

"The friend I was with was a priest of that temple, and he had once been a Chaldean wise man. For some reason he had been shunned by them, and Ur had been pretty much abandoned as a Chaldean worship center, in favor of Babylon."

"Still, he knew about the eyes – at least that they were important to the Chaldeans. If he knew more details about them, he never let on to me that he did. He did explain to me, however, how precious they were to the ambitions of the Chaldeans."

"'They will kill for them,' he told me. And they needed two. I suppose that makes sense, they are eyes, after all."

A slight, ironic smile crossed his lips

"Among those cylinders was one that caught my eye. It showed a machine to transport water – even uphill! That cylinder is under what was my bed in the house you now live in. It might be of use to you some day."

His voice was fading back to its former weakness; his face now farther from mine as he lay back in the bed. I leaned forward to hear him better.

"Kasher," his voice almost a whisper now, "remember this one thing: Jehovah has provided forgiveness to all who will accept it. In spite of all my failures, I go to my God in peace."

His last word hung in the air as my dear friend stopped breathing.

Tears filled my eyes. I wept for my loss, but there was something more. I also wept because of the realization that I did not have what he said he had. As I looked down at his lifeless face, I sincerely believed I saw peace.

I had seen death many times, but never like this. There was no contortion of fear, no horror stamped on those unseeing eyes. There was no other word for it. Utanin appeared to have died in peace.

I allowed myself a moment to compose, and then turned to leave the tent. Just outside, the elder Ma'adan stood, his eyes cast down to the ground.

"He is gone, then?"

There was a sadness in his voice I had not expected.

"Yes. He died very…" the word actually caught in my throat for a moment. "peacefully."

I did not notice any signal, but a wheeled cart was brought immediately to the front of the tent. Two women also appeared, and entered.

"They know how to prepare a body with dignity," I was informed. He took my shoulder and guided me toward the fire.

The other men were there, and one of them spoke.

"We are sorry for you," he stated simply. "We have come to think of your friend as one of us. He was always thankful, apologizing for being an inconvenience. In his better moments he was a good storyteller. Sometimes it was difficult to know when he was inventing and when he was telling a true story."

"Once he even said he was a personal friend of Nebuchadnezzar! He became agitated when we didn't believe him, but such a story could not be real."

"Oh, but it is real – very real indeed. He and Nebuchadnezzar grew up together in the palace in Babylon, I said."

"You can confirm this? Maybe he made the story up for you as well!"

"I am a member of the palace guard. I have been with Utanin and Nebuchadnezzar in the palace. I assure you, it is true."

"And the overturned boat – breathing through reeds with sand piling on his body! That was also true?"

"It was I who placed the reed in his mouth."

"He was so gracious to us. He laughed with us when we thought he was inventing. He was a truly good man."

"Yes, he was."

As we waited for the women to finish their work I explained our presence in that place, leaving out the fact that the queen was with us, of course.

"So, those boats were yours?" asked one of the Ma'adan.

At that moment there was movement at the tent door. Two men disappeared inside, returning quickly carrying Utanin's body. He was covered, all but his head, with a cloth so white is seemed to reflect the light of the fire.

Gently, they placed him on the cart. I made my way there, and prepared to make the long journey back to Nineveh.

"But how will you and your men get back to Babylon?" one of the men asked.

I had been thinking a lot about that, of course, but I did not have a concrete answer as yet. There was no way the three remaining boats could carry us all, but I wanted Amytis to have all the protection possible.

"I suppose most of us will have to go on foot. I do not like the idea of splitting up our group, but we will do what we must."

"You must pass by here, or at least down where your boats were moored as you go, yes?"

"Yes, I suppose that is true."

"Then leave Utanin with us tonight. There's no need for you to pull the cart all that way now. We will meet you at the docks at first light."

After a final look at the peaceful face of my dear friend I expressed my gratitude for all that had been done. "The king will know of your kindness to his friend and to me his servant."

With that I left their encampment, following the river until I came to the docks, then turning inland towards

Nineveh. One word rang in my head the whole way there
– peace.

Chapter 35

I made my way back without the aid of a torch. It was a clear night, and there was some moonlight to go along with the stars. A torch could have brought unwanted attention.

I followed the river back to the dock area and had a look at the three boats still there. I could only imagine that Sirrah had come on hired boats and had left these for his own transportation. He wouldn't be needing them now.

Attentive guards challenged me as I reached the perimeter of our camp. After confirming my identity one of them showed me to my tent. I was so tired – in so many ways – that I went straight to bed, leaving orders for the guard to inform Asphenaz of my return.

I awoke in the early morning to someone entering my tent. My dagger, always ready beside me as I slept, was in my hand before I was even completely awake. The high-pitched voice that greeted me let me know all was well.

"I am glad you made it back alright," Asphenaz said. "I know you are a capable soldier, but to be out there on your own at night – well, I was worried about you. Did you find your friend?"

I proceeded to give him an abbreviated version of the night's events, and he listened with great interest.

"I am truly sorry about Utanin," he said when I had finished. "He and I have clashed frequently – verbally, of course - through the years, but I always respected him greatly. The king will mourn him. They were very close."

"Well," Asphenaz continued, "let us be on our way.

"How should we proceed, Asphenaz? The queen would not be safe enough with only three boats worth of soldiers, I think."

"We will discuss it as we make our way to the river, young Kasher. A solution will be found, I assure you."

Even Amytis was ready quickly. She didn't say anything, but I was sure she was anxious to get back to Babylon. For my part, I was ready for her to be back within the safety of those great walls.

I tried to talk with Asphenaz on the way, but he put me off every time. I was getting frustrated with him as we topped the river embankment. From there, an amazing sight greeted us.

The three boats I had passed by the night before were still in their places, but they were teeming with activity. I would have been extremely worried by the fact if I had had the opportunity, but there was so much more to see I could not really think about it.

There were six more boats, all about the same size as ours. On the shore a man stood with his legs spread wide apart, hands on his hips. He was barking orders at the men on the boats. I could not see his face, but his voice was distinctly Ma'adan. He turned, having heard our approach, and I saw it was the leader of the group I had been with the night before.

I realized (to my shame) that I had not asked any of the good people at the campsite their names. I was spared any embarrassment when this one addressed himself directly to Asphenaz – and by name!

"We received your message, Asphenaz. The others came as soon as they could."

Asphenaz stepped forward to him and embraced him.

"You did well, Jared. The timing could not have been better."

As he came back to where I had stopped, Asphenaz had a look on his face I had never seen there. It was a genuine smile!

"Close your mouth, Kasher; you'll let flies in!"

"But... but what... how?"

"I will explain all in a bit, but everything is in order for us to load and be on our way. We should see to that first."

Back from my astonished stupor, I agreed that should be our priority, and I set about organizing the men and equipment to be loaded onto the boats. There was Utanin's body to be dealt with as well. It was on the cart, still wrapped in the bright, white cloth, only his face exposed. The word still applied. He looked peaceful.

When everything was in order, we started for home. I went to Asphenaz as soon as I could after our departure.

"Ah, Kasher. I was expecting you. You are developing into a very efficient leader. I saw how you delegated the various responsibilities amongst the men, and all seems to be functioning as it should. I am pleased."

"Thank-you, Asphenaz. I have learned much from many; yourself included. But I have not yet learned how to make boats appear from nowhere."

We shared a chuckle, then Asphenaz explained.

"I knew there were Ma'adan in the area, but I didn't know who they were or why they were here. One of Jared's men came to see me when we returned to Nineveh – at the same time you were going to their camp as it turns out. He brought news of Utanin and the boats, but you were well gone, and I knew you would find out soon enough. I sent the man north to where the rest of their boats had been sent. The group you met and talked to were the rearguard. Jared was coordinating their effort from there."

"Jared's man explained that they were on an information gathering expedition – at the request of our king. They pretended to be merchants, unusual for Ma'adan, but not unheard of these days. Our 'land' is under almost constant attack so our people do venture out more than in the past."

"Why would anyone want to attack these people? Surely no one wants to take the marsh away from them. I can only imagine the harsh life they lead in there."

"True, Kasher, I wouldn't say anyone wants to simply conquer that territory and claim it for their own; but the marsh's location, right on the edge of Nippur, makes it very important to the kingdom - and to our enemies. If they could gain control of the swamp (and learn their way around in there) they could mount attacks throughout that area. It would certainly give them a base to attack Nippur, and that city - your city – is critically located for our defense."

"And then, there are these," he said, pulling out his green stone. "They are emeralds, and they are highly prized, especially amongst the royalty. They are abundant throughout our swamp, if one knows where to look."

"Thankfully, we Ma'adan are loyal to Nebuchadnezzar, and these people were assessing potential threats here in the north. Another detail that might help you put all these pieces together is the fact that we Ma'adan and the Armenians are closely related. In fact, the city we just came from, Kafan, was originally named Ma'adan. It was settled soon after the great flood. There are stories about two brothers and a dispute between them that led one of them to move to our marshland. "

We made it back to the river-exchange crossing in good time and without incident. Traveling with the flow of the river allowed for a quick trip.

When we reached Ops, there was a lot of activity – much more than we had experienced on the way north.

Just east of the docks was a large but temporarily installed military encampment. I recognized the standard immediately. Since there was a permanent troop stationed here, I was puzzled by Nakhti's presence. I didn't have to wait long for answers as the powerful one was on the dock to greet us.

"Greetings, Uncle," I called out to him. I expected him to be very grim, given his unexpected presence here, but he seemed relaxed, if a bit serious.

"It's good to see you, Kasher. I trust the queen is well?"

"She is, sir. I'm afraid we lost a lot of good men protecting her,; but with the help of her own people she has returned safely to this point."

"Word came of your difficulties. Nebuchadnezzar insisted I come to escort you back. We got only as far as the Enki gate before we were engaged by a small but fierce army. We had only just settled that issue, and were preparing to head north when you appeared on the horizon. Come, let's get things organized and we will talk more."

I looked over the encampment once more. It was very large. News of the attack on his queen had obviously motivated Nebuchadnezzar to redouble her protection. I fought off a feeling of resentment. There were big troubles afoot, and I had witnessed first-hand the lengths some were willing to go in their fight against Babylon. I could see the wisdom in sending more protection for Amytis, especially with the news that Nakhti had had to fight his way here. I only hoped that the great city would not be in danger with so many of its troops so far away.

In the middle of the encampment was a tent that had obviously been set up for the queen. Amytis would be happy the pretense and hiding were over. She could – once again – live like a queen.

Chapter 36

The joy of reuniting with my family was dimmed by the news I had to share of Utanin's death. I hadn't realized what an impact the boatman had had on the one named for him, but the boy took the news very hard.

I didn't have much time to deal with the issue as I was called to the palace shortly after arriving at our home. I had to leave it to my wife and my mother to help the boy through his grief. I knew they were better equipped for the task, at any rate. A thought passed quickly through my mind as I hurried to my summons. A combination of my own observation just concluded and some of the things Utanin had said right before his death were trying to push me to some sort of conclusion, but I couldn't get a solid grasp on it for now. Still, that one word was ever-present – peace.

A call to the palace was something we trained for often, but seldom became a reality. Each soldier of the guard had a specific set of functions to perform when called. My job at this time was to first ensure the safety of the queen, verify that the requisite number of guards were posted at and near her door (I had developed a multi-layered defense of her quarters) and then report to the doorway that led from the great hall to Amytis' quarters.

When I reached that doorway, I nearly went in with sword in hand. The scene that greeted me was of Nebuchadnezzar and Belteshazzar seated on a raised platform towards the far entrance from my position. That, in itself, was not alarming. It was what stood before them that caused me to start. That, and the bluster and animation emanating from those in audience with the king.

I was looking at their backs but I could see them well enough – they were taller than any of us. Only now did I notice that the platform was higher than usual. Someone had worked fast to maintain the proper perspective.

Though I could see no faces, the voice that spoke left me no doubt as to who its owner was. I hadn't seen him since the day Nakhti joined forces with Babylon. Seren was back.

"We must know of his whereabouts!" the big man shouted.

I knew from my other experience with this man that he was not nearly as angry as he sounded. I had heard him angry, and the voice I remembered would shake the columns of this great hall.

Apparently, the heads of Babylon, there on the stage, understood this fact as well. They did not react as if they had been threatened. No matter how large they were, these men would not leave the room breathing if a real threat was posed.

"We are sympathetic to your need, Seren," I was amazed that it was Nebuchadnezzar himself who addressed the giant. "and we have dispatched men to inquire at every place we can imagine he might be, but

410

we have no word about your prince as of yet. Please, accept my hospitality as we continue our search."

It appeared I had arrived at the very end of this situation; a fact that did not sadden me. I wanted nothing more than to be with my family for a while. That was not to be.

"We accept your gracious hospitality, O King, but we will not be able to rest until Ludim is found."

The name came repeated from somewhere in a voice that sounded bewildered. It took a moment for me to realize it had come out of my own mouth.

Apparently, I had said the name with a fair amount of force. An opening spontaneously appeared between me and the Philistines. They stared at me through the human corridor with a look that made me consider flight. That, of course, was not an option.

"Did you say, 'Ludim'?" bellowed Seren.

I cleared my throat, lifted my head and said, "yes sir."

"Well, get up here, man!"

My legs responded reluctantly, but at last I found myself looking up into the four massive faces. The king and his minister remained silent as the center of attention shifted to the floor before them. Seren spoke at once.

"How do you know that name?"

"He... he was a friend."

"What do you mean 'was'? Are you no longer friends?" Seren's voice rose as he spoke, and I was feeling more and more vulnerable.

"No, sir. I am afraid that my friend, Ludim, is dead."

I expected a roar of rage at this news. But, instead, there were more questions. The giants even looked as though they had been given some very grave news.

"What is your name, man?"

"I am Kasher. Ludim befriended me several years ago. He was working with a trader at the time, and later he worked with another friend of mine to establish a settlement on the outskirts of Babylon."

"You said he was dead."

"Yes. I am very sorry. He saved my life just a few short weeks ago. He was travelling with me and my men as we escorted the queen Amytis to visit her father. We were attacked, and Ludim saved my life. Unfortunately, it cost him his own."

"And who was attacking you?"

"It was a group called the 'Umman-Manda' led, at that time, by a traitor to Babylon named Sirrah."

"This man, Sirrah; where can we find him?"

"You would have a difficult time finding any trace of him. I left his carcass to the jackals in Nineveh. As I said, Ludim was my friend."

The next thing that happened was not one that I would have ever expected, and it scared me as much as anything ever has. Seren reached forward in an amazingly swift movement and grasped me about my midsection. I thought I was going to be crushed - and I did in fact nearly black out from having the air removed suddenly from my lungs - but Seren was actually thanking me with a hug. He later apologized for the breach of protocol; but, he explained, "that's how it's done in Philistia."

Not a word had come from the platform during this entire exchange. At this point Seren seemed to recognize what bad form it was to ignore the king, and he turned, apologizing profusely.

"Do not worry yourself about it, my friend," Nebuchadnezzar said, dismissing the lapse with a wave of his hand. "I am sorry for your loss."

"I am afraid, great Nebuchadnezzar, that the loss of Ludim will be grievous for all of us, in time. You see, the reason for our haste and insistence is that Lord Golinis is dead. Ludim was his only son. He never really wanted the royal life, but we hoped to persuade him to return with us and take the throne. In his absence it appears Krona, the Edomite will finally be able to take over the city of Gath. He has developed close ties with Egypt, and I fear he will cause much trouble for all of us. I will do my best see to it that he is controlled. Our alliance with you, that of the other four cities, remains steadfast."

I thought about how easily things can change. Just a short time ago, we had been fighting these very men. Now, they were our allies.

After the Philistines withdrew, I turned to leave the palace. A voice called my name from the raised dais, and I turned to see it was Belteshazzar who had called.

The room was nearly empty now, and I was only a few paces from him. He had moved to the front edge of the platform and awaited me there.

Inviting me to climb the steps, he spoke again.

"The king wishes a word with you."

We made our way to where Nebuchadnezzar was still seated. I went to my knee before him, and he immediately bade me rise.

"So, we meet again Kasher. I wanted to thank you for your protection of the queen, especially during the trip north. I am sorry that Sirrah's deception was not known beforehand, but all the reports I have received on the subject say that you handled the situation well."

"Thank you, my king. It was my duty."

"Yes, and well carried out. I had already learned that Sirrah died at your hand, as you confirmed today. And Utanin is lost. He was a great friend to me."

"To me as well, my king."

"Belteshazzar, proclaim a week of mourning for our fallen friend. Our court shall fast."

"Kasher, I would like for you to remain on the queen's detail, at least until all the new security measures are in place. You are to oversee all that work, and you will now be the captain of her guard. Thank you for your loyal service. Now – make sure her quarters are well guarded and then go spend a few days with your family. You have earned them."

Chapter 37

Seren's prediction proved true. The next few years were tumultuous. Gath, under Krona, and with the help of Egyptian troops, became a real menace in the region, and a thorn in Nebuchadnezzar's side.

The areas surrounding Babylon were constantly sacked and harassed. If it were not for Nakhti's intimate knowledge of Egyptian warfare tactics, there would surely have been much more damage inflicted. We were able to keep the city relatively free from direct attack, though there were small raids at the gates during high traffic moments. Still, those of us living behind the great protective walls did not experience any great disturbance of our normal routine.

Nebuchadnezzar kept a close eye on the work adjacent to the queen's quarters. I had many moments with him; often just the two of us as we discussed the details of our new garden. The king seemed careful not to take the project out of my hands, which both surprised and encouraged me. I was learning from him, as I had begun to do with Nakhti, what true leadership was all about.

This day was no different.

"Kasher, how do you envision imitating the snow at the top of the 'mountains'?"

"That will be the most complicated part, my king, but Armo tells me they have come up with a solution. He won't say what it is, but they are expecting a trader to bring it any day now."

I had brought Armo and Kartan together for this project, and they had proven to be complimentary one to the other. Armo knew the look we were going for, and Kartan knew the realities of creating such a wonder in the conditions of Babylon.

Armo had been able to secure dark, lush green plants from up north, and Kartan had advised on how or if certain plants could be used here. They had done a great job up to this point, but the queen was adamant that there should be 'snow' atop the 'mountains'.

This problem had vexed the two gardeners for quite a while, and the garden's flora was beginning to climb very near the peaks of our man-made mountains.

"The queen must not be disappointed, Kasher," said the king with a wry smile. The smile notwithstanding, his pronouncement was serious.

"Yes, my king; the search has been exhaustive… oh, here are the gardeners now!"

"So, do we have a solution, my friends?" asked Nebuchadnezzar."

"Indeed we do, my king," said Kartan. "And we have Asphenaz to thank for it!"

"Is there nothing my strange minister does not get involved in?" the king said good-naturedly. "Now he tries his hand at gardening?"

"Well, you see, my king, one day he happened to be here watching our progress, and he asked us why the plants didn't go to the top. When we explained our dilemma to him, he shrugged and said, 'all you need is white grass from the marsh'. Then he walked away without another word."

"We assumed, correctly it turns out, that he was referring to a plant that grows where he is from. We have just received our first plants!"

With that Armo pulled a sheet off the wagon they had brought with them. The grass was indeed white, with just a thin green stripe running the length of each white leaf.

"It looks great," I said, "but if it is a marsh plant, it will need a lot of water, right?"

"Yes, and we have been working on that problem since we found out about the plant," Armo answered. "It will actually work well for us to have a swampy area at the top of the 'mountain' – a trough that will hold enough water for the marsh grass and also provide for water to trickle down to the other plants. We were always going to need to get water up to the top one way or another. We have had our men watering as we go, but it isn't practical to do that in the long run. We are looking for a better solution. Something to get the water up there!"

We all looked as he pointed to the top of our new structure. It was a long way up there, and the building went all the way down the edge of the queen's quarters, joining to the back wall of the Southern Fortress (so named because it sat on the south side of the north wall. Another stronghold, the Northern Fortress, was actually outside the north wall; a stroke of military genius designed by Nebuchadnezzar himself. It allowed for a special kind of defense – one that could push out into the attackers' ranks without exposure). On the eastern side of our construction Nebuchadnezzar was already building a great road for ceremonial purposes, the 'mountain' serving as a very impressive wall for it. Our work ran more than one hundred paces in length. We needed a lot of water.

"I may have the answered," I stated simply, turning to go before any questions could be asked. "I will be right back," I called back to them, painfully aware that I had just walked away from a conversation with the king as though we were equals. There was no going back from it, and I just hoped my new information would smooth out any insult I might have caused.

I went straight to our house and into my bedroom. I had looked at the cylinder several times since Utanin told me about it, but I didn't really understand what it was trying to explain. All I really knew was that Utanin had said it would transport water uphill, and that was what we needed to do.

Armo took one look at the images on the cylinder and became very excited.

"It will work! I can see it! My king, this will take some time to build, especially at the scale we need, but we can get the water to the top with minimal manpower. I promise it."

"All speed possible, my friends. The queen grows impatient."

Our children had grown into beautiful young adults. We never had more, just two, but Ruhamah and I were very pleased with what we had.

Utanin had spent most of his time within the walls of the palace compound. His mother complained at times of seeing so little of him, but we were both pleased with how he was turning out.

He was not inclined to the warrior's life. A part of me wished he was – another part was relieved.

I was privileged to be able to spend quite a bit of time with him in the palace compound. He told of his study time with Evil-Merodach. A prince needed to be learned in many subjects, and even though he and Utanin had never gotten very close as friends, he apparently found studying more pleasant with another student present. Utanin seemed to be taking full advantage of this arrangement, and his knowledge astounded me at times.

They were taught most of the time by Chaldean priests, but Utanin especially enjoyed their classes with Belteshazzar. I was concerned he might become confused since there was a considerable difference between the beliefs of the Chaldeans and those of the Hebrews, but I had to suppose that the king knew what he was doing with his heir, and Utanin was learning exactly the same things.

During one of my discussions with him, I asked Utanin about this. His answered went a long ways towards reassuring me. It also gave me confidence in my son's wisdom.

"Daniel, or Belteshazzar if you prefer, does teach us theology, but not only. His lessons on the natural world are amazing! He almost never contradicts anything the Chaldeans teach us, but many times he gives us a deeper explanation of what is behind a particular idea."

"For example," he continued, "the Chaldeans know much about astronomy, but Daniel has knowledge in that area that they don't seem to possess."

"Once, I was alone with him for a couple of hours. The prince had been called away for some ceremony or other during our lesson, and I took the opportunity to ask some things I had been wondering about."

"I asked him the source of his knowledge, and he explained that he was of a noble family back in Israel, and had been trained from very young to serve at court. His attitude is different from almost any I have ever encountered. He believes so strongly in Jehovah that he accepts his captivity as the will of his God without question. Apparently Nebuchadnezzar has no problem with that, and this has led to a very interesting relationship. Daniel is doing what he was trained to do; just for a foreign king."

"He told me that in Jerusalem, in the temple to Jehovah, there are writings explaining many things – including the celestial bodies. I asked where these writings came from, and he said they had been passed down for generations, and that they had been written by the third son of the first couple. His name, he said, was Seth, and Jehovah instructed him to write down the knowledge of the stars and moon; that these things were meant to show and teach truths – many of them prophetic!"

"He said that other peoples, including the Chaldeans, knew many of these truths, but that over the years they had mixed them with other beliefs and legends. That is why, according to Daniel, what we learn from the Chaldeans and what we learn from him have so much in common: both teachings come, ultimately, from one source. The truth, he said, is still in those writings, and that Noah's son, Japheth, had them on the ark with him during the great flood, and that the followers of Jehovah try to preserve the truth, but others (for their own advantage, he said) change it to meet their needs."

"So, Utanin, what do you make of all of this? Do you believe in Daniel's God as well?"

"I don't know for sure yet, Father. I see a lot of sense in what Daniel says, and Mother seems quite convinced that Jehovah is the one true God, but I see so many things that make me doubt that. There seem to be several ways to interpret what the stars say, for example. And I have seen some amazing things that were attributed to other gods – especially Marduk. I think there may be some truth in all these beliefs, but I am not sure."

"Daniel is also teaching us the First Language."

"Daniel knows that? Did he explain how he knows it?" The boy had my undivided attention at this point.

"Those writings – about the stars and all – are all in the First Language. He and his companions at court in Jerusalem were taught in that language!"

"And you are learning it from him? You and Evil-Merodach?"

"Yes, but Daniel has made us swear not to let the Chaldeans find out. He said it could actually be dangerous for us of they did. I have no idea why that would be, but I try to be careful not to talk about it."

"Utanin, I know, at least some of why it could be dangerous, and it really could. My time in the palace, along with some other discoveries I have made, has taught me that the Chaldeans are hungry for power, and ruthless in their attempts to achieve it."

"Shortly before he died Utanin warned me about them, but I had already seen how they are with my own eyes. They hide behind their religion, as though everything they did was for the good of the realm; but I see the power-lust in their eyes, especially their chief priests.

"Daniel says they are following the will of Marduk, and that he is using them to try to overthrow Jehovah," said Utanin.

"Whatever their motivation, son, they want to control the kingdom. We need to be very careful around them."

"You, Father? Do you know the Ancient Language too?"

"No, son, but I have something written in it! We will have a look at it the next time we are both at home."

Chapter 38

Nebuchadnezzar had had enough of Egyptian interference. Hophra didn't have the might necessary to do permanent damage to the empire, but he became a destabilizing force for quite a while. I found his kind of action to be cowardice. Not only would he not go out to war, he financed other, smaller nations to raid our towns and fields instead of using his own men.

This tactic played right into the aspirations of so many lesser lords. They were weak men, weakened mostly by their own grandiose image of themselves. They would never be able to forge a strong alliance capable of overthrowing a great empire like Babylon; but with the right patronage, they could weaken it, and the whole region as a result.

Petty lords like Krona.

Nebuchadnezzar had had enough. He just rode out with his army to cut at the root of this turmoil.

Nakhti captained his army. I had to stay behind this time, still in charge of the queen's safety. I expected to be disappointed at not going, but was not. No one had to tell me how important it was to stay at Babylon, and I suppose I had seen enough war not to long for it. I had no fear of doing battle when it became necessary, but I would have been very happy to live the rest of my life in peace.

Of course, my family was happy I did not go. I was required to spend a lot of time at the palace, but I saw my family almost every day. Ruhamah said she was glad not to be worrying about me, wondering if a messenger would arrive with bad news from the battlefield.

One evening I brought the piece of tablet out. Utanin and I looked it over carefully, and he was able to translate almost everything that was not cut off by the break in it. I was very proud of his ability, and I had no doubt that he had done a good job of translating, but the message didn't seem to make much sense.

"It must be because it is only part of the tablet. It would surely make more sense if we had the whole thing," I suggested.

"I didn't want to say anything before, Father, because I wasn't sure until I saw this, but I think I have seen the other piece of the tablet."

The boy's voice trembled as he spoke.

"Where, Utanin? Where did you see it?"

"The king pulled it out from a hiding place in the floor of the great meeting room. Evil-Merodach and I were just walking through, going to a lesson, and there was the king – on his knees in a corner of the room! He had pulled something out of the hole in the floor and was replacing a cover that blended in perfectly. Then he pushed a small table over it. When he saw us, he jumped up quickly, hiding the tablet in his robes, and turned to go without a word. I never saw it again, but it looked just like this one."

"I asked Daniel about it one day when we were alone. He said he didn't know about it, but that he had suspected for quite some time that Nebuchadnezzar possessed the 'Table of Destinies', or at least part of it. He claimed it was the instructions for building the Etemenanki."

My hands trembled slightly as I took the tablet back from my son. There was power involved in this piece of clay, but there remained so many questions.

Why were there so many towers like Etemenanki? What was so important about them? What part did the 'eyes' play in all this?

I asked Utanin if he knew anything about the purpose of the tower, but he said he had always assumed it was nothing more than a religious monument. He, of course, had not had my experience of seeing buildings like it in various places, so his curiosity was not at the same level as mine. And mine was growing at an amazing pace.

Chapter 39

It seemed conflict was becoming almost commonplace in Babylon. News from the war Nebuchadnezzar was waging against Egypt was that Hophra had been forced to retreat south from his fortress at Sin to Memphis. Nebuchadnezzar had destroyed the temples of Amun at Sin, a bold move which seemed to indicate a confidence on his part that his victory was complete.

But, if Hophra was subdued in Egypt, others were still in rebellion against Babylon – some of them closer to home.

Zedekiah, appointed by Nebuchadnezzar himself to govern Jerusalem, declared himself king in Judah, and denounced all allegiance to Babylon.

Hophra may have been greatly weakened, but Nebuchadnezzar, by taking the war directly to him, marched right past a large number of Egyptian troops that had been spread around to destabilize Babylon. The tactic is obviously sound, but it means there were still pockets of Egyptians – some of them large and strong – in places like Gath, Susa and Jerusalem whose desires of independence from Babylon were growing.

My expectation was that Nebuchadnezzar would battle those places on his way back to the city, assuming demoralization on their part from his victories against Egypt. He did not; he came straight home.

Meanwhile, in his absence, a lot of the city's inhabitants (notably the Chaldeans and their supporters) were becoming much more vocal in their dislike of 'outsiders'. Fueled by the rebellion of Zedekiah, Hebrews were particularly targeted.

There had always been resentment towards Belteshazzar and others the king had brought as captives from Jerusalem, and subsequently placed in positions of power in the kingdom. I had never felt that resentment.

Possibly I still considered myself something of an outsider. But much more compelling to me was the record of these men's service to the king. I had seen Belteshazzar up close in his role, and I had no doubt he was as competent a vice-regent as anyone would ever find. His dedication to Babylon still astounded me. Nebuchadnezzar was a wise man to use him thus.

Belteshazzar was untouchable; the king's guard was completely loyal to him, and I had never heard an ill word about him from any member of the army. News was coming in, however, of Hebrew people being harassed in other areas of the kingdom.

I was with Belteshazzar and Asphenaz, going over palace security questions, when the king returned.

I had never witnessed anything quite like this royal entrance. Nebuchadnezzar strode purposefully into the great hall, still in battle gear. His face showed what could only be described as extreme annoyance, bordering on outright rage.

The irritant seemed to be the gaggle of men, mostly Chaldean priests and ministers, who trailed behind him in a roughly cuneiform mob. The highest ranking, of both religious and civil position, followed closest, but the sheer numbers of them was something I never thought I would see Nebuchadnezzar allow at his heels.

He made his way to our position at a pace that necessitated that some of his shadowers jog to keep up. If not for the look on his face, it would have been a comical scene.

I thought to leave, but the crowd made it impossible to do so without causing more confusion, so I waited to see what would happen.

The king stopped abruptly in front of us and, without a word to us, spun on his heel and started barking and pointing.

"You, you… all of you over there, out! Now!"

There was an attempt at protest by those closest to the king, but even from my vantage point, behind the king, it was clear that his expression would brook none of that.

You, you…" On he went until the band was reduced to about ten men of those that had entered with the king.

I started to go out with the last group dismissed, but Nebuchadnezzar spoke.

"Stay, Kasher. I will need you in this discussion."

Next, he spoke to the remnants of the group.

"I have heard your complaints, and I will not be listening to any more of them at this moment. Later, when there has been more opportunity for my council to consider the matter, we will call for you."

"Now, I will be briefing my ministers concerning affairs of state – which do include the matters you have just brought to me!" The last comment was in response to one of the Chaldean's attempt to interject a comment. "I said I will not be listening to you right now; and if you have any expectation of standing in my presence in the future, you will learn to hold your tongue!"

The king's voice reverberated off the walls of the hall. The effect was powerful, especially coming from a man as imposing as Nebuchadnezzar. The effect was even stronger given the man was dressed for battle, his huge sword hanging within easy reach of his right hand.

"Now, my court, I would report of our triumphs and our continuing challenges."

The seat he used for these meetings was brought into the hall and placed before us all. Only Belteshazzar and Asphenaz remained with him on the raised platform.

I stood to one side of the assembled Chaldeans as the king related his victory over Hophra's army. They were not destroyed, but they had been greatly subdued.

"My men carried my every order to the enemy's face, and we triumphed over them. Great is Babylon!"

"Great is Nebuchadnezzar!" we all shouted in response.

"I believe we will have no trouble from the Egyptian army for quite some time to come, but the pockets of soldiers scattered about the region continue to stir up rebellion in the minor kings. Not the least of which, that ingrate Zedekiah in Jerusalem. I promoted him myself! And now he takes my absence from Babylon as an open door to walk away from his allegiance to me!"

"Belteshazzar, these hens who came in cackling behind me want me to go to Jerusalem personally and deal with this traitor. They tell me that there is strong support within Babylonia for this rebellion – that the Hebrews are sending financial help so that Jerusalem can be 'liberated' from my reign. What do you know of this?"

"My king, I cannot say with absolute certainty that nothing like that is occurring, but I do not have any knowledge of such activities. All the reports I have received of late point to loyalty amongst the Hebrews for your throne. You know yourself of my position."

"Yes, Belteshazzar, you believe your God has me on the throne for his own purposes. If I didn't need you so much you would be in a precarious position right now. You have the luxury of believing in just one god. I have my own beliefs, and I have all of these," pointing to the Chaldeans, "to try and 'help' me please a dozen gods or so more than I actually believe in myself!"

"Call in your Hebrew administrators and let us see if there is any foundation to these rumors. As you call them, prepare yourself for a diplomatic journey. It would not be good for me to leave Babylon again right now. The people need to see their king on his throne sometimes. AND, yes, Pheron," speaking to the high priest of the Chaldeans who had dared to open his mouth once more, "I know there are ceremonial duties to be performed to keep the trust of the people! We will see to it in its proper time."

"Belteshazzar, you will go talk sense into your brother Zedekiah!"

Daniel didn't look terribly pleased at the command, but he bowed his acceptance to the king without a word.

"Asphenaz will choose members of the royal guard to escort you. Not you, Kasher. I need you here for now."

"You may have noticed that Arioch has not been around lately. I took him with me on this venture into Egypt. I was able to do so without fear for the queen as you have been in charge of her safety."

"Unfortunately, Arioch was killed in the battle to take the fortress of Sin. We lost a large number of good men that day."

"Kasher, you have proven yourself faithful to me and to the kingdom. You have also shown great ability and resourcefulness. You are to keep the queen's safety paramount, but you are hereby promoted to be captain of my palace guard."

Chapter 40

I was stunned. I wanted to protest to the king that I had not fulfilled the requirement of the four areas of duties for the palace guard, but it was as if my tongue was fused to the bottom of my gaping mouth. To hide my discomfort (and my gaping mouth), I bowed my head in subjection to my king.

It was Asphenaz who saved me further embarrassment by declaring, "Great is Babylon," to which all others present replied, "Great is Nebuchadnezzar!"

"Great also is my need for a moment alone. Go, now, all of you. Kasher, Asphenaz will explain your new role in detail. I will speak more with you when I have had my rest."

I already knew what my new position entailed, but I listened attentively while Asphenaz explained it to me.

"You have been trained well, Kasher. Your combat experience is well known, and the circumstances of our journey to the north with the queen has left no doubt in any member of the court's mind as to your qualifications all around. You are ready to be Captain."

"Basically, you protect the king, just like you have done the queen. You will be at his side, or at least at his door, for most of your waking hours. On the rare occasions when you leave his protection to others, there will be a guard close to you, and others posted at short intervals between you and the king so that you can be called to his side at a moment's notice."

"Your family will be well taken care of by the kingdom, but you will see very little of them. I know you are close to them, but you have chosen a life of dedication to Babylon, and that life comes with a price."

"Nebuchadnezzar instructed me to give you one opportunity to refuse the posting. You may, if you choose it right now, be transferred back to the regular army. You will be given command of a unit of men under your uncle. You will never return to the Palace Guard if you leave, but there will be no retribution toward you or your family if you go. What is your decision?"

"I am not a religious man, as you know Asphenaz, but I can't help feeling I have been fated to this position some way. Even if not, this has always been my goal in life. I have never hidden this ambition from my family, and, as much as they will dislike some aspects of it, I know they will understand. I accept my role as protector of the king."

Belteshazzar left for Jerusalem the following day. I had never known him to be out of the city. Nakhti (now Nebuzaradan) led the party of soldiers and diplomats through the same gate we had entered all those years ago with no ceremony at all. If not for the considerable size of the group, their exit might not even have been noticed. The king was not there to see them off.

He was in the throne room that morning, his new captain by his side. After consulting with Asphenaz and a few other ministers of the realm for about an hour, he called the Chaldeans in.

They had, obviously, been waiting at the door for their invitation. Their pace as they entered showed impatience and determination.

After the requisite greetings, the chief priest began delineating their concerns and desires.

Most of it was a rehash of the complaints against the Hebrews, at least at first. These Nebuchadnezzar tolerated for a time, but then told the priest to move on. He had, after all, already stated that a full inquiry would be had, and he had already taken the step of calling the principle Jewish leaders to the city for consultation on the matter.

The next item on their agenda seemed unrelated at first, but I soon saw a clear connection back to the first question.

"We are saddened, my king, by your lack of participation in the religious ceremonies of the realm. Your father (may the gods continue to light his way!) saw the great benefit to himself and his people in the open manifestation of devotion to our deities – going so far, as you well know, to bring back lost practices that the Chaldean people hold dear. Surely you do not wish to dishonor your father's memory by allowing the celebrations to lapse."

"You pretend to speak to me of honor – and of my father? Maybe you don't remember, priest, why you are still allowed in my presence at all! It certainly is not by any merit on your part. I need you – for now. And never forget that should I ever find I no longer need you, your end will not be a pleasant one."

"My king! I do not understand how I could possibly have offended you so. I am your loyal subject!"

"You are loyal only to yourself and your cause – the promotion of Chaldean control of the kingdom. If it weren't for the fact that so many of our people look to you for 'spiritual orientation', you would have been sent away the day Marduk first spoke to me! Now, let's move on. What specific ceremonial acts do you deem essential for me to continue this necessary charade?"

There was a moment of silence, broken only by throats being cleared.

"We believe," continued Pheron, "that you should honor Ishtar at the Spring Festival."

"Of all the festivals, that one requires the most – of me and of the city! Can't we have a smaller ceremony? Even the Marduk festival doesn't take that much."

"Yes, my king, but you know that it was Marduk himself who established the day of Ishtar – through your esteemed father, of course! Besides, it will be just the thing the people need to take their minds off the difficulties the kingdom is going through. If you give me leeway in the planning, I promise to deliver to you an adoring throng of Babylonians."

The preparations went into full speed. There was less than a month to go before the spring equinox, and the holy day was the one leading into the night of the first full moon after it.

I asked to have Kartan and Armo brought in to discuss some ideas I had about the festival. Knowing Nebuchadnezzar's lack of excitement about all of this, I was concerned about whether or not I should, but I put it to the king that, since there was to be a festival anyway, "shouldn't we try to get it right?"

First, I asked about the progress on the work for the queen's garden.

"It looks wonderful," said Kartan. "And the queen is delighted with it. If she was contented with the fact we were building it, you should see how she has responded to it now that it is basically finished! She and the prince spend hours out in the garden. Most of Belshazzar's lessons are now conducted there."

"We must go and see it for ourselves, Kasher, and the first opportunity," replied the king."

The next afternoon we did exactly that.

"A good excuse to finally get some fresh air. I need it badly, Kasher."

"As do I, my king. We are men of the outdoors, you and I."

I would never have dreamed, back in Nippur, that one day I would be on such familiar terms with the great Nebuchadnezzar. I had always known he was great, but I was learning that he was also good – at least to his friends.

There was a passageway from just outside the back door of the great hall that led directly into the new garden. It seemed impossible that it could be so close all this time without either of us experiencing it, but Babylon was going through difficult times, and the king was a very busy man. For my part, the few moments I had free were spent soaking in the presence of my loved ones. I never tried to justify my decision to my family, but there could be no denying that the fact we had so little time together made us appreciate each other even more.

Neither of us truly expected the sight that greeted us as we stepped out into the open air.

The entire space between the palaces, extending to the opposite wall of the palace enclosure, was now thick with grass. There were sheep grazing in one corner. An area that had been dry as the desert around us had been transformed.

Looking to our left along what had been the wall that led to the north from the palace there was now an ascending array of deep green plants, culminating at the peak in tall white grass which moved gently in a breeze not felt here at the bottom.

Not that we felt heat – there was a coolness here that I had not known in daytime Babylon. At first I thought it was just a sensation created by the environment; but there was more to it than that.

The king and I stepped out into the garden and examined the 'mountain' more closely. At irregular intervals there were paths that wandered in gentle curves up the side of the structure, terminating in flat openings just at the edge of the 'snow'. There, benches were placed facing the garden.

The green wall extended north, past the temple of Nabu, blended in with one wall of Etemenanki, and then continued on, all the way to the outside wall where the north and south forts joined.

The ancient tower blended in beautifully with the new wall. Etemenanki means "House of the foundation of heaven on earth"; and, whereas it had always looked to me like pile of brick, it now seemed to live up to its name.

Water trickled down through the green plants with no apparent courses, flowing at the end into a wide trough that ran along the edge of the structure. Small wooden bridges connected the upward-leading paths to the floor of the garden.

Mostly hidden in the thick grass that now carpeted the garden were tiny rivulets cut in the ground, carrying the precious substance from the trough out through the area like veins.

All of this combined for a spectacular view, but also had the effect of keeping the temperature much lower than it otherwise would be.

As we stood looking up the artificial slope, a soft voice from behind said, "Are you pleased, my king?"

Turning, we saw the prince and Utanin standing just behind and to the side of Amytis. It was she who had spoken.

"The question is, are you?" answered Nebuchadnezzar.

Her smile was answer enough for me.

"I do love Babylon, I want you to know that, my king. And I serve my lord and his kingdom with all my heart. But this has made it easier for me to be content. It is wonderful. Thank you for being so considerate."

"I did not see you come into the garden," said the king, his eyes scanning from one opening to another.

"We came directly from my quarters," she responded. "Can you not see the door, my king?"

She smiled broadly as Nebuchadnezzar looked down the wall.

"That section, there," he said, pointing, "must be the outside of your wall, but all I see is stone and vegetation."

"Come; you will see."

The queen held out her hand and Nebuchadnezzar took it in a very natural way. I had served both of them for a long time, but I had actually spent very little time with them together. Asphenaz and Belteshazzar had both told me how much the royal couple was in love, and, from this simple display, I believed it. They seemed very comfortable with each other which, I think, is only possible when there is something special between the two.

I had felt that way with Ruhamah from the beginning: only now did I really see it so clearly.

We had grown older, and our relationship had changed along the way. We had not been called on to face death together for quite some time. Our lives were, generally speaking, much more sedate than early on. I cherished those exciting times, but (as I was seeing now between Nebuchadnezzar and Amytis) we were still in love: a deep, comfortable love.

The queen led our little party to the wall. Though it had been my idea originally to give Amytis and Evil-Merodach an escape route from the palace, I was not involved in the details of the work. I was about to see an impressive feat of architecture.

We stood looking at a mossy wall. There seemed to be no break in the rocks that made it up, but this was obviously where the queen had brought us to show us her passageway.

Utanin glanced at the queen, and she nodded.

As he moved forward to the wall, I noticed, for the first time, a single strand of vine hugging the wall just in front of us. It was there that Utanin's hand went, and with a solid pull downward, things began to happen.

A section of the ground in front of us began to sink. There had been no seam to mark the position of this platform, and the sod on top of it was the same as all around. But there it was; clearly outlined now as it dropped below the level of the garden. There were no stairs to climb down, as indeed there could not be for it to remain hidden as it was, but the queen jumped, unceremoniously, down onto the platform. The ground level was now a little higher than her waste, and she beckoned for the king to follow her.

Bending, their faces toward the wall, they quickly disappeared. The rest of us followed, and I saw that my idea had been implemented well.

Underneath the wall now, there were torches placed at intervals along a wide corridor – apparently the whole width of the wall. I stepped forward off the platform and was now on a floor that was level with the sunken entrance.

Looking back, I could now see the mechanism that had brought us here. It was a complicated system of levers and chains moving weights into their needed positions for raising and lowering the platform.

The king and queen had already moved down the wall to an exposed staircase, obviously leading to her quarters.

Everything was examined carefully, and Nebuchadnezzar declared his complete approval.

"I will rest better knowing you are not trapped in your quarters, my queen," he said. "We will leave you now, but I will do my best to come to you this evening. I would like for us to dine together if possible."

As we turned to go back towards the garden, the king called to Kartan.

"Walk with us, please. I need to ask you a few things yet."

Outside again, Nebuchadnezzar addressed himself to Kartan.

"I am very impressed, sir. You have done a fine job. Tell me this – and, please, do not tell the queen I have asked this – If it became necessary for the queen to leave the city, could that be done from this construction? I can see that she would have a good measure of safety down there, and could hide for quite some time if proper provisions were stored, but what if she needed to leave?"

"I have thought that possibility through, my king. I did not move forward with such planning, but I did place some elements in the structure that I believe could help get us there. Please, follow me."

He led us down the wall. Well before we reached the Etemenanki he turned in at a gap in the bottom tier. Steps led up through the foliage to the next level. A quick turn and we were ascending more stairs. It was the same at every level, which, for one thing, gave the appearance of almost continuous greenery growing down the side of the wall.

After a few of these turns and ascents we were at the top looking down into a trough of water – and across the city of Babylon.

"We have not yet made an opening to it, my king, but we built this trough with a tunnel underneath. It is small, but large enough for anyone but a Philistine to crawl through. An access could be made from inside the wall, and an exit at whatever point along the top that would be useful. Obviously, this is only the first step in an escape route from the city, but we will work on it if it is your will."

"It is. Kasher, keep me informed about this. Once again, your king thanks you."

We five spent the rest of the afternoon relaxing in the garden, much of the time at the top of the 'mountain'. We could see most of the city from there, and Nebuchadnezzar's attention seemed drawn to the gate to our north, the one that led between the walls that separate the two halves of the Northern Fortress. We could tell there was activity beyond the fortress, but we could not see what was happening from here.

"The Chaldeans are there," said my son, "directing the reconstruction of the New Year's House."

No one seemed upset at Utanin for making the proclamation, but all of us fell silent at the implications of what he had said. It was particularly awkward in the presence of both monarchs.

We all knew what the purpose of that house was; I having learned it since arriving in Babylon. Such things were part of the training the palace guardsmen received from Asphenaz.

Following the tradition established by Nimrod's son, Erech, Nabopolassar had reinstated the Spring Festival, including the symbolic mating of the king and the high priestess of Ishtar. Nebuchadnezzar had allowed that tradition, along with all of the buildings associated with it, to recede from the life of the city. Now, he was being pressured – hard – to reinstate the festival.

The king did not seem to feel the need to discuss the less than savory aspects of the festival; that which would transpire within the New Year's House. Instead, Nebuchadnezzar began discussing some practical matters, particularly one that was directly related to our position at that moment.

"See how the plants flow over the top and hang down the wall on the other side. What a wonderful effect it

442

would create if there was more of that. This wall could be one side of a great processional way leading from the Etemenanki, through the gate, and out to the New Year's House."

"What if," I ventured, "some of the plants could be made to appear through the wall in some places? That would add to the garden effect on that side."

"I will speak with Armo about it at once," said Kartan. "If we are to reintroduce the festival, it should be the best it has ever been."

The king was looking south now.

"Look, down the river there, Kasher. What do you see?"

I see Borsippa, my king. I have never been there, but I know it has a close connection to Babylon. But wait – I see a tower, like Etemenanki!"

"Yes, Kasher, just like Etemenanki. I have been building – or rebuilding, rather - both towers at once. They are identical."

Chapter 41

After what seemed like hours of negotiations, the Chaldeans agreed to let our people create the inner passageway and the inner part of the new gate. They would control everything from there outward.

"We were just wondering what we would be doing next," said Armo. "I miss home, but I must say it has been wonderful transforming desert into garden. I enjoy the challenge, and it doesn't hurt that we have a practically unlimited budget! I would be glad to stay a while longer and help with this project."

"The processional way will not be as personal for you as the garden was," I told them, "but you will still have a lot of creative input. You will, however, be limited by the necessity of displaying specific religious symbols."

"Ishtar is to be represented by her traditional lion figure. But, I believe this could be an opportunity - with some stylistic enhancements - to make that and other symbols our own. They should maintain their tie to the religious history, but I think they should make a statement that they belong to Nebuchadnezzar and his reign specially."

"I couldn't agree with you more, Kasher," interjected Kartan. "I have been examining and cataloging minerals for years, and I know where to find some stones that will bring religious symbolism a new face."

"And I have a friend who is a great artist. I will ask him to begin creating a new lion worthy of our king. He and I have been working on a procedure to grind up lazaward and mix it into brick to get a blue tint. We have also developed a way to glaze the bricks that will both give them a shiny surface and help avoid erosion. Are there other symbols we should use as well?" asked Armo.

"I was instructed – by the council of the Chaldeans – that Gugulana, the great bull of the weather god Add, must be involved somehow. And of course, Marduk's dragon needs to be represented. I will let you know if they have other symbols they want."

From time to time, I would venture outside the city to see the progress the Chaldeans were making. There was movement everywhere. I felt like I was standing next to a hive of hornets. I understood most of what they were doing, but there was a huge pit being dug, the use of which I knew nothing. It was being dug next to a rock that rose from this plain. It was fairly narrow at this point, but extending away from the city for quite a distance. The face near the pit was, I estimated, at least fifty cubits high.

I did not like the Chaldeans, did not trust them; but one day I finally needed to satisfy my curiosity, and so I asked one of the younger priests what the pit was for.

"Marduk likes fire," was his only explanation.

Belteshazzar had been gone for a week when the first report came to the throne.

"The lord minister Belteshazzar sends his greetings from Jerusalem. He wishes to convey his continued loyalty and…"

"Get on with it, man!" the king demanded. "I don't have either time or patience for pleasantries at the moment – at least not when it comes to Jerusalem. Now what is your report?"

The messenger shifted through the information he had brought with him, finally discovering where the protocol ended and the information began.

Clearing his throat, he said," Belteshazzar has established indirect communication with king Jehoiakim. The king has thus far refused to meet with him face-to-face, but through emissaries talks are proceeding in an effort to establish a new alliance with Babylon."

Before the courier could speak further, Nebuchadnezzar stood to his feet, towering over the man down on the level of the floor. The look on his face would have frozen the tongue of any man, and the messenger was left with his mouth partially open, as if a word that had been forming there was suspended in time.

"I have one message for Jehoiakim, and it will be communicated only once through my minister. If he does not bow to me – not form an alliance, but bow to me as his sovereign – by the end of the New Year's Festival, I will be making a visit personally to bring these negotiations to their proper end. You will deliver that message – and only that - to Belteshazzar."

The senior of the Chaldean priests were present for this exchange, and, even though they were wise enough not to get involved at that moment, I couldn't help noticing they looked pleased by the way things were going.

Chapter 42

"Normally," said Asphenaz, "Belteshazzar deals with these 'complications'. I have seen the king become agitated like this before. Once, he stayed out of the public eye for several months."

"That must have been right before I came here. My uncle was prepared to attack Babylon, partly because he thought the king had either become incapacitated or was no longer the man he had been. Either way, he believed the kingdom needed a new leader."

"What would Belteshazzar do when the king got this way?" I continued.

"First of all, I have seen him much worse that this; and maybe we won't have to do anything. So far all he is doing is muttering to himself – unsettling enough for us who know him well and know how out of character it is for him; but an outsider would probably not think it so important. I say we just observe him for now. If he deteriorates, we will try the Hebrew's methods."

We were less than a week from the beginning of the New Year's celebration and I was very concerned that he would not be up to his public duties. Asphenaz and I decided that one of us would be with him at all times until then.

Asphenaz had called it 'muttering to himself', but it seemed like more than that to me. I did not claim to understand the workings of the mind, but the king's seemed very troubled.

In fact, he didn't seem to be talking to himself, but to someone else; and not to anyone I could see. There were loud protestations on his part, during which he seemed oblivious to the fact that I was there.

"You and your festivals!" he screamed one time. "If you are so great, why do you need all of this? I think you are weak!"

After just a moments delay, he screeched, falling to his knees and holding his head with both hands. I had not seen this level of disturbance before, and I wanted to go for Asphenaz; but I also feared to leave Nebuchadnezzar alone.

There was more ranting; then he stood to his feet, all at once, as composed as if nothing had happened. Then he spoke again, this time in a normal tone and cadence.

"I have tried to finish the Etemenanki, but I do not have the whole tablet! Get the other part of it for me and I will make it happen. Until then, there is no more to be done. It is no good speculating about what the rest of the tablet says."

With that declaration, he sat down and closed his eyes as though asleep.

I did not want to disturb him: After such an emotional outburst, I was sure he needed rest. So I waited.

The king seemed to recover very quickly from his ordeal, and after just a few minutes with his head down on his chest, he moved on to other matters.

As soon as he was able the doors were opened for him to receive those who had pressing business with the king. My new position meant that I was right at his side during almost all of these discussions, and I was learning much about the state of the kingdom.

I waited for things to quiet down, and then asked Nebuchadnezzar if I could have a word with him in private.

I was very uneasy about making such a request – I was not one of his ministers or someone with whom the king would normally conduct business – but I had information no one else in the realm had.

He looked at me with surprise at my request, but acquiesced gracefully, commanding me to close the doors of the chamber.

"First of all, Kasher, I want you to know that you have this type of access to me because I trust you implicitly. Now, what is on your mind?"

"I know about the tablet, my king."

"Oh, that business about not having the whole tablet. I was just having a bit of a dream, Kasher. Nothing to worry about!"

"No, my king. I do not know why you were talking about it, and if you say that was dream, I accept that, but I know that you do have a tablet, and I know what it is."

I had his full attention at this point, and he was obviously not pleased with what I was saying. I continued quickly.

"My son, Utanin – he is the prince's companion here in the palace - he and the prince saw you one day placing the tablet back in its hiding place. He told me about it."

I was trembling at the potential reaction from the king, but pressed forward so as to get the whole story told without interruption.

"I have the rest of the tablet, my king."

His countenance went from near outrage to complete wonder in one very short, moment.

"You have the rest of the Tablet of Destinies?"

"Yes, my king. I found it in Nippur; hidden in a space in the wall of a tower there – one that looks just like Etemenanki. I have kept it since our campaign there, but I only discovered recently that it held importance to you. When my son told me what he saw I showed him the piece of tablet that I found, and he said it looked just like what you held that day. Then when I heard you talking about the missing piece – well, it must be the piece I have!"

I finally felt I could stop talking for a moment and allow the king to respond. He considered all I had said for a long moment.

When he finally spoke, he was solemn.

"No one else must ever know about this until I say so. If you have what we think you do, it could determine how long I am on this throne. When you can safely bring it to me, please do so."

"Yes, my king."

Chapter 43

The measurement of Entemenanki is to be the gar, which is the same as the sa, as it was known before. One gar is equal to 12 cubits.

In the center of these groups of temples will stand the grandest portion of the whole pile, the great Ziggurat, or temple tower, built in stages, its sides facing the cardinal points.

The bottom or first stage is to be a square in plan, 15 gar in length and breadth, and 5 gar in height. This stage is to be indented and ornamented with buttresses.

The next or second stage of the tower must also be square, being 13 gar in length and breadth, and 3 gar in height, with gently sloping sides. The third stage differs widely from the lower ones, and commences a regular progressive series of stages, all of equal height. It is to be 10 gar in length and breadth, and 1 gar in height

The fourth stage is to be 8 1/2 gar in length and breadth, and 1 ...

We had met in the area under the new wall, a space that very few people knew about. The king had commanded us not to reveal it to anyone.

"These instructions we were able to ascertain from this piece of the tablet. There are a few of the Chaldean priests who are somewhat knowledgeable in the ancient tongue. I have often doubted their ability; but, of course, was not able to verify my doubts. Your piece does seem to be the missing part of the tablet."

"Why did you not consult with Belteshazzar about the translation, my king?" asked Utanin. "He is our teacher, and he knows the language perfectly."

"I could not, my young friend. It would be completely unacceptable to the Chaldeans to have a Hebrew involved in the construction of Etemenanki. Besides, it would be an affront to him. He knows the purpose of the tower; probably better than the Chaldeans do."

"I see, my king, and you are surely correct about all of these matters. The translation is good enough, as it deals mainly with numbers and such. That is the easiest part of any language I think. There are mistakes, though. Things that have to do with star positions and names of constellations. Some of them are correct, but some have been mistranslated. As they tend to see things in religious terms, those differences may not be important to them. I would, if it please the king, like to retranslate your segment some time."

"Are you not religious, then, Utanin? Perhaps it is because of your name. My good, late friend, for whom you are named, was not one for talk of gods and spirits. Although your father tells me he was inclined toward the god of Belteshazzar on his death bed, isn't that so, Kasher?"

453

"It is my king."

"So, young Utanin, what are your thoughts on religion. I need all the input I can get in this present climate of worship."

"I am a seeker, my king."

"Of what, son? The truth? Or just an expedient belief system?"

"I seek truth, my king, but I am not sure there is only one system that reveals it. My mother and grandmother are devout followers of Jehovah, and I have read their scriptures. If it is a true record, then Jehovah is the only one worthy to be followed. Belteshazzar has also instructed me, both from the Hebrew holy books, and from things he learned as a child at court in Jerusalem. I have learned much from him, but I think some of his conclusions are a bit simple – forgive me, my king, for speaking of your minister that way. I got carried away with my thoughts."

"You may speak freely, Utanin. I share your impression of Belteshazzar, but I respect him greatly and count him the most loyal man in my kingdom. That is, to my kingdom. He tells me he believes Babylon is Jehovah's instrument to carry out much of his plan. So, his complete dedication to Jehovah equates to complete devotion to Babylon – and to me, as long as I wear the crown."

"Thank you, my king. As you know, your son and I have also been instructed by Chaldeans. I see much in their teachings that appeals to my own perspectives. Perhaps there is something to be learned from both of these religions, and others as well. This is what I mean when I say I am a seeker. I feel I must dig through all these voices to see the real truth."

"It sounds as though you are dedicated to this idea," said Nebuchadnezzar.

"I am. Two seers have pronounced over me; Belteshazzar and the Chaldean priest, Pushan. Belteshazzar's was the simpler of the two, and was delivered with what appeared to be sadness on his part. He said I would lead many, but not to war. He said that my army would grow very large, in time, but that our battles would be of the mind, and of the spirit."

"What was the warning?" I asked.

"That I would not lead men directly to the truth, but that some would find their way, through my teaching, to the truth. He said I would not be among those."

"And what of Pushan's prophecy?" asked the king.

"Pushan went to much greater religious lengths than Belteshazzar. During one of our classes on astrology, he seemed to go into a sort of trance for several minutes. When he came around, he left the room for several more minutes, leaving Evil-Merodach and me alone, wondering what was going on."

"When he returned, he held a bowl, from which he proceeded to spill out onto the floor before us a mixture of blood and organs. He said he had been instructed by Marduk to perform 'extispicy' concerning my future. We did not need to ask what that was as he proceeded to show us."

"The lungs and liver of some small creature were there before us on the floor. Pushan proceeded to push the organs around, obviously looking for something specific."

"Finally, he stopped, picking up one of the livers."

"He brought it to me, his eyes wide with delight. 'The lower part of the liver, as I now hold it, guided by

Marduk's spirit, is called *sibtu,* the revealer. Do you see this mark, running all the way from top to bottom, diagonally, left to right, on *sibtu*? I have searched for it during hundreds of divinations since I learned of its meaning. It means you will cause the Chaldean name and fame to be spread throughout nations! You will find the answer to the question of *Nisslin'. "*

"*Nisslin*? What is that?" I asked.

"I can explain that one, Kasher," the king said. "*Nisslin* is the legend that tells, in very vague terms, of the return of Nimrod. According to the Chaldeans, he will set up a *true* Chaldean empire which will usher in peace; albeit through a very strong hand. There is more, but that is the gist of it."

"But, my king, are you not known as the 'Chaldean king'? Why do they not consider you to be Nimrod?"

"Ah, Kasher, now you come to the real reason we are here in hiding, both from the Chaldeans and from Belteshazzar. I am not truly Chaldean."

There was a pause in which no one seemed willing to speak. I certainly had no inclination as my lower jaw was embarrassingly inoperable, allowing my chin to nearly rest on my chest. Nebuchadnezzar smiled and continued.

"We are not of the same blood as Nebuchadnezzar I. He was, indeed, a Chaldean. My father, Nabopolassar," he continued, "was the leader of a small tribe to our south, in the area formerly known as the 'houses of the Chaldeans'. His wisdom became legendary in that region, and the Chaldeans, who had been banished from Babylon after the death of Nebuchadnezzar, prevailed upon him to lead them in the retaking of the city – and the empire."

I finally found my voice.

"That must explain the tense relationship you have with them. It seems you need each other. A precarious balancing act that makes the kingdom function well. But they cannot - as you cannot - give over too much power. If they proclaimed you to be Nimrod, you would no longer need them to manage the religious side of things; am I right?"

"Precisely. And I accept this arrangement gladly! I have no interest in being deified. I do want to finish Etemenanki; and there is a religious component to it, of course, but there is much more. It has always been a symbol of great power."

"Eventually, I will be forced to tell the Chaldeans that I have the whole tablet – if that proves to be the case. I will not do so until I have to, though. Now, let's have a look at this tablet in its complete form."

The two parts fit together perfectly. We laid carefully them on the floor, and I took a lit torch from its holder on the wall so we could see the strange writing better.

Nebuchadnezzar and I waited patiently as Utanin examined the tablet.

"The part my father found contains the instructions you seek, my king. There are plans here for the construction of the top layer. It seems to be designed as a temple; at least there are religious expressions involved. I will need time to translate this completely, and I want to ensure I do a good job."

"I trust you that you will do your best, and I understand it will take some time," said the king. "I have waited this long, and I can wait a while longer. I am relieved to finally be this close to ending this project."

"Would it be acceptable, my king, to ask Belteshazzar for help with some specific words that might confound me? I could say I read them on some sort of document in the royal library."

"As long as you raise no suspicion with him, that would be fine. Belteshazzar must not know of the tablet for now. Do you have your own quarters here in the palace?"

"No, my king, I stay with the prince when I am here."

"I will speak to Asphenaz right away and instruct him to arrange a space for you to stay by yourself. I don't believe anyone will think it is so you can translate the Tablet of Destinies."

Chapter 44

It was day 4 of the month Nissannu. The first day of the New Year's celebration went smoothly enough. I made sure we had high security for all the areas involved, and yet, as per the king's instructions, the soldiers were not an obvious presence. Those who knew could easily identify them by their loose-fitting cloaks under which they carried weapons, but with so many priests running around in fancy robes, such details were not glaring.

The šešgallu, the high priest of the Chaldeans, had opened the door of Esagila, the temple of Marduk, at sunrise, declaring loudly that the New Year had begun. He then proceeded to give a prolonged speech on the importance of recovering this festival, stressing Babylon's need of Marduk's favor. Afterwards, dignitaries from around the empire were 'invited' to hear the reading of the *Enûma eliš,* the creation portion of the *Gilgamesh Chronicles.* My understanding was that any minister or tribal leader who did not attend this reading would be committing a grave offence to the realm.

While this was going on, one of my biggest headaches was also playing out. The king's role in this day's events was to go by boat to Borsippa, a short distance downriver. There, Nebuchadnezzar was to spend the night in the temple Ezida, dedicated to Nabu,

Marduk's son. I decided I should be with him on this journey.

"The temple was built by Hammurabi himself," the king told me. "I enjoy going there; to the city that is. It's a calm, refreshing sort of place."

"There has not been, at least in my lifetime, any political activity there. The priests of the city make up a large part of its population; but they are very different from those in Babylon. They let me know, on my very first visit here, that they are of a different 'house' from those power-hungry priests in the capital. I have always got along well with them."

"And then there is the lake. The name of the city actually means 'horn of the sea'. The lake is large, and considered a sea, and there is a horn of water that joins to it, fed by the river. Sometimes when I am particularly troubled about something I go to Borsippa and sit outside the temple, looking out over the lake. It is one of the most calming experiences I have ever had."

The king and I spent a peaceful night in the temple, and at first light were on our way back to Babylon. A statue of Nabu, about half the height of a man, accompanied us home.

We stopped just as we passed the inner wall of Babylon, and there we offloaded the statue. It was placed, with great ceremony, in the Uraš Gate, the same one Nebuchadnezzar had exited to speak with Nakhti all those years ago. From there we made our way to the Esagila where we were to meet up again with the high priest.

As we neared the temple, Nebuchadnezzar stopped to talk with me.

Taking me to one side, out of the hearing of the others of our party, he said, "Kasher, I need to explain the next part of the ceremony to you. I wouldn't want you to be shocked into doing something you shouldn't; though it would be very natural for you to do so."

I was shocked just from hearing what was about to happen, and it was a good thing the king had warned me.

Arriving at the Marduk Temple, the king lay down his weapons, crown and scepter before the šešgallu, professing his loyalty to Marduk, and declaring that he had not sinned against him. The priest then proceeded to slap Nebuchadnezzar across the face with all his might.

Even forewarned as I was, it was all I could do not to attack the high priest. There were actually tears in the king's eyes, so hard was the blow. The outline of šešgallu's hand was beginning to show in red on Nebuchadnezzar's cheek.

I hadn't noticed until that moment, but Asphenaz had arrived and was standing beside me.

"It symbolizes the superiority of Marduk, and the king's subservience to him. A rather effective way of demonstrating it, don't you think?"

The king was led away into the temple, and Asphenaz explained that he and the priest would only come back out at sundown in order to perform the 'Rite of the White Bull'.

My inquiries as to the nature of that rite were not answered. Asphenaz explained that he knew nothing of it – and that almost no one did. There were secret rituals involved that only the king and a few of the Chaldeans, those in the higher ranks of their priesthood, could know. As the king's protector it made me nervous that something involving a bull was being played out without my presence, but my instructions were clear.

Nebuchadnezzar had commanded me not only to leave him for the entire night there in the temple, but I was also to go outside the north gate. Two reasons were given for my presence there. I was to confirm that the Chaldeans had their part of the celebration under control, and I was to have one final look at the safety concerns for the royal family.

"The queen and prince must be present, but not so close to me as to endanger them if I am attacked," he had said.

Reluctantly, I left the door to the temple and made my way outside the walls.

I had seen much of the progress that Kartan and Armo were making on the processional way from Esagila to the gate. There had been much progress just since I last passed by the place, and it was indeed impressive.

Both walls were decorated with one hundred and twenty beautiful tile representations of lions: their white bodies rippling with power as they strode majestically toward the gate, protecting the great city from harm and escorting her citizens out to their tasks. Their ruddy manes were carefully carved down from their heads, flowing back along their flanks. Their size was uniform;but, as I examined closely, there were minor differences. These were not from poured molds; each figure had been carved by hand and place in relief over the sky-blue tile background.

Above and below the lions there were rows of tile in various colors. A row of daisies was placed above and below the lions, on a field of deep blue.

Green tendrils both escaped from unseen holes in the wall and cascaded down the side of it. The effect was magnificent; beyond anything I could have imagined.

As I approached the gate I saw Kartan and Armo standing looking up at it.

"Admiring your handiwork, I see."

Both started at hearing my voice, so intently were they looking at the gate.

"I suppose so," said Kartan, "but we feel a great responsibility for this project, and we come back time and again to make sure everything is as it should be."

The gate had already existed, of course, but they had transformed it.

"The queen instructed us that it should be dedicated to Ishtar, as she is said to give Babylon her glory. We have done our best to comply."

Amytis had been listening to our conversation. At this last declaration, she smiled in our direction.

From where I stood I could see that the original gate had been masked by what was immediately in front of me. The new facade mostly hid the outer part of the wall. It was covered in the same kind of tiles as the walls of the processional way. The figures, however, were different.

"The lion is Ishtar's symbol, but she is protected by Marduk and his dragon. Adad, represented by the bull, is also at her side, favoring her with good weather for her followers and tremendous storms for her enemies. Her priests tell us that Adad actually invented the whirlwind to defeat an enemy of her people in one battle."

I looked at the gate and saw there were thirteen rows of beasts going up it, alternating between bulls and dragons. All this was bordered, like the way, by yellow bricks and white daisies. The background was again blue, but there were various shades. The overall effect was overwhelming.

"There are five hundred and seventy five figures, in and outside the gate," explained Armo. "By royal decree we had an army of craftsmen, every one we could find with any talent, and they followed our directions better than we could ever have imagined. This is truly a monument."

I left my friends and proceeded out through the massive cedar doors hung from huge cedar beams. In contrast to the commotion I had encountered the last time I was here, I saw almost no movement in most of the area.

Everything seemed organized; at least the things I knew about and could see at a glance. My attention was drawn once again to the open pit on the north edge of this zone, now glowing red with fire, a wisp of flame appearing over the rim from time to time.

A raised platform stood facing the rock, about twenty paces away. The face of the rock was obstructed by a wooden scaffolding which did not allow any view of the considerable work that was obviously going on there.

There was a structure between the pit and the promontory now, obviously hastily thrown up out of clay bricks. There was no door visible to me, but I saw men hurrying around both corners, coming and going. Most of those headed into the building (I supposed that must be where they were going as they did not reappear right away, on any side of the building) were carrying materials, mostly in baskets suspended on poles across their shoulders. Others carried water pots or pushed small wagons whose contents I could not see. That they rode heavily was obvious. There was also a steady stream of men, also heavily laden, carrying steaming pots to the scaffolding in carts.

I made my way closer, but was confronted by a squad of military men.

"No one past this point without authorization," the leader said in a firm but even tone. He had obviously been well trained.

"Do you know who I am, soldier?"

I was always in full military dress, sword at my side, when by the throne, but Nebuchadnezzar did not like me to be too conspicuous when out in public. Those who did know me could try to use me to get to him.

"No, sir, I do not, but my orders are directly from the king. No one is to pass without authorization of the Chaldean council."

"Very well, soldier; I will respect your orders. Tell me your name so I can commend your service to the king."

Trembling slightly now, he told me his name and those of his men. I thanked them, and then turned to leave.

"Sir – could we know your name?"

"Kasher," I threw back over my shoulder without stopping.

Chapter 45

The next morning there was music on the air. I had slept on the ground outside the temple where Nebuchadnezzar had gone the night before. I was surprised at how sore I was. Sleeping on the ground hadn't bothered me at all a few years before.

The king appeared shortly after the first horn blast. There was no time to talk as things were developing rapidly, so I took up station at his side and joined in the procession that had seemed to appear out of nowhere.

The coordination of this event was amazing. From several directions, groups of priests appeared with images of gods held high and fell into the ever growing parade without any hesitation or confusion. Each group was dressed in a different (always bright) color. The procession just kept growing and growing, as did the music.

In just the same way as the priests, musicians joined in with a variety of instruments. Besides the original horn there were pipes and various types of small harps.

The king led the way with one hand always on the cart that carried the image of Marduk. By the time we all came to the Ishtar Gate (for so it had become known), we were a spectacle indeed. The statue of Nabu had arrived just before we got underway, having had (I was informed) a couple of religious duties to perform before arriving. The two - Marduk and his son, Nabu - led the throng down the Processional Way.

There were other priests awaiting our arrival, just outside the gate. They were dressed in somber robes; a shade that looked like it had once been black, but that now was simply drab. We stopped as we came up before them.

It seemed to me that the contrast between the procession and the welcome party here at the gate would certainly have stopped our merrymaking all by itself – and stop it did – but even this detail seemed to have been scheduled.

The various gods now present were displayed in a circle around Marduk and Nabu. There was plenty of room in the middle of the circle for the crowd to stand, and the area was jammed with people.

The statues of the gods were subjected to a change of clothing, with much merrymaking involved. Their new clothes were dazzling, and it appeared there was competition among the different groups to have the best costume on their god. The spectators began walking around the inside of the circle, looking at each statue in turn.

The mood grew more and more festive as comments flew about the new clothing and the manner in which each god was displayed. It looked as though there might be a fight at one point - no doubt a dispute over which god looked the best - but the priests of the two idols in question stepped in and calmed the situation.

Pheron, the šešgallu, standing on a platform in the middle of the circle, was the first to speak when all had quieted down.

"Great is Babylon!" he declared forcefully.

"Great is Nebuchadnezzar!" The cry rose spontaneously from all present – a considerable number.

Pheron launched into a long list of achievements - supposedly of the king, but the word 'Chaldean' came up a lot in the speech. This went on for three full hours. No one dared to leave, but all trace of interest was gone in the faces of those present after the first twenty minutes or so.

"There will be," said Pheron, finally concluding his oration, "a recital of the kingdom goals for the following year tomorrow morning. Until then, the gods will be taken to their respective stations, and the people will rejoice that they are Babylonian!"

A great cheer broke out, and, simultaneously, skins were pulled from off of wooden structures placed around the area revealing food and drink for sale. Nebuchadnezzar leaned in to my ear and said, "This is what they have been waiting for."

I escorted the king's party back to the northern fortress. Designed for defense, it also served us well as a safe location from which we could both see and be seen. We settled in to observe the people at play.

"Kasher," said the king, after we had taken some refreshments, "I have no official function tonight. Perhaps we could look at that matter with your son?"

"Certainly, my king. I will send word to him now."

"Have him meet us at the base of Etemenanki at sundown."

Chapter 46

Back inside the protective walls of Babylon there was very little movement. Most of the people of the city would spend the night in revelry in the area of the New Year's House. That gave us a helpful level of security for the discussion we were to have.

"Are you comfortable in your new quarters, Utanin?" asked Nebuchadnezzar.

"Very much so, my king, thank you."

"I know you have not had a lot of time for the translation, but perhaps you have something for me?"

"Yes, sire, I do. The tablet, as you know, is not extremely large, but it is packed with information. When I put the two pieces together I learned that some of the understanding the Chaldeans had of its meaning were totally incorrect."

"You mean they mistranslated?" I asked.

"No, not exactly. They did what any translator would do under the circumstances and extrapolated certain words and ideas from what they had when there was an incompletion. I can see clearly why they assumed some of what they did, but they were wrong in almost every case!"

"But how," asked the king, "could they go so far off if, as you said, they used accepted methods?"

"I have wrestled with that question myself since I saw this problem, my king, and my answer is that this tablet is unique. It cannot be translated like a normal piece of literature. There are subtleties in almost every word, and those are often carried forward into unusual understandings in phrases. I don't know if I am making myself understood, sire, but this is a special work. It may sound strange of me to say, but I don't believe this was written by a mere human. The only conclusion I can draw is that its author is divine."

The king and I were silent for a long moment at this declaration. Finally, Nebuchadnezzar broke the silence.

"How much do you think you now understand of it, Utanin?"

"Quite a lot, my king. And, please, know that when I say that the Chaldeans misunderstood a lot of things, it did not directly affect most of the construction so far. There are some changes to be made, but they are mostly aesthetic – and yet these details are given considerable importance in the document. I am not completely sure why yet. That is part of the complication in translating this, the interconnection of ideas; of the physical and the spiritual, the form and the function, the conceptual and the concrete. I hope to understand it all someday, but I wish I had some help with it. Is Daniel... I mean, Belteshazzar – my apologies my king, he asks me to call him Daniel – is he due back any time soon?"

"I hope so, son. I need his counsel, too. I have had no word from him for quite a while now, and I am concerned for his safety. The Jerusalem problem is still very unstable. In the meantime, do your best for your king. Come, let us climb this great and terrible monument. Perhaps you will gain some insight in that way. With all you have in your head about Etemenanki, you should, I think, let it inspire you to understanding it."

The three of us made our way up the great staircase that made up the face of the tower. There were landings at each level and, like in Nippur, there were inscriptions placed in the walls alongside the stairs.

Unlike in Nippur, where I only saw dedications to one goddess, Innana, and the city's chief god Enlil, here there were several gods represented. Even without stopping to examine closely I could see various names of gods and goddesses, Nabu and Ishtar holding prominence by the size and beauty of their inscriptions. Marduk himself did not appear in any of these at the lower levels, but his dragon was carved into nearly every section of stone visible from the staircase.

We sat at the summit of the tower. It was a flat surface, six levels above the ground, but I knew from the 'Tablet of Destinies' that another level was to be built here: a temple to Marduk.

The view below is was spectacular. We all commented on the various works that we had seen come to pass; many of them only recently. Older projects included the new section of wall enclosing the area to the west. It was built with four gates, but the most notable of them was the Royal Gate. As its name implies, it was a work of grandeur, only eclipsed now by this new one dedicated to Ishtar.

Turning our attention to the construction related to the New Year's Festival, our perspective from so high up just increased our sense of awe. Seen from up here, we seemed to be looking at a paradise.

I couldn't help my attention being drawn to the fiery pit outside the Ishtar Gate. Nebuchadnezzar had never referred to it, so I decided not to ask him about it.

Instead I asked, "What, my king, is the real purpose of this marvel on which we now sit? Surely there is more than the view of things below – as wonderful as that is."

"You are a clever man, Kasher. This view is one of the reasons for building Etemenanki. Such a perspective brings great glory to the kingdom, and I intend to bring all visiting dignitaries up here to truly see Babylon. But, you are correct. That is not all there is to the tower. There is also the impression it makes from below, but neither of these things is the real purpose for so much work and expense."

"I saw, in the tower in Nippur," I said, "scenes from the heavens painted on the ceiling of the underground level; a map of the stars, it seemed."

I could not get past the warning my old friend Utanin had given me just before he died about the *eyes of Nimrod*. Even though it was Nebuchadnezzar, and not the Chaldean priests, I was still hesitant to speak of them just yet.

"There you have it, Kasher. There is indeed a celestial purpose to this building. That scene you saw there is in this tower as well. Not having seen the one in Nippur I cannot confirm that they are identical, but as all these towers have the same origin; and, with minor differences, the same purpose, I would imagine they are at least very similar."

"Just as when Nimrod first put hand to build his tower, Etemenanki is to be our gateway to the heavens."

Nebuchadnezzar proceeded to speak of the gods and how they grace certain humans with their power and favor.

"Marduk will be triumphant, I am sure of it. I have witnessed his great power firsthand, and he will not rest until he is the lord of lords. With the help of his son, Nabu, he will rule the heavens and the earth."

"He has promised me great power as well: both in this world and the one to come."

I slept well that night. The security I had in place gave me a sense of confidence that no trouble could penetrate the walls of the palace.

We left early having eaten little. The king seemed to share my feeling of anticipation concerning the events this day might bring. I was to be disappointed – there was to be no dramatic moments today.

We spent the day among the people; a rare moment for Nebuchadnezzar's subjects to see him as human. He explained to me that this was a large part of these ceremonies; that the leader, though chosen by the gods, was one of the people. On one hand, the gods could choose anyone; a thought meant to encourage everyone to great loyalty to the kingdom. On the other hand, Nebuchadnezzar was worthy of being displayed. His presence and demeanor certainly inspired confidence, and confidence inspired obedience.

It was after sunset that the mood changed. There was no obvious signal, but there was a calming of the festivities which seemed to have an immediate effect on us all. At one point, the king moved toward the New Year's House, apparently without prodding of any kind -

473

yet he moved with purpose, as though having been summoned.

I remained at his side, but as we reached the door, he turned and spoke gently to me.

"I must go alone from here, Kasher. What awaits inside is the will of Marduk, and it must be accepted. Please be here at the door for me at sunrise."

I did not like leaving the king in such a place – outside the city walls – but I had to respect his order. I comforted myself in the knowledge that security measures were in place all around the House, and I would be sleeping on the ground at this very door tonight.

In the morning Nebuchadnezzar appeared at the door. He was not alone.

The Ishtar priestess was at his side in the doorway, dressed as Ishtar always appeared in reliefs and statues. The king was also in special clothing. He looked astonishingly similar to the images of Marduk.

Nebuchadnezzar stepped forward, and the priestess faded gracefully back into the House. A trumpet fanfare sounded, and Chaldean priests rushed to face the king.

The chief priest declared, "O great Nebuchadnezzar, defender of Babylon, blood of our blood, descended also from on high! We accept you once again as the chosen of Marduk, chief of all gods. We accept your union with him as displayed by his union, through you, with the glorious Ishtar, mother of us all. May you reign forever!"

A swell of cheers filled my ears. Only now did I realize just how many people were present. There was barely room to move, and I quickly moved to Nebuchadnezzar's side in case I was needed.

The acclamation of the people seemed unanimous, but my training caused me to be very wary about the situation. I calmed a bit as the first few moments passed. Surely, a people so enamored with this man would not allow any harm to come to him.

The priests had claimed a section of the area about 10 men wide between the king and, of all things, that pit filled with fire. As the trumpet blew once more, they separated in the middle, pushing the crowd away on each side, creating a corridor for the king.

Nebuchadnezzar did not seem to know what was happening, but the high priest came to his side and, taking his arm gently, began speaking to him, guiding him forward through the priests forming the way.

Evil-Merodach was brought through the crowd to be at the king's side. I was pleased to see my son accompanying him. Utanin was not trained as a fighter, but through the last few years I had noticed the prince relying on him as an adviser and, seemingly, as an emotional pillar. I was aware that there did not seem to be anything like a real friendship; but neither did Evil-Merodach treat him as inferior. I think he needed Utanin.

The queen was not present this time.

"We have a surprise for you, o king. We wish to make clear our pleasure at your gesture of allegiance to Marduk and the Chaldeans. Come - please, sire."

We looked down through the corridor of priests, and there, at the end, was the raised platform, the rocky hill face just behind. The fiery pit was not visible for the press of people.

Led by Pheron, we made our way to the platform and up the stairs.

I could see the pit really well for the first time. It was large, and still glowed, though it was nothing like the inferno it had been a few days ago. There was a ramp in the middle, accessible from behind the building. At the bottom of the ramp there were several landings with large iron pots on them. I could not make out any more, but it seemed it had all been for smelting metals.

The rock was still hidden from view by all the wood. I was convinced they had carved an image into it, and it must be (logically, I thought) of Marduk.

There was another seemingly interminable speech by the high priest, during which workers spread something (it looked to be pitch) on the bottom layer of the scaffolding.

The speech rose to a fevered conclusion of 'great is Babylon', to which all the assembled people cried, 'great is Nebuchadnezzar'!

The cheers continued, increasing in volume, as Pheron descended from the platform and made his way (other priests opening the way through the crowd) to the pit. He walked deliberately, ceremoniously, down the ramp and onto one of the platform areas. On his way down he pulled a torch from the wall of the pit. At the bottom, standing on one of the platforms, he extended the torch into an area of the pit that still burned.

He made his way to the scaffolding, lifted the torch as high as he could and screamed another declaration. This one was completely lost in the noise of the crowd, but the gesture was sufficient in itself. I would not have believed that the noise level could still rise - but it did. And there was even more to come.

The area just in front of the rocky face was cordoned off by soldiers. Pheron stepped a few paces back and launched the torch at the base of the scaffolding. Instantly, flames shot up the wooden structure, causing the soldiers to move farther away from the heat. The crowd obliged them. It was also moving back due to the great heat being generated – heat we even felt all the way back on the platform. Pheron stayed where he was, apparently oblivious to the danger. The crowd noise rose and rose at the spectacle, the fire licking its way up the scaffolding, revealing from bottom to top the figure of a man.

Pheron was finally driven back by falling chunks of wood, but stayed within the line of soldiers, closer than anyone else to the rock.

People were dancing now, chanting 'Marduk, Marduk, Marduk'. All at once though, as the smoke cleared enough to reveal the face of the image, there was a stunned silence. The face carved into the rock was obviously that of the king.

The recovery took only an instant, and the chant began, 'Nebuchadnezzar, Nebuchadnezzar, Nebuchadnezzar, Nebuchadnezzar, Nebuchadnezzar, Nebuchadnezzar'!

The carving occupied the whole height of the promontory, including a representation of the world at the bottom on which the king stood, and was correctly proportioned as to height and width. The crown Nebuchadnezzar used for the most formal occasions adorned his head.

The entire image was covered in gold.

Chapter 47

The revelry lasted two full days and well into the second night until people began to fall asleep all over the celebration grounds.

A throne had been placed on the platform before the image, and Nebuchadnezzar observed the proceedings from there the entire time. His subjects were treated to his presence like never before, and they obviously adored him. He invited them, a few at a time, up onto the platform to speak with him. It was a security nightmare for me, but there were no incidents beyond a few who complained a bit loudly about what they saw wrong with the kingdom. Most who joined us were obviously too awed just to be in his presence to even speak, and the king, ever wise in these matters, thanked them for their loyalty and for their contributions to the greatness of Babylon.

As we saw the crowd begin slowing that second night, I was able to convince the king to come in with me to the palace for some much needed rest. After checking on the guards at his quarters, we slept well into the next morning.

If we had any thoughts that everything would return to normal right away, we were mistaken.

Asphenaz entered while we were finishing our breakfast and, apologetically, informed the king that the Chaldeans wished a word with him.

There had been no conscious decision that I should accompany the king at all times during this season, but it had happened spontaneously, and I did not see that we had reached a stopping place for the policy just yet. The king exited his chambers through the door that led directly into his private conference room with me at his side.

A group of six priests awaited us there, and their faces showed both excitement and concern.

"O great Nebuchadnezzar," began Pheron, "we trust you were pleased with our part in the New Year's celebrations."

"I was truly overwhelmed, my priest. The carving in the rock was something I never could have imagined."

"It is about that image that we have come today – begging your forgiveness for interrupting your rest, of course."

"Think nothing of it, Pheron. These are special days, and we all make sacrifices."

"My king," continued the priest, "the acclamation for your image has been overwhelmingly positive, and yet... there are detractors still."

"How can anyone be against a display of honor directed to our king?" asked Asphenaz who had followed us in from the king's quarters.

"It is true, my lord. There are some, it seems, who believe our love for our great king has gone too far with this act of homage. And what is worse, they are reported to be ministers of my lord's realm."

479

"Who are they?" asked the king, growing angrier by the second.

"We do not know for sure, my king, but we have reliable sources who tell us it is so."

"Find out who these people are!"

"We have been considering how to do that, and we think we have a plan that will work. We have taken it upon ourselves to draw up this declaration for you to sign – if you are in agreement. It says, 'I Nebuchadnezzar, by the will of Marduk, prince of Babylon and her supreme benefactor, do require the presence of all his ministers and their assistants in the area of the New Year's House during these last three days of festivities.' We will make that part of the declaration today; the king permitting. The rest we will declare tomorrow morning – 'At moments to be determined by the king or his representative, the herald instruments of the realm will sound. At such sound, in order to give his subjects opportunity to further honor him, all present are commanded to bow down to his image. Anyone who refuses this demonstration of loyalty to me and my realm will be cast into the fiery furnace to die.' Is this acceptable, my king?"

"It seems to me both reasonable and usual an order. It will also give all my ministers the opportunity to affirm their loyalty to me. Here, I affix my seal. Proclaim this edict at once, and inform me if there are any who dare defy it."

It didn't take the priests long to make the first declaration. The following morning the second part was read in the hearing of all. As if to punctuate the order, the instruments sounded their fanfare as soon as the edict was read.

It also didn't take long for a problem to manifest itself.

Within a half hour of the edict's proclamation, Pheron was back in the king's presence with three men in tow.

"O great Nebuchadnezzar, worthy of all honor and praise, these three have refused your most correct and worthy decree. They will not bow before your likeness!"

I remembered one of the men. It was the Hebrew administrator I had met in Chebar.

The king's face was red, I presumed with anger. I soon learned there was another reason as well.

"You three! Did I not promote you above others of my own countrymen? Have I not treated you with grace, even allowing you to rule over many of your own affairs? And this is how you repay me? Even Belteshazzar has declared me rightful king over the Hebrews – the hand of Jehovah for the chastisement of his people! And yet you will not bow to me?"

I could see that the fact that it was these men who had defied his order was an embarrassment to him. I knew there were many Chaldeans who had resented their promotion from the very beginning. They now had their opportunity for revenge. It seemed that this was their plan all along.

"O, king, live forever!" said one of the men. "We do not dishonor you! We are your loyal subjects, and we claim no other earthly king."

At this, all three fell to their faces before Nebuchadnezzar.

"Pheron, what means this?" The king's anger now turned toward his high priest. "What sort of game are you playing?"

"No game, sire, I assure you. They bow before you; but I have hundreds of witnesses to the fact that they would not bow before your image."

"Shadrach, what have you to say to this?" asked the king.

"The great Nebuchadnezzar is not ignorant of our ways, my king, You must be aware that we are forbidden by Jehovah to do homage to any graven image. I know you trust Daniel – please, consult him and see."

"Alas, I cannot at this moment. You see he is away at Jerusalem, supposedly trying to convince some other Hebrews that I am their legitimate king! It would appear I have misjudged your loyalty as a people. Do you so defy me still? I have decreed that you will die in the pit of fire, the very one that was used to forge my image in the rock, if you do not comply. I have had respect to your god along with the others I follow. Are you not capable of the same? What do you say? This is your last chance."

"O, Nebuchadnezzar," said Meshach, "we are not careful to answer you in this matter. If it be so, our God whom we serve is able to deliver us from the burning fiery furnace, and he will deliver us out of your hand. But if not, be it known unto you, that we will not serve your gods, nor worship the golden image which you have set up."

I had never seen any man - not just Nebuchadnezzar - that angry before. He stood to his feet and moved to the back of the room, his back to us all; but I could still see the fury stamped on his face.

I moved to his side in case he should have need of me, but stayed at a respectful distance. His face was actually contorted with rage. I thought he would be able to curb his great anger in a few moments and return to the question with his usual dignity, but I was wrong.

After a short moment, alone at the back of the room, he turned, his face still burning.

"These three who know not the meaning of loyalty will be burned! Pheron," (even he jumped at the sound of his name spoken this way) "you will see to it that the furnace is sufficiently hot enough to burn these men instantly. You have three hours. Bring the pit it to the level that was used to melt the gold, and then make it seven times hotter! Leave me now – all of you!!"

I looked into the king's face as if to ask the question, and he understood and answered.

"Yes, Kasher, even you. I will be alone for these three hours."

Chapter 48

The king emerged in the same regalia that I had seen him in when he met with Nakhti that day outside the south wall of the city. Asphenaz and I were at the door waiting, and we fell in behind him as he made his way solemnly out of the palace, through the Processional Way, out through the Ishtar Gate, and straight to the platform before his statue – all without a word.

He climbed the steps of the platform slowly, finally breaking his silence as he reached the top.

"Kasher, have the throne moved into a position facing the furnace, if you please."

As that operation was being completed Pheron emerged from the crowd of people present, the three Hebrews in tow. They came meekly, their heads down as if in submission.

The king sat, and addressed himself to the people.

"Be it known this day that Shadrach, Meshach and Abednego, ministers of the realm by the good hand of their sovereign, have been accused of, and have admitted to the crime of refusing my royal declaration to bow before my image. They were made aware, both by the decree itself, and by further explanation three hours ago, that they were to die by burning in this fiery furnace for their crime. They have heretofore refused our magnanimous attempts to help them see the right path. I now give them one more opportunity. Bow!"

The last word carried such power that the assembled crowd bowed their knees, whether misunderstanding what was happening or desiring to comply with the wishes of their king (probably a combination of these factors). Anyone who had not knelt immediately, upon seeing their compatriots doing so, made all haste to get to their knees as well.

Only three remained upright.

I now was struck with something of the anger I had seen in the king's face. *How dare they! So many chances to make things right, and they remained alone in their arrogant defiance of my king!*

I moved to leave the platform, saying to Nebuchadnezzar, "I will cast them in myself!"

My move caught the king by surprise, and I almost made it to the bottom of the steps when I heard his voice call out, "Kasher!"

I stopped, confused by all that I was feeling, but the king motioned for me to return to him, and for the first time in my life I hesitated to obey my sovereign.

Of course, I obeyed.

Standing by Nebuchadnezzar once again, the king bade me lean down to hear him speak.

"I am deeply sorry, my friend. You deserve the honor of dispatching my enemies more than anyone. But we must all play our role in this story."

"There may be others involved in this treachery who would take advantage of the moment to attack me or Evil-Merodach, and I must have my captain at my side for that eventuality. Please forgive this slight. I need you here."

The moment brought me to the greatest level of dedication ever to my king. This was no ideal; no mere representation of the grand idea that is Babylon. Nebuchadnezzar truly was the greatest man I had ever known. I was wounded that I could not be the instrument of his vengeance; but I would honor my king. I would stand by his side forever.

I said, simply, "Yes, my king." I believe he heard the complete dedication in my answer.

"Bind them!" shouted Nebuchadnezzar, "hand and foot, neck to ankle, and cast them into the fire!"

I had about a hundred palace guardsmen stationed around our present position, and I called to six of them by name that I saw standing near the Hebrews to do the king's bidding.

Ropes were brought, quicker than I would have thought possible. They were handed to my men by Chaldean priests.

A turban fell from the head of one of the condemned, and someone made to toss it aside. The king stood and yelled, "No! Put it back on his head! I want no trace to remain that these men ever walked upon this earth."

The fire was incredibly hot already as well; something that seemed to imply a readiness on someone's part for this action to take place. These details would come back to me later when I would reflect on whether there had been manipulation involved. For now, I was concentrated on ridding the kingdom of these who had dishonored my king.

The Hebrews were bound, and each was lifted by two of my men. All three were taken to the brink of the pit unceremoniously, and without even a backward glance, they were cast in.

At that very moment, there was a huge roar; but it was not from the crowd or any other human source. Instantly, a massive tongue of fire flew up into the air and spread outward in our direction. My six men were caught in the inferno, and were completely engulfed in flame instantly. Before anyone had time to react, they all lay motionless on the ground, their bodies still on fire.

Others of my men rushed to help them, ignoring the danger to themselves, but they were too late. All they could do was drag their lifeless bodies a short distance from the edge of the pit.

I was shaking all over. I was no stranger to death, but this was an awful spectacle. I was also instantly struck by the fact that I could have been – should have been – one of those burned to death but for Nebuchadnezzar's order to return to his side.

But if all that had set me trembling, what happened next turned my insides to water.

All eyes had been, naturally, on the men who had just been killed by the flames. If any thought had been directed to Shadrach, Meshach and Abednego, it would have simply been that they were already burned to ashes.

I heard the king gasp, then he was on his feet, moving forward to the edge of the platform. I followed his gaze, and nearly fainted at what I saw.

Nebuchadnezzar found his voice and said, "Did we not cast three men bound into the midst of the fire?"

"Yes, my king," I managed to say feebly.

"Lo, I see four men loose, walking in the midst of the fire, unhurt; and the form of the fourth is like the Son of God."

On the ground level, only those closest to the pit could see into it at all; and their view was limited. Pheron

487

was there, just outside of the fire's major influence, and he had also seen what we saw.

The crowd was beginning to murmur. No one knew what to make of what was going on. Many could not see into the fire, but it seemed that everyone had heard Nebuchadnezzar's affirmation.

Pheron ascended a few steps of the platform and addressed the crowd.

"A great sign has taken place. The men who were cast into the fire live, as our king has declared. It is so! The great and wise Nebuchadnezzar has also seen the hand by which this miracle is done. He has declared it the work of Nabu, son of the mighty Marduk!

Even as he was finishing this speech, the king and I were pushing past him to get closer to the pit. I had to restrain Nebuchadnezzar at one point from going too close. He recognized what I was doing and accepted my action.

"Shadrach, Meshach and Abednego, servants of the most high God, come forth from the furnace. Come and stand before me."

I only saw three men at this point, and I began do doubt what I had seen before. I knew, though. There had been four.

The Hebrews made their way to the ramp. They still had to pass through a considerable amount of fire to get there, but they appeared not to notice.

Up the ramp they walked, solemnly, and around the edge of the pit to our position. There, they bowed before the king.

The prince and Utanin were there, having followed us down the ramp. Every other minister and priest of rank was also gathered around the scene.

There was not even a smell of smoke on those men. Their clothes were completely intact (even the turban Nebuchadnezzar had commanded put back on Meshach's head). There was no sign whatsoever of the ordeal they had been through.

Once again the greatness of Nebuchadnezzar's character shown through. He recovered his composure far faster than anyone else there.

"Stand, servants of Jehovah, and accompany me."

The king turned back toward the platform. He called to Pheron and several of the higher-ranking dignitaries to come with us.

Back on the platform, the king caused the three Hebrews to face the silent crowd. Everyone could see now what had happened.

Ignoring the high priests previous declaration about which god's son was involved, he spoke.

"I make a decree: That every people, nation, and language, which speak anything amiss against the God of Shadrach, Meshach, and Abednego, shall be cut in pieces, and their houses shall be made a dunghill: because there is no other God that can deliver after this sort."

The very next day, Belteshazzar returned.

Chapter 49

The three that had survived the ordeal in the pit had all been promoted to high positions, all within the city. If there had been jealousy when they were in minor posts in the outlying provinces, there was a sense of near revolt among the Chaldeans now.

Of course, they had no one to blame but themselves; Nebuchadnezzar had done everything they wanted. I could only imagine the frustration they felt, not even able to complain about the outcome; but I was sure they were primed for action if an excuse presented itself. My primary concern was the direction that action would carry them.

If they found a way to move against the Hebrews, that would be worrisome. But if they dared go after the king – well, that would automatically involve me directly.

Belteshazzar was ushered into audience with the king as soon as he arrived. He was obviously weary from traveling, and his clothes showed the same weariness, but Nebuchadnezzar did not seem to take notice, and Belteshazzar made no protest to the king's desire to speak with him.

"I take it you have been made aware of the events concerning your countrymen."

"The news of their deliverance has spread throughout the whole world, my king. I know not if there has been exaggeration, but I have heard the tale as it is being told, yes."

"I doubt this story could be exaggerated, Daniel. Three men were rewarded by their deity with a miraculous salvation. Any distortion of what happened could only diminish the true event."

The king had used Belteshazzar's Hebrew name; something I had never heard him do before. I wondered if it was because of some new respect he had for their god, as the name Daniel was specific to the Israelites – 'God is my Judge'. Not something a strong king would like to acknowledge, either for himself, or for his subjects. I still marveled at the power Belteshazzar wielded in Babylon; and how the Chaldeans tolerated it.

I was in for more surprises that day.

Nebuchadnezzar had been exceedingly angry of late concerning the king in Jerusalem. Belteshazzar had been sent specifically to deal with that issue. Naturally, a report of his time there and an assessment of the situation were the main subject of discussion at this meeting. What surprised me were the relative positions taken by the two men.

"Zedekiah will not listen to reason," said Belteshazzar. "I fear my time there was wasted. He finally, reluctantly, spared me a moment of his time for us to speak in person a few days ago. Until then, I had only seen low-level ministers. There is no respect for Babylon in Jerusalem at this moment."

"Surely the people do not share their king's views about us," said Nebuchadnezzar.

"There is, my king, a confidence among the people that Egypt will back them against you. They seem to be behind Zedekiah, in the main."

The man who had been railing against everything Hebrew just a few days before seemed reluctant now to see them as his enemy.

"Surely there is a solution, Daniel. Kings can be deposed, but the people either fight or surrender. What can we do to bring them back to our side?"

I would never have expected the next words to come from one of their own countrymen.

"They must be broken, my king. There is no other way, and it truly seems to be the will of Jehovah; no matter how harsh that sounds. They must accept that your rule over them is for their purification. I suggest another siege of Jerusalem, and this one, I believe, will not be over so quickly as the last one."

I had seen both the efficacy and the cruelty of sieges, and could not have believed that someone would want that imposed upon their own. Did this man truly believe so strongly in the importance of Jehovah's will being done?

I had seen strong military action taken to impose the will of one on another. I had heard the names and wills of gods invoked as justification for such actions. But this was different.

It was as if Belteshazzar placed more value on the desires of his god than the wellbeing of his own people. I could not grasp that concept, but it seemed to resonate with Nebuchadnezzar, albeit with great reluctance.

"If you think it is the only way…"

"I fear it is, my king. My people can be very stubborn, and Jehovah has often had to use strong correction to bring us back to Himself. As I have told you many times, you are the rod of God for the salvation of His people at this time."

Details went on for some time, but the principle decision had been made. After a few hours more, the conference ended with the king's order, "Kasher, make ready to move the court. We march on Jerusalem."

The decision was made to move in one month's time. I petitioned the king, and was granted my request, to move the rest of my family back into the palace. I felt they could be exposed to danger without that protection in my absence. Several rooms were made available near Utanin's quarters, and though she said she would miss living in her own home, Ruhamah seemed to be pleased with the new arrangement.

"It will be nice to see Utanin once in a while. We have had so little time together of late."

My Armenian friend, Armo, had not returned home yet. His work on the gardens and the gate were finished so far as I knew, but he had found time for romance somewhere in all this work, and he was soon to be married to a distant cousin of the king.

Armo had proven to be a man of many talents, and I called upon him to work for me once again.

"I want you to head up the queen's detail. I can think of no one more qualified. Amytis will surely feel comfortable with her own countryman protecting her; and I, knowing you, will feel better about my own family's safety within the palace as well."

With my mind at ease concerning my family, I was able to concentrate better on the plans being made for the move on Jerusalem.

493

"Your uncle, Nebuzaradan, is in Riblah at the moment," said the king. "That serves our purpose well. We will meet him there to begin the action."

As anyone with knowledge of Nebuchadnezzar's military achievements, I knew well of the place. Necho II of Egypt had established Riblah as his northern stronghold upon taking control of Assyria during Nabopolassar's reign over Babylon. As his father's general, Nebuchadnezzar routed him from that position, fighting a series of battles in the area. The final blow was a crushing defeat of Necho's army at Carchemish, just north of Riblah.

The fortress became a powerful tool for the Babylonians, as it had been for the Egyptians. It was situated in a fertile valley with springs that ran all year round. Nearby were great woodlands, extending westward into the famed cedar forests of Lebanon. All of the usual industries that spring up alongside a military installation were in place for many years now, and the conditions were ideal to sustain a large army.

Riblah held other advantages for our endeavor. It was protected from attack on its south by a mountain range that had only one good pass; easily defended if Jerusalem's allies should want to attack – assuming she still had allies.

It was also on two principle trade routes, cutting off trade from much of the Western Sea and the Euphrates. Control of this spot would allow both the limiting of supplies to Jerusalem and the continued reception of all that our army would need. We were already in control of the land south of Jerusalem as well, so it had all the elements of an effective siege.

And effective it was. There was defiance and resistance for the first few months. That settled into a quiet stalemate that lasted about two more years. But, finally, hunger brought what hunger brings: desperation.

Nebuchadnezzar had decided to stay at Riblah for most of the siege, and I, of course stayed with him there. At first I longed to be with Nakhti – Nebuzaradan – in the fighting, but I was accepting more and more my pace alongside the king as more than my duty. It appeared to be my destiny.

I had seen the same miracle the others saw, and I could not deny there had been a great power behind it. I was certain, now, that there were indeed supernatural forces. Unlike some, I was not yet convinced that these powerful beings should be worshiped.

I also doubted what my mother, Jeremiah, Ruhamah and other followers of Jehovah said about his goodness. Certainly, he had saved his three followers from the fire, but some of my best men perished in that pit; and as far as I could see they were guilty of nothing deserving of their fate. I wanted to avenge those men. They were killed by the Hebrews' god, so I wanted to participate in their deaths as well. I especially wanted to be involved in tearing down that great monument to Jehovah – Jerusalem.

The time wore on slowly, with messages flowing back and forth from the besieged city. If Nebuchadnezzar had grown a little more tolerant of the Israelites, that feeling faded with the intransigence of their king. Message after message was sent to Zedekiah offering relief for his people if they would but surrender. Stories of people eating their own children in order to survive began trickling out of Jerusalem with the few people that did defect. Nebuchadnezzar's ire was as hot as the fiery furnace at these reports, and his will became more and more settled, as if forged in those very fires – Jerusalem would cease to be.

There should have been no doubt about either his resolve or his terror when defied. His destruction of Ashkelon of the Philistines should have served as warning to any who did doubt.

After Carchemish, Nebuchadnezzar had pursued an unusual battle strategy. He had fought on, even though winter was upon him. Even Necho had counted on the heavy rains of the season to keep him safe for a few months more in Carchemish. But not only did Nebuchadnezzar keep fighting until Necho was completely defeated, he immediately turned his fury on the Philistines.

No one in Ashkelon had expected an attack at that time. Fighting first the torrential rains and resulting mud that posed great hazard to horse and chariot, as well as the soldiers, the prince of Babylon came upon the Philistines like a surprise whirlwind.

The depth of his resolve was only the first thing the world learned about Nebuchadnezzar in that campaign. The Egyptians had tried to turn the whole region against his father, and the Philistines had provided them with every possible aide in their quest. The devastation of Ashkelon was legendary. As I saw my king's eyes burn at the defiance of these Hebrews, I expected nothing less for Jerusalem.

Asphenaz had stayed behind in Babylon to counsel Evil-Merodach who was getting his first taste of power and responsibility, dealing with the mundane matters of the city. Anything weighty would come to the king's attention, but it seemed a good training experience to me.

Belteshazzar was with us. I still did not know how I felt about him. He was a Hebrew, and yet his dedication to Babylon created an affinity between us.

Jeremiah showed up at one point in Riblah, and, after a few days, Belteshazzar sent him to Jerusalem with instructions to convince Zedekiah to surrender.

I was present as they said their goodbyes: Belteshazzar stern and calm, as always; Jeremiah deeply emotional.

"I had a dream last night," began Belteshazzar. "Jehovah has confirmed this mission. You will not be listened to, but He will be justified that His truth has been spoken in their hearing. You go in the power of His Spirit."

Finally, the news came. A breach was almost made in the north wall with no resistance coming from inside. We set out at once for Jerusalem.

Chapter 50

It took us five days to reach the hills overlooking the north wall of Jerusalem. Everything was quiet – deadly so. Our troops were awaiting the arrival of the king before breaking through.

There were small fortresses that had been erected all around the city by our men. The news coming to us told that there had been a few attacks on them, of no real consequence. They made an imposing impression.

Nebuzaradan met us in our encampment the night of our arrival to go over plans for the final assault.

"Take the city without concern for life, but do all you can to bring me Zedekiah alive. We will see to the destruction of the city afterwards. Right now I want that stubborn rebel."

Our men were all around the city walls, but, somehow, as we broke through in the north, Zedekiah and a sizeable portion of his army managed to sneak out in the south.

We stayed for two more days during which all those who were not in pursuit of Zedekiah went about the systematic destruction of the city.

Just as Nebuchadnezzar had done to the Philistines, my uncle led his men straight to the center of the city; their energies focused first on the temple, then the palace, the two great symbols of Jerusalem's greatness. I watched as those magnificent structures – built in the glorious reign of Solomon - became mere heaps of rubble.

The question came into my mind unbidden: would Babylon someday suffer such a fate? It was unthinkable to me; yet, there must have been many in Solomon's day who had felt the same about Jerusalem.

This was the seat of our enemy, yet I felt a sense of loss as I saw the destruction. Was nothing worthy of permanence?

I had come face to face with my own limitations on numerous occasions. I knew I was not immortal, but I managed not to give it a lot of thought – most of the time. But at moments like these, it was impossible for me not to contemplate the ideas of time, beginnings and endings, life, death – and after.

I had heard many explanations of these questions, and, admittedly, much of what my mother and wife said made some sense to me. There were also those moments I had witnessed for myself; including the fiery pit. Could it be that Jehovah was the one I had to deal with?

But here, now, his own temple was being destroyed by mere men. He must not be so powerful if he allows this. Belteshazzar and Jeremiah seem convinced that this is actually his will! What kind of god is that? Doesn't that show weakness?

Ruhamah's words came often to my mind, that Jehovah, among all the gods, was different in that he was concerned about his people. There did seem to be something to what she said. He had saved the three from the fire. Other gods don't seem to be so beneficent.

And still, here are his people, those who did not flee with the king, wandering in and out of the broken down walls, their weak voices begging for a crust of bread from any who will listen. Where is the love Jehovah is supposed to have for his people in that?

I sent them prophets, Kasher.

I froze with fear. I had heard the voice as surely as I had heard anything in my life. I didn't need to look around to know that it had not come from a human source. Even to say I had *heard* it might not be completely correct. It seemed more to be a conclusion voicing itself; a summation of so many things I had seen and experienced.

I waited for more, not sure I wanted to hear it. But that was all there was.

Chapter 51

The next day we made our way back to Riblah. Nebuchadnezzar had left Nebuzaradan there to finish the operation. He would be bringing more captives as soon as he had established someone there to be in charge of what was left.

On the way I was bold enough to ask the king why we would go back there, and he was not rough with his reply. Not to me, at least.

"That dog will never see his beloved Jerusalem again. Nor will he see the glory of Babylon. Either would be too good for him."

The day after our arrival back in Riblah, Zedekiah was brought to us. We went out to an open area in front of our tents.

"O king, live forever! We have brought your enemy to face his fate."

At the sight of the Hebrew king, I spoke up.

"Could you not have cleaned him up a bit before bringing him before the great Nebuchadnezzar?"

"With respect, sir, there is an explanation. Nebuzaradan discovered the means of his escape, and thought it appropriate that he be brought here in the full shame associated with it."

"Go on," said Nebuchadnezzar. "Explain this assault on our senses."

"Yes, my king. The king and his men escaped through a small gate that we had - unfortunately, yet understandably - ignored in the main. You see there is a point in the southern section of the city wall where two walls join near a fountain. That fountain has been rendered unusable - apparently for some time now - as there is a small opening in the area where the two walls meet where the offal of the city has been disposed of, running down a trough and into the well. We have, since its discovery, heard it referred to as the Dung Gate. That was their means of escape, and that is their shame. We found them to the east of the city, headed for Jericho. They had not stopped to bathe, and Nebuzaradan thought it appropriate that they carry their shame all the way to your presence. My apologies for the stench".

"We shall endure what we must for this fitting shame upon so vile a person as Zedekiah," declared the king.

"I do not fear you!" shouted Zedekiah to everyone's surprise. "I may be debased before you, but I have the word of Almighty God Jehovah that you, Nebuchadnezzar, shall lead me to Babylon where I shall stay unto the visitation of the Lord!"

"Really? And who has been bold enough to make such a pronouncement, my lord Zedekiah?"

"None other than the prophet of the Lord, Jeremiah!"

"And so it shall happen, my friend," said Nebuchadnezzar. "You indeed shall be ushered into glorious Babylon."

I was astonished at these words, as the king had told me Zedekiah would not see Babylon.

"Who else have you captured with him?" asked Nebuchadnezzar.

"O king, live forever! We have his four sons, and several of the nobles from his court."

These all were ushered into the king's presence.

"Your prophecy does not say your sons will go to Babylon; nor your princes, my friend. Kill them."

There was much screaming, and Zedekiah looked completely shocked as his sons were run through with swords before his very eyes.

"Hold him down," commanded Nebuchadnezzar, after the other Hebrews were all dead.

The lone remaining captive seemed in too much shock to fight or even cry out at this point. Several soldiers held him down on the ground, face up.

Nebuchadnezzar walked to a nearby fire and pulled out a metal rod. He then made his way to stand over the man he had placed over Jerusalem.

"The prophecy of Jeremiah shall indeed be fulfilled. You shall be led by my hand to Babylon. You shall need to be led, because your traitorous eyes will never behold that which I have built!"

With that, Nebuchadnezzar burned out both of Zedekiah's eyes.

We made our way back to Babylon, Zedekiah forced to walk the whole way. Belteshazzar and Asphenaz met us at the Royal Gate, which led into the new part of the city, west of the river.

People lined the road as the disgraced Hebrew king was paraded through that part of town, across the bridge that spanned the Euphrates, and up to Etemenanki. There we stopped, and Nebuchadnezzar addressed the huge crowd that had assembled.

"People of Babylon, hear me. We have seen the greatness of the Hebrew god. We have heard the declarations of his prophets that I, Nebuchadnezzar II of Babylon, am his instrument for the chastisement of his people."

"I do not, this day, tell you whether or not I believe this message. What I do declare is that those who would mock our good graces, pretending to be a friend to this kingdom and yet aligning themselves with our enemies – as though we were too weak to react; these shall meet an end such as you see before you. Their line cut off from the face of the earth; their eyes unable to behold any more the glory that this kingdom has created."

"And yet there is a way with kings. This traitor was lifted to the throne of Jerusalem by my hand, and brought down from it the same way. He shall join his nephew, Jehoiachin, whom I deposed to make him king, as our guest for the rest of his life."

Zedekiah was led away. I had not even been aware of the presence of this other king here in Babylon, and I never saw Zedekiah again.

Immediately following the king's speech we were in conference in the palace. I suppose I expected some reaction from Belteshazzar, but he proceeded with the business of the kingdom as if nothing out of the ordinary had happened.

As night came upon us, I asked for, and was granted, leave to go and see my family, but was called back after just a few minutes .

Nebuchadnezzar was in his bedchambers, and, as I approached the door, I could hear the moans of agony emanating from inside.

Asphenaz was there, and he informed me that it had started almost immediately upon the king's lying down.

"I have gone in unto him, but I cannot even awake him," he told me. "I don't know what else to do but wait it out, but I want you near while this is going on."

"Of course; I will be here as long as necessary."

There was no sleep that night for Asphenaz and myself. We entered the king's room periodically to see if there was anything we could do, and he seemed to be sound asleep, but he rolled slowly from side to side as he continued his ordeal.

Finally, just as the sun began warming those spots in the palace lucky enough to have windows, the moaning ceased.

We immediately knocked at the door, not knowing if the change was a good thing or not.

"Come in," the king managed to say, barely above a hoarse whisper.

We found him sitting on the edge of the bed, still in his night clothes. He was trying to look unconcerned, but failed miserably.

"You have had a difficult night, my king," Asphenaz began. "What can we do to help you prepare for the day?"

"Help me, old friend, to get dressed. Kasher, go and call Pheron. Tell him I have had a dream -a very troubling dream - and I need an interpretation."

"My king," said Asphenaz, "should we not call Belteshazzar? You remember from before that he was the

505

only one able to tell you the meaning of the vision of the giant statue, don't you?"

"Of course, Asphenaz, I remember." There was no trace of irritation in the king's answer, just an acknowledgement. "But, first of all, they would never leave me alone about it if I bypassed them completely. I will let them try, and when they fail – and I have no doubt they will – they will not have anything to say when I call for Daniel."

Chapter 52

We assembled in the main meeting hall. Pheron had brought over twenty priests with him. Surely one of them would have the ability to understand a dream. It did not seem to me a great degree of difficulty for someone known as a seer.

I was actually hopefully they could do it. I admired Belteshazzar, and I recognized that Jehovah must, indeed, exist, and that he was very powerful. But I was a bit tired of Hebrews at the moment.

This nights disturbance had come on the heels of something that could have – should have – been avoided. Many people, children included, had died because of the stubbornness of Zedekiah and his followers. Their own prophets counseled against defying Nebuchadnezzar. What would it take for these people to accept their rightful king?

"I have had a troubling dream. I need to know its meaning."

Pheron was next to speak.

"Great Nebuchadnezzar, as you know, your people - we, the Chaldeans – have been blessed by the gods with many spiritual gifts. I have assembled the seers form amongst us. They will give you what you seek."

Before the king could answer, he continued, "Only, please, my gracious and reasonable lord, do tell us the contents of the dream this time. It is only fair."

"Very well, my priest. You shall hear the dream this time, but I do hope you are able to help me. Your very use to your king is on trial."

"I saw a tree in the midst of the earth; an exceedingly tall tree. The tree grew, and was strong, and it reached its branches upwards to the heavens, and it was visible to all on the earth. Its leaves were fair to look upon, and it bore much fruit; enough to feed the whole world! The beasts of the field had it for shade, and the fowls of the air dwelt in its boughs; and all were well fed from it."

"I saw a holy man watching, and he descended from heaven, crying aloud, 'Hew down the tree, and cut off its branches; shake off its leaves, and scatter its fruit. Let the beasts get away from under it, and the fowls from off its branches. Nevertheless, leave the stump of its roots in the earth, even with a band of iron and brass, in the tender grass of the field; and let him be wet with the dew of heaven, and let him feed with the beasts in the grass of the earth."

"Let his heart be changed from that of a man, and let a beast's heart be given unto him; and let seven times pass over him. This matter is by the decree of the watchers, and the demand by the word of the holy ones, so that the living may know that the Most High rules in the kingdom of men, and gives it to whoever he will, and sets up over it the basest of men.'"

"This dream I, king Nebuchadnezzar, have seen. Now, give me its meaning."

"We will return with an answer for you in a few hours, my king. We must consult the omens."

Nebuchadnezzar sat there, in the great hall until they returned. He would not be convinced to eat or to return to his chambers to rest. Suggestions of the latter were met with a look that bordered on panic. Understandably, after the previous night's events, sleep was not among the things Nebuchadnezzar longed for at the moment.

Finally, late in the afternoon, the Chaldeans returned. Pheron once again took the initiative to start the conversation.

"Our men have consulted every writing we have; they have analyzed the positions of the celestial bodies; the entrails of dozens of beasts have been read. There is nothing within our art that would explain such a vision."

The king started to rise from his seat.

"My lord – might it not have been simply a bad dream? There seems to be no meaning to it!"

Pheron seemed genuinely worried. I wondered why they had not simply invented something to appease the king; but, I supposed, if it turned out not to be correct, that might lead to worse consequences than saying they did not know.

Nebuchadnezzar rose to his full, imposing height. I expected a roar of rage, but he spoke calmly and in a level voice: "Bring Daniel."

"I must protest, my king," began Pheron. Echoing my earlier thoughts he continued, "How long must we be subjected to the scorn of these Hebrews?"

Still calm, his voice rising gradually in power, the king answered, "Have you forgotten, Pheron, that it was because of this Hebrew that your lives were all spared when I had the other vision? I suggest you shut your mouths, seat yourselves over against the wall, and hope that his interpretation is not a command from Jehovah for you to finally be destroyed!"

A suggestion from Nebuchadnezzar was normally sufficient. This one was no exception.

Belteshazzar was brought quickly; he was never far from the king as long as they were both in Babylon.

He walked in slowly, stopping in the middle of the room. I did not know if he had been informed of the dream, but he obviously knew the mood was somber.

Nebuchadnezzar rose and descended the stairs from the platform. His demeanor matched that of his minister. Crossing to where Belteshazzar stood, he stopped, paused for a long moment, took a deep breath, and then said, haltingly, "I've... had another... dream, Daniel."

He proceeded to repeat what he had already told the Chaldeans. All the rancor that he had displayed to the priests was gone. There was nothing but anxiety in his voice now.

"These men," he continued, his voice regaining its former strength, "were not able to tell me the meaning of my dream. All of these wise men! Where are their gods when they need them?"

Lowering his voice again and leaning in close to Belteshazzar's face, he said, "But you can do this for me. There is a spirit within you that these others know nothing about."

"I require some time, my king."

Nebuchadnezzar called me over.

"Kasher, go with him. I want there to be no possibility of any interference in this matter," he said, casting a suspicious eye to the Chaldeans still sitting at the edge of the room.

We were gone about an hour, Belteshazzar pacing in a small, empty room a little ways down the corridor from where the king waited. I stayed in the doorway, and tried to be inconspicuous, but I couldn't help hearing the groans coming from the man. He seemed to be in genuine agony.

Returning to the meeting hall, I waited at the door as Belteshazzar entered. His head was bowed, and he moved very slowly forward until he occupied the same spot where the king had recounted his dream to him.

Nebuchadnezzar came to meet him, and the two men reached the spot at the same time.

After another long pause, Belteshazzar lifted his eyes to those of his king.

"My lord, I fear the dream favors your enemies."

"Clear the room!"

I hardly recognized my own voice. Who was I to make such a demand? But I knew it was necessary. There were some present whose loyalty I did not take for granted, and I would not stand by and let them get an advantage over my king.

There was some shuffling and complaining, but I was adamant that my command should be obeyed. Neither Belteshazzar nor the king said a word – they simply stared into each other's faces.

When I had finally managed to oust all of the Chaldeans, Nebuchadnezzar finally spoke.

"You stay, Kasher; and Asphenaz."

I closed the door behind me and remained just inside to insure our privacy.

"Speak, my friend. Hold back nothing. If there is a message in this dream, I need to hear it; be it good or ill."

"O king, live forever. Here is the interpretation that the Spirit of Jehovah gave me: The tree that you saw, in all its glory, is you, O king. Your influence has spread far and wide, as has your fame. Your kingdom has made it so that we can live in peace and prosper."

"The watcher you saw – a holy man – did not, in reality, command that the tree be cut down, but rather saw it happen. He saw your future, my king."

"He saw you driven from among men for seven years, living as a beast. He saw you eating grass as the oxen, covered in the dew of morning for refusing the shelter of human habitation."

"The stump remains; your kingdom will endure this trial. You will be given this sign to help you see that it is the Most High God, Creator and Sustainer of all, that sets up and takes away kingdoms. Seven years living as a beast will make this truth real to you."

"Daniel, you said the watcher saw all of this. Does that mean there is nothing I can do to avoid this fate?"

"I do not know the answer to that for sure, my king. My counsel is that you cease from any arrogance and accept the sovereignty of Jehovah. Leave off any unrighteous acts or thoughts you may have; allow His peace into your heart and into your kingdom. Humble yourself, showing mercy to those who need it. It may be that this trial can still be avoided."

The king spoke not another word; he simply turned and slowly left the room.

Chapter 53

Life in Babylon returned to what could be described as normal. Nebuchadnezzar went about his royal life as before, and the rest of the city followed his lead.

I noticed a difference in him, though - a melancholy of sorts. I also knew that he continued to struggle within himself. Troubling sounds emanated from his room at night. There were no more of the fits as before at least not during the daytime. The sounds I heard from my post outside his door might have simply been bad dreams, but they reminded me clearly of those dreadful moments I had witnessed before.

One morning, allowing myself to be replaced at my post for a few hours, I decided to have a talk with Belteshazzar.

"Almost no one knows it, Kasher - not even the Chaldeans – but the king has been in a spiritual struggle for a long time. The prophetic dream he had, and certain events of late, have combined to intensify that struggle."

"Our king was 'encouraged' by his father into an alliance with Marduk – one even Nabopolassar did not really understand. Nebuchadnezzar has known for a long time that Marduk is indeed real, and he has come to know the god quite well."

"I have, through the years, tried to help him understand that Jehovah is the true God; that all these others are no more than rebellious angels, fighting in vain against their Creator; and, ironically, amongst themselves for preeminence. Until recently, he dismissed these ideas, preferring to hold onto what he knew for sure; that Marduk is real and powerful. Since the incident of the fiery furnace, he has new knowledge."

"He now knows that Jehovah is indeed real and that He is indeed a great God. He has always had a struggle between his own will and that of Marduk, resulting in his crisis moments. I believe that he, as everyone, also struggles with the fact that deep down he knows there is a Creator God, One who is above all. Jehovah put that understanding in our being, but most people run form it, preferring their own way to that of their Maker."

"But, now, Nebuchadnezzar – and, indeed, all of Babylon – has been given a demonstration of just how great Jehovah really is. He defied the worshippers of Marduk and prevailed."

"But," I interjected, "the Chaldeans perform miracles, too. I have seen some of them myself."

"That is true. I do not deny that Marduk, and the other gods, are powerful. But I think anyone can see that this miracle was different."

"When the Chaldeans perform a miracle, what is its purpose, Kasher? Is it not to enhance their political power and position? And what of this thing wrought by Jehovah? Admittedly, it did lead to my brothers' advancement in the kingdom, but they had not asked for that. Surely no one would risk death in that way just to be promoted. They didn't even claim to know they would be rescued by Jehovah, just that they knew their stand was the right one, come what may."

"Miracles are not enough," I said pensively.

"A very astute statement, Kasher. The Chaldeans perform miracles, but where is the peace?"

Chapter 54

I am being sent away.

I'm not sure how to take this move. I don't believe I have done anything to deserve a punishment, and I do not know that it is one; but something doesn't feel right about being sent away from my duties of protecting the king.

I am probably reading too much into the move. I should be honored that the king trusts me to go with his son.

Just as his father did with him, Nebuchadnezzar wants to move his son forward in his preparations for the throne.

Evil-Merodach will need people like me around him if he is to succeed. He does not seem to be made of the same stuff as his father; but perhaps, given the right experiences, example and counsel, he will be a ruler worthy of Babylon.

But it still feels like I am being sent away. I wonder if the king is uncomfortable with how intimately I know his personal life. Again, my mind is probably exaggerating the whole issue.

We are going to the fortress in Riblah. There are still issues to be resolved concerning Jerusalem; and Tyre, which has been a thorn in Nebuchadnezzar's side for decades, is waxing bold again. The war talk has been that they need a taste of what Jerusalem went through; so, among other things, Evil-Merodach is to lay siege to that city. Asphenaz will go with us as well.

It seems much longer, but it has only been about a month since Jerusalem fell. I can't imagine that Tyre will be much of a problem. They surely know what took place in Jerusalem. They surely will surrender quickly.

I certainly hope they do. Maybe then I will be allowed to return to Babylon. I will miss my family; but more than this, my place is at Nebuchadnezzar's side.

The siege turned out to be a prolonged event after all. Altogether it took thirteen years. Twelve of those years were not much of a hardship on the city. It was only in the beginning of the thirteenth year that Babylon was able to complete a fleet capable of cutting it off from the sea. Evil-Merodach was actually the one who finally discovered the problem and how to deal with it.

But the early days in Riblah were not so brilliant for him.

To his credit, he did not make rash decisions. If anything, he was too hesitant when it was time for action, seemingly afraid to make a mistake.

Shortly after we arrived, Nebuzaradan arrived with some captives from Jerusalem.

"My lord, we thought it best to bring these by here before taking them to Babylon. There are prominent men in this group, and the other roads from Jerusalem to Babylon have become extremely perilous. This route we have been able to secure much better."

"Bring them before me," said the prince.

A group of about seventy men was brought into the open space in the middle of the fortress. My uncle explained who they were.

"At your illustrious father's orders, as soon as the walls were breached I made my way with a force of my best men to the temple. These Hebrews seem to hold it in very special regard."

"This group of men barricaded themselves inside the temple. We had already been ordered by the king to destroy the temple and the palace, cutting out the very heart of the city. I gave them opportunity to surrender and declare allegiance to Babylon, which they decided was in their best interest. We then burned the buildings."

"We have here the five main priests of their religion, including the high priest, Seraiah. We have brought the principle scribe of the temple, and these other sixty or so were in the temple with them. Also, this is Bensalem. He was in charge of the city defenses, and I he is a member of the 'Army of Jerusalem'.

"Would you like to address this accusation?" asked Evil-Merodach.

Bensalem stepped forward a few paces and spoke clearly.

"The 'Army of Jerusalem' is the arm of the Lord! We do His will, and none shall thwart us. Umman-Manda is formed, and will be the next kingdom of Assyria, Israel and Babylon."

I had been staring at the man the whole time, believing that I had seen him before. Now I remembered.

"You are an Edomite!" I declared. He was one of the Jackals!

"And what if I am? I am a child of Abraham. Jerusalem is Jehovah's throne. We are His servants."

At that he lunged forward in the direction of the prince. Without hesitation I drew a dagger from my girdle and plunged it into his heart.

Evil-Merodach seemed completely confused by all of this, and he was obviously enraged as well.

"Kill them all!" he shouted.

Before Nebuzaradan or I could do anything to stop them, the other guards present, believing that an attack had been made on the prince, fell to slaughtering all the captives from Jerusalem.

I stood looking at my uncle in disbelief. There were important men lying on the ground now, covered with their own blood. Some of them would have had strategic value to the king. The fact of the slaughter would be valuable to his enemies.

Somehow, one of men from amongst the captives was still standing, right in the middle of the others, apparently untouched. I recognized him as well. It was Jeremiah.

His head was down, and he was silent. I could tell, however, that he was weeping.

"Who is this man who yet lives, and how is it so?" the prince demanded.

I rushed to Jeremiah's side before anyone else could attack him.

"My lord, this man is a friend of Babylon and loyal to your father. His name is Jeremiah, and I know him," I said.

"Very well, see to him yourself. Now, someone clean up this mess!"

The prince turned and went to his chambers. Bodies were carries off to be disposed of. I took Jeremiah, shaking like a leaf in the wind, to my uncle.

"I know this man," Nebuzaradan said. "He has been our emissary to Zedekiah on many occasions."

"Old friend," he continued, "what would you have me do with you? We can give you safe passage to Babylon, or you can return to Jerusalem to help in the reorganization process. You are free to choose."

Jeremiah lifted his eyes for the first time since I went to him. "The Lord God would have me return to the Holy City – what is left of it."

"As you wish."

"No; it is not my wish to see Jerusalem in ruins, but it is the will of Jehovah."

We took him to a small house nearby where he could prepare himself for the journey, then returned to speak with Evil-Merodach.

It was decided that Nebuzaradan and I would lead a troop to Jerusalem to set up a governing body.

"I know a man, Gedaliah, who has the trust of the people. He stayed in Bethlehem during the siege, and always showed allegiance to Babylon."

"I trust you for these decisions, Nebuzaradan. You have more experience with these people than most. You have full authority to act."

My uncle asked me to go along.

"I need someone to watch after Jeremiah for a few days. Hopefully he will be alright; but after all he has seen, we must verify his loyalties. He still has a lot of influence with a certain segment of the Hebrews."

The next day we made our way toward Jerusalem. I arranged a mule for Jeremiah to ride, and he did not speak as we traveled. He seemed in better spirits, but it was always hard to tell with him.

We stopped at the summit of the hill the Hebrews called Har HaTsofim which had a clear view of the palace and temple – what was left of them.

Smoke still hung in the air from several places around the city center, and very few buildings still stood in that area.

Military camps had been set up in strategic locations, one of them farther down the ridge on which we now stood. Nebuzaradan started forward again, evidently heading for that encampment. Jeremiah held his mule back from following.

I dismounted and went to him, but he simply sat there, unmoving for a long time. I did not feel I had the right to interrupt whatever he was experiencing.

Finally he spoke.

"Would it be alright if I stayed here for a while?"

"Of course; stay as long as you like. What do you require? Some food perhaps?"

"No, thank you. I have plenty of water, and that will suffice me for now. I do have one request, though. I don't know if he will still be around, but my scribe was with your army when I was carried away to Riblah. He was in the camp on the Mount of Olives. He would be a great help to me if he could be found and brought here. His name is Baruch Ben Neriah."

"I will ride there at once and see if he may be found."

I asked for Jeremiah's scribe in the camp on the Mount of Olives, and he was not difficult to find. I arranged a horse for him and took him back to his master.

The reunion was, surprisingly, without emotion. Jeremiah simply declared that a prophecy was forthcoming, and that Baruch should write down what Jehovah would say through him. Baruch brought papyrus and ink from a bag he carried, sat them down on a relatively flat rock, pulled another rock close to the first, and sat down ready to write.

I did not know what to expect. I wanted to ask Jeremiah of I should move away from them, but he had already moved away himself – not physically, but he was no longer with us.

After what seemed like an interminable pause, he began to speak with his eyes shut tightly.

"How the city that was full of people sits solitary! How is she become as a widow! She that was great among the nations, and princess among the provinces, how is she become tributary!"

"She weeps sore in the night, and her tears are on her cheeks: among all her lovers she has none to comfort her: all her friends have dealt treacherously with her; they are become her enemies."

"Judah is gone into captivity to feel affliction, and is sold into servitude: She makes her dwelling among the heathen; she finds no rest. All her persecutors overtook her in her distress"

He paused here, and looked once again upon the destruction of the city.

"The streets of Zion mourn, because none come to the solemn feasts. All her gates are desolate: her priests sigh, her virgins are afflicted, and she is in bitterness."

"Her adversaries are the best warriors; her enemies prosper. For the LORD has afflicted her for the multitude of her transgressions. Her children are driven into captivity before the enemy."

"And all beauty has departed from the daughter of Zion. Her princes are become like harts that find no pasture, and they have run without strength before the pursuer."

"In the days of her affliction and of her miseries, when her people fell into the hand of the enemy, and none did help her, Jerusalem remembered all her pleasant things that she had in the days of old. The adversaries saw her, and mocked her Sabbaths."

"Jerusalem hath grievously sinned; therefore she is removed: all that honored her despise her, because they have seen her nakedness: She looks back, groaning."

His lament went on and on. Occasionally a phrase would catch my attention.

"For these things I weep; mine eye, mine eye runs with water, because the comforter that should relieve my soul is far from me. My children are desolate, because the enemy prevailed."

"Zion spreads forth her hands, and there is none to comfort her. The LORD has commanded concerning Jacob that his adversaries should be round about him: Jerusalem is as a menstruous woman among them."

"Jehovah is righteous, for I have rebelled against his commandment. Hear, I pray you, all people, and behold my sorrow: my virgins and my young men are gone into captivity."

My mind drifted away again. There was much to occupy my thoughts. Once again, something the prophet was saying brought me back.

"This I recall to my mind, therefore have I hope."

Hope? How can this man speak of hope at a time like this? Is he not seeing what I am seeing?

"It is of Jehovah's mercies that we are not consumed, because his compassions fail not. They are new every morning: Great is Your faithfulness.

"Jehovah is my portion, says my soul; therefore will I hope in him."

"Jehovah is good unto them that wait for him, to the soul that seeks him."

"It is good that a man should both hope and quietly wait for the salvation of Jehovah. It is good for a man that he bear the yoke while he is young. He sits alone and keeps silence, because he has borne it. He puts his mouth in the dust in a search for hope. He gives his cheek to the smiter. His reproach is complete."

"For Jehovah will not cast off forever. But though he cause grief, yet will he have compassion according to the multitude of His mercies."

I could not comprehend this message. It seemed contradictory to me to speak of Jehovah's wrath and his salvation at the same time. This is what Ruhamah and my mother were always trying to get me to understand; but as I stood overlooking his wrath (if Jehovah indeed did have something to do with the destruction of Jerusalem by Babylon), I did not see any trace of mercy, love or peace.

Chapter 55

A year has passed since that awkward day when Daniel had to give the king the interpretation of a dream predicting Nebuchadnezzar's collapse. I have seen enough of the Hebrew to know he does not pretend. I have also seen enough of Jehovah to know what he is capable of. But, even though I've seen my king troubled, I can't imagine his going over the edge for seven years.

Daniel's words seemed to leave room for the dream not to come true. Jehovah apparently wanted him to be more equitable with the people. He has indeed taken many measures since that day to assure everyone a fair hearing in any matter. The old code, originally written by Hammurabi, has been updated, with less privilege to the ruling class.

I returned from Jerusalem shortly after Jeremiah's moment on the hill. There has been more turmoil there. Gedaliah and his closest followers were murdered by a group insisting that (contrary, apparently, to prophecies by Jeremiah) the Hebrew's hope was to be found in Egypt. News from Jerusalem says that Nebuchadnezzar is being blamed for the slaughter committed by his son in Riblah.

Those looking to Egypt are led by a man named Ishmael Ben Nethaniah: a man, it is reported, with a horrendous vertical scar on his face. They took Jeremiah and some others captive, and headed south. My uncle has been acting governor of Jerusalem since then, bringing some stability to the situation.

I have enjoyed being back with my family, and Utanin and I have been working with the king on finishing Etemenanki. It looks like we have come to the place where we will have to enlist Daniel's help with the translation.

"Daniel is loyal to me, but we will be asking him to help us build a monument to a god he will not follow."

"Maybe you can copy the symbols you don't know, Utanin, and we can show those to Daniel out of context," I suggested.

Two days later we met again.

"He wasn't suspicious about the translation?" asked the king.

"He must have been, my king, and it showed in his face; but I told him it was requested by you personally, and he asked no questions."

"Do you now know what the tablet says?"

"I do my king. That is, I know what the words mean, but there is a part here that I do not understand, even knowing what the words are. It is here – it says that the final dedication to Marduk is to place the eyes into Orion's face, and then to follow these numbers to know the power of the gods. I do not know what that means."

"I think I do," I said.

Nebuchadnezzar and Utanin turned to look at me in wonder, I could only imagine what they must be thinking as I was not able to read anything on the tablet and had not even been involved in the early phases of the tower's construction. But I had been places neither of them had.

"Both in Nippur and in Nineveh, inside their towers, there was an owl painted on the ceiling of the lower level: an owl with two holes for its eyes."

"I remember that, now that you mention it, Kasher. I remember when we started rebuilding - with only part of the tablet - that we had to make two holes in the outside edge of the first layer, coming through the flat, horizontal area beneath the second layer. And there is an owl! We had no instructions about that, but we could make out a faint outline on the ceiling inside, and decided to repaint it as we found it, assuming it would be on the other part of the tablet. It turns out it is not, but there must be some reason for its existence. But whether the eyes are of an owl or of Orion, the instructions are to place eyes in the holes. We have no eyes to place there."

All of a sudden I realized that I had been carrying those eyes around for years.

"My king, I have an urgent errand. I will return very quickly, I promise."

Chapter 56

We pushed hard to complete the temple at the top of the tower. The instructions of the tablet were that it was to be dedicated to the god Bel; but that was pretty much redundant as Bel just means a deity. Nebuchadnezzar said that it obviously meant Marduk, as he was the chief of the gods, but I was inclined to believe it had been left ambiguous on purpose.

All three of us were anxious to put the eyes in the owl's face, but the king was adamant that we should follow the tablet to the letter, and it said to do that after all else was complete.

There was too much going on now to keep it a secret, at least from the Chaldeans, so Utanin was consulting with some of their best mathematicians about the numbers at the end of the tablet. They could not read the tablet, so he was able to keep the part about the eyes from them.

"The first part is an angle measurement," he told us after one of their sessions. "A mirror must be placed on the pedestal under the eyes at an angle of exactly fifteen degrees. Then, there is an astronomical calculation that, I have been informed, can only relate to the position of the sun. It would appear that the light from the sun, hitting the eyes in just the right the right way, will reflect onto the mirror, sending that light upwards to the ceiling to reveal there a location in the night sky. A map of the stars is painted there, and this light will reveal something important – but the tablet does not say what."

"Marduk will reveal it to me." The king was deep in thought. "He told me he would give me the secret to eternal life through this project, and that the final explanation would come from his own mouth when my work on Etemenanki was finished."

We all three needed a moment to digest this sober declaration.

Chapter 57

The tower was finished.

The sun would pass by the correct position in the early morning hours of the next day, and the king would descend into his creation to see the secret of the ages revealed.

It was a beautiful, clear night, and Nebuchadnezzar invited me, Utanin and Daniel to climb Etemenanki.

We all looked around us at the great beauty of the city, glowing softly in an almost full moon.

The king spoke. "Great is Babylon, the city I have built for the seat of my great kingdom!"

Something was different about the way he spoke. Nebuchadnezzar was a great man, but not needing to, he rarely called attention to that fact.

"Have I not have built this great house by my strength, and for my deserved honor?"

Before his last words stopped ringing in our ears, the three of us accompanying the king heard a great, booming voice coming from somewhere well above our position at the top of Etemenanki. It was as clear a voice as I had ever heard, and more powerful than any I had ever heard. I couldn't be certain, but there seemed to be a slight tone of sadness as well.

"O king Nebuchadnezzar, hear what I say to you this day: The kingdom is departed from you."

"You shall be driven from among men for seven years, living as a beast. You shall eat grass as the oxen, covered in the dew of morning for refusing the shelter of human habitation. All of this is so that you may know of a certainty that it is the Most High God, Creator and Sustainer of all, that sets up and takes away kingdoms."

The king began moaning, holding his head in agony. Then, after just a few short seconds, he fell to his knees.

We all rushed to his aide, but he was incoherent. He seemed not to see us at first, then he became violent towards us.

We restrained him with as little force as was absolutely necessary, and were finally able (with great difficulty) to bring him down from the tower.

Chapter 58

Seven years went by slowly.

At first we were able to keep the king in his own quarters, but, after a short while, he could not be restrained from hurting himself, and there was too much noise. Comments began to circulate about what must be happening in there, so we decided to build him a small house out in the gardens. It was well known that they had been built for the queen, and she had always been very jealous to keep them to herself.

As soon as we took him out there, we saw a dramatic difference in his behavior. All the while that we were leading him through the garden, he was relatively peaceful. As soon as we tried to get him into the new building, he began fighting us wildly again, endangering us and him.

We decided to let him roam the garden area, leaving the door to his new house open should he desire to go in. He adamantly did not.

Just as had been predicted, he began eating grass; grazing as if he were an ox. We made sure he had other things available to eat, which he did at times, but mostly he just grazed.

Either Daniel, Utanin, Asphenaz or myself was with him at all times, day and night. We tried to bathe him, but he would have none of it. After a while he really did start to look more like beast than man.

We managed to keep the fact a secret. Rumors we could not stop. Daniel was the face of the kingdom, and that wasn't unusual, but the fact that the king never appeared was causing a lot of consternation.

I don't know what he suspected, but we were able to keep Evil-Merodach out of the loop, too. We used the kings official seal to send him messages from time to time, the first of which stating that he would be the regent of Riblah, Tyre and Jerusalem, answerable only to Nebuchadnezzar. That seemed to content him for quite a while.

The biggest problem was with the Chaldeans. There was nothing directly they could do against Daniel's governance, but I was getting reports back from some of my men outside the city walls that some Chaldeans were communicating a lot with someone in Egypt.

Three years in. As unlikely as it seems, even this has begun to seem somewhat normal. Everything stays the same, day after day. Nebuchadnezzar's hair grows long and is matted from lack of washing. Even his fingernails are grown hideously long. We continue to try, periodically, to bathe or groom him; but he will not accept. He is amazingly strong for a man who eats mostly grass.

The fourth anniversary of the king's madness has come and gone. Daniel and Asphenaz are masters at keeping the public from growing too concerned by not seeing their king.

My mother passed away this year. She died in her sleep. I was too busy trying to hold Babylon together to know she was even ill, but Ruhamah said she simply didn't wake up one morning.

Both of my sisters had married Hebrew men from the provinces. We hardly knew each other as we met at Mother's funeral.

Our youngest son died this year as well. He was always a weak boy, but we never could have expected him to simply fall over dead one day as he did.

Nebuzaradan is back in the city.

He simply appeared one day with no warning. He was traveling alone; a perilous thing for him to do.

"I disguised myself as a mercenary," he explained to our little group. "It seemed the best idea for not being challenged too much."

"But, if you are here, who is in charge of Jerusalem? We haven't heard of any change by Evil-Merodach," said Asphenaz.

"There has been no official decree, but I was recalled to Riblah, and then allowed to leave; I think only because the prince was afraid of recriminations if I was harmed. My sources tell me that the man named Ishmael, the one who led the group of Hebrews to Egypt, is back in Jerusalem, and that there seems to be some sort of alliance between him and Evil-Merodach."

"I have heard that the prince is also communicating with some of the Chaldeans – the same ones who were sending and receiving messages with someone in Egypt," said Utanin.

"It all comes down to this Ishmael," I said.

"We must continue to keep our secret safe," said Daniel. "Any word of the king's weakness could bring an attack; and if we lose the Chaldeans, anything can happen."

Chapter 59

The seventh year; at last. I wondered if anyone else had doubts about the back end of the prophecy. Would Nebuchadnezzar really come back to his senses? Would it be literally at the time the dream said?

We were kept informed about the fighting in several areas of the kingdom. At one point we discussed having Nebuzaradan put together a force to quell some of the troubles, but we all decided, in the end, that our primary concern had to be the city itself.

My uncle went about securing our walls; and I, when I was not with the king in the garden, went over our plans for the safety of the royal family – with the exception of Evil-Merodach, of course.

Ruhamah's quarters were adjacent to those of the queen, and I developed a plan for her to accompany Amytis out of harm's way should that become necessary.

At first, she resisted, but I was firm.

"I need you for this. The kingdom needs you to be prepared to do this."

"I'm not a warrior, Kasher. I don't know anything about fighting!"

"I have men to send with you to do the fighting. I need you because of who you are. Imagine if it were you, all alone except for some soldiers. Amytis is a strong woman, but nothing like you. She will need you if she is fleeing Babylon. I also need to believe that you are safe if things get bad here. If you are able to escape, I can concentrate on winning the battle – and staying alive!"

That seemed to convince her.

"Very well, I will prepare for the worst – but I will pray for the best!"

The next day, Kartan and Armo met us in the garden.

"Were you able to work out the escape route?" I asked them.

"Come," said Kartan, "it will be easier to show you than tell you."

I had brought Ruhamah and Utanin along, but decided to leave Amytis out of this for now. We would tell her the details once I was confident of the plan, but she might panic if she had to confront the idea right now. She was a strong woman - I had learned that during our trip up north. But she was also given to overthink things, and I could not leave the decision of when to run up to her.

We climbed the artificial mountain just as we had earlier with Nebuchadnezzar. We paused about two-thirds of the way up, and, looking back into the garden, I could see the king huddled in a corner.

It was the way he usually spent his days. Food was taken to a place close to him and left. We had tried time and again to feed him ourselves, but he would either ignore us, or, occasionally, try to attack the food bearer.

We always left his food in large, clean bowls, but the first thing he would do upon reaching it was to throw it out of the bowl onto the ground. Then he would eat little bits of it at a time; circling it, snarling at it, and eventual pouncing on it as if it needed killing.

My attention was brought back to the task at hand by someone gently prodding me forward. It was Ruhamah, who was just behind me in our little procession.

"Kartan is calling for us to follow him, my love."

She had seen the source of my distraction. So complete it had been that I hadn't yet noticed that a door had opened before us.

"I didn't see a door here before," I mused aloud.

"And that is as it should be," answered Armo.

"Don't worry, Kasher," Ruhamah consoled, "I know where the door is and how to open it. I am the one who needs to know, after all."

The light was dim, and I hoped it was dim enough for the redness of my face not to show. If anyone did notice, they said nothing. Kartan led us into the mountain.

A ladder went up just inside the door, leading us into a tunnel at the top of the structure. It was almost tall enough for me to stand without bending over. There were holes at regular intervals in the roof letting in a small amount of light and air. Water dripped in in places.

We followed the tunnel to its end, and, upon exiting another door and lighting a torch that awaited us there, discovered that we had entered another tunnel, perpendicular to the first.

"We are inside the north wall," explained Kartan. These tunnels were already here, built into the original wall, but it seems no one knew about them. The new walls on the other side of the river do not have them."

There were no holes in this one. The air was stale, but it was a large area, and there would be plenty of air to breathe for a long time, even if it were sealed tight.

The floor sloped gently away from our position in both directions, indicating that, among other things, we were at the center of the wall's expanse.

"We have developed two escape routes from here," said Armo. Going to the left will take you to the river, and we have a contingency to try to get the fleeing parties onto a boat, sailing north. We have a network of people loyal to the king and queen from here all the way to Armenia; more or less on the same route you took going there, Kasher. If that way is not viable for some reason, going right will take you to a guard station at the northeast corner of the wall. We have made sure to have the right people stationed there, and it is the strongest point in all the perimeter. From there a network of traders will take over with the final result the same: safety in Armenia."

We discussed the rest of the plan for a while. I was pleased with the effort, but hoped we would never need to take advantage of it.

"Armo," I said, "I would appreciate it if you would lead them if it becomes necessary to go. You know the way, you are a fighting man, and you would be going home!"

"I would be honored, my old friend. You can count on me to give every safety possible to the queen – and whoever goes with her."

"Kartan, I won't ask you to go, but it would be further comfort for me if you did."

"We will see where I am most needed at the moment, should it come. I will do what I can for my kingdom."

We made our way back to the garden. Just as we got there, I realized why I had been looking so intently at the king before we entered the tunnel. He was, indeed huddled in his corner, but there had been a slight difference in his posture. His back was straight – something I hadn't seen for seven years.

From the landing outside the door I could see him again. He was in the same place; the same posture was evident as well, but there was one more difference:

He was looking up at us.

Chapter 60

The king made no move to rise no matter how close we came to him. Before, he would have lashed out if we got too close. This time, we walked right up to him. As I stood quietly at his side, he looked at me. There was no sign of the madman in his eyes.

"Hello, Kasher!" he said, his voice extremely weak. It seemed it was an effort for him to speak. I presumed it was from lack of use, like muscles that do not get exercised properly.

I soon found out that was a problem as well.

"May I help you up, my king?"

He reached a hand up to me. His arm was very muscular from the life he had been leading; his fingernails amazingly long, deformed, and, of course, filthy.

Kartan came to his other side; Armo took up position behind Nebuchadnezzar. As we tried to lift him to his feet, he groaned in agony. The looks that passed between us indicated that we all understood the problem: he had not walked upright for seven years.

We massaged his muscles, and patiently helped him up. After about ten minutes, the king was finally able to stand without great pain, and we guided him gently toward the palace door.

None of us spoke as we made our way there, though I was bursting with questions only the king could answer – questions he was probably the only person who had ever lived could answer.

Once in a while as we walked I would look at his face. I'm not sure what emotion I expected to find there, but it was certainly not the one I discovered. The only word I could come up with to describe it was… peaceful.

We eased him into a sitting position on his bed and Armo left to bring food and drink for the king. None of us knew quite what to do or say, but after a few moments, Nebuchadnezzar looked at me and said weakly, "I need Daniel and Asphenaz."

I immediately left him to find his two trusted ministers, irritated with myself that I hadn't anticipated his command. They were both involved in meetings, but I managed to communicate to them what was required without rousing too much suspicion from others. I said simply, "It has been twelve months." They understood.

The king's spirits lifted visibly as Daniel and Asphenaz entered the room. He was beginning to look more like himself, even without losing all the hair and accumulated filth. The rest of us waited outside the room as the three most powerful men in Babylon conferred for the first time in a year.

Asphenaz appeared at the door and asked for water – lots of it – and a sharp knife.

"I am sorry to ask this of people like you. You are not servants, and I hope you don't think I see you that way. It's just that we still need to limit the number of people involved."

"Of course, Asphenaz, we understand completely. Ruhamah will see to it. If anyone asks, she can say it is for the queen and no one will question her. The rest of you should go on about your normal business. No one will find my presence here at the king's door to be odd, so I will stay." I said.

A few hours later I was summoned into the room. The transformation the king had undergone was astounding. I could still see evidence of his ordeal in his face, but even that was quickly fading away. In a few days' time, Nebuchadnezzar should be able to be seen in public without alarming anyone. Babylon had survived the ordeal.

We all agreed that meetings with the king should begin slowly; one a day for a few days, increasing in frequency as his recovery allowed.

The first few days, particularly, allowed me a lot of time with the king. I had missed being with this man I so admired.

Daniel was almost always present now. Before he had been a force that swept in and out of the king's world like a summer breeze through the palace windows, but he stayed with us now. Nebuchadnezzar seemed to want him there more than ever before, and Daniel seemed to believe he should be there. I had to admit that it felt right to me as well.

They seemed completely at ease talking about Nebuchadnezzar's experience of the last year. They also spoke much of Jehovah.

"There were several factors that led to your fall, my king," said Daniel. "Not giving glory to Jehovah for honoring you as his vessel, as your dream explained, was of course the principle reason. But you were battling on at least two spiritual fronts at once."

"Yes, I see that now. My arrogance was my downfall, and I always admired Jehovah, but in reality it was only for what I thought I could get from him. Marduk was my god, not Jehovah, and I thought I could use the power of both of them for my own means."

"Do you remember," I asked, "anything about the time out there in the garden, my king?

"Some things, Kasher. It was as if I was two people during that time. My mind still functioned in a certain way, but not all the time. The times I remember like that, I had no control over what my body did. It seemed to just follow what it had been given to do – like the beast it was. But those moments when my mind was clear, it was completely human; spiritual."

"It is very hard to explain, but somehow Jehovah allowed me to think and reason during that time. And He spoke to me. At one point my inner turmoil was greater than anything you might have seen on the outside. Jehovah kept reminding me of all I knew about Him – from you, Daniel, and from Jeremiah and others. He reminded me that I really did know quite a lot about Him; but He was not my God."

"Marduk was there too. He reminded me of all the power he had given me. He reminded me of all the great signs and wonders done by his ministers, the Chaldeans. I had to admit it was true. I had seen powerful works from both him and Jehovah."

"Finally, in one of those moments, I cried out in anguish: I see all the miracles; but where is the peace?"

"There was silence in my mind at that point; a silence like I have never experienced before. Every day, since my first encounter with Marduk as a young man, my mind has been filled with a chaotic chorus of voices, all

544

fighting each other for dominance. Finally, I was alone with my own thoughts."

"From somewhere close to me (I can't explain it any better than that), I began to hear, in calm yet powerful words, a message that felt authoritative, and yet encouraging at the same time."

"The gist of the message was that even though there were many gods, only one of them was the Creator. In fact, I began to understand that all the other gods had in fact been created by Him."

"The other part of the message (and it became clearer and clearer that it was Jehovah Himself speaking) was that the created gods were like I had been: arrogant. Everything they did was to promote their own selves."

"'But I created you as well, Nebuchadnezzar,' He told me, 'and I created you with special love and care. You have served me without submitting to me, for I am sovereign over the affairs of men - and gods. But if you will serve me with your heart, you will find peace as well.'"

"I understand now. It makes no sense - and certainly brings no peace – to place my own will ahead of the will of my Creator. He truly is God! He is worthy of all praise and service. That day, as my body was bowed to the ground by my years of self-serving, my heart knelt before the King of kings and Lord of lords. At long last, peace is mine."

Daniel had held his tongue during this revelation, and neither did he speak afterwards. I waited in what was, for me, an uncomfortable silence for a time, then asked the king a question that had been in me for quite some time.

"My king, you have explained yourself marvelously, but – if you will be patient with me – I would ask you a question related to your spiritual journey."

"Of course, Kasher. Ask me what you like."

"I have heard in many religious discussions – including some of your own in the past, my king, of the desire for immortality. How… forgive me my boldness… how does your new belief affect your understanding of that concept?"

"A very interesting and pertinent question, my friend. I tell you truly that I have not even considered that aspect since giving myself to Jehovah. Frankly, it has been enough for me to be at peace here in this life. But your question is certainly an important one. Marduk offered me immortality and great glory in the afterlife, as a lesser god myself under his command. I know now, that since he is not the Creator, he certainly cannot give life; not in this world or any other. Jehovah has not spoken to me to this point. Daniel, can you shed any light on the subject?"

"I can, my lord. You have great understanding already, and you have reached right conclusions with the help of Jehovah's servants and His Spirit."

"It is recorded in the first book of Moses that Jehovah created all, crowning it all by molding our first father, Adam, out of the clay with His own loving hands. This man, along with our mother, Eve, was deceived by the prince of darkness, Lucifer, the lord over all of those called 'gods' excepting only Jehovah Himself. Man sinned against his Creator, and was separated from Him by that sin. Only Jehovah had the power to bring about the redemption Adam needed. Not Marduk; not Ishtar; not Nebu – and not even man himself."

"It would have been hard for us to lay any guilt at Jehovah's holy feet if He had not seen fit to pardon Adam's sin. But He is always true to His own nature, and loves His creation in ways we humans cannot comprehend."

"So, as was always His plan, He provided salvation. Adam hid from his God in the shame of his sin, but Jehovah called to him, giving him a way back. Adam confessed his sin, and Jehovah pardoned him – just as He does everyone who comes by the same path."

"The price was still to be paid for Adam's sin, however. No act of violence against the perfect Law of the Creator can be ignored – there must be an atonement. There, in the beauty of Jehovah's pardon, was a prophecy of how that redemption was to be carried out."

"Jehovah declared that there would be a great conflict between Lucifer and One who would come through the seed of woman – not man. There will be a redeemer, anointed by Jehovah to give spiritual life to those who will accept it. As Isaiah wrote, 'As for our redeemer, the Lord of the hosts is his name, the Holy One of Israel.'"

"There is a sense, in the Holy Scriptures, of Jehovah's redemption of His chosen people, Israel. But it goes much deeper and much broader than the Nation. Redemption is before, during and beyond Israel. Adam and the other fathers before Abraham found Him willing and able to save them individually, before there was an Israel. And you, O king, are brought to Him as many are; having no claim to the promises of inheritance given to my people. You rule over God's people by His decree!"

"Now, to get to your question specifically, Kasher. As there is a redemption that goes beyond lands and peoples, what is its nature? It is, of course, spiritual, and there is a salvation that goes beyond this mortal life."

"After creating man's body, Jehovah breathed into his nostrils the breath of life; and man became a living soul. None of the animals received such a gift. Only man."

David wrote of Jehovah, 'You will show me the path of life: in Your presence is fullness of joy; at your right hand there are pleasures forevermore.' Forevermore! Not just until our bodies of clay cease their breathing. He also said, 'Surely goodness and mercy shall follow me all the days of my life: and I will dwell in the house of the LORD forever.'"

"The prophet Job declared, 'I know that my Redeemer lives, and that He shall stand at the latter day upon the earth: And though after my skin worms destroy this body, yet in my flesh shall I see God.'"

"We don't know all that is involved in Jehovah's plan of redemption, Kasher, but we do know what He has revealed. There will be life everlasting in His presence for those whom He has saved."

Chapter 61

The king did not hide his new-found faith from anyone. I cautioned him that he might create for himself new enemies - and strengthen the animus of the old ones - if he was too publicly forthcoming with such a radical change.

He would hear none of it.

Just one week after his recovery began, Nebuchadnezzar called a great assembly. Speaking from the wide porch of the palace - the gates to the compound open for all to enter - He declared that Jehovah, alone, was the True, Almighty, All-Knowing and All-Present God. The love of Jehovah was something to be embraced by all the peoples of the earth. He did not go so far as to pronounce an edict demanding that Jehovah be worshiped, but the god of the king was the god of the realm.

As I feared, the Chaldeans were immediately emboldened by this declaration. Their ever present fiery criticisms of the king were fanned by the knowledge that Nebuchadnezzar had abandoned the god they followed; the god from whom they derived their power and influence.

There were other voices, ranging from concern for the king's mental state (ironic, given his past troubles) to ire in the face of such a great change of religious stance.

One group had complaints that I had not anticipated. There were those among the very followers of Jehovah who were angry. It soon became clear that at least some of these people did not welcome company to their special world. They were 'the chosen', and there was no room for outsiders – not even a king.

Nakhti – Nebuchadnezzar had asked him to go back to his old name since the one he had given him was tied to 'the old gods' – came and went from the palace to places outside the city walls. The news he brought back was never comforting.

"My king, your enemies have taken great strength from your new position. Some of them are uniting around it."

"There are new alliances that have been forged between some of the Philistines, Egyptians and Assyrians. So far, Lebanon has remained neutral; possibly due to the presence of your son in the region."

"There is renewed talk in the north about the revival of Umman-Manda. They have a new champion; a Mede called Darius. He is gathering a considerable following, and has declared himself to have some claim to the throne of Babylon."

The king's demeanor was peaceful through all these reports.

"Jehovah's will shall be accomplished," he would state calmly.

"But, my king," I ventured, "surely, since you reign at Jehovah's pleasure, He would not expect you to give up your kingdom without a fight?"

"Of course not, Kasher, we will fight when we must to preserve our realm. But we must not fret over it as though the All-Mighty God has no say in it."

I was comforted – a little – by his declaration that we could still fight. I just wondered what we would be able to do against so many enemies at once.

I didn't want to believe that the great Nebuchadnezzar was becoming soft, but I could not help entertaining the thought at times.

I felt like I was back in the sandstorm all those years ago – trapped; trapped by my own fears as much as by the external forces that held me prisoner. I had reached out to Jehovah at that time. Was it he who had saved me alive then? Would he bring me – us – out of this trial too?

Or was he the cause of all this trouble? We had managed to keep peace in the region with the king completely out of the picture, and now that he was back – with Jehovah now – things had gone mad.

I could almost feel my throat closing, clogged by the millions of grains of sand working together in harmony, fighting for my destruction.

One relatively calm day I asked the king if we might not be able to still use Etemenanki and the eyes of Nimrod for the city's protection. I still did not understand exactly how it was supposed to work, but there had been talk of great power there.

"I don't know, Kasher. Let me call in Daniel and see if he has a perspective we haven't heard about this."

Daniel had been kept out of our discussions concerning Etemenanki before because of his strong religious stand. Now, the king shared his views, and so he was to be seen as an ally, even in this question. I had my reservations, but I didn't have any concrete reason to advise against it, so I called for him to come.

"I am very aware of this phenomenon. We were taught all about Nimrod and the towers at court in Jerusalem. The Scriptures tell us some things about them, but there are other pieces of information that do not have the weight of Jehovah's revelation behind them, but that are nevertheless deemed to be quite reliable."

"One of Adam's sons, Cain, is said to have been given a tablet by Jehovah, or by Lucifer (depending upon which story you accept as true) with the instructions for the building of the original tower. He then passed it on through the next generations. It is said to have made it onto the ark; and then, after the flood it came into the possession of a great-grandson of Noah - Nimrod."

"Was it Jehovah, or was it Lucifer who wrote the tablet?" asked Nebuchadnezzar.

"I can't say with certainty, my king, but since everything having to do with it has led men to rebel against Jehovah, either it was Lucifer himself who wrote it, or he has done a masterful job at what he does best – twisting the truth."

He proceeded to tell us the rest of the story, and it was, indeed fascinating, but it never seemed to come to my question. Finally, he ended, and I asked, "But what is its actual function?"

"We were taught that, with the eyes in place, at a certain time of day the sun's rays would strike a mirror placed on the floor of the inner chamber. Their lights would then combine in some forceful way that I don't understand, and the new light would be reflected onto the ceiling to a spot on the star map painted there."

"That spot was said to hold a key to where and when Jehovah's Redeemer would be born. It was said that whoever held that knowledge would have tremendous power. They might even rule the world, or at least they could manipulate world powers for their profit."

"Marduk promised me everything – even immortality – if I built it for him," said the king, "but I now know he does not have that power. This all fits together with what I have learned about the 'gods'. They use men, not love them."

"Kasher, I appreciate your bringing this matter up. I know you are looking after my wellbeing, as always, but we will not speak again of Etemenanki."

Nakhti left for one of his assessment trips and did not return right away. There were rumors flying everywhere; not only about his whereabouts, but also of open threats against Nebuchadnezzar.

One morning, just three months after the king's recovery, a messenger came through the Ishtar Gate.

"We are ten nations strong and growing. We demand that Nebuchadnezzar place himself and his city under our headship. We intend a peaceful relationship, but we are prepared for battle if the king is not willing to submit to us. You have two days to respond. If we are not respected in this matter, a siege will be laid and you will be humbled before all the earth."

The messenger turned on his heel the way he had come – completely without ceremony.

Nebuchadnezzar brought in all of his normal counselors and some new ones as well. Conspicuously absent were the Chaldeans. Whether they had been invited or not I did not know, but they were not present.

"We can hold out to a siege for quite a while, my king," Asphenaz said, "due to your wise preparations of the city, but if we are indeed surrounded in an efficient manner, we can do nothing to help our subjects elsewhere."

"Our most recent information indicates that this threat is real," one of the captains of the army added, "and that it is already too late to try and bring anyone in from the nearby towns. This is unfortunate, but there is nothing to be done about it at the present."

Ideas were debated for hours in an attempt to find a solution that did not include our subjugation. Through all the talks, one idea kept coming up.

"If we can hold out for a while," another of the captains said, giving voice to the idea many of us were contemplating, "Evil-Merodach can come in from behind the enemy and break them up. Then we can go out to meet them, squeezing these usurpers in the middle."

That seemed to be the only hope we had if we would not surrender. I did not know if it was hope enough for Nebuchadnezzar to hang his decision on, but as the second day was drawing to a close he said, "We will hold out. My son will come."

Just as a messenger was being prepared to take our word to the enemy camp, Nakhti arrived.

He looked half dead - beaten, cut and exhausted - but even so our spirits were buoyed by his arrival. Our joy was to be short-lived, as was my old friend and mentor.

He struggled to speak, supported on either side by the men who had managed to get him back inside the city.

"O great Nebuchadnezzar, live forever!"

"My faithful general, "said the king. "What news do you suffer so to bring us?"

"I have only one thing to add to the king's knowledge; and it pains me more than anything I have ever felt to bring you this news. Your son, my king, has betrayed you."

An uproar filled the room: doubt, anger, disbelief all mingling in one great deafening chorus. The king stood and help up his hand for quiet.

When the chaos finally abated, he spoke.

"Nakhti; speak. And say true what you must. We must know where we stand."

"My king, these lords who surround your great city have somehow perverted your son against you. He is to be their vassal here in Babylon. I spoke with him at length concerning his decision, and he is convinced that he will be able to regain full sovereignty in time; but that you never would. He tried to have me killed when I spoke against his plan, but I managed to escape."

With that, my uncle collapsed to the floor, never to rise again.

There was no time for grieving, and Nakhti would have understood that better than anyone. When his body had been removed a heated debate ensued. Our last hope for a victory seemed out of reach, and there was nothing like unanimity amongst us concerning the path forward.

As it turned out, all our talk was for nothing.

A breathless attendant rushed in through the door. Several swords were unsheathed, but the king recognized him and appealed for calm.

"My lord! The Chaldeans have opened all the gates to the enemy!"

A new chaos ensued. I was, as usual, standing by the king, and I grabbed his arm and pulled him toward the door to his chambers.

"No," he screamed at me. "I will fight them to my last breath!"

"Yes, my king, I am sure you will if that should become necessary, but for now you must let your army defend the city and repel this enemy. You must let me protect you so that they will still have a king when the battle is won."

My argument seemed to convince him, at least for the moment. I was glad to see that his new faith had not erased the man of war and action that I had admired for so long.

As we moved, Nebuchadnezzar reached out and took Daniel by the arm, bringing him along with us. I looked for Asphenaz, but could not see him. There was no more time.

My men knew what to do, and a cordon was formed to get the king and myself into his chambers, closing behind us as barrier of iron.

Inside his great room, we did not have long to wait for the attack to reach us. I was impressed, as a military man, at the speed and efficiency with which the enemy had managed to get this deeply into the palace compound. They had to confront elite soldiers all the way from the gate of the compound to this very door. Somehow they had managed to neutralize all my preparations, and they were pounding at the door in front of me.

I turned to look at the king. He was now dressed just as I had seen him that day outside of Nippur. A ray of sunshine had found its way onto one shoulder of his armor, and it reminded me of the sunlight playing on the ripples of the river.

His sword was in his hand, and he smiled broadly at me.

"Let's have them, eh Kasher?"

I could not help but smile back; confidence, even now, filling me at a word from this man.

I was standing forward and to Nebuchadnezzar's left. Daniel was directly behind me. He was not a fighter, and refused when I tried to offer him a dagger.

"Thank you, Kasher. This is not my fight. I wish I could help, but I would be useless to you. Do not even consider me if you must fight. I would not have you or the king endangered by trying to protect me."

The door came open with a great crash. It was large – almost as wide as it was tall – and three at a time poured through.

There weren't as many as I expected, but still I counted eight of them.

They spread out before us. I knew there would be more if we were somehow able to survive this fight, but I also knew I would kill several men before I was through.

One more man stepped through the door; alone.

He had a scar above his nose, running all the way to the top of his forehead.

The noise of battle outside was loud, but in this relatively small space, everything came to an eerie halt.

"Well, well; you again. And here with the king himself! You've done well for yourself I see. And I'll bet you have learned a bit about fighting since that day the arrow saved you from my sword."

"We will all know soon enough, I suppose," I retorted," but don't think you will have so easy a time with me now."

I was fighting to keep my emotions in check. I almost let myself wonder about my family, but there was nothing I could do for them at this moment. I just hoped the plans we had in place would be sufficient for them and the queen to get to safety.

"And look who is hiding in the corner," said the man with the scar.

"Not hiding, brother. Just trying to stay out of the way."

"You look surprised, my young friend. You did not know that Daniel and I are brothers? For shame, Daniel. Do I embarrass you so? We both serve Jehovah, after all."

"You serve only yourself and Beelzebub, Ishmael. You have no right to even utter the Holy Name!"

"Just because our methods are different doesn't mean we don't want the same thing, brother. I fight for Jerusalem with the sword; you fight... well, you do at least love the holy city, don't you, brother?"

"Jerusalem is holy because of the presence of Jehovah in her. She has lost that presence. My God has chosen other vessels to bring his erring wife back to Himself. Jehovah fights for me, and I bow to His will."

"Go, you coward! Leave this battlefield at once! You are not worthy to die here. Men will be victorious here, and men will be defeated here, but you will not be among them!"

Daniel looked at Nebuchadnezzar. The king spoke softly.

"My dear, dear friend. Go. Whatever the outcome here today, we will meet again; with Job, Isaiah, Abraham and our Redeemer. Now go, and know you have my eternal gratitude and love."

"My king…"

"Your king commands you to go, Daniel, servant of the All-Mighty God. Obey your lord, and thus fulfill His will. Babylon may have further need of you."

Ishmael's men looked as though they might attack Daniel as he moved to exit the room, but their commander called them down.

"Any man who harms my brother will have his entrails up to the hilt of my sword before I dispatch this heathen king."

With that, Daniel was gone.

The attack came without further conversation, and it came ferociously.

Four men went after Nebuchadnezzar and four straight at me. I saw Ishmael move toward the king, and, fighting off four slashing swords, I placed myself between them.

He and I were now engaged, and the others tried to come at me from the sides as we fought. There was no opportunity for me to look at the king to see how he fared.

I fought with everything that had ever been placed in me. I fought like the powerful Nakhti. I summoned up all the finesse that I had learned from Enusat. I tried to make myself as large as Ludim. I remembered the cunning of my friend Armo.

One of my adversaries went down – on my left, victim of the dagger refused by Daniel, still in my left hand. I had been able to conceal it until the right moment, and it struck home in his heart, even as I blocked two swords at once in front of me.

There was no time to retrieve the dagger, but he had been the only attacker on that side of me, so I now a little more room to maneuver. One of the other attackers lunged from the right, and I was able to slide quickly out of his path, stepping over his fallen comrade. He was not so lucky as his momentum carried him dangerously close to my right side and beyond me, tripping over the dead man on the floor. Without taking my eyes off the other attackers I switched the sword to my left hand, grabbing the falling man by his hair with my right as he fell, jerking violently upwards as his weight propelled him downward.

There was no respite. I had to fight with my left hand for a moment, but I had trained extensively to be able to do that. Nakhti had insisted on it. He had claimed that ability had saved his life on several occasions.

Fighting left-handed did seem to throw them off a bit. Though they did not have the same force behind them, my thrusts came from different angles than before, and I used their moment of confusion to reach down and recover one of the swords now left without an owner.

As soon as I stood I charged into the remaining three before me with all my might. I had never stopped working on my body, and even though I was considerably older now, I was almost as strong as I had ever been. Two more men fell to the floor before me, and I could not say exactly how it had happened. What I did know was that I was facing that scar once again.

I heard a gasp from behind me, and I recognized it as coming from the king. For a split second I forgot all my training, and looked in the direction of the sound.

There were two men on the floor, and the king was still on his feet fighting the other two. He looked exhausted, but I did not have time to assess the situation further because I was falling to my back.

There was a horrible pain in my left shoulder, but I only had time to pull my sword up before Ishmael's arrived at my chest. I drove a knee hard into his groin just as I parried his thrust, with the result that he landed with all his weight on my stomach his sword now high in the air, where I had caused it to go by blocking it.

He was in obvious pain, but I could see he would soon be able to fight through it to deal me the final blow, and I was in no position to do anything about it. I could not breathe, and there would be no arrow coming through his back to save me this time.

Everything was spinning around me. I had no control of my arms – or anything. And evil grin crossed Ishmael's face, and he grunted, "Finally."

Suddenly there was something different about the image I saw before me. I was still having trouble focusing, but there seemed to be something protruding from the scar now.

I shook my head to clear my eyes, and, sure enough, something had perfectly divided that awful scar all the way from his crown to his nose. I followed the object back from his head to above my own, and, about halfway along, I realized that it was a sword.

The hilt was poise just above my eyes, and as I began to take in what was going on, it started coming towards my face.

I jerked hard to my right, away from the pain earlier inflicted on the other side, and pushed with my good hand and my body the other direction against the dead weight trying to fall on me.

I had just managed to avoid some potentially devastating injuries from a dead man, and, my head clearing some more, I noticed that the room was quiet.

I managed to push Ishmael's body off of me.

"Now that will leave a permanent scar," I managed to joke.

As I got to one knee, I saw Nebuchadnezzar standing before me, his hands bloodied, but empty.

"My king," I said, standing tenderly to face him, "we have managed it – and you saved my life."

Nebuchadnezzar smiled at me, put out his hand, and collapsed.

I managed to get him to his bed, and I was relieved to see he was still breathing. As I examined him, however, I saw a large amount of blood seeping out from under his chest armor.

I managed to get the breastplate off him. He was dead weight at this point, so it was no easy task, especially in my present condition.

Thankfully, the bleeding had almost stopped by this point, but the wound was very serious.

There was nothing more I could do for him.

The noise of fighting in the streets came once again to my hearing. I had to try to do something; but what?

One of the windows in the king's chambers had been designed to allow Nebuchadnezzar to look at Etemenanki; the great work of his hands. I was desperate.

I went to the chest where I knew he kept the eyes. They were in a cotton-lined box for their protection. I took the box and headed out the door.

The carnage in the king's room was repeated over and over as I made my way out to the door leading into the garden. Apparently the fighting had been concentrated here, but now had mostly moved elsewhere.

I encountered no resistance as I walked deliberately towards the tower, box in hand. I was weak, but I was on a mission for my king – the only mission I could come up with. It had to work.

I made it to the base of the great monument, still without opposition. I placed a tired hand on a tile in the wall inside the stairway. It was inscribed, "I Nebuchadnezzar, did build this monument to honor my god, Marduk the Ever-Living."

My only hope now was that Marduk would come back to us and rid us of our enemies if I could please him by placing the eyes in their sockets. Then he could see the information he craved on the roof inside.

I was almost at the top when I felt something burning in my right leg. I didn't need to look down to know it was an arrow.

I struggled on, finally to a place just a few paces away from the eye sockets. Night was coming on, but I could just make out where the eyes should go.

Another arrow; this time in my side. Can't they just leave me alone? They can't even know who I am!

The next arrow hit me in the chest. Breathing became almost impossible, but I had reached my destination. Close enough anyway. Lying on my stomach, I reached forward and placed the first eye in its place.

I could hardly see as I reached into the box to take out the other eye. *It has to work. There is nothing else left to us.*

Just then another arrow streaked in. It missed my prone form, hitting instead the box still containing the other eye. I watched, absolutely amazed, as the box was carried down off the ledge where I lay to the ground below.

I thought I saw a huge, white owl fly off from somewhere along the tower there. Yes, there he goes, over the city wall - gone.

Rolling onto my back, I looked up into the clear night sky. It was so hard to keep my eyes open. A cold crept into my body like I had never felt before.

Straining, I saw Orion. For just a moment, there was a bright spot just below his girdle.

I have seen all the miracles, but where is the peace?

Epilogue

It's been Lucifer all along. I will never understand him fully. When we joined his rebellion we thought it was us against Jehovah, but it seems the Bright One likes to toy even with those who are on his side.

The towers were never even necessary. Jehovah has given Daniel even more prophecy about the Messiah, and it includes dates! Micah already said He would be born in Bethlehem. Jehovah apparently doesn't feel the need to hide this information from us. The tablet – Lucifer now admits it: He wrote it. Anything to get people's attention away from Jehovah, even if it comes at our (or my) expense. So much effort for so little gain.

I still think I will get some more use out of that tablet. They still haven't translated all of it correctly – not even Daniel. Someday I will get one of my followers to make the instrument described there and get the full use of the 'eyes'.

I have lost Babylon, that's for sure. Evil-Merodach might have been faithful to me, but I knew he was weak. Barely lasted a year.

That brat of Kasher's, the one who changed his name to Zoroaster; he came back from the east with such a mixture of beliefs, I can't even sort it out. But Enlil is heavily involved. When he went to the east, I took over everything here – including the 'owl' persona.

And he got to Cyrus before he took Babylon.

Ishtar went east, out to where Zoroaster had his enlightenment with Mahavira and Gautama. Some there have embraced her in her new role as Laksmi, wife of Vishnu. She is so weak. She accepts second place wherever she goes.

I'm looking west. Greece is rising, and I'm too late to get very high in their structure, but Rome will soon be strong, and here I will look to Lucifer for a model. He imitates Jehovah, deceiving many. The Romans want their own Zeus, but he is busy there in Greece. I will be their supreme god. I think 'Jupiter' sounds good. If I get enough people and gods behind me, who knows? Maybe Lucifer's day will be over.

•

•

Proof